Delight in the

✢ *Secrets of the Tudor Court Series* ✦

"Emerson captures the pageantry and the politics of the Tudor court, portraying real-life characters who negotiated turbulent times and giving historical-fiction fans a first-rate read."

—*Booklist*

"Emerson wields a sure pen when it comes to Tudor England, and laces the story with just the right amount of period detail."

—*Historical Novels Review*

"Rich and lushly detailed, teeming with passion and intrigue. You can happily immerse yourself in another time and place."

—*RT Book Reviews*

✢ *At the King's Pleasure* ✦

"Emerson knows her stuff."

—*Historical Novels Review*

"A wonderfully absorbing novel that is full of enough historical detail to satisfy even the most hard-core Tudor fan. Emerson beautifully depicts the difficulty of living in a treacherous period in which one had to do what the king's pleasure demanded, in spite of the risk of losing one's head."

—*Library Journal*

"I continue to be awestruck by each and every book."

—*Historically Obsessed*

✥ By Royal Decree ✥

"Another captivating novel. . . . Emerson skillfully manages to keep Elizabeth's life as the central point and never loses track of her faith in love and happy endings."

—*RT Book Reviews* (4 stars)

"Appealing . . . a refreshingly willful, sexually liberated heroine."

—*Publishers Weekly*

"Presenting the tempestuous and often scandalous court through the eyes of Bess Brooke . . . the author paints a confident, realistic picture of the king. . . . A valuable addition to the current popular interest in all things Tudor."

—*Historical Novels Review*

"Another beautifully written Tudor secret love . . . everything I could have hoped it to be and more."

—*Historically Obsessed*

✥ Between Two Queens ✥

"Emerson skillfully crafts a strong heroine who maintains careful command of her sexuality and independence. Nan's behavior is as brave as it is scandalous for the time, and Emerson makes readers appreciate the consequences of Nan's choices."

—*Publishers Weekly*

"Emerson's sharp eye for court nuances, intrigues, and passions thrusts readers straight into Nan's life, and the swift pace will sweep you along."

—*RT Book Reviews*

"Filled with intrigue, mystery, and romance. . . . A quick, fun read that was perfect for a rainy weekend, it provides Tudor fans with yet another viewpoint of the fascinating lives of those closest to Henry VIII."

—Historical Novels Review

⤜ *The Pleasure Palace* ⤛

"A riveting historical novel of the perils of the Tudor court, vividly fictionalizing historical characters and breathing new life into their personalities and predicaments."

—Booklist

"Jane Popyncourt is not the idealistically virginal heroine but a skillful player in the intrigues of the Tudor court. . . It is this heroine that separates the book from the pack."

—Publishers Weekly

"Emerson's lively 'fictional memoir' . . . includes many vivid descriptions of the clothing, comportment, and extravagant entertainments . . . and adds to these lighter moments a subtle undercurrent of mystery and political intrigue."

—Historical Novels Review

"Beautifully researched. . . . History, love, lust, power, ambitions—a pleasure indeed."

—Karen Harper, author of The Irish Princess

All the gripping historical novels in the
Secrets of the Tudor Court series are also available as eBooks

Also by Kate Emerson

At the King's Pleasure

The Pleasure Palace

Between Two Queens

By Royal Decree

↣ The ↢

KING'S
Damsel

KATE
EMERSON

GALLERY BOOKS
New York London Toronto Sydney New Delhi

G

Gallery Books
A Division of Simon & Schuster, Inc.
1230 Avenue of the Americas
New York, NY 10020

First Gallery Books trade paperback edition August 2012

GALLERY BOOKS and colophon are registered trademarks of Simon & Schuster, Inc.

For information about special discounts for bulk purchases, please contact Simon & Schuster Special Sales at 1-866-506-1949 or business@simonandschuster.com.

The Simon & Schuster Speakers Bureau can bring authors to your live event. For more information or to book an event contact the Simon & Schuster Speakers Bureau at 1-866-248-3049 or visit our website at www.simonspeakers.com.

Manufactured in the United States of America

10 9 8 7 6 5 4 3 2 1

Library of Congress Cataloging-in-Publication Data is on file.

ISBN 978-1-4516-6149-1
ISBN 978-1-4516-6152-1 (ebook)

This book is dedicated to the memory of the historical novelists who gave me my first taste of history in fictionalized form—Margaret Campbell Barnes, Thomas B. Costain, Anya Seton, Jan Westcott, and Frank Yerby— and to Dorothy Dunnett, for creating Lymond.

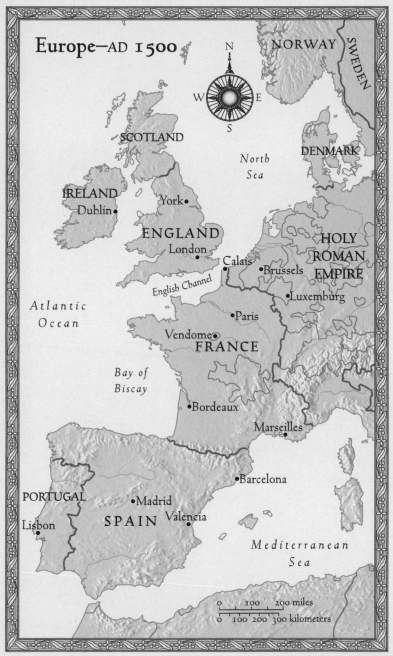

Europe—AD 1500

NORWAY

SWEDEN

N
W   E
S

SCOTLAND

North
Sea

DENMARK

IRELAND

Dublin

York

ENGLAND

London

Calais

Brussels

HOLY
ROMAN
EMPIRE

Luxemburg

Atlantic
Ocean

English Channel

Paris

Vendome

FRANCE

Bay of
Biscay

Bordeaux

Marseilles

Barcelona

PORTUGAL

Madrid

Lisbon

SPAIN

Valencia

Mediterranean
Sea

0   100   200 miles
0   100 200 300 kilometers

Map by Paul J. Pugliese

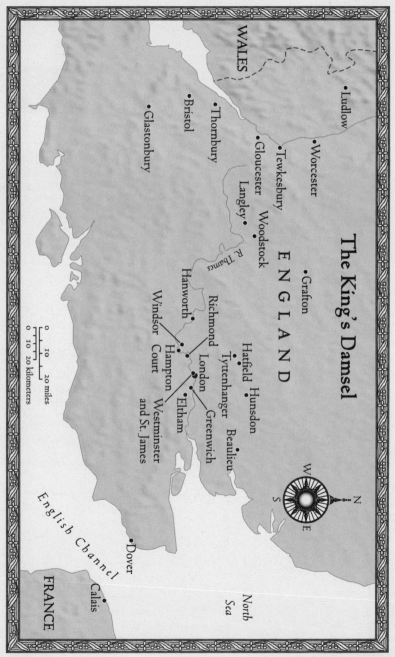

The King's Damsel

WALES

ENGLAND

• Ludlow
• Worcester
• Tewkesbury
• Gloucester
Langley
Woodstock
• Grafton
• Thornbury
• Bristol
• Glastonbury
R. Thames
Hanworth
Richmond
Windsor Court
Hampton
London
Tyttenhanger
Hatfield
• Hunsdon
Beaulieu
Eltham
Greenwich
Westminster
and St. James

0 10 20 miles
0 10 20 kilometers

English Channel

• Dover
Calais •

FRANCE

North
Sea

W
N
S
E

Map by Paul J. Pugliese

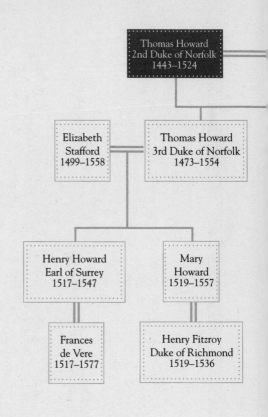

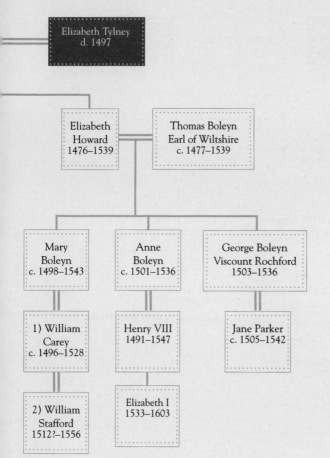

Elizabeth Tylney
d. 1497

Elizabeth
Howard
1476–1539

Thomas Boleyn
Earl of Wiltshire
c. 1477–1539

Mary
Boleyn
c. 1498–1543

Anne
Boleyn
c. 1501–1536

George Boleyn
Viscount Rochford
1503–1536

1) William
Carey
c. 1496–1528

Henry VIII
1491–1547

Jane Parker
c. 1505–1542

2) William
Stafford
1512?–1556

Elizabeth I
1533–1603

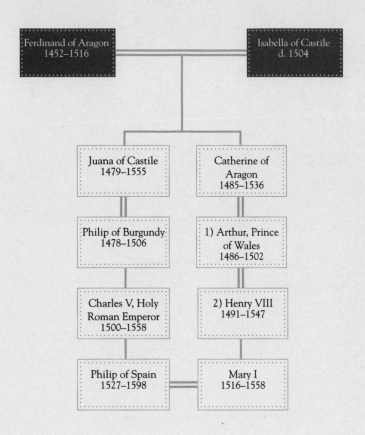

✦ The ✦
KING'S
Damsel

1

*S*tar of Hartlake sensed my troubled spirit. He turned his massive head toward me and nickered close to my ear as I curried his long, thin mane with a hedgehog skin brush. It was all I could do not to bury my face against his warm neck and weep.

"Do you know?" I asked him. "Do horses sense it when their owners have died?"

Star had been my father's favorite, the mount he invariably chose, even when we were only riding out for pleasure. My brother used to chide Father for that, saying that Star of Hartlake was too valuable an animal for everyday use. He was a courser, bred for warfare. He had the stately appearance of his breed, all black except for the star-shaped blaze on his forehead, with a broad breast, a long, arched neck, small upright ears, and large black eyes.

Father's answer to Stephen had always been the same. He'd laugh and ask what sense it made to own such a marvelous beast and not enjoy him.

They were both gone now, Father and Stephen, and I missed them more each day.

My father was Sir Arthur Lodge. It still seemed impossible to me that he could be dead. He had always been a strong and vigorous man. But three months ago, he fell ill of a fever. The most learned physicians in Bristol and Glastonbury were consulted, but none of them could do anything for him. After two weeks of suffering, he died.

My older brother, Stephen, inherited everything but the widow's third that went to my stepmother, Blanche, and my marriage portion of four hundred marks. As we three grieved together, Stephen assured Blanche that he intended to make no drastic changes. She did not need to move into her dower house unless she wished to. I was to have the run of all the properties that now belonged to Stephen. It had not occurred to me until he told me this that matters might have been otherwise.

I was thirteen years old when Father died and not yet betrothed to anyone. That made arranging my future marriage Stephen's responsibility. He said he was in no hurry to find me a husband, nor was he in any rush to be one himself. Stephen was only ten years my senior and had inherited our father's zest for life. He soon resumed his normal round of activities. A few weeks after Father died, Stephen lost his own life in a hunting accident. Of a sudden, I found myself sole heir to the wealth amassed by three generations of the Lodge family.

I sighed deeply and resumed my steady, rhythmic stroking of Star of Hartlake's mane. I should not have been in the stable at all, let alone performing such a menial task, but it soothed me to be with the horses. Father had taught me to ride when I was barely old enough to walk. We'd gone out together on horseback at every opportunity, sometimes to visit tenants, other times simply to explore. I knew the rugged Mendip Hills north of Glastonbury almost as well as the cottagers who lived there.

Both a love of hearth and home and a yen for new experiences ran in my blood. My grandfather and great-grandfather had been among the most successful merchant adventurers of Bristol. As a young man, Grandfather had sailed all the way to the New World across the Western Sea and brought back captive savages to present to the king. My father, on the other hand, had been the first in his family to acquire land instead of trade goods. He bought estates in Somersetshire and Gloucestershire and a town house in Glaston-bury. All those properties, as well as his chattel, were mine now. I'd have relinquished every one of them—even Star of Hartlake—to have my father and brother back again.

At the sound of footfalls on the planked floor behind me, I turned. I expected to see one of the grooms, although I'd given them permission to retire to their room above the stable and had imag-ined them passing their time gaming with dice or cards.

Instead of Peter or Barnaby, it was Blanche who appeared. She looked as ill at ease as I'd ever seen her. I hurriedly put away my brush and my wisp and returned Star to his stall. My stepmother had always been uncomfortable around horses. Born and bred in a town, she'd had little to do with large animals and had never learned to ride.

Blanche wrinkled her nose at the smell of soiled hay. The scent did not bother me, but I took her arm and led her out into the cob-bled courtyard. It was there, in the brightness of full sunlight, that I finally saw why she had braved the stable to seek me out. In one plump hand, she held a letter. She was clutching it so tightly that she'd cracked the seal.

Father had, on occasion, received written communications, but I could think of no reason why anyone would correspond with his widow. She never exchanged missives with friends. Like most women, she had never been taught to read or write.

"Who sent it?" I asked as we continued across the courtyard toward the house.

"That is what you must tell me, Tamsin. The boy who brought it from Glastonbury said it was delivered to the town house, but he knew no more than that." She thrust the letter at me and put her hands behind her back the moment I took it, as if she feared I'd try to return it to her.

Curious, I looked first at the mangled seal. It was a blob of plain red wax. No signet ring had been pressed into it to tell me the sender's identity.

I wish I could say that I felt a deep sense of foreboding as I unfolded that piece of paper, but I had no warning of what was to come as I stood there on that warm summer afternoon, a light breeze riffling my long brown hair, loosely held back from my face in a net, the air redolent with the smell of new-mown hay from the surrounding fields. All unsuspecting, I began to read.

"It is from someone called Sir Lionel Daggett," I announced.

I was proud of my ability to read. I had been taught by the nuns of Minchin Barrow. Another of our manor houses lay close enough to the priory at Barrow Gurney for me to have been sent there for lessons. For more than a year, I had gone every day to be taught by Sister Maud and Sister Berengaria. The sisters were, in fact, my father's aunts.

"I do not know the name." Rather than go inside, where the servants could overhear our conversation, Blanche seated herself on the stone bench beside the door. She arranged her voluminous black skirts with great care before she patted the seat beside her in invitation for me to join her.

I barely noticed the gesture. I had come upon my own name—Mistress Thomasine Lodge—in the letter from the mysterious Sir Lionel. I felt my brow furrow and heard my breath hitch as I continued to read. Then I blinked and focused again on the astonishing words on the page before me. They did not change.

"I do not understand," I said aloud, at last sinking down onto the bench at my stepmother's side. "Sir Lionel claims that I am his ward. He writes that he is coming to Glastonbury to take up his duties as my legal guardian."

Beside me, Blanche went very still. "That cannot be. Your father entrusted your care to me." But worry creased her face, leaving my confidence shaken.

My stepmother was a gentle soul. She had been born Blanche Good, the youngest daughter of a Bristol clothier. "Good her name and good her nature," my father had been wont to say of her. She was plump, sweet-faced, and even-tempered, with thick golden hair—hidden now beneath the gable headdress she wore—and dark blue eyes that were very nearly the color of violets. As she'd been Father's second wife, they'd married for love.

"If this man is a fraud," I said, "we will have him seized by the constable and whipped for his effrontery." I spoke with the brashness of youth and ignorance and my bold words did little to reassure my stepmother.

"We must consult with someone wiser than we are. A man of law, perhaps, or one of the learned scholars who visit the abbey. We will go to Glastonbury."

"But that is where Sir Lionel will be," I objected. "He writes that he will meet with us at the town house in four days' time." The demand that we present ourselves there at his convenience displayed an alarming arrogance. Even more disturbing was his apparent confidence that we would obey.

"Then we must leave here tomorrow at first light," Blanche said, rising.

"Send for Master Wynn," I suggested as I followed her inside.

"Perhaps he can make sense of the letter." As steward, Hugo Wynn managed the lands that were now mine, just as he had for my brother before me and our father before him.

Blanche went straight to the solar, where several large embroidery frames were always set up to hold works in progress. For once, however, she made no move to pick up a needle. I did not understand why she was so upset, but her distress was even more palpable indoors than it had been in the courtyard.

"Do you know more of this matter than you have said?" I asked, dreading her answer.

"I do not, and it is that which alarms me."

I called for Edyth, one of the maidservants, and ordered her to dispatch a kitchen boy to fetch Master Wynn with all speed and then prepare a reviving posset for my stepmother. Edyth Mells was a big-boned, moonfaced country-bred girl with freckles and a toothy smile. She goggled at Blanche, who appeared to be on the verge of tears, and had to be told twice before she followed my orders.

After Edyth brought the drink, Blanche and I sat side by side on the window seat, close enough that our skirts were touching. One of the dogs sprawled across our feet, as if she knew we were in need of reassurance.

"Hugo will know what to do." I tried to sound confident but I do not believe I succeeded.

"Will he? I wonder." Blanche's features hardened into a grim expression. "I *do* wonder. I wonder if perhaps Hugo knows more about this matter than he should."

Before she could explain what she meant by this enigmatic statement, Hugo presented himself. I stared at him, searching for anything suspicious in his manner, but he looked the same as he always had. He was short for a man, with a wiry build, and slightly bow-legged. This gave him a rolling gait when he walked. His long, thin face was unremarkable, save for a bump on the bridge of his nose to show where it had once been broken. I had known him all my life. He and my father, who'd been close in years, had been friends . . . as much as servant and master can be. Hugo had taken it hard when Father died and had been even more distraught over Stephen's demise.

As soon as Blanche told him about the letter, he asked to read it for himself. A deep frown marred his features even before he reached Sir Lionel's boldly inscribed signature. Hugo's naturally florid complexion darkened to an unhealthy red.

"What do you know of this fellow Daggett?" he demanded.

Hugo's voice was unexpectedly deep for a man of his stature, a rich, rumbling bass. I was accustomed to it, but the barely contained rage beneath the words had me sitting up straighter and staring at him in consternation.

"I know nothing at all," Blanche replied. "I have never heard his name before today. That being so, how is it possible that he has any right to interfere in Tamsin's inheritance?"

She had set her goblet aside, the herbal brew it contained untouched. Her hands, clasped tightly together in her lap, betrayed how tense she was. I realized then that she feared to hear what Hugo would say. She suspected that the claim in the letter was true, even if she did not understand how that could be possible.

"If he has the legal papers to back up his claim, then he may have every right." Hugo snapped out his answer, the words striking like angry lashes of a whip.

"But who could grant him Tamsin's guardianship?" Blanche asked. "I am certain her father never did."

"Daggett must have purchased her wardship from the king."

The ferocious scowl on Hugo's face would have warned most people not to ask any further questions. I was too astonished to be wary. "The *king?"* King Henry, eighth of that name, lived far away from Hartlake Manor. He'd never even visited Glastonbury or Bristol. All the great royal palaces were nearer to London, a journey of many days to our part of England. "Why should the king take an interest in me?"

"Because you are a considerable heiress, too young as yet to manage your inheritance on your own and lacking a husband to do it for you." Calmer now, Hugh's wrath was tempered with bitterness.

"What business is that of the king's?" I demanded, building up to a fine rage of my own.

"He makes it his business because there is profit in it. Once his high and mighty grace has declared that someone is a royal ward, he can then sell that wardship to line his own pockets. This Sir Lionel Daggett, Mistress Thomasine, has bought the right to manage your estate until you come of age."

"But I have no need of such a person," I protested. I had Blanche. And Hugo himself.

"You have no say in the matter, mistress." He still looked as if he wanted to kick something across the room. Before he could give in to the urge, he abruptly excused himself and left us.

I turned to my stepmother, who had finally availed herself of the posset. The faint scent of ginger and herbs calmed me a little, too. I waited until she had drained the goblet.

"There must be some mistake," I said in as steady a voice as I could manage. "How could I have been made a royal ward and know nothing of it?"

"If Hugo's rage is any guide, such a thing is very possible, but we will not take his word for it. We will go to Glastonbury. I will consult Sir Jasper."

Sir Jasper Atwell was Blanche's favorite priest. Her choice made sense. But something else still puzzled me. "Why do you no longer trust Master Wynn?" I asked. "Father never complained of his stewardship."

"Your father had a blind spot where Hugo Wynn was concerned. He relied on him far too much."

She rubbed at her temples, as if her head ached, and then, as we were alone, she removed her hood and the pleated barbe she wore beneath it to signify her widowhood. The late afternoon sun turned her hair the color of spun gold.

"If there is something I should know about Hugo, you must tell me," I insisted.

"You are so very young," she whispered.

"I am old enough to marry," I reminded her.

Blanche sighed. "Ah, well. My suspicions will bear fruit soon enough, and then there will be no hiding their deceitful scheme." She began to pull pins from her hair, which had been braided and wound tight around her head. "That you have noticed nothing speaks well of your maidenly innocence, Tamsin, but you cannot remain in ignorance much longer. I believe Hugo's daughter is with child."

My eyes widened at this news. "Griselda? But she is not married!"

Blanche gave a short bark of laughter. "No indeed. All her hopes in that direction were dashed when your brother died so unexpectedly. Griselda Wynn will bear Stephen's bastard, not his heir."

I had seen them together, I realized, my brother and the daughter of our steward. Griselda kept house for her father, living with him in separate lodgings on the grounds of Hartlake Manor.

I could understand what had drawn Stephen to her. Big brown eyes dominated Griselda's fine-boned face. Although it was usually covered, she had lovely long dark hair, almost black in color. She was a tiny woman, soft-spoken and delicate in appearance. Only the way she pursed her lips when she was displeased, so that they formed a hard, thin line, gave away her true nature. She'd never troubled to hide that side of herself from me.

"Hugo pushed his daughter into Stephen's path after your father's death," Blanche said. "He hoped by their marriage to advance himself and his posterity. When Stephen died, he lost his chance, but he still had charge of the estate. Now he fears he will lose even that. If Sir Lionel Daggett truly has control of your inheritance, he has the authority to replace Hugo with a steward of his own choosing."

"But what Hugo told us *cannot* be right. The king of England is no kin of mine. How can he decide what is to become of me and mine?"

Weary of questions she could not answer, Blanche closed her eyes and rested her head against the window behind her. "I do not know what to tell you, Tamsin. I understand no more of the workings of king and court than you do. I can only pray that we will hear better news tomorrow in Glastonbury."

2

The church of St. John the Baptist in Glastonbury does not have a vicar. It is staffed with a parochial chaplain and four stipendiary chaplains. One of the latter, Jasper Atwell, called Sir Jasper for courtesy's sake, had held his post for many years. Blanche trusted him as she did not trust Hugo Wynn. As soon as we arrived at the Glastonbury house, she sent for him. He came within the hour.

In contrast to our steward, Sir Jasper was tall. He was also bald as an egg and thin as a beanpole, with a long, narrow nose, a negligible chin, and a splotchy complexion that was the result of a long-ago bout with the swine pox. He listened to Blanche's account of events without interrupting and then squinted at Sir Lionel's letter—he was extremely shortsighted—while Blanche and I once again sat side by side, this time with my right hand clasped tightly in her left.

"Well," he said, after he handed the letter back to me. "Well."

"Does Hugo have the right of it?" I demanded. "Must I accept this stranger as my guardian?"

"I fear you are obliged to, Tamsin." Sir Jasper had a soothing tenor voice, but his words had me springing to my feet in agitation.

"It is not fair! My father's widow should be my guardian!"

Surely that was what he and Stephen had intended.

"My dear child, you will discover that life is rarely fair."

Sir Jasper reached out to me but I avoided his touch. I could not meet his eyes, either. I did not want to confirm what I already knew—that he felt sorry for me.

"It is a great pity," he added, "that you had not yet attained your fourteenth year before your father and brother died."

"What difference would that make?" Blanche asked.

"All the difference in the world. Under the law, a girl who is fourteen or older when she inherits, so long as she is not yet betrothed, is granted control of her own lands and chattel. She needs no guardian."

I calculated quickly. I knew the date of my birth. I could remember my mother, who had died when I was eight, telling me that I had been born on St. Valentine's Day, when birds traditionally choose their mates and all true lovers rejoice. "Then, in six months' time," I said, "I will be free of the odious Sir Lionel!"

Even before he spoke, the sadness in Sir Jasper's expression told me it was not to be that simple. "As matters have fallen out, you must now remain under your guardian's control until you are of full age to inherit. During that time, he will have complete authority over both your inheritance and your person. Most guardians take their wards to live in their own households. If Sir Lionel has sons, he no doubt intends to marry you to one of them, for by purchasing your wardship from the king's Court of Wards, he has also acquired the right to choose your husband."

I stared at him in disbelief, but his solemn countenance and the tears that sprang into my stepmother's violet eyes confirmed that he was not likely to be mistaken in what he told us. A sense of utter helplessness gripped me, hard as a fist squeezing my heart. Appalled, I realized that I had more in common with Star of Hartlake than I'd realized. We had both suffered loss and neither of us had any control over what happened to us next.

3

I disliked Sir Lionel Daggett intensely from the moment I first saw him striding arrogantly toward us through the garden of the town house in Glastonbury. No, I will use a stronger word—I *despised* my guardian. At that early stage in our acquaintance, I could not have said why. As yet, he had not even announced that he intended to separate me from my stepmother and remove me from all that was familiar to me. For a few more minutes, that was only a possibility, not a fact. And yet, there was something about him that immediately set my teeth on edge.

"You must be pleasant to Sir Lionel, Thomasine," Blanche warned me in a low voice as we watched him approach. "A smile is more likely to be rewarded with kindness than a frown."

Seated on one of the two wooden benches beneath the rose arbor, she appeared calm, her hands steady as she embroidered flowers on a sleeve. She never missed a stitch in the intricate design. No lines of worry or care marred the cream-colored smoothness of her brow.

I strove to keep my expression equally impassive as I studied my guardian. At first glance, he was not unattractive. He was lean rather than burly and not at all threatening in any physical way. He had rich blue-black hair that surrounded a deeply tanned face dominated by dark brown eyes.

Very properly, he bowed first to my stepmother and then turned slightly to show me the same courtesy. My bench and the one Blanche occupied were arranged at an angle to each other, so that he had to step back to see both of us at once. The placing was deliberate. We wanted to keep him at a distance.

"A delight, Mistress Thomasine." His voice was raspy, like one suffering from a catarrh, but the absence of any coughing suggested that this was the way it always sounded, so rough that it flayed the ear.

Because I was seeking flaws, I soon found another. He had a calculating look in his eyes. He answered my bold stare with a slight lift of soot-colored eyebrows.

When he turned again to my stepmother, I saw that, from the side, his face was far less pleasing than in the front view. His features in profile put me in mind of a rat.

"Have you traveled far to reach us?" Blanche asked, in part to be polite and in part because we knew nothing about Sir Lionel, not even where he lived.

"From London," he answered, which told us nothing. He cut short any further inquisition with a blunt announcement: "I leave Glastonbury at dawn tomorrow. Mistress Thomasine will accompany me. She may bring with her one maidservant."

Blanche's needle faltered. Although Sir Jasper had warned us that Sir Lionel might take me away, my stepmother had spent the night on her knees in prayer and come away from her devotions convinced that she could persuade my guardian to let me remain in her custody. "She is too young to leave home."

His eyebrows shot up to his hairline. "She is thirteen, is she not? Some girls are wed and mothers by that age."

"Not Thomasine, Sir Lionel. It is well known that too-early breeding produces sickly children and unhealthy mothers."

His gaze shifted to me, giving me a long, assessing look. "Perhaps you are right. As it happens, I am not taking her to be wed, but I *am* taking her. The decision has been made."

With a visible effort, Blanche rallied. "Then I will accompany my stepdaughter, wherever she may be going."

"No, Lady Lodge, you will not."

"I do not understand why it is necessary to take Tamsin away." There was a quiver in her voice. "A girl's place is with her family."

Sir Lionel continued to stand while we sat, his back stiff and his mien arrogant. His lips curled into a sneer. "I beg to differ, Lady Lodge, and the girl is my responsibility now." Once again, his tone brooked no argument.

Blanche's eyes filled with tears. "You cannot mean it," she whispered.

"Oh, but I do."

The distaste in his expression made it clear he did not care for weeping women and would not be swayed by any such display of emotion. But then, to my surprise, he suddenly dropped to one knee between the benches. Showing me his back, he touched his gloved fingers to the underside of Blanche's chin. He lifted her tear-stained face until she was obliged to meet his eyes.

"Dear lady, you have no cause for sorrow. I only wish to help Mistress Thomasine advance in the world. Surely you know that most girls of her years have already entered some gentle or noble household, there to learn the social graces and meet others of like station."

Say rather to fetch and carry for higher-ranking ladies, I thought.

I had no desire to become someone's unpaid servant, even if it was under the title "waiting gentlewoman" or "lady-in-waiting."

Blanche drew in a deep breath. She held his gaze. "Given Tamsin's wealth, perhaps she should stay at home with me and invite other young women to enter *her* household."

My heart swelled with pride. My stepmother might have been reduced to tears by Sir Lionel's reluctance to compromise, but she was neither weak nor witless. For a moment, I thought this last game attempt to change his mind might even succeed.

He rose slowly. His voice almost sounded regretful. "Forgive me, Lady Lodge, but your stepdaughter has not the age and you have not the consequence to make such an arrangement feasible."

This blatantly offensive remark stunned me. I wanted to protest that it was not my stepmother's fault that she had not been born a gentlewoman. She was a knight's lady by marriage. Surely that was all that should matter.

Before I could speak, Blanche bowed her head, silently acknowledging the truth of Sir Lionel's words. Satisfied, my guardian returned his attention to me. This time his study of my appearance was so intent that I wanted to run away and hide. I remained on my bench, motionless, glaring at him in defiance. I went weak with relief when his gaze once more shifted to my stepmother.

"They did not lie when they told me Mistress Thomasine was beautiful," he said, "but I had not realized her stepmother would rival her in looks."

To my astonishment and dismay, Blanche colored prettily at his compliment.

I could not understand why she should feel flattered. The praise had come hard on the heels of an insult. Besides, it could hardly be a surprise to her that men found her attractive. My father had been accustomed to tease her about her power over such poor, smitten creatures, knowing full well that she had no interest in anyone but him.

I considered Sir Lionel's praise of *my* appearance to be arrant nonsense. My looking glass assured me, morning and night, that I had only middling beauty, especially when I compared myself to my stepmother, with her thick golden hair and her violet-blue eyes. I had my father's coloring—very ordinary light brown tresses and eyes of a plain pale blue, and if my current height was anything to go by, it seemed likely I would end up being as tall and gaunt as my two great-aunts who were nuns.

Clearly Sir Lionel preferred looking at my stepmother. After a moment, he even presumed to settle himself beside her on her bench. Blanche did not object. I was the one who squirmed uncomfortably, watching them, although I could not say why seeing them sit so close together both disturbed and alarmed me. Sir Lionel took no further liberties and all their conversation seemed to center on me.

Although I could not catch every word they exchanged in low voices, I could tell that Blanche had not yet given up hope of persuading Sir Lionel to change his mind. She seemed to be trying to charm him into seeing things her way.

"Is Mistress Thomasine trained in the domestic arts?" Sir Lionel asked.

"Every gentlewoman learns those skills—to manage the still house, the bake house, and the brew house," Blanche replied. "Tamsin is most adept in all that a wife needs to know to run a household."

She exaggerated. I was adequate.

"And is she proficient in music and dance?"

"She has been taught the social graces, as any gentlewoman should be."

I waited for Blanche to mention that I could read, but she did not. It was a somewhat rare ability for a gentlewoman and not all gentlemen were schooled in it, either. I could not write, of course. That required separate instruction and was a skill even more rare among young gentlewomen than reading. Few of my acquaintance, male or female, were able to do more than sign their own names. What need had they of an ability to write when clerks and secretaries were plentiful?

An occasional nod of Sir Lionel's sleek black head seemed to indicate that he was satisfied with the answers Blanche gave him. When he cast a speculative look my way, I thought he was about to ask me to demonstrate my talent by singing or strumming my lute, but the moment passed. I was relieved that he accepted my stepmother's word for it that I had sufficient talent not to embarrass myself when I performed in public. My music master had deemed my skills acceptable but said they lacked heart.

As the interrogation continued, it became ever clear to me that Sir Lionel was not about to change his mind. I would be leaving Glastonbury with him. But where would we go? It was all I could do to remain seated on my separate bench. My embroidery abandoned, I twisted my hands together in my lap. When I could wait not another moment to learn my fate, I blurted out a question.

"Where is it that you propose to take me?"

Sir Lionel found my outburst amusing. My stepmother blanched. She glanced from my guardian to me and back again, all the while worrying her lower lip with her teeth.

Now that I had Sir Lionel's full attention, he stood and closed the distance between us, ending up uncomfortably close to me, near enough that I could smell the cloves he'd chewed to sweeten his breath. As he had with my stepmother, he lifted my chin on his gloved fingertips and stared into my face. I glared back at him, defiant. His eyes narrowed and he closed his fingers in a pinch. It hurt, but I did not cry out. I would not give him the satisfaction.

His lips twisted into a parody of a smile and he gave a curt nod. "You'll do."

"I beg your pardon, Sir Lionel," Blanche said in an anxious voice. "She'll do for what purpose?"

He drew back a little and once again bowed, first to me and then to my stepmother. "My apologies, Lady Lodge, and to Mistress Thomasine, for keeping you in suspense. I had to be certain, you see, that she would suit."

"And have I passed inspection?" I did not trouble to hide my irritation. I felt he'd been playing games with us, teasing us the way a cat toys with a mouse before it pounces on it for the kill.

"You have. On the morrow, I will escort you to Thornbury Castle."

Blanche frowned. "Thornbury? Why there? No one has lived in the castle for four years or more. Not since the Duke of Buckingham, who built it, was beheaded for treason." She crossed herself.

Intrigued, I leaned a little forward on my bench. Thornbury was said to be haunted. Everyone knew that the late duke had consulted seers and asked them to predict the death of King Henry. Had the castle been granted to Sir Lionel by the king? I could think of no other reason why he would take me there.

"All that Buckingham owned became the property of the Crown when he was attainted," Sir Lionel said, "and now Thornbury is to house the court of the Princess of Wales."

This news took a moment to sink in.

"Do you mean King Henry's little daughter?" Blanche asked.

Sir Lionel beamed at her, as if she had just said something clever. "Indeed I do, Lady Lodge. Princess Mary now has her own household and her court will take up residence first at Thornbury, then at other locations in the Marches of Wales. As for your stepdaughter, Mistress Thomasine has been appointed, through my influence, as one of the princess's maids of honor."

Blanche's relief was so obvious that I stared at her in puzzlement, wondering what she had thought Sir Lionel intended. I had no time to contemplate that small mystery. Sir Lionel began to lay out his plans for the journey, waxing eloquent about the great advantages I was to have as one of Princess Mary's attendants. I would be issued clothing made of luxurious fabrics, be waited on by my own tiring maid, and, should I desire it, keep a lapdog as a pet. My duties would be negligible. The primary purpose of a maid of honor, according to Sir Lionel, was to look decorative.

"The princess is a child of nine, Mistress Thomasine," he told me. "When she is not at her lessons, she will have need of companionship. Those who win her trust and affection will then be in a position to influence her when she visits her father's court."

"It is a great honor to serve royalty," Blanche said hastily, trying to fill the gap left by my silence.

"I do not want to leave you," I whispered. During the three years Blanche had been married to my father, she had become my friend as well as my stepmother. In a rush, I crossed from my bench to hers. Her arms came around me and held me tight.

To serve royalty *was* a great honor. I knew that. And yet I would still be going to live among strangers. And I would be at the beck and call of a mistress. That Princess Mary was younger than I was made that prospect even less appealing.

Sir Lionel snapped out a command. "Enough of this nonsense, Mistress Thomasine. You will do as you are told."

"Perhaps, Sir Lionel," Blanche said in her mildest voice, "you might leave us alone so we can make preparations for the journey. And we must decide which maidservant Tamsin will take with her."

"Edyth," I mumbled into the fabric of her gown. "I want Edyth." Of all our servants, I had known Edyth Mells the longest. Her mother had once been tiring maid to mine. If Edyth came with me, I would not feel so alone.

Sir Lionel, having succeeded in winning our cooperation, left us to our packing. He had taken a room at the George, the commodious inn that had been purpose-built to house those making pilgrimages to Glastonbury Abbey. It also catered to those on secular errands.

4

At dawn, wrapped in a heavy cloak against the morning chill, I stepped out into the courtyard. Edyth was right behind me, so close that I felt her shiver of fear at the sight of all the mounted men waiting for us. A luggage cart containing my possessions had already been hitched to a nag.

"Where is my palfrey?" I asked Sir Lionel.

I had resigned myself to the fact that I must be decorous on this journey to Thornbury and a palfrey's gait never approaches a trot or a gallop. They amble. I'd expected to find Amfilicia waiting. The dapple gray mare had been a gift from my father to Blanche, purchased before she convinced him that she preferred to travel in a litter.

"You will ride on a pillion behind one of my men," Sir Lionel said. "You have no need of your own horse."

I opened my mouth to protest, but Blanche caught my arm and pulled me into a final farewell embrace. "You need not obey him forever," she reminded me in a whisper. "Bide your time until you are free of his control."

Now that the moment of parting had come, I felt tears well up in my eyes. I let them fall, as did my stepmother, and we clung to each other, weeping, until Sir Lionel lost patience and ordered that I be lifted onto the pillion at once. Edyth was already mounted behind another of Sir Lionel's men. She clung tightly to his waist, fearful of falling, and looking even more unhappy than I was.

I scrubbed at my eyes, dashing away the moisture, and twisted my head as far around as it would go as we rode away. I watched my stepmother, a brave smile in place and waving, until we passed through the gate.

I'd ridden on a pillion before, but not since I was a child. In the country, my favorite mount was Bella, a swift horse of a golden dun color. Father had put me on her back, astride, as soon as he deemed me old enough not to fall off. With my skirts kilted up, I'd enjoyed as much freedom as a boy throughout my girlhood. It had only been during the last year of his life that my father had insisted I learn to ride like a lady.

I did not much care for the sidesaddle, but I preferred it to a pillion. I owned a particularly nice one, high in the back for support and with a hollow to support one knee. The pillion, by contrast, was naught but a hard wooden frame padded with a leather cushion scarcely softer than the wood. It was strapped to the back of the horse behind the saddle. My feet rested on a footboard hung from the offside instead of in the velvet sling that was part of my sidesaddle.

My grief at being separated from hearth, home, and family was thus made worse by acute physical discomfort. Riding on a pillion meant that I had to turn my upper body at an awkward angle in order to grasp the waist of the man in front of me. I had no choice but to do so. If I did not hold on, I would tumble off. I had to cling

ever more tightly to him as we descended the little hill just outside
of Glastonbury.

He was a burly fellow wearing a leather jerkin. He turned his
head to look at me when we started across the quarter mile of low-
lying ground beyond. He seemed curious and not unkind and I
forced myself to smile at him. I consoled myself with the fact that he
did not stink of anything worse than leather, sweat, and horse.

When we slowed to cross a small bridge, I addressed him. "We
would both be more comfortable if I had my own horse." I could already feel bruises coming up on my bottom. "Perhaps I can persuade
Sir Lionel to stop at Hartlake Manor." We would pass quite near the
home farm on the main road from Glastonbury to Wells.

He hesitated before he spoke, then kept his voice low. "Best not
to anger him, mistress."

"Why? What would he do?" I whispered, too, keeping a watchful
eye on Sir Lionel, who rode some distance ahead.

"Beat you, mayhap."

"He would not dare!"

"Do not be so certain of that." He shrugged. "And he could pun-
ish you in other ways—by selling that pretty little palfrey he made
you leave behind, mayhap. He could sell all the other horses, too, if
he had a mind to. He has that right."

The thought of losing Amfilicia and Bella and Star of Hartlake
weakened me. I fell into a brooding silence that lasted all the way
to Wells, five miles from Glastonbury, where we stopped to dine.
When we continued on our way afterward, we skirted the Mendip
Hills. I knew the route we followed well, at least as far as Bristol,
having been there many times. Thornbury, I'd been told, lay ten
miles farther along the River Severn.

From my pillion, I did not have much of a view of the passing countryside, although I did occasionally catch a glimpse of a pud-dingstone cottage or a bank of white ramsons. Once I caught a whiff of wild garlic growing nearby. The journey was long and wearying and inescapably dull. From time to time, I dozed, in spite of the uneven gait of our mount and the roughness of the road, my head resting against the leather jerkin. The steady clop of hooves, the murmur of the many streams we had to cross, and the whisper of the wind stirring the leaves overhead lulled me into a sort of trance.

We spent the night in Axbridge. Edyth and I shared a bed.

She had been a mere girl when she first came to work at Hartlake Manor and was still no more than five and twenty. She sniffled far into the night, but I could not tell if she was weeping. Edyth sniffled a great deal of the time, especially when she was anywhere near a field of grain or a patch of wildflowers.

In the morning, as she helped me dress, she ventured to ask a question that made me wonder if she was as distraught as I'd be-lieved her to be about leaving home. "Bean't the princess a snicker?"

"A pretty girl? I suppose so. We will know soon enough, when we meet Her Grace."

I glanced at Edyth over my shoulder—she was tightening my laces—and saw that her moon-shaped face was pink with excite-ment. Edyth was no beauty. In addition to her other physical flaws—the pale, watery eyes, the squadron of freckles that marred her nose and cheeks, and the large teeth—she had oversized ears, although those and her straw-colored hair were mostly hidden by her coif. I wondered if she thought she'd find a husband in the princess's household.

"Aught to do with she be passing vine," Edyth said. "Be we going to the king's court do 'ee think?"

Her excitement at the "passing fine" prospect of meeting a prin-cess, mayhap even a king, made me examine my own feelings more closely. I resented that I'd not been given a choice about my future but, now that we were on our way, I could not help but remember how much I had enjoyed my lessons with the nuns, and previous journeys from manor to manor, and my father's tales of the traveling he'd done in his younger days. He had been to London more than once and had even crossed the Narrow Seas to France. He'd gone to fight the French, and been knighted after the Battle of the Spurs.

I continued to think about these things on that second long day of riding apillion and by the time we neared the end of our three-day journey and were riding through the final flat, tree-filled stretch of land, I was resigned to my fate.

No—I must be honest.

I was young—not yet fourteen years old—and adaptable. I had begun to imagine the pleasures inherent in my new life. As Edyth had said, it would be exciting to meet Princess Mary. I envisioned her household as a place filled with gaiety and laughter. There would be masques and tournaments, feasts and festivals. And as a maid of honor, I would be at the center of them all.

5

We reached Thornbury Castle on the twenty-fifth of August, just one day after the princess's entourage arrived there. As we rode across the last stretch of countryside, I gaped at the magnificent stone gatehouse rising ahead of us. It had some kind of inscription over the gateway, but I did not have time to make out what it said before we passed beneath to enter the huge outer courtyard.

I had heard that the late duke had meant to raise an army and make himself king. It was easy to imagine hundreds of men and horses gathering in this space. There was a fair amount of bustle and noise as it was. Princess Mary's many baggage carts were still being unloaded. Servants in blue and green livery and carrying parcels and chests hurried to and fro, delivering their burdens to the royal wardrobe, the chapel, even the kitchens—everything from prayer stools to brass pots.

We had no sooner appeared in the courtyard when one of the servants dropped a chest. It struck the cobblestones and cracked open. To my amazement, books spilled out—more books than I'd ever seen in one place before. A spindle-shanked gentleman in a clerical gown paled and let out a screech, acting as if his firstborn son had just tumbled to the ground instead of a collection of leather-bound tomes. With loud exhortations to be more careful, he supervised the repacking of the chest and accompanied it when it was carried through to the inner courtyard.

"Dr. Richard Fetherston," Sir Lionel murmured. "He is the princess's new tutor. Make yourself pleasant to him, Thomasine. He will likely have considerable influence in the days to come."

On the journey from Glastonbury to Thornbury Castle, my guardian had repeated this lesson in various ways until I was heartily sick of the subject. I must make myself pleasant. It was my duty to assure that everyone liked me. I should ingratiate myself with those who mattered. Further, I was to keep my eyes and ears open, seeking opportunities to advance myself—and through me, Sir Lionel—at the Princess of Wales's court.

I nodded to let my guardian know I had heard him, but my mind was elsewhere. There was so much to see. My head swung back and forth as I tried to take in everything at once. Once again I wished I had ridden my own horse. The bulk of the henchman in front of me—he'd unbent enough on the second day of travel to tell me that his name was Oliver—obscured much of my view.

Although I had never seen an outer courtyard quite so opulent as this one, the arrangement of domestic offices was familiar to me. I felt certain that those who worked here were housed in the rooms on the upper level. Where there were stables below, there would be living quarters for grooms in the rooms above. If I craned my neck, I could see flights of wooden stairs climbing the exterior of the building at regular intervals.

That was all I had time to observe before we passed beneath a second gatehouse and entered the inner courtyard. The shield of the

Stafford family adorned the top of the archway above the portcullis. I knew enough of heraldry even then to recognize the four badges the dukes of Buckingham had used for generations—the golden knot, the silver swan, the blue-ermined mantle, and the spotted antelope.

The porter came out of his lodge to greet us. Sir Lionel demanded to know where the princess might be found. His imperious attitude made me wonder if the lodge had a dungeon beneath. I imagined my guardian confined for his effrontery, but it was not to be. The porter did no more than tell him to wait in the second courtyard while he relayed word of our arrival.

This courtyard was much smaller than the first, no more than half an acre in size. Oriel windows opened out onto the open space from the first floor apartments on every side. These would be chambers for the steward and for guests, I surmised, and rooms for upper servants. I had no idea where a maid of honor fell in the hierarchy.

When I dismounted, I was able to see my surroundings in more detail. My nose twitched as I caught the scent of cooking meat and I had no difficulty picking out the entrance to the kitchen. There would be wet and dry larders and a bake house nearby, all on the ground floor. I wondered if Mary Tudor dined, even now, in the great hall. At the thought, my stomach growled. It had been a long time since we'd broken our fast.

The liveried servant who came to fetch us led us away from the succulent smells and into the royal lodgings to the right side of the inner court. I gawked at the luxury surrounding me at every hand. I had heard that large sections of the castle had been left unfinished at the Duke of Buckingham's death, but it was obvious that he had completed the construction of his own living quarters before his execution. They were very grand and occupied both the ground and upper floors of one entire wing of the castle.

When I'd thought of Princess Mary during our journey, I had imagined a larger-than-life little girl ensconced on a bejeweled throne. It seemed to me that a king's daughter must always sit in state, anticipating visits from her father's subjects, even if she was only nine years old.

The first floor presence chamber did indeed contain a chair impressive enough to be a throne, but it stood empty. The princess sat with her women. They were gathered around a large embroidery frame, hard at work stitching religious symbols onto an altar cloth.

Everyone looked up when we entered, but I had no difficulty picking out which one was the princess. She was by far the youngest person in the room. Even if her age had not given her away, her clothing would have. Her kirtle and sleeves were made of white satin and the gown she wore over them was purple damask. The sun shone through the bank of windows behind her. Where it struck the fabric, tiny golden threads glinted merrily. So did the many jewels she wore—rings on every finger, pearls, and a diamond-studded cross on a gold pendant.

When I shifted my attention from Her Grace's clothing to her face and form, I felt a stab of disappointment. The princess was small for her age, a thin, pale child with eyebrows so fair that for a moment I did not think she had any. As was proper for one of her years, she wore neither coif nor hood. Her best feature, her long, auburn hair, was held back by a jeweled band. Her nose was rather flat, although it was turned up at the end. Her lips were thin and unsmiling.

I gleaned only the most vague impression of the other women and girls in the room. They were all much more simply dressed than their mistress, for the most part in black or russet.

The servant who had conducted us to the presence chamber

presented Sir Lionel to the princess and he, in turn, introduced me. I sank hastily into a deep curtsey. My forehead nearly touched the tiled floor.

"Welcome to my household, Mistress Lodge." The princess had a high-pitched but musical voice.

"I am honored to be here, Your Grace."

Daringly, I lifted my head and sent her my best smile. It was met with a hard stare. Disconcerted, I stared back until it came to me that, like Sir Jasper Atwell, Princess Mary was extremely shortsighted. My guess was confirmed when she squinted, trying to make out my features. No doubt the bemused expression on my face remained a mystery to her.

I would have liked to move closer, so that Her Grace could see me more clearly, but when she dismissed me, saying that Lady Salisbury would see me settled, court protocol demanded that I back away from her. Sir Lionel reinforced the rules by grasping my upper arm to guide me to the side of the room. The princess returned to her ladies and the embroidery frame.

We were escorted from the presence chamber to a smaller room. After a considerable wait, a formidable-looking old woman all in black joined us there. In spite of the color, her kirtle, sleeves, and gown all reflected wealth. They had been made of the finest materials and were heavily embroidered. And although it was summer, the sleeves were trimmed with fur. I thought it might be sable, which was forbidden to all but those of noble descent. Her gable headdress was the most elaborate I had ever seen and her fingers were weighed down with heavy rings. When she moved her hands, the scent of jasmine wafted my way.

"So, Sir Lionel," she said in an acerbic tone, "I see that your suit to the king was successful."

"His Grace was most obliging." Sir Lionel's voice might be rough but his manner was smooth and well oiled. "As were you, my lady. A token of my gratitude is on its way from London. The goldsmith was putting the finishing touches on it when I left."

She responded to this announcement with a regal nod.

"May I present my young ward, Mistress Lodge. Thomasine, this is Lady Salisbury, lady mistress of the princess's household. You will obey her in all things."

"I will do my best to please you, my lady," I promised, and made my obeisance to her.

"Excellent." The old lady looked down her long, thin nose at me. She did not even glance at my guardian when she dismissed him with a wave of one bejeweled hand: "Run along, Sir Lionel. We will manage quite well without you from now on."

Although I was not sad to see the last of him, or to hear him put so neatly in his place, I felt a distinct twinge of trepidation at being left alone with this formidable woman. Without my having had any say in the matter, she had been given complete control of my life.

Lady Salisbury had a long, narrow face to match her nose, and an authoritarian manner. She made a visual assessment of my person first, then began an inquisition into my qualifications to be a maid of honor.

"Princess Mary speaks Latin, French, and Spanish," she informed me, "and understands Italian. She can read Greek. What accomplishments have you in language?"

"I can read English," I mumbled.

"Speak up," she snapped.

For a moment, I thought her lips twitched, but I must have been mistaken. She did not strike me as a woman much given to amusement.

"The nuns at Minchin Barrow taught me to read. And I can write my own name."

"You will learn to write more than that while you are here. Her Grace sings and plays several instruments, including the harpsichord, the virginals, and the lute. You will join in her music lessons and those with a dancing master and you will be expected to acquit yourself well."

"Yes, my lady." I thought about telling her that I already knew how to play the lute, but decided against it. Something told me that my performance would fall short of her exacting standards.

Apparently satisfied, Lady Salisbury turned to a page who had been waiting, forgotten and very nearly invisible, in a shadowed corner of the room. "Fetch Mistress Rede," she ordered.

A moment later, as if she'd been waiting for the summons, a young woman presented herself. Like the princess, she wore her hair uncovered, as maidens everywhere are permitted to do. For the journey from Glastonbury, my own hair had been tightly braided and confined beneath a hood. Three days of hot sun beating down on me had left me longing to wash the long strands and scrub my face and scalp, too.

"Mistress Rede is also a maid of honor," Lady Salisbury said. "She will show you the way to the maidens' dormitory, answer your questions, and help you settle in."

I curtseyed yet again as I thanked her.

Lady Salisbury sniffed, wrinkling her nose in distaste. "You stink of horse, Mistress Lodge. I will have a bathtub sent up. You will bathe before you enter the princess's presence again."

6

"Here we are," my companion said in a cheerful voice. "This is the maidens' dormitory."

Mistress Rede, a rosy-cheeked individual no more than a year or two my senior, sent another friendly smile my way. She wore what I supposed must be the livery for Princess Mary's maids of honor—a russet kirtle, bodice, and sleeves under a plain black gown.

The room we entered was large, long, and sunlit. It contained three beds and numerous wardrobe chests. My trunks and boxes made an untidy pile in one corner.

"Mistress Rede—"

"You must call me Anne," she interrupted. "We will be great friends. I am certain of it."

She seemed so eager to have me agree that I did so at once.

"My father is Sir William Rede of Boarstall in Buckinghamshire. Was that your father who brought you to Thornbury?"

I shook my head in vehement denial. "He is my guardian, Sir Lionel Daggett. My father was Sir Arthur Lodge of Hartlake,

Somersetshire. He died." The words were painful to say aloud. I tried to mitigate the feeling by adding, "I am an heiress."

"That is of little consequence here." Anne grinned at me. "Did I hear him call you Thomasine?"

I could not help but smile back at her. "My Christian name is Thomasine, but my friends and family call me Tamsin."

"Tamsin it will be, then. Did you bring your tiring maid with you?"

"Oh," I gasped. I had forgotten all about Edyth. "Do you think someone will escort her here? I hate to think of her lost in such a large and frightening place."

"No doubt she has been taken to the servants' quarters. The maidservants have their own lodging, as there is not enough room in the maidens' dormitory for truckle beds. Do you need her to help you unpack?"

I could tell that Anne was curious about me and my belongings. I obliged her by delving into my baggage and showing her some of the special treasures I'd brought with me from home. Anne admired the small handheld looking glass Father had sent for all the way to London, and the deck of brightly painted playing cards he'd given me one Yuletide, but she was much more impressed by the jeweled pendant my grandfather had taken off a French ship during the brief period when he'd sailed as a privateer. I was happy to recount the stories behind each of these items and soon Anne and I were chattering together like old friends.

Before long, I dared to ask the question that had been bubbling up in my mind ever since my interview with the princess's lady mistress. "Who is this Lady Salisbury that she can command such instant obedience from Sir Lionel?"

"She is the *Countess* of Salisbury. She was Margaret Plantagenet before her marriage and she is cousin to King Henry. She is high in His Grace's affection and in that of Queen Catherine."

Anne chuckled at my abashed expression. Even though I'd taken note of the sable trim on her gown, I truly had not thought I was speaking to so great a noblewoman.

"And she is in charge of the princess's household?"

"She controls the distaff side. You would be wise not to give her any offense. If she takes you in dislike, you will be sent home."

My fingers tightened on the sleeve I'd been about to return to the largest of my trunks, which would now serve as my wardrobe chest. A wave of homesickness swept over me, so sudden and so intense that for a moment I had to close my eyes. Tears sprang unbidden into my eyes. I dashed them away with my free hand, but I could not seem to stop myself from speaking. "I am not certain that would be such a bad thing."

I missed Blanche terribly, and I also missed all the privileges I'd enjoyed as Father's only daughter. In each of our houses, I had my own chamber, my own bed. I'd not had to share either, as it was clear I would have to at Thornbury. And I had never had to be someone else's servant, either.

"Sent home in *disgrace*," Anne clarified.

A chill passed through me as I realized that I would not be returned to my stepmother. If I displeased the countess, I would be sent to Sir Lionel Daggett. I had no doubt but that he would retaliate for my failure to follow his instructions. If I did not make myself pleasing to those I met here, he would marry me off to the first man who offered him a large enough bribe.

With excessive care, I put the sleeve into the chest, resolved to make a success of myself at Princess Mary's court. "What am I to wear to serve the princess?" I asked.

"Someone will come and measure you and within a day or two you will have clothing just like mine." She swept a hand down her body to indicate the russet and black garments. "This livery is provided by the Crown and we each earn ten pounds per annum, besides. It is paid quarterly, but we can borrow against that expectation if we need to buy anything the princess does not supply."

At this interesting juncture, we were interrupted by the arrival of two burly servants carrying a wooden tub. They were followed by a dozen more bringing buckets so full of water that it sloshed onto the floor as they walked. They dumped these into the tub until it was half full and left the remaining buckets for rinsing. Edyth brought up to the rear of the procession, armed with packets of fennel and bay to add to the bathwater, a ball of sweet soap, a sponge, and two towels.

"Is bathing common at court?" I asked Anne as Edyth began to help me out of my travel-stained and reeking clothing. Although many people thought total immersion in water was dangerous, I saw no harm in the practice. In the ordinary way of things, however, all my washing was done with no more than a basin and ewer.

"More so than elsewhere." She sounded faintly disapproving. "I have heard that King Henry is most particular about cleanliness."

I thought that odd in a man, but I did not say so. I was too relieved to have the chance to scrub off the dirt and smell of days on horseback. I stepped gingerly into the tub, pleased to discover that the water was neither steaming nor cold, but just comfortably warm.

Anne perched on one of the wardrobe chests, her legs tucked beneath her. "Have you more questions for me?" she asked.

Sunk in the delightful luxury of having my hair soaped and rinsed by Edyth—a process I usually had to carry out by kneeling on a towel and bending over a basin of water set on the floor of my chamber—I needed a moment to realign my thoughts.

"What are our duties?" I asked.

"We do whatever the princess requires of us," Anne answered. "You will be asked to swear an oath of allegiance to Her Grace. The

Lord Chamberlain will administer it. He is the one in charge of the entire household. If you ever want to leave court for any reason, you must apply to him for permission."

"Where would I go?" I asked. "Thornbury is too far from my home for me to return there on my own."

"Oh, we will not be here long. The princess will not remain in any one place for more than a few weeks. Her Grace has been given her own household so she can be seen in her role as Princess of Wales."

"Then shouldn't she be *in* Wales?" I asked. On our way to Thornbury, Sir Lionel had pointed out the distant Welsh hills . . . on the other side of the Severn. This castle was in Gloucestershire.

"I expect we will go there," Anne said as Edyth poured more water over my head, "but it is to the city of Gloucester that we travel next."

Would we visit Bristol? I wondered. Blanche would hear of it, if that city were included in the princess's itinerary. She'd make a point of removing to our town house there . . . unless Sir Lionel prevented it. I still thought it unfair that he, not my stepmother, controlled all the property I'd inherited. Then I remembered—he could not forbid her to occupy the Bristol house. It was part of her widow's third of my father's estate and hers to do with as she would. Should she choose to remarry, she'd make her second husband a wealthy man.

While Anne prattled on about the plans for Princess Mary's ceremonial entry into Gloucester, which had required weeks of preparation, and the pageantry that the citizens of that town were likely to provide, Edyth dried my body and began to comb out the tangles in my hair. Since it fell nearly to my waist, this was no simple task.

"It will make a nice change," Anne said.

The odd note in her voice caught my attention. "A change? To what are you accustomed?"

"Boredom!"

"But we serve a princess. Surely there are disguisings and banquets and tournaments to amuse us at her court."

Anne laughed and shook her head.

"No? What about entertainment by jugglers or players?"

Another head shake answered me.

"Surely Princess Mary has her own fool."

"Not even that, although there is one musician assigned to the household. For the most part, Her Grace has lessons. Endless lessons, to some of which we must accompany her. And when we are not listening to Her Grace learn to speak some foreign language or going with her to church or on her daily walks in the garden, we sew shirts for the poor or embroider altar cloths or vestments."

"What of lessons in dancing and music? Those must be enjoyable."

"They do not occupy enough hours to dispel the boredom."

Although Anne painted a far less exciting picture of life at court than I had imagined, the reality did not sound all that dull to me. "There is that ceremonial entry into Gloucester," I reminded her.

She laughed. "Oh, yes. We'll have to ride right behind Princess Mary. We'll watch the pageants—endless pageants. We must smile the whole while . . . and hold our water."

I saw her point, but I still looked forward to the experience. As Edyth dressed me in fresh, sweet-smelling clothing, I wondered how Anne Rede had become so jaded. Since the princess's household had only just been formed, she could not have served Her Grace for very long.

I thought back over what she had said and suddenly began to smile. "We ride behind the princess, did you say?"

Anne blinked at me in confusion. "How else should we enter the city?"

"In a litter. Apillion. Sir Lionel would not permit me to bring any of my horses." I thought of Bella with sudden longing. "Should I send for one?"

"The princess has an excellent stable. Suitable mounts are provided for us."

Palfreys, then. Still, this was the best news I'd heard yet. My smile stayed in place as Edyth made one last adjustment to my kirtle and left us, explaining that she had to return to the servants' quarters if she wished to sup.

The reminder of how long it had been since I'd eaten had my stomach growling again. I glanced toward a cupboard with a perforated front. I'd spied it on my first survey of the chamber. It was the kind of cabinet used to store wine and cheese. "Is there anything to eat in there?" I asked Anne. "I have had neither food nor drink since we broke our fast at dawn."

"You should have said something sooner," she chided me, and produced a wedge of cheese and a pitcher of barley water. "We are well fed here," she assured me, "but only after the princess and the highest-ranking ladies in her household have been served. All of Her Grace's meals are conducted with great formality—another lesson. One day, after she marries some foreign ruler, she must preside over his court as queen."

"So, like all of us, the princess is in training."

"But unlike us, she can *never* be private. I feel sorry for her sometimes."

Anne summoned servants to remove the tub and mop up the water that had sloshed over onto the floor. Moments after they left, the other maids of honor joined us. They were all dressed alike and all appeared to be nearly the same age. At first glance I saw little to distinguish one from another, but Anne quickly remedied that situation.

"This is Cecily Dabridgecourt," she said, catching hold of a girl with green eyes. "She is the oldest of us at nineteen."

"I come from Solihull, near Coventry," Cecily said, speaking so softly that I could barely make out the words.

"You'll have no trouble remembering Christian names," Anne continued, gesturing to the three remaining young women. "The others all share the same one."

"I am Mary Fitzherbert from Derbyshire," said the first girl. She had a small mole on the left side of her chin.

"I am *Maria*, not Mary," the second girl insisted. "Maria Vittorio. My father is the queen's physician." She spoke with a the slightest of accents, but it was enough to betray her Spanish origin.

The third Mary had sad brown eyes. "And I am Mary Dannett of Leicestershire," she said.

Later I learned that her father, like mine, had died too young.

We had no time to exchange more than the briefest of life histories at that first meeting. We might not sup with the princess, but we were required to be in attendance upon Her Grace while she ate. When the others left the maidens' dormitory, I went with them.

7

I found it difficult, that first night, to fall asleep in a strange bed, especially when I was sharing it with a stranger. I was paired with Maria. She turned her back to me and feigned sleep, but after a few minutes I could feel her shoulders shaking and knew that she was crying.

"I miss my home, too," I said aloud. "Thornbury does not have the same magic."

That got my bedfellow's attention. "Magic? Do you mean sorcery?" She lowered her voice on the last word, as if to speak it aloud would bring curses down upon our heads.

I giggled. "No. Good magic. Miracles. The kind of magic the church approves of."

And I began to tell her about Glastonbury, stories my father had told to me. I was barely launched upon the tale of how Joseph of Arimathea came to England after the crucifixion of Our Lord Jesus Christ, bringing with him the Holy Grail, when the bed curtains parted and Cecily joined us. She was quickly followed by the two Marys and Anne.

I had to admit that no one knew where Joseph had hidden the sacred chalice. "But we know he was there, at Glastonbury," I insisted. "He was sent by the Apostle Philip to establish the first Christian church in England. Joseph was a very holy man. One night, he planted his staff in the ground on Wearyall Hill and by the next morning it had taken root. It grew into a hawthorn tree and it is still there today. Every Christmas, it bears green leaves, just as if it were summer. And there is a walnut tree near the Lady Chapel that comes into leaf each year on St. Barnabas's Day."

I had no idea if the walnut tree had any connection to Joseph of Arimathea, but my companions were mightily impressed by these wonders, and by the fact that the life of St. Joseph had been written up in a book. A monk at Glastonbury had composed it when my father was a boy. It now served as a sort of guidebook to the abbey, encouraging pilgrims to visit. This benefited both the abbey and the town.

"Are there other marvels at Glastonbury?" Anne asked when I'd finished recounting all I knew about Joseph of Arimathea. She followed the question with a jaw-cracking yawn.

"Oh, yes," I assured her. "King Arthur is buried there, you know."

"*The* King Arthur?" We were in darkness, but Mary Fitzherbert sounded so awed that I was certain her eyes had gone as round as saucers.

I would have launched into still more stories of Glastonbury had not a quiet rap at the door interrupted me. A woman's voice, sounding amused, spoke from the other side. "It is well past time to sleep, young ladies."

Anne sighed. "That is Lady Catherine, Sir Matthew Craddock's wife. She occupies the chamber next to this one."

"Will she report us for keeping her awake with our talking?" I felt I was well on my way to becoming friends with the other maids of honor, but if my storytelling led to all of us being dismissed, the cost was too high.

"I do not think so." Cecily's near whisper was clearly audible in the quiet dormitory as she and the others crept back to their beds. "She is very kind."

Then silence fell in earnest and in a little while we slept.

8

The next day, I was duly sworn in and was subjected to a lecture from the Countess of Salisbury on my duties and responsibilities. Summed up, they were simple enough—be loyal to Princess Mary and willing to die to protect her should the need arise. It was a theme the countess would expand upon frequently to the maids of honor and ladies of the privy chamber. She took her responsibility as the princess's guardian very seriously.

Two days after my arrival, my new clothes were ready. Thereafter, I wore only the livery colors—russet and black—that identified me as one of the princess's female attendants.

Within a week, my fellow maids of honor habitually gathered on my bed in the maidens' dormitory as soon as the candles were snuffed. There, careful to keep my voice low, I spun stories about King Arthur, who had been taken to Avalon, the old name for Glastonbury, when he was mortally wounded in battle.

I told other tales, too. Before two weeks had passed, although we'd all sworn to keep our private entertainments secret, I noticed that people were staring at me. Even that most august personage, Dr. Butts, the princess's physician, sent me curious looks. Everyone from Lady Catherine, chief gentlewoman to the princess, to the stable boy named Thomas, whose title was "keeper of the princess's nag," seemed to know how we spent the first part of the night in the maidens' chamber.

It was Lady Catherine who first approached me openly. Even though she was almost as old as Lady Salisbury, her face was still largely free of lines. She was, in fact, a beautiful woman, but both she and the countess had already passed beyond the half-century mark. As I was not yet fourteen, that seemed very ancient to me.

"Princess Mary has heard that you are a storyteller," Lady Catherine said. "A veritable bard."

The comparison pleased me. I preened. But I also had sense enough not to overstate my skill. "I do not sing of great battles or ancient warriors," I warned her, "but I can tell tales of King Arthur and his knights, of bold explorers among the men of Bristol, of saints and miracles, and of the wonders of Glastonbury."

And so, a short time later in the princess's privy chamber, all sixteen of her ladies and gentlewomen gathered around me in a circle, prepared to be entertained. The princess sat on a chair. I was allowed a stool. Everyone else sat on cushions on the floor.

Thinking to flatter Her Grace, I chose a story that included one of her ancestors.

"During the reign of King Richard the Lion Heart," I began, "the bones of King Arthur and Queen Guinevere were discovered in the graveyard at Glastonbury Abbey."

Everyone knew some stories about King Arthur. The princess's grandfather, King Henry VII, had revered him, even naming his firstborn son Arthur in his honor. My father, too, had been named for the ancient hero-king.

"It was the song of a Welsh bard that contained the clue to finding them," I continued, "and the monks of Glastonbury managed to decipher it after many years of trying. They dug in the ground near the Lady Chapel and there they found a stone slab. Beneath it lay a leaden cross and on the cross was an inscription. It read: *Here lies buried the renowned King Arthur in the Isle of Avalon.*"

"In what language was the inscription?" the princess asked, interrupting me.

Happily, I knew the answer. "In Latin, Your Grace. The monks translated it so that everyone would know what it said."

She gestured for me to continue. Her shortsighted brown eyes remained fixed on my face. She did not smile.

"The monks continued to dig and in a little while they came to a coffin made from a hollowed-out log. Inside they found two skeletons, one of a tall man and the other of a woman."

A gasp, hastily stifled, came from one of the princess's ladies. I thought it was Mistress Pole, who had been the princess's wet nurse years before and had stayed on in her household as a waiting gentlewoman after Her Grace grew too old to need her original services.

"Although they were much decayed," I went on, "the remains were determined to be those of King Arthur and Queen Guinevere."

Princess Mary seemed untroubled by the suggestion of moldering bones. In truth, she took an almost ghoulish interest in the condition of the bodies. "How was King Arthur slain?" she asked. "Could the monks tell after so much time?"

"The skull was damaged." My brother, as boys are wont to be, had been fascinated by such details and had duly relayed them to me. "Learned men came to view the bones and they determined that the king had been killed by a blow to the head."

"Ahh," the princess said.

"Both sets of bones were put on display. Hundreds of people came to see them. Thousands. Even a king came."

"Which king?" Lady Salisbury's avid voice assured me that she was as caught up in my story as anyone else in the privy chamber.

"It was some years after the first discovery. The king who came was King Edward the First and with him came good Queen Eleanor."

Observing the satisfied expression on her face, I remembered that King Edward and Queen Eleanor were the countess's ancestors, too.

"Edward the First was the king who so loved his wife that when she died he erected crosses to her memory at every stop made by her funeral cortege," I added, remembering Sir Lionel's instructions to please and flatter the most important members of the household.

These ornate "Eleanor Crosses" still stood. When, later, I saw one for the first time—in the city of Westminster, hard by London—I understood why both the princess and the countess took such pride in their heritage. Never had I beheld such a marvelous creation—all statues and carvings and standing higher than any other monument.

I had planned to launch into another tale of Arthur and the Round Table, after I recounted the discovery of the king's bones, but Princess Mary was not through asking questions: "How did he come to be buried in Glastonbury?"

"The town was built on the ancient site of the Isle of Avalon, Your Grace. Another old name for Glastonbury is the Isle of Glass."

I spoke with confidence. My father used to say that it is always best to sound as if you know what you are talking about, especially if you are not at all certain of your facts. Inside, I was beginning to panic. I had already revealed every detail I knew about King Arthur's bones.

Before anyone could ask another question, I blurted out a related tidbit: "In those days the deep channel of the River Brue was surrounded by shallow swamps. The Perilous Bridge was once the only way to enter the city by land from the south and it was from this bridge that the knight Bedwyr returned the sword Excalibur to the Lady of the Lake after the Battle of Camlann."

Happily, this information diverted my audience and allowed me to launch into the tale of how King Arthur acquired his famous sword—which was not the same sword he pulled out of the stone. I followed that story with others, including the one about Joseph of Arimathea and the hawthorn tree. By the time I'd finished the latter, my throat was dry and my voice had gone hoarse from too much talking.

Lady Butts, the physician's wife, regarded me with concern. She was a tall, exceedingly plain-faced woman with a decided chin, a prominent nose, and a brusque, no-nonsense manner. She served as one of the princess's waiting gentlewomen. Before I could begin another tale, she reminded the princess that she had missed her morning walk: "It was raining earlier in the day, Your Grace, but there is just time now for a brisk stroll before supper."

As this daily constitutional had been prescribed by Dr. Butts for the young princess's health, a regimen that had the full approval of her mother the queen, the hint was sufficient to recall Princess Mary to her duty. She rose with a resigned sigh.

We all stood with her. The maids of honor always accompanied Her Grace on her perambulations, along with two gentlemen ushers, two gentlemen warders, two yeoman ushers, and two grooms. I took my usual place, at the end of the line of young gentlewomen, lowest in precedence as well as the last to join the household, but Lady Butts caught my arm as we started to file out.

"You should stay indoors, Mistress Lodge. I will send one of the servants for a hot drink containing honey and lemon juice to soothe your throat."

"That is kind of you, Lady Butts."

She snorted. "There is nothing kind about it. I should like to hear more of your stories, too, and you cannot tell them if you lose your ability to speak."

But Her Grace, just as she reached the door to the garden, looked over her shoulder to fix her nearsighted gaze on me. "Come walk at my side, Mistress Lodge," she piped in her high, child's voice. "I would hear more of this magical hawthorn tree at Glastonbury."

Lady Butts released me. I heard her sigh as I hastened to obey. Belatedly, I recalled that the hawthorn was also a *Tudor* symbol.

9

nne Rede's prediction about state visits proved correct. Such spectacles may be exciting to watch but they proceed with agonizing slowness for those obliged to participate in them. Even riding on horseback was not the treat I'd expected. I was assigned a plodding palfrey whose only show of spirit was to nip my shoulder when I finally dismounted.

After we left Gloucester, the Princess of Wales's court traveled another seven miles to Tewkesbury and settled into a pleasant manor house built of timber and stone and situated in the middle of a park belonging to the local abbey. By then I knew that Anne had also been right when she called life in the princess's household dull.

Her Grace's previous tutor had set up a strict regimen, one Queen Catherine had ordered Lady Salisbury to maintain, to the best of her ability, in the Marches of Wales. This accounted for the standing order that the princess's clothes, chamber, and body be kept pure, sweet, clean, and wholesome, a requirement that extended to her closest attendants. We were also instructed, in Lady

Salisbury's words, "to practice honor, virtue, and discretion in words, countenance, gesture, behavior, and deed."

Frivolity of any sort was discouraged. The only approved pastimes were playing the virginals and other instruments, and dancing, which was considered healthful exercise. Is it any wonder that my stories became so popular?

Although amusements were frowned upon, learning was not. In addition to lessons in music and dance, I was taught to speak French and began instruction in penmanship. I had never expected to learn to write, but I caught on quickly. Within a few weeks, I was proficient enough to pen a short letter to my stepmother, trusting that she would find someone to read it to her.

The season of Advent was strictly kept in the princess's household. Everyone was obliged to fast and attend church with even more frequency than usual and our meals contained far less variety. As the days grew longer and darker, I found it increasingly difficult to appear cheerful and willing to please. Indeed, on some cold, candlelit mornings I would not have arisen from my bed at all had Lady Catherine not made it her responsibility to make sure all the maids of honor reported for duty at the appointed time.

I began to feel better once the winter solstice was past. Supper on Christmas Eve, although there was still no meat or cheese or eggs to eat, marked the beginning of a more joyous season. Very early on Christmas Day, the princess went to Mass, attended by all six of her maids of honor. As it was well before dawn, we each carried a lighted taper, scented with juniper, and held it throughout the service. The sermon seemed endless, but when it was finally over we broke our fast with a veritable feast—boiled chine of beef, bread, beer, cheese, butter, and eggs.

In honor of the birth of our Lord, we had no lessons that day. There were two more masses to attend, but I expected the time between to be spent in pleasurable pursuits. At home, Yuletide celebrations customarily lasted twelve days, all twelve filled with games and entertainment. Instead, after we ate, the princess and her ladies turned to embroidery, just as if this were an ordinary day. I looked with distaste at the needle in my hand, but I perked up when Princess Mary asked for a story.

"During the Twelve Days of Christmas in the country, Your Grace, all work save for looking after livestock is forbidden, not to begin again until Plough Monday. Even spinning is banned. People twine holly branches around their spinning wheels to keep them from being used." I sent a pointed look at the embroidery frame and wondered if I dared do likewise with it.

"If they have no work, what do they do?" the princess asked.

"They bring in the Yule log and light it. They visit their neighbors to partake of wassail. They gather to dance and make music. Sometimes traveling minstrels entertain."

"If the servants do no work, how do their masters eat?" Princess Mary asked. "Someone must prepare food."

"They bake much of it in advance. There are minced pies, a traditional dish that has thirteen ingredients to represent Christ and his apostles. It always includes chopped mutton, too, in remembrance of the shepherds."

"Last year," Her Grace said, a faraway look in her eyes, "we ate of a large bird called a turkey. My father the king was much taken with the taste and ordered that a flock of them be raised for food on lands he owns in East Anglia."

I had never heard of a turkey, but when the princess had described what they looked like, I had no difficulty envisioning huge numbers of these birds being walked to London from Norfolk and Suffolk, just as was the practice with other livestock. Sometimes the journey to market would begin months in advance.

"At court the king appoints a Lord of Misrule. He wears motley and organizes the most wonderful entertainments," Her Grace continued. "I had my own Lord of Misrule one year, when I was six and spent Yuletide at Ditton. My parents were nearby, at Windsor Castle, but John Thurgood, one of my servants, was put in charge of my celebrations. Under his direction, I hosted a feast that was just like the king's, only in miniature. I even had my own gilded and painted boar's head. And there were mummers and morris dancers and disguisings."

I did not understand why the princess should be denied such trappings here. Surely there was no harm in them. As the other maids of honor shared their own memories of past Yuletides, I watched Her Grace closely. She had been animated when she spoke of her parents. Now her spirits visibly drooped. I knew, from listening to the older ladies talk, that in some years Princess Mary saw her father and mother *only* at Christmas and Easter. Had she expected to join them at her father's court this December? No wonder she looked so sad.

Her Grace was in dire need of distraction. I hesitated only a moment longer before I reached into the pouch suspended from the chain I wore around my waist and pulled out a velvet-wrapped object tied closed with a ribbon. I had taken it out of my wardrobe trunk that morning because it had been Father's gift to me one New Year's Day and keeping it with me made me feel closer to him. This was the first Yuletide since his death, and the first I'd been away from my stepmother.

"What have you there?" Maria asked, peering over my shoulder.

"A deck of cards, fifty-two in number." I unwrapped my treasure, revealing the blank back of the top card. When I was certain every eye was fixed upon it, I turned it over to reveal a full-length figure painted in bright colors.

"This is the king," I said, perhaps unnecessarily, since the man in the illustration was dressed in old-fashioned finery and wearing a crown.

The expression of delight on Princess Mary's face made her almost pretty. The instant passed far too quickly. She was a serious child by nature. After a moment both the quick smile and the twinkle in her eyes were only a memory. "He does not look anything like my father," she said.

"That is because this deck of cards was made in France. My father brought it back with him after he crossed the Narrow Seas to fight for Your Grace's father in a war against the French."

The princess fingered the painted face, marveling at the detail. "Perhaps this is King Francis, then. I may one day wed one of his sons. We were betrothed when I was barely out of swaddling clothes, but the arrangement fell into abeyance." Even at the age of nine, Her Grace had long since learned that such alliances shifted and changed like the wind, no matter how solemn the vows that had been exchanged. Then she added, "I have never played a card game."

Hearing the wistfulness in her voice, I at once offered to teach her the ones I knew.

Princess Mary hesitated. She actually glanced over her shoulder to make certain that the Countess of Salisbury had not yet returned from her meeting with the Bishop of Exeter, head of the council that governed Wales in the princess's name. The other older ladies of the household were likewise absent, although I did not know where they had gone.

Aside from the princess and her maids of honor and the ever-present gentlemen ushers, gentlemen waiters, yeoman ushers, and grooms, the only other person in the presence chamber was Princess Mary's Welsh musician. Ushers, waiters, grooms, and musician all wore the princess's green and blue livery. Only the highest-ranking gentlemen of the household were permitted black velvet doublets under black camlet gowns furred with black budge.

We were in luck. All of the black-clad officers were also busy elsewhere.

"May I borrow one of Your Grace's goblets to hold the wagers?" I asked.

She nodded, looking intrigued.

"This game is called Maw, a simple trick-taking game my father taught me. Each player must put in a penny, or some marker good for an equal amount. A bit of ribbon or a pin will do."

There was momentary confusion while everyone found something to wager. None of us had a coin on her person, not even a ha'penny. Few of us had any anywhere.

"Now we each receive five cards," I said. "The goal is to win three or more tricks. Failing that, you try to prevent anyone else from winning that many." I shuffled the cards and dealt.

"What happens if no one wins?" Anne asked.

"Then what is in the goblet carries over to the next game."

"But what is a trick?" Maria wanted to know.

When I realized that I was the only one among us who had ever played a game of cards before, I grew quite puffed up with my own importance. I answered Maria's question and went on to explain that the Ace was the card with the highest value and the Deuce the lowest and that a King outranked a Queen and a Queen was of greater value than a Jack.

"There are four suits," I continued, using the cards in my own hand to demonstrate. "Clubs, hearts, diamonds, and spades. If the first card played, by the player to the dealer's left, is a heart, everyone else must follow suit, unless you have no cards in that suit. Then you put down a card from any suit. The highest card in the suit that started the hand wins the trick and the winning player takes all those cards and leads the first card of the next trick."

I started to add that there were many variations of the game. The player who won three tricks could choose to claim the pot or lead to the fourth hand and by winning five tricks require all the players to pay a second stake. There was also such a thing as a trump. But looking at the faces surrounding me, their expressions ranging from deep concentration to baffled puzzlement, I decided to keep this first game simple.

We played for an hour, all of us sitting in a circle on the floor, even the princess, before we were caught. Fortune smiled on us that day. It was Lady Catherine who returned to the presence chamber first. Her eyes widened when she saw what we were doing, and she scolded us, but she did not confiscate my deck of cards and she did not tell Lady Salisbury.

"Do you know other card games?" the princess whispered when I stepped close to her to adjust her gown, which had become wrinkled where she'd been sitting on it.

"A great many of them," I assured her, thinking of Primero and Pope July and One and Thirty.

"Then you will teach them to me, too, when next we have opportunity for leisure."

As it happened, that was sooner than anyone anticipated. King Henry had not, after all, forgotten his daughter on the faraway Marches of Wales. He sent her a Lord of Misrule, with orders to provide all the delights of the Yuletide season. The fellow arrived late that afternoon and for the next twelve days, the usual regimen did not apply. We gave ourselves over to the enjoyment of the season.

On the first of January, called New Year's Day even though the new year did not truly begin until Lady Day, the twenty-fifth of March, we exchanged gifts and gave gifts to the princess. My second letter to Blanche had asked her to send a leaf from the holy hawthorn tree of Glastonbury in a reliquary as a New Year's gift for the princess. It arrived that very morning, along with a message my stepmother had dictated to Sir Jasper.

I found a quiet corner to read that she was well and that she missed me. Sir Lionel Daggett had visited her both in Glastonbury and in Bristol and had been seen several times at Hartlake Manor and the other properties that made up my inheritance. I winced at that, but kept reading. Then I sat up straighter. Hugo Wynn had been allowed to remain as my steward . . . and his daughter, Griselda, had given birth to a fine, healthy girl child she'd named Winifred.

This news affected me oddly. The baby was kin to me, my niece. If she had been the product of a lawful union . . . and a boy . . . I'd have been disinherited. As matters stood, the child had no claim to my family's estates and would be raised by her mother and grandfather in the steward's lodgings. I might never even meet her.

That thought engendered others. I had heard nothing from Sir Lionel since he'd left me at Thornbury. That made me suddenly nervous. Was he, even now, arranging a marriage for me? I did not care for that idea. I knew I must eventually wed, but once I did, my husband would control everything I'd inherited from my father. A wife owned nothing in her own right. If she had fallen heir to land and chattel, jewelry and household goods, as I had, all that became the property of her lord and master . . . as did she.

It was fortunate, I suppose, that I did not have much time to brood on such matters. The princess required the presence of her maids of honor as she accepted offerings from all her household and half the countryside, as well. She seemed pleased by my gift.

Princess Mary gave presents, too, mostly cups and bowls of

various sizes. For each of the maids of honor, she'd chosen a more personal gift, individual rosaries blessed by her chaplain.

On Twelfth Night, the day began with a mass and ended with a feast and a mumming. It was the last celebration of the Yuletide season. The Lord of Misrule departed the next day, and soon after we moved to Battenhall Manor, located in the countryside near Worcester. The journey was a short one, only some twelve miles, but once we were settled there, Lady Salisbury's strict regimen resumed. Once again, my stories were one of the few entertainments the princess was permitted.

As the days passed, I recounted the further adventures of Joseph of Arimathea and of King Arthur and his knights, then branched out into tales of St. Dunstan, whose body had been translated from Canterbury to Glastonbury. I also delved into the legends and lore of the Mendip Hills. I delivered these in a broad local accent that sent all the ladies off into gales of laughter.

I'd heard the speech of Somersetshire and Gloucestershire all my life, and still did every day, from Edyth. She regularly substituted *z* for *s* and *v* for *f*, dropped the *w* in *wood*, added an *h* to *egg*, and replaced the word *are* with *bist*.

"Thee bist sprack as a banty-cock, zur," I was declaiming, as part of a story I'd heard at Hartlake Manor, when I noticed that my tiring maid had joined my audience in the presence chamber. In a sea of rapt expressions, hers alone reflected deep distress.

I faltered, recovered, and went on with my tale, but the praise and laughter at the end did not please me as much as they usually did. As soon as I was free to do so, I went looking for Edyth, who had left soon after I noticed her, her eyes glistening suspiciously in the candlelight.

I found her in the maidens' dormitory.

"I bin looken out var thee," she said in a choked voice.

"Edyth, you must not mind what I say to the others. They are not from these parts. I am certain, were you to hear the native accents of the counties they come from, you would find them most strange to the ear."

"Thee'll kill I wi' laughing." Edyth sniffed. "If I'd a-known, I 'ooden never a-went wi' thee."

"Do you want to leave?" I asked. "I can send you back to Hartlake Manor, though that would never be my choice."

Edyth did not answer me.

I sighed. "I do beg your pardon, Edyth, for making mock of the way you speak, but we live at the princess's court now. Even the Welsh here try to talk like the London gentry." I smiled at her, hoping to encourage a similar expression in return. "You could learn to speak that way, too, if you did but try."

She remained silent, but I could tell by the tilt of her head that she was listening.

I might have said more, had my fellow maids of honor not returned to our lodgings just then. I did not want to embarrass Edyth further. When she slipped out of the room a few minutes later, she was still sulking, but I could not help but notice that, afterward, whenever she was with me, she paid close attention to the way the maids of honor spoke to one another.

For my part, I no longer used dialect to elicit laughter at my tales. I realized that I had no need to do so. If the story was engrossing enough, it did not require embellishment.

10

In a rare departure from the austerity of the princess's household, we were allowed to celebrate Valentine's Day. It had nothing to do with that date, the fourteenth of February, marking the beginning of my fourteenth year. No one at Battenhall Manor was aware of that fact and they would not have cared if they had been. Except for the king, hardly anyone celebrated their birthday. I had no cause to rejoice in any case. It was a bittersweet accomplishment to have attained, too late, the age that would have kept me out of wardship after my father and brother died.

Copying the manner Valentine's Day was observed at King Henry's court, gentlemen's names were written on slips of paper and placed in a gilded bowl. Then each of the ladies and gentlewomen in attendance on Mary Tudor took a turn to pull one out. Princess Mary, who would enter her tenth year in a few more days, was the first to take her turn. She drew the name of Sir Ralph Egerton, her treasurer of the household.

Anne Rede and I exchanged an amused look and Anne had to

turn away to hide her laughter. Sir Ralph was very likely the oldest man in the princess's retinue. His short hair was grizzled, his face was deeply lined, and his shoulders were stooped. I could not think of anyone more unsuited to be Her Grace's partner for the day.

At least Sir Ralph's clothing was grand enough for his role. He had a love of rich fabrics and bright colors. He most often wore a gown and jacket of tawny velvet, pearled with gold and lined with black satin, but he also had a very fine jacket made of cloth of silver and blue and russet velvet. In honor of Valentine's Day, he wore a green velvet gown lined with green sarcenet and guarded with cloth of gold.

Princess Mary gave every evidence of being delighted with the luck of the draw. "Sir Ralph, for today you are my husband *adoptif* and I am your pretend wife." She cried as she sank into a deep court curtsey.

He bowed in response, but his eyes widened at her declaration.

The drawing continued. Anne picked Thomas Pereston, the princess's apothecary. She read out his name and when he came to stand at her side, she was polite to him, but the moment he looked away, her face crinkled up in distaste. Master Pereston carried the stink of his medicines with him. It permeated his clothing. Even his hands reeked, in spite of frequent washings.

When it was my turn, I found myself unaccountably nervous. I was not accustomed to spending much time with gentlemen, even though there were always several of them present in the princess's chambers. I'd never had to make conversation with one of them.

The name I drew was that of Sir Giles Greville, controller of the household. He was almost as important as Sir Ralph Egerton, and formidable-looking besides, being one of those men who always stand very stiffly, back straight and chin up. When I read his name aloud, Anne caught my arm and pulled me closer.

"Oh, that we could trade 'husbands,' Tamsin," she lamented in a low wail. "Above all men, I find Sir Giles most appealing."

At first I thought she was jesting, but the expression on her face conveyed nothing but genuine admiration for the older man. He was not so ancient as Sir Ralph, but neither was Sir Giles blessed with youth. I had heard he had a grown daughter, already married.

"He sent me a token of his esteem," Anne confided as the drawing continued.

"A locket with his portrait in miniature?" I guessed, although I thought that unlikely.

Anne pinched me, hard, between the stays of my body-stitchet where the material of my bodice was thinnest. When I jerked away from her, she lifted the pomander ball that hung from the belt at her waist. It was a pretty thing, latticed to allow the sweet-scented herbs that filled it to waft out. Only then did I realize that it had replaced the more ordinary-looking one she usually wore.

It was a gift of some value and made me wonder how Anne and Sir Giles had contrived to meet in private. He had not given her such a costly bauble when any of the other maids of honor were present to witness it. Did Lady Salisbury know that a courtship was in progress beneath her very nose? I doubted it. She would not approve. She did not approve of much of anything.

Sir Giles joined me, a fixed smile on his grizzled countenance. He bowed to all the maids of honor, since we stood together in a group, but his gaze went straight to Anne. He could not seem to keep his eyes off her.

When all the princess's women had picked their valentines, Her Grace called for the dancing to begin. She had only one official musician, but two of her gentlemen waiters had previously been lute players in the king's household and regularly accompanied the Welshman. They played a variety of instruments, from viol and rebec to virginals and tambor.

"I beg your pardon, Your Grace," Sir Ralph said, "but I am unable to execute even the simplest steps. You must choose another gallant to partner you."

"Nonsense, Sir Ralph." Princess Mary's voice was that of a young girl but nonetheless carried authority. "As your pretend wife, I am duty bound to stay true to you."

"I am an old man afflicted with the gout, Your Grace. I cannot dance." Sir Ralph's quandary was apparent to all. He did not wish to insult the princess, but his pain was quite real. "I . . . er . . . that is, my wife of many years . . . my real wife . . . does not demand so much of me, Your Grace."

"I can scarce believe that the gout would prevent a good husband from showing his love to his wife." The young princess was completely innocent of any double meaning to her words, but the rest of us had to stifle our laughter.

"There are other ways than dancing, Your Grace." His eyes brightened as inspiration struck. "A good husband gives instruction to his wife."

"He means he orders her about," Mary Fitzherbert whispered, sounding disgruntled. Her tone made me think her father must be a tyrant, but I had no time to ponder the matter. My attention swung back to the unlikely couple on the dais.

"Well, then," said the princess, "I beg you to teach me what a good husband ought to teach his wife. You may begin with the definition of love."

"Love, Your Grace?" Sir Ralph sounded as if he were choking on his own question.

"Yes. Talk to me of the ideals of courtly love."

Sir Ralph sagged in relief. "As you wish, Your Grace." He launched into a long and convoluted lecture about loyalty, worship from afar, and the satisfaction of performing well in a tournament while carrying a lady's favor.

I heard nothing new in what he said. Although we'd had little chance to put our knowledge into practice, we were all familiar with the favorite pastime of courtiers and ladies at the royal courts of Europe. A courtier picked out one lady in particular to be his "mistress," wooed her with gifts, wrote poems to her, serenaded her with song, and vowed to be faithful only to her. If she accepted him as her "lover," he was allowed to joust in her honor and she, especially if she was older than he or superior to him in birth, advanced his career at court. This flirtation, which might even include passionate declarations of love, was all a game. Most of the time, both "mistress" and "lover" were married, although never to each other.

"The perfect knight honors his beloved, ofttimes from afar," Sir Ralph concluded, "and so I shall worship you, Your Grace, as I watch you dance with another."

Once the elderly knight had persuaded Princess Mary to choose a different partner, a young gentleman waiter, the music began. We all joined in the dancing. I was pleased to discover that Sir Giles knew all the steps and executed them with precision. Even better, he was uninterested in conversation. His attention strayed with the least provocation to my friend Anne Rede, and when the first dance was succeeded by a second, abruptly abandoned me to partner her.

I evaded Master Pereston before he could offer himself in Sir Giles's place. After that, I tried to make myself invisible. It was not all that difficult to blend into the shadows at the side of the chamber. I sought a window alcove where I could observe without being seen.

It was already occupied by Lady Catherine.

"I beg your pardon, my lady. I will—"

"Stay, Tamsin. There is room for us both." She slid over on the window seat and patted the cushion beside her. The princess had given permission for those of her ladies who were not dancing to sit in her presence.

I could not, in politeness, refuse, but I felt awkward perched there at her side. Sensing how ill at ease I was, she sent a reassuring smile in my direction. "Shall I tell you a tale for a change?" she asked.

"I am always interested in hearing stories."

I wondered if she would speak of herself. I had observed, from time to time, a sadness in Lady Catherine that hinted at an intriguing past. It was, however, Sir Ralph Egerton's history that she recounted. Or rather, that of his wife.

"She was born Margaret Bassett, daughter of Ralph Bassett of Blore, Staffordshire, and her first husband was an important Leicestershire sergeant-at-law named Thomas Kebell. He was a very rich man, and after his death, because she was a wealthy heiress, she was abducted from Blore Hall by a band of men brandishing swords. It is said there were a hundred and twenty in the raiding party and it was led by Roger Vernon, son of Sir Henry Vernon of Haddon Hall in Derbyshire. Roger wanted to marry Margaret, even though she was already planning to wed Ralph Egerton of Ridley. In fact, at the very time Margaret was kidnapped, Ralph—he was not yet *Sir* Ralph then—was staying at Blore with his father to celebrate their upcoming betrothal."

"How terrible!" I felt a deep sympathy for Margaret. Like her I was an heiress. Like her, I had been taken away from my home against my will.

"Margaret's mother and grandfather and brother set off in pursuit of the abductors, but they were outnumbered and were unable to rescue her. Roger Vernon forced Margaret to marry him and then sent her to his uncles in Leicestershire and later into the Welsh Marches, to hide her from pursuit. Margaret, however, was a clever young woman and she managed to escape on her own and travel to London."

The music and the noise of the dancers faded away as I listened, rapt, to Lady Catherine tell the tale. I felt certain there was a happy ending in the offing. "Did Sir Ralph find her there? Were they married at last?"

"In time they were. First the case had to go before the court of the Star Chamber. Do you know what that is?"

I shook my head.

"That is where cases involving rich and important people are settled, sometimes by the king himself. There charges and countercharges were made. The legal wrangling went on for more than seven years but, in the end, Margaret Bassett was allowed to marry Ralph Egerton. Her forced marriage to Master Vernon was declared null and void."

"And they lived happily ever after," I concluded, remembering Sir Ralph's reference to his wife. I sighed in satisfaction.

Lady Catherine chuckled. "They have had as good a marriage as most, although I understand that Sir Ralph has a number of bastard children."

I frowned, disliking this ambivalent ending to the tale. "What happened to the band of kidnappers?"

"Vernon was fined. Then the king pardoned everyone who was involved in the abduction."

"I prefer stories where evil is punished."

Lady Catherine laughed aloud at that, but it was a sound so devoid of humor that I became more convinced than ever that she had herself lived a life worthy of a *roman*. She had experienced, I was certain, more than her share of sadness. I wanted very badly to ask her why she looked so unhappy. To stop myself from speaking out of turn and offending her, I turned my gaze toward the dancers.

It was only by chance that I noticed the princess slipping away from the crowd. She was alone.

I hastily excused myself and followed Her Grace. Protocol demanded that at least two attendants be with Princess Mary even when she visited the stool chamber, which seemed likely to be her destination. She passed through her bedchamber and on into the smaller room where her close stool was housed. I stopped short when I heard voices. I hesitated on the threshold, suddenly unsure of myself.

It never occurred to me that the princess might be in danger. She was well guarded here in her innermost chambers. No one could gain access who was not already part of the household. Still, there was something strange about the rhythm of the words I overheard, even if I could not quite make them out. When I listened harder, I realized what it was that seemed so peculiar—the princess and her companion were not conversing in English.

Still unsure whether to advance or retreat, I took a step away from the inner door. My foot struck a cushion left carelessly on the floor. It made no sound, but I was so startled by the unexpected contact that I gasped.

An abrupt silence fell on the other side of the door. I longed to creep quietly away, following the distant sounds of lute and viol and the faint ripple of laughter that filtered in from the presence chamber, but I was frozen to the spot. Before I could force my legs to move, Maria Vittorio emerged from the stool chamber.

I sagged in relief. They had been speaking Spanish together. That was all. I had no cause for alarm.

But Maria gave me a long, hard stare and showed no hint of the friendliness I'd come to expect from her. Then she spoke over her shoulder to the princess. "It is only Tamsin, Your Grace."

With a rustle of brocade, Princess Mary appeared behind her. She smiled, just as she had smiled at Sir Ralph when she'd drawn his name. "I could not hold my water," she said with a little laugh. But if she was embarrassed by her lack of control, she showed no other sign of it. "I am ready to return to the dancing now."

That night in our shared bed, neither Maria nor I mentioned the strange little incident. I related the story of Sir Ralph and his Margaret to the other maids of honor and then we all settled ourselves to rest.

For a long time, sleep did not come.

Maria and the princess had been speaking Spanish, a language no one else in the household understood. I could not help but wonder why.

11

We left Worcester on the seventeenth of April to travel to Hartlebury Castle, principal country residence of the Bishop of Worcester, which was seven miles distant. I liked Hartlebury at once. It had good ponds, a rabbit warren, and a deer park. While we were there, we hunted and fished, but we were soon on our way again. We traveled northwest to Mitton, where the River Stour divides into several streams that drive mills, then rode on to Bewdley through wooded countryside and newly planted fields. We stayed at Tickenhill Manor, just west of Bewdley, a house built at the very top of the hill on which the town is built, among trees in a good park.

Thus, by slow stages, we made the journey to Ludlow Castle, twenty miles from Worcester and the official seat of the government of the principality of Wales. Building had been going on there for months, but Lady Salisbury still deemed the castle unfit for occupation by a royal princess. We settled in instead at Oakley Park, a few miles to the northwest. It was the Shropshire residence of Sir

William Thomas, who moved his family out for the duration of our stay.

As spring turned into summer, I gradually forgot about Maria's odd behavior. We were easy with one another again.

I continued to spin stories at bedtime and as we sat and wrought, too. One day in early summer, I told the old tale of Floris and Blauncheflour, one my father had told to me, about a king's son who risks his life for the girl he loves. Surrounded by avid listeners, I recounted how Blauncheflour was sold to merchants and taken to Babylon and how Floris followed her there, found her among the maidens in the sultan's palace, and rescued her. This happy ending provoked sighs of rapture. In the realms of legend and lore, as well as in real life, the triumph of true love is never a sure thing.

"All men should be so loyal to their sweethearts," Cecily said.

"My suitor is." Anne's strident voice dared the rest of us to disagree.

I exchanged a speaking glance with Mary Fitzherbert. We'd all of us heard more than enough about the trouble that Sir Giles Greville's desire to marry Anne Rede had caused. Lady Salisbury disapproved of the match, but that was not the greatest obstacle. It was that Anne's mother, Lady Rede, insisted upon a huge jointure for her daughter in the marriage settlement. Sir Giles wanted Anne as his wife, but he had no desire to give in to his future mother-in-law's demands. Since Anne's father was too ill to take part in the negotiations, they dragged on. A happy ending was by no means certain.

"It is not the lot of a woman to choose her own husband," the princess said. As was so often the case, she sounded more like a prim and proper woman of five and twenty than a ten-year-old girl.

"No woman should be forced to wed someone repugnant to her," Cecily, who had just turned twenty, said in her usual soft whisper, but with more force than was her wont. I wondered if she had rejected such a suitor. At her age, her father must already have tried to arrange a match for her.

"We must obey our elders." Her Grace kept her eyes on her embroidery. "When I am older, I will marry a foreign prince, just as my mother did, and perforce leave my homeland behind forever."

I thought I heard a catch in the princess's voice at the last. I glanced her way in time to see her miss a stitch. In no other way did she betray her reluctance to be sent away from England and all she held dear.

I frowned, considered a moment, and then spoke hesitantly. "Your Grace, you are the king's only heir. Surely you must remain here. Why, one day you could be queen in your own right."

Everyone stared at me. I wondered if I had suddenly grown another head. Feeling mutinous, I pursued the thought.

"If a girl is the only child, she must inherit her father's estate. As I did."

"Hush, Tamsin," Anne hissed at me. "It is treason to speak of the death of the king."

"But I was not—" I fell silent. Heat flooded into my face as I realized that I *had*. How else should Princess Mary become queen except through the death of her father? "I beg your pardon, Your Grace. I simply meant that if there should be such a misfortune as to be no sons, in any family, then a daughter becomes the rightful heiress to all that remains."

"I am certain that, one day, my father will have a son to succeed him." Her Grace sounded confident but looked unbearably sad when she added, "I had a brother once, before I was born, but he lived only a few days. I would like to have another. I pray to God for that blessing every day."

"You would no longer be Princess of Wales if you had a brother," Mary Fitzherbert pointed out.

"I would still be a princess. In truth, I think I should be happier, for I could live at my father's court. And I could see my mother again."

Maria lifted a hand, as if to pat the princess's arm, but remembered herself just in time and pulled back. "Your Grace's father will find you a handsome prince to marry, Your Grace. No matter who he is, you will have children of your own and that will be your happy ending."

There were general nods and murmurs of agreement, for we had all been taught, since our earliest years, that children were what every woman most desired in life. *Be fruitful and multiply?* I wondered. I had never had much to do with babies, being the youngest myself. Then again, from what I had gathered since coming to the princess's court, royal mothers spent little time with their children after they were born.

"I know whom I would wed, if it were up to me," Cecily murmured.

"Who?" I thought it best to turn our conversation away from royal matrimony.

"His name is Rhys Mansell. He is Welsh," she added, unnecessarily.

"Where did you meet him?" Princess Mary was suddenly a little girl again, as curious as the rest of us.

"He is not a member of this household," Mary Dannett said.

"No, he is not," Cecily agreed, "but he has ties to it. Lady Catherine's husband is Sir Matthew Craddock and Sir Matthew was Rhys's guardian when he was a boy."

"Why is she Lady Catherine and not Lady Craddock?" I asked. I had wondered about the princess's chief gentlewoman for months and this seemed a perfect opportunity to discover something of her mysterious past. "Is she a duke's daughter?"

The daughters of dukes and earls were addressed by their Christian names, with the honorary title "Lady" as a prefix, no matter the rank of their husbands. If Lady Catherine had been of lesser birth than Sir Matthew, she'd have been addressed as Lady Craddock.

"He was an earl," Cecily said. "The Earl of Huntley."

"But that is not an English title," Mary Dannett objected.

"Lady Catherine is Scottish by birth."

None of us had known that and our demands for the whole story persuaded Cecily, once she had looked around to make sure none of the older ladies-in-waiting was within earshot, to tell us the tale.

"She was born Lady Catherine Gordon," Cecily began, "far away to the north in Scotland. She was the daughter of an earl whose first wife was a royal princess of that land. Because of her high station, the king of Scotland—I do not remember which one, but his name must have been James; they are all called James—married her to a young man who claimed he was the rightful heir to the English throne. He said he was Richard, son of King Edward the Fourth, and that he had miraculously escaped from the Tower of London."

We all nodded, knowing full well that this was not true. *Everyone* knew that Prince Richard and his older brother, who was briefly Edward V, had been murdered there by their wicked uncle, the evil usurper who had made himself king in little Edward's place and called himself Richard III. King Richard, to the joy of all true Englishmen, had been defeated in a great battle by Henry Tudor, Princess Mary's grandfather, after which Henry took the throne himself as King Henry VII.

"The man who married Lady Catherine," Cecily continued, "was really a lowborn foreigner named Perkin Warbeck. When he attempted to invade England, he was captured and executed."

I do not know which of us was more astonished, myself or the princess, to learn that Lady Catherine had once been married to that notorious pretender to the throne of England. We were all listening so intently that the sound of a pin dropping would have sounded like a cannon shot in the quiet of the room.

I wondered that the other ladies did not suspect something was amiss, but they remained where they were, on the far side of the presence chamber, engrossed in a complex piece of embroidery stretched on a large frame. Lady Catherine was one of the women seated in a circle surrounding it, but she never looked our way.

"Perkin Warbeck," Cecily continued, "brought his poor wife with him from Scotland. She was captured, too, but instead of imprisoning her, Your Grace's grandfather made her a lady-in-waiting to his wife, Queen Elizabeth of York."

The princess's expression had darkened. Her lips were pursed in disapproval.

Mary Dannett missed these signs. "But she is married to Sir Matthew now," she exclaimed. "Oh, I do hope that is a happy ending."

"Perhaps it is," Cecily said, sounding doubtful, "but Sir Matthew is her third husband. Her second was a knight named Strangeways." She lowered her voice still further, until it was almost impossible to catch the words. Only because I was sitting right next to her did I hear her say, "She wed Sir Matthew Craddock only a month after Sir James Strangeways died."

Into the little silence that followed Cecily's revelations, Princess Mary spoke. Her voice was nearly as soft as Cecily's but it vibrated with barely contained emotion. "She was married to a pretender to the throne. She tried to become queen in my grandmother's place." Had the look she sent in her chief gentlewoman's direction shot daggers, Lady Catherine would have bled to death on the spot.

"A wife must do as her husband commands," I reminded Her Grace, "and Lady Catherine could not have been wicked herself, else Your Grace's father would not have entrusted her with Your

Grace's care." As chief gentlewoman, Lady Catherine was second only to the Countess of Salisbury, both in precedence and in authority.

"Perhaps no one told him her story," the princess said. She had already regained control of herself. Princesses are taught young to hide their true thoughts from the world.

"The king knows everything." Anne said this with perfect confidence. When we all looked at her askance, she pouted. "Well, he does. Sir Giles told me. It is part of being a king to have spies everywhere."

Princess Mary's eyes narrowed. "My father would never spy on me."

Anne made haste to agree with her. "No, Your Grace. Why should he?"

Mollified, the princess picked up the shirt she had been hemming—we were always making clothes for the poor, although I never saw a poor man wearing anything I stitched—and muttered, "Someone should have told me Lady Catherine's history ere now."

"Perhaps they did not wish to distress you, Your Grace," Maria suggested.

Princess Mary considered that for a moment, plying her needle industriously as she did so. "Perhaps, and yet I think it must be better to know things than to live in ignorance."

I wondered if she would ever look upon Lady Catherine in quite the same way again.

12

Some weeks after Cecily told us the story of Perkin Warbeck, I ventured out alone at Oakley Park. The princess
had sent me to search for the friendly striped cat that had been
a regular visitor to her apartments since we moved in. It had not
been seen for several days. Tender-hearted as she was, Princess Mary
feared that Foolish, as she'd named it for its antics with a bit of lace
it had stolen to play with, might have been killed by one of the
hunting dogs.

Lady Salisbury was of the opinion that cats were unsuitable pets.
In addition to a lapdog, she kept a monkey, a foul-tempered, dirty
little beast. Cats, at least, cleaned themselves.

After an hour of looking high and low, I finally located Foolish in
the stables, nestled in a bed of straw, nursing a litter of kittens. This
came as a surprise to me. I'd thought the cat was simply getting fat
from a surfeit of rich table scraps. Bemused, I left mother and babies
where they were.

It was early August. The trees in the garden that lay between the stables and the house were bursting with good things to eat, everything from pears to filberts. Flowers grew there in profusion, in particular roses and gillyflowers, planted among the knots and mounds, the carved wooden beasts, and the ornamental pools.

At the center of the garden was a bower. The wooden pillars that formed the arch were ten feet high and boasted four turrets, each housing a birdcage. When they were so inclined, the feathered occupants filled the air with song. On this day, however, they were silent.

For greater privacy, a quickset hedge had been trained over the frame of the arch. All in all, it was a peaceful place, well hidden from casual view. I headed that way with the intention of stealing an hour for solitary contemplation, a rare treat for anyone who lived in the large household attached to a royal princess.

I had almost reached my goal when I heard the murmur of voices. A man and a woman already occupied the bower, seated on the wooden bench beneath the arch. I stopped in my tracks, prepared to retreat, but I changed my mind when I recognized one of the speakers as Lady Butts, the physician's wife.

"But he is a bastard!" she exclaimed, her tone of voice suggesting outrage.

Intrigued, I crept closer, until I could see that Lady Butts's companion was her husband. Although he'd received livery of blue and green damask, he wore the black robe and cap of a physician. In common with his wife, he had a plain, strong-featured countenance. From my place of concealment behind the hedge, I caught only a glimpse of them, but I could hear their conversation as clearly as if I sat beside them.

"You must not say such things, my dear," Dr. Butts warned his wife. "Your words might be misconstrued as treason."

"I speak nothing less than the truth," Lady Butts protested. "The king himself has acknowledged the boy as his son. He's called Henry Fitzroy by one and all."

"He's called the *Duke of Richmond*. King Henry gave him that title more than a year ago." Dr. Butts made an odd little sound, somewhere between a snort and a laugh. "Dubbed him Duke of Somerset, too, and Earl of Nottingham. Grand titles for a lad barely seven years old."

"He's Bessie Blount's bastard," Lady Butts insisted. "No more than that."

"My dear, I know you are loyal to the queen and the princess, as am I, but you must face facts. The king's intentions have been clear ever since he set up a separate household for the boy at Sheriff Hutton Castle in Yorkshire. If His Grace has no legitimate son, he will find a way to make the Duke of Richmond his heir."

Although I was caught unaware by this news that the king had an illegitimate son, I could not say that I was surprised. Men took mistresses and babies were the result. I had only to remember Lady Catherine's comments about Sir Ralph Egerton. Dr. Butts's prediction that Henry Fitzroy might one day rule England, however, came as a shock. That a bastard could deprive a legitimate child of her inheritance was a terrifying notion.

"Princess Mary is heir to this kingdom," Lady Butts insisted. "And do not tell me that a woman cannot rule. Look at Isabella of Castile, Queen Catherine's mother. Isabella not only ruled Castile in her own right, and left it to her eldest daughter, Joanna, but she drove the Moors and the Jews out of all of Spain. She was a *warrior* queen."

Silently, I applauded the idea that a woman could rule. Had I not said so once myself? But I did not think the opinion of a physician's wife or a princess's maid of honor would carry much weight with

King Henry. Moving as silently as I could, I backed away from the bower and fled from the garden.

Back in Princess Mary's presence chamber, I pondered what to do with my newly acquired knowledge. Should I tell Her Grace what I had learned? I remembered well what she had said when she'd heard Lady Catherine's story—that it was better to know than to live in ignorance. But the princess, for all her grown-up ways, was still only ten years old. And the king and queen might yet have a legitimate son.

I debated with myself for two days, unable to decide what to do. It was only when I was alone with the princess, with no one else save Maria Vittorio, in the relative privacy of the stool chamber, that I finally made up my mind. As I approached Her Grace with a bowl of warm washing water scented with chamomile flowers boiled in orange peel, I said in an urgent whisper, "Your Grace, there is something you should know."

She dipped her hands into the bowl. "Speak."

I told her what I had overheard, although without naming Dr. Butts or his wife. Maria dried the princess's hands with a towel, her lips pursed tightly together in disapproval. I could not tell if she was wroth with me or with the king.

Her Grace absorbed the news with seeming equanimity, although her pale complexion went a trifle whiter and her fingers shook a little as she freed them from the towel. Princess Mary had an uncanny ability, even at that young age, to affect calmness.

When her steady, unsettling stare came to rest on my face, I feared my days in her household were numbered. I lowered my eyes and waited for the ax to fall. Nearby, I could hear Maria's quiet breathing, but she did not speak.

"I value honesty above all else," Princess Mary said after a lengthy, nerve-racking pause, "even when it distresses me. You have done me good service this day, Tamsin Lodge. I will not forget it."

13

From Oakley Park, the princess's household moved on to Worcester, where it remained for nearly two weeks. We left there in late August to journey to Evesham Abbey, but Evesham was only a stop on the way to Langley in Oxfordshire. The princess was as impatient as I had ever seen her, and no wonder, for at Langley we were to join the king's annual progress. For the first time in over a year, Princess Mary would be reunited with her parents.

I confess I envied her. I had not seen my stepmother in all that time, either. There were days when I even had difficulty remembering what Blanche looked like. I had always been my father's pet, spending long hours in his company. The last few years of his life, Blanche had been there, too, but well in the background. By the time our first year apart had passed, I rarely thought of her at all. I had become part of a new family. Instead of parents, I had sisters, all of them as dear to me as my own kith and kin.

Since Yuletide, I had received only one letter from my stepmother. She had dictated it to a hired scribe. It had told me little except that Blanche now spent all her time in her dower house in Bristol. She had not visited Hartlake Manor since Sir Lionel Daggett came into our lives.

I had spared a thought or two for my estates during this same period of time, but as there was nothing I could do to override any decisions Sir Lionel made concerning them—not until I attained my majority—I'd soon turned my mind to more immediate concerns. Foremost among these had been the need to keep coming up with stories to tell. Although the princess liked to hear her favorites again and again, fresh material was always welcome. I soon taught myself how to elaborate upon the framework of an existing tale. I even created a new story or two out of whole cloth.

At Langley, I expected to enjoy a respite from providing entertainment to the princess and her ladies. King Henry and Queen Catherine went on progress every summer, traveling to various parts of the kingdom to be seen by their subjects. They took with them their fools and musicians and their hosts provided other diversions along the way.

Going on a progress was also a good way to avoid being in London and its environs during the months those heavily populated areas were most likely to be visited by outbreaks of the plague and other vile sicknesses.

Langley was located a mile from Burford, right on the edge of Wychwood Forest. It was a beautiful spot, but when we first arrived there I had little interest in the scenery. Like the princess, I was eager for my first glimpse of King Henry VIII of England.

His Grace was the tallest man I had ever seen. That was my initial impression. In the months I had been with the princess, I had myself shot up in height, but King Henry towered over me. Everyone around him seemed small and insignificant in comparison.

The second thing I noticed about the king was the flash of jewels. Every article of his clothing glittered, calling attention to his face and form. Above a richly ornamented doublet rose a striking countenance. He was clean-shaven, as were most of the men at court, which displayed a forceful chin. His hair was burnished copper. Although his complexion was fair for a man and his features were almost delicate, there was nothing feminine about him. He had the physique of an avid jouster, which he was. His arms and chest were well muscled and his legs strong. He exuded masculinity and good cheer and he seemed genuinely pleased to be reunited with his daughter.

Princess Mary made her obeisance, her smile stretched wide. Had she been an ordinary girl and he just another father, I am sure she would have flung herself into his arms. Court protocol discouraged any such display.

"By St. George, Mary!" King Henry exclaimed. "You have grown apace in your time away from us."

"Yes, Father. I have been very well cared for."

The king gave a booming laugh that echoed off the rafters of the great hall at Langley. "Well and good, my girl. Well and good."

Queen Catherine, who had gone almost unnoticed in her husband's presence, now stepped forward to greet her daughter. Her Grace was some years older than the king. Repeated pregnancies had left her stooped and stout. What little I could see of her hair beneath an enormous gable headdress appeared to be a faded reddish gold shot through with gray. She was also extremely short. Princess Mary, for all that she was on the small and dainty side, already surpassed her mother in height.

A bevy of the queen's maids of honor hovered nearby. They were all younger and more physically attractive than Her Grace. Their presence made Queen Catherine seem even older and more worn out than she really was. Some of these young women appeared to be close to my own years, while others were clearly older, but almost all of them had pink and white complexions and a tendency toward plumpness.

There was one exception, a slender woman whose skin was almost olive-hued. She had eyes so large and dark that they appeared to be black. These characteristics should have made her ugly, but she had an elegance about her, and an air of self-confidence. I found myself staring at her, studying the high cheekbones, the strong nose, and the wide mouth, all set into a long oval of a face. She was no beauty, but her countenance suggested a forceful personality that might well make up for her lack of conventional prettiness.

When my wandering attention returned to Queen Catherine and Princess Mary, they had finished exchanging formal greetings and the princess had begun to tell her parents about her sojourn in the Marches of Wales. The queen listened with avid attention to every word, but His Grace soon grew bored.

King Henry's interest shifted to his daughter's assembled ladies. He narrowed his blue-gray eyes when his gaze fixed on me. Disconcerted, I quickly sank into a curtsey, but I still felt the king's hard stare boring into the top of my head. The sensation seemed to continue for a very long time, although I suppose it lasted less than a minute. Only when I was certain he had lost interest did I dare look up.

I breathed a sigh of relief. His Grace had engaged his cousin, the Countess of Salisbury, in low-voiced conversation. I told myself I was being fanciful. The king had no reason to take any notice of me.

The king, the queen, and the princess soon adjourned to a more private chamber to continue their reunion. The rest of us were left to our own devices. I was examining a particularly fine tapestry in the presence chamber assigned to Princess Mary when I was ordered to present myself to Their Graces.

The king and queen were seated in comfortable chairs with a

table between them. The princess, her legs curled beneath her, sat on a cushion at her mother's feet. There were at least a dozen courtiers and servants in the chamber, but they stayed well in the background.

"You are Daggett's girl, are you not?" the king asked when I rose from yet another curtsey.

His abrupt question caught me off guard. I wanted to deny that the odious Sir Lionel had any connection to me, but in the sense His Grace meant, I *was* his "girl."

"Sir Lionel Daggett is my guardian, Your Majesty." Together with all the princess's ladies, I had been forewarned by Lady Catherine that King Henry preferred this form of address to "Your Highness" or "Your Grace."

"Has he arranged a marriage for you?"

"If he has, Sire, he has not told me of it." I could not quite keep the tartness out of my reply but, to my relief, the king only smiled.

"I would not wish to lose Mistress Lodge from my service, Father," Princess Mary said. "She tells the most wonderful stories and entertains us better than any bard."

Queen Catherine frowned. "These are improving tales, I trust?"

Because the king and queen sat behind their daughter, they could not see the twinkle in the young princess's eyes. "Oh, yes, Madre. Tamsin comes from Glastonbury. She knows all about the holy relics that are kept there."

I remained silent, for I doubted that the queen would approve of some of the stories I'd related to her daughter. My father had been widely read and had seen no reason to censor the tales he told me. I'd repeated these as closely as I could remember them, and I had a very good memory. In doing so, I had never considered their content. Faced with the princess's protective mother, I now had belated second thoughts. *The Squire of Low Degree*, in which a king's daughter falls in love with a lowly squire, was unlikely to meet with Queen Catherine's approval. Even worse was *William of Palerne*, a tale featuring an evil queen of Spain as the villain—she turns the hero into a werewolf by the use of sorcery.

"We must hear one of these stories someday," the king said.

Then he dismissed me.

Feeling a trifle dazed and most certainly dazzled, I backed out of the chamber. It was my intention to retire to the tent that had been set up in the garden as temporary housing for the princess's maids of honor, since Langley was a simple manor house that did not have indoor accommodation for everyone who'd accompanied the king and queen, and now the princess, on their summer progress.

I got no farther than the outer chamber.

A man emerged from among the crowd of men and women, local people and courtiers alike, who were awaiting their opportunity to present petitions to the king. It had been a little more than a year since I'd last seen Sir Lionel Daggett, but I had no difficulty recognizing him. I stopped dead and stared, an unreasoning dread rendering my limbs incapable of movement.

He made me only the most cursory of bows. "Mistress Thomasine. You are well, I trust."

I dropped into an equally brief curtsey. "Sir Lionel." His name came out as a croak. "I am as you see me."

He smiled, but the expression did not reach his eyes. "Come aside with me awhile, Thomasine."

He gave me no choice in the matter, seizing my arm in a painful grip. Anne Rede was watching us from the other side of the presence chamber, a look of alarm on her face. I smiled at her to let her know I did not need help, but I also took comfort in knowing that someone had seen me leave the chamber in the company of my guardian.

I do not know what I expected. I did not think he was likely to try to take liberties with my person, but I grew more and more uneasy as our distance from the protection of the crowd increased. He did not slow down until we reached a quiet corner of the courtyard where, by standing in front of me, his bigger body blocked mine from view. No casual passerby would even know I was there.

"You have blossomed in the last months, Thomasine," he said in his raspy voice. As usual, that alone set my teeth on edge. "You have indeed lived up to your promise. You have become almost as pretty as your stepmother."

I had learned something of decorum in the princess's household. I kept my composure and said only, "You flatter me, Sir Lionel." His compliment was every bit as insincere as it had been when we first met, and he still had that calculating look in his eyes.

"The king noticed, too," he continued. "Thus am I well pleased with my purchase."

It took me a moment to realize that he meant the purchase of my wardship. Hidden by my skirts, my fists clenched. It was a struggle to repress the sharp retort I wanted to make. What good would it do to tell him that I was not his property? In all ways that mattered, I was.

I sought to change the subject. "I have had little news of home since joining Princess Mary's household. Is all well at Hartlake Manor?"

"Your estates flourish," he assured me.

"And my steward? Does Hugo Wynn still occupy that post?"

"He remains in place . . . for the moment."

"And the horses?" I asked. "My brother intended to breed Star of Hartlake."

"I found a better use for him."

"He's been sold?" I had been warned Sir Lionel had the right to dispose of my cattle, but this news still came as a shock. As I struggled to come to grips with an acute sense of loss, I almost missed the import of what Sir Lionel said next.

"The princess will travel with the king and queen for the next few weeks. That should give you ample opportunity to push yourself forward."

Frowning, I ventured to correct him. "A maid of honor is expected to remain in the background."

"That has never troubled the *queen's* damsels." His smirk offended me, although I was not certain why that should be so. I knew nothing to the detriment of Queen Catherine's maids of honor. Not then.

"What is it you expect of me?" I demanded.

"That you impress the king as favorably as you have his daughter. Find a way to linger in his memory. Serving the princess is but a stepping-stone. You must contrive to serve the queen. And then, should you be presented with the opportunity, use your wiles to become the king's damsel as well as his wife's."

My stomach twisted in revulsion. The enormity of what he was suggesting left me speechless. I tried to tell myself that I had misunderstood him. He could not be advising me to—I could scarcely put words to the thought. "I am no whore," I whispered.

"Every woman is a whore," he said in equally low tones. "And you will do as I tell you or I will marry you off to an elderly beggar afflicted with the pox." Sir Lionel's insincere smile had vanished and with it any doubt of his sincerity.

"I . . . I have little opportunity to—"

"You will make your own opportunities and you will use whatever position you attain to my advantage. The king, if he is approached in the right way, can be persuaded to dispense grants of land and licenses to import or export goods. Annuities, too. I have been able to win some favors. I have been awarded a lucrative post in the West Country. But my duties will require my presence in Cornwall. That leaves you, Thomasine, as my advocate at court. The Princess of Wales will not remain in the Marches much longer, nor will you. Play your cards well, my girl, and we will both prosper."

14

We were to remain at Langley until the tenth day of September. To my great relief, Sir Lionel left on the fifth. I saw him only in company after that dreadful interview in the courtyard, but although I could avoid close physical contact with him, I found it difficult to stop thinking about what he had said.

I knew when he was to depart and from the concealment of an upper window I watched him ride away. When he at last disappeared from sight, I nearly wept with relief. Leaning against the casement, I rested my forehead against the decorative woodwork.

"He is an appalling creature, that man," said a voice from behind me.

I turned around so fast that I nearly lost my balance. The queen's olive-skinned maid of honor stood a foot away. If the knowing look in her dark eyes was any indication, she understood why I had wished to confirm that Sir Lionel was truly gone. The hint of a smile curved her unusually wide mouth, as if she was pleased to have rattled my composure.

By that time, I had learned her name. She was Mistress Anne Boleyn, daughter of Thomas Boleyn, Viscount Rochford. Rumors abounded at court that Rochford owed the acquisition of his title to his older daughter, Mary, the wife of William Carey. Until the previous year, Mistress Carey had been the king's mistress.

"Sir Lionel Daggett will find little favor at court," Mistress Anne said, "in spite of his open purse. Everyone was surprised to hear he'd been able to place his ward in the princess's household." Her disconcerting gaze swept over me, as if she was searching for whatever elusive quality had made me suitable to serve Princess Mary.

Offended, I blurted out a tart response. "I must suppose that a great heiress can always find a welcome."

She laughed. The sound of that low, throaty chuckle made the hair on the back of my neck stand up. Much later, when I knew more of the world, I would realize that Mistress Anne's laugh could have a pronounced effect on gentlemen, too, although not quite the same as the one I experienced.

"You are bold," she said. "I admire boldness. The meek inherit nothing."

I did not know what to say to that, so I said nothing. After studying me intently for a few moments more, she turned away. I supposed she had to return to her duties with the queen.

"Wait!" I called. "What more do you know of Sir Lionel?"

"Are you certain you wish to hear the story?" Once again I had the feeling she found me amusing.

"Not at all, but I believe I should." I hurried after her, wrinkling my nose when I was engulfed in the strong, sweet smell of her perfume. I recognized the scent as that of meadowsweet flowers, also called bridewort because it was the herb most often strewn at weddings. It seemed an odd choice, both too cloying and too ordinary for an exotic creature like Mistress Anne.

Side by side we resumed walking at a slower pace. We would

have little time to be private. The moment we entered the great hall, we would be surrounded by courtiers.

"The tale is well-known among the queen's ladies," she began. "It was a great scandal at the time. That was some seven years past. Sir Lionel Daggett kidnapped an heiress and forced her to marry him."

I barely suppressed a gasp.

"The marriage was allowed to stand because by the time the matter came before a court of law the bride, doubtless intimidated by her husband, insisted that she was content with the match. Still, the king was much displeased and Sir Lionel had to pay a huge fine."

"Why was such a man allowed to purchase my wardship?" Outrage made my voice louder than I'd intended. A nearby yeoman of the guard shot a suspicious look our way.

Mistress Anne laughed again. "Why, because it brought money into the royal coffers. Sir Lionel also paid well for his new post in Cornwall, but he will have to be more generous still if he expects an appointment at court. King Henry does not like the fellow."

This was the best news I could have heard. I took my leave of the queen's maid of honor with a lighter heart. I was grateful for her intelligence about the wicked man who controlled my inheritance. I would not aid him in any way, I vowed. I would do nothing to help his advancement at court. And if he tried to marry me off, as he had threatened, I would appeal directly to the king to save me.

15

At Ampthill in Bedfordshire, on the first of October, the princess's entourage broke away from the king's and returned to Hartlebury. Once back in the Marches of Wales, with our second winter there coming on, we resumed our dull routine. I was prevailed upon to provide entertainment for the household and told stories old and new to the princess and her maids of honor. When the older ladies-in-waiting were not present to stop us, we also passed the time with card games, setting aside our needlework to gamble. By February, when the Princess of Wales was summoned to join the king and queen at Windsor Castle, I had won several of Her Grace's vouchers and an assortment of trinkets from my friends.

Not all of the princess's household—more than three hundred people—accompanied her to Windsor Castle. Lady Catherine left to rejoin her husband, Sir Matthew Craddock, at Swansea, where he had built himself a fine new house. And, the negotiations finally complete, Anne Rede married Sir Giles Greville and left Her Grace's service. Sir Giles himself had been replaced as controller the

previous year so that he might assume other duties in the government of South Wales.

"I do not see why I cannot remain with the princess," Anne
complained as her trunks and boxes were loaded into a cart for the
journey to her husband. In another part of the courtyard, similar
conveyances stood waiting, filled with Princess Mary's possessions
and those of her remaining attendants.

"You will be too busy," Cecily teased her. "By spring, you will be
breeding, you mark my words."

Cecily herself was now happily betrothed to Sir Rhys Mansell
and expected to marry him later in the year. We all wondered who
would replace Anne and Cecily in the ranks of the maids of honor.
Shortly after we reached Windsor Castle, we had a part of the answer. No one arrived, nor was expected, to fill the vacancy Anne
Rede had left.

A reduced household was necessary, I soon realized, if Princess
Mary was to remain at her father's court. With both the king and
queen in residence at Windsor, the castle had been overflowing with
courtiers even before we arrived. When we moved on to Richmond
Palace in March, the overcrowding was even worse. More of the
princess's Welsh servants were sent away. They were told to remain
ready to resume their duties in the Marches, but I doubted Her
Grace would ever return there. More likely was a journey to France,
for negotiations had been resumed for her marriage to a French
prince.

Princess Mary's first betrothal had been to the French Dauphin.
When that match was broken off, she'd been betrothed to her
cousin, Holy Roman Emperor Charles V. He ruled over the Low
Countries, the German city-states, eastern Burgundy, Savoy, and
much of the northern part of Italy . . . or at least, he tried to. France
laid claim to some of those same territories. When Charles ended

his betrothal to Princess Mary, King Henry once more wished to ally himself with Francis I of France. Marriage being the traditional way to seal a treaty, a French delegation had been sent to inspect the prospective bride.

We traveled to Greenwich for St. George's Day and there Princess Mary received the Viscount of Turenne and his companions. In her own presence chamber, Her Grace sat on a chair of estate under a canopy. She was now eleven years old and greeted the ambassador with aplomb, speaking to him in Latin first, and then in French. Later she played the virginals for him.

Watching from my post a little behind and to one side of the princess, I had a clear view of the viscount's face. For the most part, he smiled and nodded, but there was a troubled look in his eyes.

When the audience was nearing its end, I slipped away from my companions. Since the floors were covered with rush matting from wall to wall, my steps made no sound as I scurried into hiding. I concealed myself in an alcove hidden behind a tapestry showing a scene from the Trojan War. I knew that the French delegation would pass by the spot after they left the princess's lodgings. From my vantage point, I could overhear bits of their conversation. I understood French quite well, having shared the princess's lessons in that language. As soon as the delegates moved out of earshot, I hastened to report to my mistress.

Maria, who had seen me leave, suspected where it was I had gone. "Well?" she asked when I reappeared. "What did they say?"

It would have been futile to deny that I had spied on the Frenchmen, but for a brief moment I considered lying about what I had heard. I glanced at the princess. I could tell her that they'd said nothing of importance. Princess Mary was an intelligent girl, but she was also more naïve than most. It was my duty to protect her from unpleasantness and to preserve her innocence. That said, my own inclination was toward honesty, and Her Grace had made clear that she preferred knowledge over ignorance.

In this instance, I decided there was no harm in forewarning her. "The French viscount thinks Your Grace is too physically immature to marry for at least three years."

The princess grimaced and sent her rueful gaze slanting down along her small frame. She was healthy, but exceedingly thin.

For myself, I was glad Her Grace was likely to remain in England longer. Soon enough, she would have to go and live in her husband's land, wherever that might turn out to be. Most of her English ladies would be left behind.

I might be sent back into Sir Lionel's keeping.

For the next week, negotiations raged. In the princess's lodgings we heard few details, even though she was the one most affected by the outcome. We could not even be certain who her betrothed would be, although the leading candidate seemed to be King Francis's second son, Henri, Duke of Orléans.

"If Her Grace becomes his wife," Maria confided one night after we'd retired to our bed, "my father says he will one day rule England as Mary Tudor's consort."

Maria's father, I remembered, was Queen Catherine's Spanish physician.

But the very next day we heard that King Henry had proposed that his daughter marry King Francis himself, since Francis was a widower. King Francis's mother, Louise of Savoy, backed her grandson's suit and suggested that the ceremony take place in Calais in August, after which the bride could return to England until she was old enough to consummate the marriage. King Henry did not care for that plan, but he did want France's help in making war on Charles V. The alliance that was finally agreed upon contained ambiguous terms. The princess would wed either Francis or his son at some as-yet-to-be-decided future date.

The successful completion of these negotiations resulted in the "Treaty of Eternal Peace," signed at Greenwich on May 5, 1527. This signing was followed by celebrations. The next afternoon there was a tournament. Afterward, the king hosted a lavish banquet in his newly built banqueting house. It had been constructed at one end of the tiltyard gallery. At the other end was a purpose-built disguising house. It was to this second structure that the king and his guests adjourned for a post-banquet recital by the singers of the Chapel Royal, a concert that was to be followed by a masque.

In Princess Mary's bedchamber, pandemonium reigned, emotions ranging from hectic gaiety to confusion to excitement to barely contained panic. Sachets and perfumes warred with each other as every one of the princess's maids and gentlewomen tried to help prepare Her Grace for her first appearance in a disguising. By the time she was attired in her cloth of gold gown and surcoat, the babble of feminine voices had risen to deafening levels and the room was so close that it was difficult to breathe.

I flung open a window. The princess's lodgings at Greenwich overlooked one of the gardens. Fresh air rushed in, carrying with it the sweet scent of flowers and the pleasant aroma of recently scythed grass.

Her Grace shot me a look of gratitude before lifting her arms, a worried look on her face. "The sleeves of the surcoat are so long that they nearly touch the floor. What if I trip on them?"

"They are not quite *that* long," I assured her.

"Sir Henry Guildford is the king's master of revels," Lady Salisbury put in. "He is a careful man and he hires only the best craftsmen to design costumes and props."

Maria distracted the princess by scooping Her Grace's hair into a net. It had already been colored silver by the addition of a fine powder. Cecily set a richly jeweled garland on top of the princess's head and Mary Fitzherbert added a velvet cap. A small silver mask, covering just Her Grace's eyes and held in place with silver points tied at the back, completed the ensemble.

I stood back to better admire the effect. So many precious stones adorned the costume that I was nearly blinded by candlelight reflecting off the facets.

"It is almost time," Mary Dannett said.

We were about to escort Her Grace to the "cave" hidden behind a curtain in the disguising house—from which the "damsels" in the masque would emerge—when Mistress Anne Boleyn, dressed exactly like the princess save she was not wearing her mask, burst into the chamber. Two maidservants trailed after her carrying another cloth of silver costume and all the accessories that went with it.

"Your Grace, I beg your pardon for intruding," Mistress Anne said, making a hasty obeisance, "but Mistress Knight has eaten something that did not agree with her and is too ill to play her part. The king has asked that one of Your Grace's maids of honor fill in for her." She cast her black-eyed gaze over the five of us clustered around the princess. It came to rest on me. "You there. The tall one. Thomasine, is it not? You are closest in size to Mistress Knight. You can be pinned into the costume with the least trouble."

"But I do not know the steps," I objected.

"Simply watch what others do and copy them." She thrust one of the two small silver masks she carried into my hands.

"You dance most gracefully, Tamsin," Princess Mary said, "and no one will mind if you miss a step, seeing as you are doing everyone a great favor by replacing another performer at the last moment."

Her Grace's reassurance bolstered my confidence and it was not as if I had any choice in the matter. The maids Mistress Anne had brought with her set to work, stripping me down to my shift and then using metal pins half an inch long to shape the cloth of silver skirts over the padded roll they'd tied in place around my waist. They created small flounces at the front and large flattened flounces at the back that fell into a train. Then they pinned lace all around the edge of the low-necked gown and tightened the fit of the bodice anywhere the proper lines were not already achieved with the help of hooks and eyes. The surcoat that went on top of the whole fit very well, but I suddenly understood the princess's concern about its hanging sleeves. I slid my feet into silver slippers as my hair was hurriedly dressed and stuffed into its net. When the garland and the jaunty little cap were in place, the princess insisted that I admire myself in her looking glass.

My eyes widened in pleasure at the image that stared back at me. The figure in the shining surface seemed older than my fifteen years. I smiled, and suddenly my reflection was a woman grown, a woman confident she could carry off her role in the evening's disguising.

A short time later, eight identically clad damsels crowded in behind a large piece of wood painted gold and shaped to resemble a cave. This cave sat on a stage behind a proscenium arch at one end of the banqueting house. I started when a trumpet blared, even though I'd expected the sound. It was the signal for the painted curtain that hid the cave from view to be drawn back.

On the audience side, an expectant hush fell over the gathering of courtiers, diplomats, and dignitaries. To the sound of fife and tabor, the princess led us out of the cave and down a few steps until we reached the floor of the stage. I stumbled slightly on the second step, having caught sight of the crowd.

They filled three sides of the building, seated in tiers that rose nearly to the ceiling. And that ceiling was a wonder in itself.

Painted upon it was a depiction of the whole earth surrounded by the sea, like an enormous map. Beneath this hung a transparent cloth painted and gilded with the signs of the zodiac. The stars, planets, and constellations glittered in the light from hundreds of wax tapers held in iron sconces and ornate candelabra. At this stupendous sight, my heart stuttered, but somehow I managed to recover my equilibrium and proceed with my part in the disguising.

From the sides of the proscenium arch, eight masked lords appeared, dressed as Venetian noblemen. We had to pretend not to recognize any of them, but I knew one of them must be the French ambassador and none but the most raw newcomer to court could mistake the king for anyone else.

Aside from his height, Princess Mary's father was distinguished by a well-proportioned, athletic body—he excelled at riding, hunting, shooting, dancing, wrestling, and casting the bar—and by the priceless gems that decorated his clothing. Even though all the "Venetians" wore bright red silk and velvet doublets with gold chains draped across their shoulders, King Henry's jewels were the most flawless and his shoulders the broadest. It was not necessary for me to take note of his auburn hair or his laughing blue-gray eyes to confirm his identity. Although he seemed quite old to me then, he was still a fine figure of a man and much to be admired.

The eight "Venetians," as they had rehearsed, joined the eight damsels already on the small stage. We were to dance for the entertainment of the court. Recorders and flutes joined the fife and tabor to provide the music. A masked gentleman seized hold of me. His face, what I could see of it, was darkly tanned by hours in the sun, but I had no idea who he was.

"You are not Mistress Knight," he whispered.

"She was taken ill," I whispered back.

He made a valiant effort to guide me through the intricate steps.

The attempt cost him dearly. Nervousness, and the fact that the floor was carpeted in silk over the rush matting—slippery underfoot for all that it had been embroidered with gold lilies in honor of the French—had me stepping on his feet and, once, kicking him in the shin. To make matters worse, one of the pins holding my gown in at the waist came loose and stabbed into his hand deeply enough to draw blood.

When the dance was over, we removed our masks. Everyone feigned surprise that the king had been one of our company. The ladies curtseyed. The gentlemen bowed.

"Sir Nicholas Carew at your service," my partner said, dabbing at his bleeding palm with a handkerchief.

Flustered, I told him my name and apologized for his injury.

"Mistress Lodge of Hartlake Manor? Then you are, of course, forgiven. Star of Hartlake is a most excellent piece of horseflesh."

"You . . . you own my father's stallion?"

"Not I, mistress. The king. I am but His Grace's master of the horse. Star of Hartlake was a gift, I believe, from your guardian."

The king's booming laugh echoed through the disguising house, causing every eye to turn his way. He was well pleased with his daughter's performance, but the display His Grace had organized for the benefit of the French ambassador was not yet over. With an affectionate gesture that appeared impulsive but was, in fact, as carefully choreographed as any dance, he removed the princess's velvet cap. His excuse was that he wished to admire the garland beneath, but he contrived to displace her hairnet in the process. A profusion of silver-gilt tresses tumbled down over Princess Mary's shoulders. With this unsubtle gesture, the king of England reminded his French guests of his daughter's virginity . . . and her wealth.

Displays of symbols and cunning conceits were part and parcel of life at court. I might have told tales of knights and ladies during our sojourn in the Marches of Wales, but here courtiers lived the fantasy. Gentlemen, even the king, wrote poems and sang songs in praise of the ladies to whom they pledged their eternal devotion. These ladies were never their own wives, but neither were they the gentlemen's mistresses, except in the sense that the gentleman humbled himself and swore to be his lady's servant.

The true knight placed his lady love on a pedestal and became her willing slave, hers to command in all things. He wooed her with adoration, devotion, and many small gifts, and wore her favor in tournaments. He expected nothing more than her kindness to him in return. Their love was of the heart and spirit, not the body. It was all a grand and gaudy game, and within a few weeks of joining King Henry's court, all of us who served the princess had begun to practice the art of flirtation, even though we did not have much opportunity to perfect it.

On this balmy May night, the formal entertainment ended with our unmasking, but the festivities were far from over. The king called for his musicians to strike up a pavane. Dancing was one of His Grace's favorite pastimes.

When I turned to look for Sir Nicholas, I discovered that he had used the distraction to slip away. I could not blame him. I would not have wished to dance with me again, either. But others were not put off by my clumsiness or by the silk floor. I fumbled with the loose pin and removed it so there would be no more bloodletting.

Once the silk became well trampled, the slipping and sliding ceased. The dancing continued until long past midnight. I had no shortage of partners. Some were young and handsome while others were old enough to have sired my father. I enjoyed every step of every passamezzo and saltarello for, in the normal way of things, the princess and her maids of honor did not participate in such late-night revels. Her Grace's parents chose to shield her from the rowdier elements of the court.

When at last it came time for the final pavane of the night, King Henry indicated that the French ambassador should partner Princess Mary. The queen, who had been present earlier, had long since retired to her bed and His Grace singled out Mistress Anne Boleyn to dance with him. There was nothing improper about his choice, but as I passed close to them in the pattern of the steps, I could not help but notice the smug and self-satisfied expression on Mistress Anne's face.

16

*L*ess than two weeks later, I heard a rumor that the king had consulted with certain prominent churchmen about obtaining an annulment of his marriage to Queen Catherine.

"That cannot be true," I objected when Edyth told me what the lower servants were saying.

"As sure as God's in Gloucester," she vowed. Edyth had been making great strides in her attempts to mimic the gentry, but she slipped into an odd mixture of dialect and more refined speech when she was excited. "The truth comed out to do with she—Mistress Anne Boleyn. Rose—"

"Mistress Anne's tiring maid?" I interrupted.

Edyth nodded. "Happen the king doan't bed his wife. Not for years."

"What does that have to do with anything?"

"Mistresses," Edyth said succinctly.

"It is no great secret that a man may take mistresses. That does not mean the king intends to marry one of them. Or anyone else, either. You must not repeat such things, Edyth, not even to me. Why, as it concerns the king, such talk is dangerous. Do you want to be accused of treason?"

A mutinous look on her face, Edyth subsided, but what she'd already told me was enough to cause me concern. It was true that Queen Catherine was past her childbearing years, and that there was no son to inherit the throne. Could King Henry really intend to set aside his queen and marry again in the hope of begetting a male heir?

I answered my own question easily enough—he would, if he could get the pope to agree that his marriage was invalid. I had no firsthand experience with such matters, but I had heard of other annulments, especially among the nobility. There had been a king of France, too, I recalled, and not so very long ago, who had set aside a barren wife in order to marry another who could give him children.

But Queen Catherine had not been barren. She had given birth to a living daughter. If the king succeeded in his quest, Princess Mary would be as much a bastard as young Henry Fitzroy. Deeply troubled by this thought, I wished I could discuss the matter with someone older and wiser, but I knew too well the folly of repeating such a rumor. I could lose my post for spreading tittle-tattle.

I said nothing to the princess, either, biding my time, praying that the story would turn out to be the most arrant nonsense and have no foundation in fact. When, in late July, Princess Mary and her parents took up residence together at Beaulieu, near Chelmsford in Essex, proposing to remain there for a month, I took this as a hopeful sign.

Beaulieu, a substantial royal house, had been refaced with red brick and enlarged only a few years earlier to provide sufficient housing for the many courtiers who always accompanied the king, queen, and princess. Among the additions had been four bathing rooms. What luxury!

The princess visited her mother daily, taking two of her maids of honor with her each time. It was when Maria and I took our turn to accompany her to Queen Catherine's privy chamber that Their Graces withdrew into a small room in the "secret lodgings," the chambers on the far side of the royal bedchamber where no one entered without an invitation. I thought nothing of this . . . at first.

Maria wandered off, approaching one of the queen's Spanish attendants. As they spoke together in that foreign tongue, I remembered that both of Maria's parents attended the queen. Comparing the faces of both women, I decided that they were indeed mother and daughter. When their features knit into identical expressions of concern, I began to worry. The feeling flared into panic when Maria returned to my side and I saw the shimmer of unshed tears in her eyes.

"What is wrong?" I hissed at her.

Maria just shook her head and would not answer me.

Impatiently, I waited for Princess Mary's return. The tension in the chamber was almost palpable. I disliked feeling uncertain and was even more irritated because I did not know *why* I felt so on edge.

As my searching gaze flitted from face to unguarded face, I recognized bewilderment on some, sorrow on others, anger on one, and on a few, satisfaction. I was not well enough acquainted with the queen's ladies to put names to most of them, but there was one maid of honor with whom I had spoken previously—Mistress Anne Boleyn. She was nowhere to be seen.

I told myself her absence meant nothing. The queen took only her "riding" household on progress, as did the king and the princess. Excess attendants returned to their homes to visit their families and were recalled when the court returned to one of the larger palaces—Richmond or Greenwich or Windsor Castle. There had been no need to send any of the princess's maids of honor away. Shortly before we journeyed to Beaulieu, Cecily Dabridgecourt had married Rhys Mansell and left us.

When Princess Mary finally returned to the privy chamber, she put up a brave façade, but I knew her well. Something had upset her. My conviction was confirmed as soon as we left the queen's lodgings. Instead of returning to her own apartments, Her Grace turned toward the ornate little chapel on the west side of the main court. Taking no note of her surroundings, either secular or sacred, the princess went straight to the altar and knelt. Head bowed, back rigid, her lips began to move in silent prayer.

As was our duty, Maria and I knelt side by side just behind our mistress, but my thoughts were in too much turmoil for true piety. Besides, I did not know what it was I was supposed to pray for. Patience was the only thing that came to mind.

Her Grace neither moved nor spoke for a full quarter of an hour, giving me time for a visual inspection of the entire chapel. In addition to the usual religious paintings, stained glass, and statues, it was decorated with the royal arms. They were carved, colored, and gilded and far outshone the trappings of mother church.

The princess swayed. With a cry of alarm, I stumbled to my feet to catch her before she could fall. Maria did likewise from the other side. Still on her knees, the princess sagged against us, tears streaming silently down her cheeks. She did not try to hide them. We were alone in the chapel and if she could not trust two of her faithful maids of honor, whom could she trust?

What bound us all together was our unswerving loyalty to and genuine affection for this twelve-year-old girl. We'd sworn an oath to protect and serve the princess, but "duty" was only a small part of the devotion I felt toward Mary Tudor. I would do anything in my power to preserve her life and keep her safe. I would slay dragons for her.

At first, I had not taken seriously the demands of loyalty about which the Countess of Salisbury had lectured us. She had repeatedly insisted that we must be willing to lay down our lives to save that of the heir to the throne. But the longer I was part of Princess Mary's household, as I came to know and love her, the less absurd it seemed to contemplate going to such an extreme.

Maria spoke softly in Spanish to the princess. Her Grace, who had recovered sufficiently to pull away from us and stand unaided, replied in the same language. Maria's face lost its color at her words.

"What? What is it?" Truly alarmed now, I heard my voice rise and quickly stifled it. The last thing we wanted was to attract the attention of some curious passerby. "What is it?" I repeated in a whisper.

Maria choked out the words. "The queen has given our mistress most distressing news. A little more than a month ago, King Henry asked Her Grace for a formal separation. He wishes to take a new wife, one who can give him sons. His Grace has already sent Cardinal Wolsey to France to negotiate with King Francis for a royal bride."

My heart went out to the princess. She looked so alone, standing there in the chapel. Hollow-eyed, lower lip trembling, she struggled to come to terms with the devastating confidences her mother had shared with her. In that moment, I did not see her as the king's daughter, but as a lost child in need of comfort. She was too young to have to bear such a burden by herself. Acting on impulse, casting aside protocol and propriety alike, I reached out to her, taking her hand, squeezing her fingers, offering in that tiny gesture all the reassurance, all the love I could muster.

With a piteous sob, Mary Tudor flung herself into my arms.

17

When the royal progress left Beaulieu, eventually to return to Greenwich, Princess Mary's household went its own way, visiting various country manors farther from London. We had little contact with the court for more than two months.

Letters to the princess from her mother were full of admonishments to be diligent in her studies. They did not report on the progress of what had already been dubbed "the king's great matter." The princess's senior ladies, particularly the Countess of Salisbury, no doubt received news of the outside world, and on occasion even ventured into it themselves, but as one of Her Grace's four remaining maids of honor, I lived almost as isolated as the princess herself.

The routine of prayers and lessons and healthful exercise resumed. The only change was that I was given responsibility for supervising the care of the princess's clothing. I soon learned that it was a constant battle to remove dust and grime from fabric, especially when we traveled. Although garments were packed in individual cloth bags and placed inside wooden coffers covered with leather, it was difficult to keep them clean. When they were worn, kirtles and gowns quickly acquired spots of grease, mud, and other even less salubrious stains. Fabric rubbed thin where jewels were attached for decoration. Sleeves caught on splinters and hems snagged on nails, or became worn simply because they dragged on the ground. Even applying a brush with too much vigor could damage the more delicate fabrics.

Fortunately, garments could be sent to the wardrobe of robes for repair. This office was located beneath Princess Mary's privy chamber and staffed by a yeoman, a groom, a page who did the hemming, and a clerk. Her Grace's clothing was stored there, along with supplies of material for making more.

The yeoman of the wardrobe of robes, Jenkin Kent, a short, stocky man with a ready smile, allocated cloth from his stores to artificers. A tailor was employed full-time to alter, reline, replace, and repair clothing, as well as make new garments. The princess also kept her own skinner and embroiderer. I came to know them all well during those weeks in the country.

In late October, we journeyed to Greenwich Palace to celebrate with King Henry when he received the French Order of St. Michael. The princess's lodgings were near her father's, but she rarely saw him and never alone. Determined to capture His Grace's attention, Princess Mary devised a plan whereby she and her ladies would play a role in the revels surrounding this event. This required costumes, and for that purpose I was sent to meet with Mistress Pinckney, a silkwoman from London, to discuss the items we would need.

Armed with a list, I descended to the wardrobe of robes. Although this room was in the same location at Greenwich as at other royal residences, it was much larger, crowded and humming with activity. Everywhere I looked, men were sewing hems or brushing skirts or cutting fabric to be stitched into clothing. The scent of sweet powder filled the air and, beneath it, the smell of smoke from the coal fires. These not only provided heat but also "aired" the stored garments.

I had no difficulty locating Mistress Pinckney. She was the only woman present. Tall and slender, dressed like a merchant's wife, she stood talking to Master Kent. He had to look up to meet her eyes.

Standing beside Mistress Pinckney, his attention clearly wandering, was a boy a year or two older than I was. In his thin arms he held a large wicker basket covered with leather and bound with iron. As I approached, eyes of the deepest brown I had ever seen shifted to me. A slow grin spread over his face when I came to an abrupt halt halfway to the little group of three, as if he knew that I found his stare disconcerting.

Frowning, I continued on. Conceited oaf! He likely thought himself passing toothsome, just because he had wavy black hair and an aquiline nose and sculpted features.

"Mistress Lodge is to make the selections," Master Kent told Mistress Pinckney. Relieved to be quit of this task himself, he made haste to return to other duties. I was left alone with the silkwoman and the boy I assumed was her apprentice.

"Display our wares, if you will, Rafe," Mistress Pinckney ordered.

The boy set down his basket and opened it. It was lined with yellow cloth and contained an assortment of silk products, everything from ribbons, braids, and points to buttons and loops to thread for embroidery. Mistress Pinckney lifted out a tray, revealing laces made from intertwining silk threads in various patterns. Other silken treasures lay beneath.

She indicated the laces. "These can be used for points, for laces to fasten coifs, ruffs, or cloaks, or as purse strings."

I was more intrigued by the silk cauls made to contain a woman's hair and the selection of fringe and tassels. There were no larger items, like gowns or kirtles or sleeves among her wares. I knew there would not be. I had been told by Master Kent that silkwomen specialized in converting imported raw silk into thread. They wove the smaller silk materials—trimmings—but did not deal in larger items or whole cloths.

I lifted out a handful of points made of Spanish silk. They were already tagged—their ends attached to aglets. The quality of the work was very fine. But all the while I was examining them, I was uncomfortably aware of Mistress Pinckney's apprentice. His steady gaze bored into my back.

I cleared my throat. "Her Grace wishes accessories and trim for costumes for a disguising. Can you also supply ostrich feathers?"

"I will provide whatever Her Grace wishes."

"Wire for skirt hoops?"

She nodded.

I consulted the list I had brought with me. "We also need thirteen yards of green ribbon and a quantity of flat gold and flat silver woven into fringes."

"Woven gold and silver costs three pence the ounce," Mistress Pinckney interrupted.

I hesitated. No one had said anything about paying for the goods. Fortunately, Master Kent was not far away. He overheard and took the silkwoman aside for a muttered discussion of terms. This left me alone with her apprentice.

"So, there is to be disguising." His voice was low and pleasant and as refined as any courtier's. "Will you dress as a Saracen maiden? Or will it be a Venetian princess?"

"Venice does not have princesses!" I blurted out.

I felt myself flushing. He pretended an intense interest in the contents of his wicker basket. If he knew anything about Venice, then he had been teasing me. If he did not, then I'd just called attention to his ignorance. Either possibility embarrassed me, although I was uncertain why that should be so. I turned my back on him to stare at my list, even though I knew every item on it by heart.

The princess wanted red silk cords for the borders of the Italian mantles we would wear for the disguising. And three gross of points to fasten sleeves, cloaks, bonnets, and buskins—not only for the revel but also for every day. Then there were blue silk buttons and silk hairnets woven with gold thread.

"Will the king attend the princess's entertainment?"

When I did not answer, I expected the apprentice—Rafe—to let the matter drop. After all, I was his better, a maid of honor to a princess while he was in service to a mere merchant. Instead, he persisted with his questions.

"I hear there is to be a tournament. Do you think the queen will preside? Or will it be her replacement who sits beside the king?"

I wheeled around to face him, outraged by the suggestion even as I was horrified to discover that a common servant lad knew more about the rift between the king and queen than their own daughter did. "You had best mind your tongue, sirrah! And remember where you are."

He should have been abashed, even frightened. There were dire consequences for speculating about King Henry's private business in public. Instead, he laughed.

It was a nice laugh, not a deep and booming roar like the king's, nor yet the false chuckle that so many courtiers used to indicate that they shared His Grace's amusement.

"I say no more than others do, mistress. The king's pursuit of Mistress Anne Boleyn has been talked of in London for months, as has His Grace's desire to divorce the queen."

Was he brave and bold or merely foolish? I narrowed my eyes and stared at him, trying to discern the truth. He grinned back. There was a distinct twinkle in the depths of his dark eyes. My belly gave an odd quiver. I told myself it was distaste and looked away, determined to focus on anything, anyone else.

That was when I realized that no one was paying any attention to me, or to Rafe. I considered for a moment and then, perhaps rashly, decided to discover what else he knew. When I turned my attention back to him, I took a deliberate step closer and lowered my voice.

"Was it Mistress Anne Boleyn you meant when you spoke of Queen Catherine's replacement?"

"Who else? Everyone knows she wishes to take her mistress's place as queen."

"Everyone?"

I doubted this. Edyth was in the habit of repeating to me the rumors she heard from the other lower servants. She had said nothing about Mistress Anne *marrying* King Henry. Then again, the tidbits Edyth gleaned from her friend Rose, Mistress Anne's tiring maid, had been few and far between of late. That made me wonder if Rose had been sworn to secrecy . . . or threatened with dismissal if she talked out of turn.

"She might *like* to be queen," I told Rafe, "but there is no possibility that she will get her wish. If His Grace should succeed in winning an annulment, he will have to wed a foreign princess. That is the way countries seal alliances. That is why Princess Mary will one day marry a king or a prince from another land." I was quite certain of my reasoning. King Henry would never wed one of his own subjects. Where was the advantage to England in that?

Rafe took a step closer, until I could feel his warm breath on my cheek. He smelled faintly of cinnamon. "Then why does the king send so many expensive gifts to Mistress Anne?"

"How do you know that he does?"

"Do you think anyone, even a king, can conjure up silks and

jewelry by magic? London merchants have received many payments of late from the king's privy purse, for everything from an emerald ring and diamonds and rubies set in roses and hearts to gilt and silver bindings for books." Apparently servants in London enjoyed greater freedom than those at court, and felt no compunction about keeping their thoughts to themselves.

"I am certain you have misinterpreted what you think you know," I said in my most haughty tone of voice. "Courtiers ofttimes play at love, even kings. They swear fealty to a lady, *call* her their mistress, and give her gifts, but it is all a game."

His eyebrows shot up. "You cannot be such an innocent! The king's mistresses most assuredly warm his bed. How else do you explain Henry Fitzroy?"

"I will concede that Mistress Anne may be the king's concubine, but surely she is no more than that. Why ever would he *marry* her?"

He shrugged. "He is the king. He can do whatever he wants."

I frowned, suddenly uncertain what to believe.

"The citizens of London do not like the idea of a divorce," Rafe said. "If a man can set aside his aging wife and replace her with a younger woman, why then where is the sanctity of marriage?"

"The citizens of London appear to have too much time for idle speculation," I shot back, trying to sound severe.

Rafe dared to smooth one callused finger over my forehead. "You should not scowl so fiercely, Mistress Lodge. Your face might stick that way, all creased and wrinkly."

I stepped quickly back, cheeks once again aflame. He was not even wearing gloves! His bare skin had brushed against mine. I opened my mouth to remonstrate with him, but his gaze abruptly shifted to a point behind me. I turned to find Mistress Pinckney and Master Kent returning.

"Is everything settled, Mother?" Rafe asked.

I completed my business with the silkwoman in short order and returned by way of a back stair to the princess's privy chamber. Pushing the memory of Rafe Pinckney's bold behavior to the back of my mind, I debated the wisdom of sharing the rumors he'd repeated to me with the princess. Her Grace valued the truth, but was what the apprentice had told me true? I did not wish to distress Princess Mary without cause.

It made sense to me that Mistress Anne Boleyn might have followed in her older sister's footsteps and become the king's mistress, but surely no lady of the court would be so foolish as to think His Grace would *marry* her. Mistress Anne was one of Queen Catherine's maids of honor. A member of the queen's household was all she could ever hope to be, no matter how much the king enjoyed her company. When His Grace tired of her, he would find her a husband, just as he had for Bessie Blount after she gave birth to his bastard son.

"Have you spoken with the silkwoman?" Lady Salisbury asked, catching sight of me still dithering on the threshold of the privy chamber.

"I have, my lady. She will supply all our needs in good time for the revel."

"Excellent," said the countess. She relieved me of the list I'd forgotten I still held clutched tight in one hand. She gave me a sharp-eyed look. "Does something trouble you, Tamsin?"

"No, my lady." I forced myself to smile to back up my claim. I had made my decision. I would not tell the princess what Rafe Pinckney had said. He'd done naught but pass on a rumor, one that seemed unlikely to prove true. Out of consideration of Her Grace's feelings, I would keep the story to myself . . . and pray very hard that it had no foundation in fact.

18

The princess lived at court throughout that November and December of 1527. She was much in her father's company, which did not please Mistress Anne Boleyn at all. Just after the feast day of St. Thomas the Apostle, she left to celebrate Yuletide at her family home, Hever Castle in Kent, some thirty miles from Greenwich. Queen Catherine presided over the festivities at court, as she always did, the king at her side.

The celebrations included a tournament, but it ended early because the light was so poor. The banquets and disguisings were more successful. Our masque and dance, for which we disguised ourselves as ladies of Mantua, was well received, but the king still managed to avoid private conversation with his daughter.

Oddly, I caught myself noticing how much silk the master of revels had used in costumes and scenery. Even the trees for one of the disguisings were made of it—a hawthorn for the house of Tudor and a mulberry representing the French royal family of Valois.

There were more celebrations when news arrived of the escape of Pope Clement VII from Rome. The Holy City had been captured earlier in the year by Emperor Charles V. As good Catholics, all true English men and women rejoiced at the Holy Father's deliverance. At the time, I was not aware of any deeper significance to His Holiness's troubles. Indeed, I allowed myself to be lulled by the appearance of harmony between King Henry and Queen Catherine into thinking that His Grace had changed his mind about setting aside his wife.

There followed an exceptionally cold and bitter winter. Even parts of the sea froze. In February at Hunsdon in Hertfordshire, the house the princess most often lived in when she was not at court, I entered my sixteenth year.

A few days later, I was summoned to the little room Lady Salisbury used for private prayer and study. Sir Lionel Daggett was waiting there, warming himself by the fire.

It had been a year and a half since I'd seen him, but I had not forgotten our last meeting. Instantly wary, I lingered in the doorway.

"Come in, child," Lady Salisbury chided me, her long, narrow face tight with disapproval. "Make your curtsey to Sir Lionel."

I made a perfunctory obeisance, rising quickly to approach my guardian. "I do beg your pardon, sir. I did not expect to see you here."

He had changed in the intervening months, and not for the better. Where once he had been lean, he now showed signs of frequent overindulgence in food and drink. The sharp point of his narrow jaw sported the beginning of an additional chin.

Nodding in satisfaction, Lady Salisbury picked up a piece of needlework and began to stitch. For propriety's sake, she intended to remain where she was. Sir Lionel scowled, but he knew better than to try to dismiss a countess with royal blood in her veins.

"Is there a reason for your visit, sir?" I asked, all sweetness. I felt braver now that I knew I would not be left alone with him.

He removed a document from an inside pocket in his doublet and unrolled it on the wooden surface of the countess's table. "You wish, I assume, to keep Hartlake Manor running smoothly?"

I frowned, staring without comprehension at the words in front of me. "I cannot read this. It is not written in English."

"No, this is Latin. To make it legal."

"What does it say?"

"You need not shoot such suspicious looks my way, Thomasine. This document does no more than confirm Hugo Wynn in his post as your steward. I assumed that would meet with your approval, but if you would prefer I appoint someone else—"

"No! It is . . . that is, Master Wynn knows the land and will do right by me."

But still I hesitated to dip quill in ink. Did Hugo resent that I had inherited everything while his grandchild got nothing? *Would* he do right by me, in truth? But I knew of no one else who was as familiar with my estate as he was. When Sir Lionel pointed to the place where I should write my name, I inscribed my signature in bold letters.

My guardian sanded the ink himself, then carefully rolled the document back up and tucked it away again.

"Is that all you came for?" I asked uneasily. Sir Lionel looked far too pleased with himself.

"What other matter could there be?" He slanted a look at the countess, contentedly embroidering in the corner.

I could have told him that Princess Mary's lady mistress had been growing ever more hard of hearing in the time I'd been a member of the household, but I did not. I did not want to encourage Sir Lionel's confidences.

He retrieved his traveling cloak from the peg where it had been hung to dry and made another little bow in my direction. "I must be on my way. I would not wish to intrude on the princess's hospitality. Besides, I have other matters of business to attend to before I return to my duties in Cornwall."

I had no idea what those duties were and I did not ask. It was enough to know that Sir Lionel would soon be gone again and that his post kept him away from both the king's court and that of Princess Mary. Although, this time, my guardian had been civil, I had no desire to spend any more time in his company than was necessary. As soon as he left, I returned to the princess's presence chamber, took up my sewing, and banished Sir Lionel Daggett from my thoughts.

19

By the time we returned to Greenwich for the annual May Day revels, spring was well advanced. No sooner had we settled in, however, than Princess Mary fell ill with a fever and a rash. Several of the queen's women suffered a similar affliction. At first the royal physicians feared it was an outbreak of smallpox. Then they decided it was the measles.

Older and more experienced ladies were set to nursing the princess. The maids of honor were left to their own devices. Maria took the opportunity to visit her mother and father.

I was alone in the maidens' dormitory when she returned. "What is wrong?" I asked, taking note of the damp, crumpled handkerchief clutched in her fist. "Have more ladies fallen ill?"

She shook her head, reaching up with the bare fingers of her free hand to swipe angrily at the new tears forming in her eyes. "If only one of them would!"

I gave her a moment to compose herself before probing further. We had long since established an unspoken bond of trust between us, based on our mutual devotion to the princess. Maria did not hesitate long before telling me what it was that had upset her.

"It is Mistress Anne Boleyn, Tamsin. The king has singled her out, again, and this time in a most remarkable way. As soon as he heard of the sickness among the queen's ladies, he gave orders that Mistress Anne was to move into lodgings off the gallery over the tiltyard. She was already living in separate rooms, apart from the other maids of honor. Clearly His Grace wishes to make certain she remains safe from any infection."

"I am not surprised. She has been His Grace's concubine for some time."

Maria worried her lower lip. "My father says she has made the king fall in love with her." She lowered her voice. "Mayhap with witchcraft. And Father does not think she *has* yielded her body to His Grace. He believes she is playing for higher stakes."

Rafe Pinckney had said that, too, months ago.

"She takes a great risk to tease the king. I have heard that His Grace has a terrible temper." Everyone at court knew that, even those, like me, who had never witnessed an explosion of his wrath.

"So, I am told, does Mistress Anne."

I felt my eyes widen at this intelligence. I found it difficult to imagine anyone brave enough to quarrel with King Henry. He was physically intimidating, with his height and girth and his booming voice. And he was the king.

"Father says that King Henry wants nothing more than to please the lady," Maria added.

"Would he go so far as to make her his queen?" I whispered.

"Pray God he will not, but who can say?"

That night, when Edyth came to the maidens' dormitory to help me undress for bed, I asked her outright if she had seen Rose lately.

Edyth made a face.

"Does she still serve Mistress Anne Boleyn?"

"Oh, yes," my tiring maid assured me, "and full of pride about that she is, too." Edyth had almost entirely lost her country accent.

"What reason has she to boast?" I asked as Edyth stepped behind me to untie my laces.

"Why, of the attentions the king shows to her mistress. What else?"

I waited.

"The king visited Windsor Castle in March," Edyth went on as she freed the last of the points holding bodice to skirt and let the latter fall to the floor. "His Grace did not even take his riding household with him, only a few favored courtiers."

I stepped out of the puddle of fabric and waited while she gathered it up. It took great effort to contain my impatience. "What of that? King Henry is wont to go off hunting with only a few boon companions."

"Mistress Anne Boleyn met His Grace at Windsor."

"In the queen's absence?" Without the queen's household in residence, there should have been no women there, except perhaps for the few courtiers' wives who had permanent lodgings in the castle.

"Mistress Anne's brother was one of the men who accompanied the king," Edyth said.

"That hardly makes his sister's presence respectable."

"Rose says King Henry sent for her, so she had to go, but she took her mother with her."

"To guard her reputation?"

"I do not think Mistress Anne cares a fig for her reputation. Her behavior while she was there was most improper."

"She shared the king's bed?"

"I do not know about that," Edyth said, freeing me from my sleeves and setting them aside so she could remove my bodice and loosen the body-stitchet beneath, "but the king and the lady went hunting together every day and sometimes Mistress Anne rode *with* the king." When I did not react, she poked me in the ribs. "On the same horse, Mistress Tamsin. On a pillion behind His Grace, her arms wrapped around the king's waist!"

Mistress Anne's audacity astounded me. One did not touch the king so familiarly in the presence of others. Not even his wife did so.

Then an image formed in my mind, born of my personal dislike of riding apillion, and I choked back a laugh. "I should have liked to see the lady trying to shoot an arrow from that position."

Edyth made a snorting sound. I'd have taken it for amusement if her expression had not remained so grim. "I do not think she was in Windsor Forest to hunt for deer."

20

We were still at Greenwich in the middle of June when the sweating sickness broke out in London. Within a day, two thousand people fell ill in the city. Then the disease spread to the court. Rose, Mistress Anne Boleyn's maidservant, was the first to be struck down.

The following day, the king left Greenwich for Waltham Abbey in Essex, twelve miles distant. The removal of his court to that smaller house had been planned for some time, but originally the king, the queen, the princess, and Mistress Anne were all to travel together. Fear of infection now outweighed King Henry's desire to keep his concubine nearby. Mistress Anne and her ailing maid were left behind in Greenwich.

"She must be furious," I remarked as Edyth brushed off my travel-stained skirts in the lodgings allotted to the princess's maids of honor in our new abode. The chamber was small and cramped, with only one bed for the four of us. Our tiring maids were in even less salubrious accommodations, for they were obliged to sleep in tents erected in the gardens.

"Frightened, more like," Mary Dannett said, overhearing.

It was no longer any secret that Mistress Anne hoped to marry the king, or that His Grace must have given his mistress reason to think such a thing might be possible. And yet King Henry carried on in public as if nothing had changed. The queen sat in her accustomed place at court functions. Her husband still spent several evenings a week in her company. They dined together and afterward His Grace played his lute while Her Grace embroidered.

Or so I'd heard. The princess's household was separate from those of her parents. Like everyone else, I relied upon my gossips for information.

"We should all be frightened," Edyth muttered.

At once, I felt ashamed of myself. Edyth and Mistress Anne's Rose had been on friendly terms for a long time and Rose, poor thing, was likely dead by now. Few survived the sweat. Anne Boleyn might be angry that she'd been deprived of the king's company, but since someone in her own household had contracted the dread disease, her very life was in danger.

The sweating sickness came on without warning. The sufferer felt pain in the back or shoulder, and then in the liver and the stomach, the head and the heart. A profuse sweating began, followed by delirium and palpitations. There was no cure. Within a few hours, you lived or died by God's will alone.

Mary Dannett, Mary Fitzherbert, and I, together with our maids, were still in our quarters at Waltham Abbey when Maria rushed in. She had made the journey from Greenwich in the company of her parents, since her mother was one of the queen's women and her father, Fernando Vittorio, was a royal physician.

"It followed us here!" she blurted out. "Two of the king's ushers and two of his grooms of the chamber have fallen ill, and so has Mistress Anne's brother, George Boleyn."

I hastily crossed myself, as did everyone else in the room.

Mary Fitzherbert seized Maria's arm. "Is there nothing we can do? No preventive tonic we can swallow?"

Thanks to her father's profession, Maria had a more extensive knowledge of herbs and their healing properties than most gentlewomen, even though we'd all received some instruction in the stillroom.

"I have heard that the king takes a medicinal powder to ward off infection," I put in, "but I suppose the cost of such a thing is too dear for any commoner to afford."

"My father says His Grace sets great store by pills of Rhazis," Maria said. "Rhazis was a famous Arab physician."

"My old nurse," said Mary Dannett, "claims that her life was saved the last time the sweat broke out, ten years ago, by a mixture of endive, sowthistle, marigold, mercury, and nightshade."

Maria gaped at her. "That combination would be as likely to kill you as save you. Nightshade is a deadly poison."

"Three large spoonfuls of dragon's water and a half nutshell of unicorn's horn," I murmured, remembering a cure I'd heard somewhere, probably in one of the old legends I collected. I managed a weak smile. "It seems unlikely we can locate either ingredient."

Maria looked thoughtful. "I have heard that a philosopher's egg is a sovereign remedy for almost any ailment. That is a crushed egg, its white blown out and mixed shell and all with saffron, mustard seed, herbs, and . . ."

"What?" I prompted when her voice trailed off.

She looked sheepish. "Unicorn's horn."

We all laughed, but the outburst did not last long.

"Any one of us could be in perfect health at dawn and dead by nightfall," said Mary Fitzherbert, her voice mournful and her face a picture of gloom.

"Sooner, in truth." Maria shrugged. "Some die of the sweat in as little as two hours after the onset of the symptoms."

In fascinated horror, I listened as she relayed still more of the information she'd learned from her physician father.

"If you fall ill, you must go at once to bed in a closed room with a fire. Cover yourself completely. It can be fatal to expose any part of your body during the crucial twenty-four hours after you sicken, assuming you live past the first few. Father said that he heard of one case where a hand, extended from beneath the bedclothes, became as stiff as a pane of glass and stayed that way, even though the patient lived."

"My mother," said Mary Fitzherbert, "swears by treacle and water imperial for fever and setwell for the stomach."

"Little help that would be," Maria said with a sniff, "but we might set out onions. They will absorb the evil in the air."

For the next month, the maidens' dormitory reeked of raw onion. We added braids of garlic, too, since that plant was said to have protective powers.

Those weeks were fraught with anxiety. Thousands more died in London and throughout the country. In an attempt to stay ahead of the rapidly spreading infection, the king and his court changed houses almost daily. From Waltham we went to Hunsdon, six miles east of Hertford, the royal residence in which Princess Mary's household so often lodged. The familiar redbrick manor house was a welcome sight, but its walls held no promise of safety.

I was returning from a visit to the stables on our first day there— a weakness of mine that I indulged whenever I could—when a messenger in Lord Rochford's livery rode into the yard. My mind was still on the gentle palfrey who'd been taking carrots from my hand, but something about the man made me take a second look at him, and then a third. His mien was somber, his expression terrified.

Combined with the lathered condition of his horse, it was not difficult to guess that he brought bad news.

But bad news for some could be the best news of all to others. If Mistress Anne Boleyn, Lord Rochford's daughter, had been taken by the sweat, then there would be rejoicing in both the queen's household and that of the princess.

I followed the rider inside. No one noticed me. I was just one more dark-clad young woman going about her business. By the time the messenger reached the king's presence chamber, I was only a few feet behind him and in good time to hear King Henry demand to hear what news he brought from Hever Castle, the Boleyn family seat in Kent. Mistress Anne, I surmised, had fled to that place after the king abandoned her at court.

"Lord Rochford has fallen ill," the messenger announced, "as has his younger daughter, Mistress Anne Boleyn."

All the color drained out of the king's usually florid face. He turned to one of his gentlemen and ordered him to fetch Dr. Butts. I remained where I was, almost invisible in a shadowy corner, fingering the rosary the princess had given me. Was it wrong to pray for someone to die? I knew it was, but still I hoped for that outcome.

When Dr. Butts arrived, the king dispatched him at once to Hever. "Save her," His Grace commanded.

"I will do all I can," the physician promised.

During the next few days, all but one of the gentlemen of the king's privy chamber contracted the dread disease. Leaving each one behind in turn, His Grace changed houses again and again. We did not stay anywhere for more than a single night at a time until we reached Tyttenhanger, near St. Albans, one of the many houses owned by Cardinal Wolsey.

In advance of our arrival, the king had ordered the entire place cleansed, first by burning fires in every room and then by scrubbing every surface with vinegar. As a further precaution, everyone at court was ordered to carry wads of linen soaked in a mixture of vinegar, wormwood, rose water, and crumbs of brown bread.

"At least this smell is an improvement over the stink of onions and garlic," I muttered, lifting the dampened cloth toward my nose. We'd been instructed to sniff it, as if it were a pomander.

Carelessly, I brought the preventive in contact with my face. With a sharp cry, I dropped the ball of linen. My skin stung and my eyes streamed. I was more cautious after that, remembering Maria's warning that some remedies could be as deadly as the disease they purported to cure.

At Tyttenhanger, the king, the queen, and the princess attended Mass every morning. They confessed their sins every day, too. I followed their example, even admitting to the sin of wishing for Anne Boleyn's death, for when one was afflicted with the sweat, there was not always time to fetch a priest. My penance was slight. For the next week, I was to pray at each of the canonical hours for Lady Anne's full recovery.

Every day messengers arrived in a steady stream. They brought word of more deaths among the king's friends. Mary Boleyn's husband, William Carey, succumbed to the dread disease. So did Sir William Compton, the king's longtime groom of the stool.

But sprinkled in among somber tidings came news of miraculous recoveries. George Boleyn, his father, and his sister Anne survived.

21

We were fortunate. No one in Princess Mary's household fell ill. The king and queen were also spared. Gradually, the fear of infection dissipated. King Henry and Queen Catherine set off on their regular summer progress while the princess and her household returned to Hunsdon.

And Mistress Anne Boleyn? The king's anxiety about her health had made it all too plain that she occupied a special place in his heart. Would she succeed in her quest for the crown? I told myself it was unlikely. After all, His Grace continued to spend quiet evenings with Queen Catherine, just as he always had. They still attended Mass together. Her Grace sat beside him on state occasions. To all outward appearances, nothing had changed in their marriage.

News from the progress and, later, from Bridewell Palace in London, where the king and queen lodged upon their return, arrived at Hunsdon in erratic spurts. In spite of the fact that the queen herself had warned Princess Mary of the king's intention to annul their marriage, the princess remained unaware of the extent of her father's infatuation with Mistress Anne. Her Grace was still an innocent in many ways. As her devoted ladies, we continued to protect her. What profit was there in repeating rumors that would distress her? The Countess of Salisbury even went so far as to warn the maids of honor against speculating among ourselves, lest the princess accidentally overhear more than she should.

In truth, we did not have much to speculate about, being so far removed from the king's court. Maria received occasional letters from her father, written in Spanish, but she insisted that they contained only recipes for herbal cures and personal expressions of affection.

The lack of news did not stop me from worrying. I prayed that His Grace had seen the error of his ways, but I feared that he had not. I kept remembering those few occasions when I had encountered Mistress Anne Boleyn. Even my limited acquaintance with her had shown me the effect she had on people. She was not a beautiful woman, but there was something about her that compelled attention. Men, in particular, flocked around her like bees to honey.

At Yuletide, we traveled to Greenwich Palace. The princess bade me meet with Mistress Pinckney, as I had the previous year. But on this occasion, the silkwoman sent word for me to come to the Great Wardrobe in London, so that I might examine the full range of her wares.

The Great Wardrobe was located just east of Blackfriars Priory, that great house of the Dominicans. It was the place where cloth for the use of the king and his court was delivered, measured, and parceled out again, the lengths going to tailors, embroiderers, cappers, hosiers, shoemakers, and skinners. The clerks of the royal wardrobes of robes, like Master Jenkin Kent, went there both to collect the results of artificers' work and to claim bolts of fabric to make into clothes themselves.

In the three years and four months since I'd left Glastonbury, this was the first time I had ventured outside the princess's retinue. Keen anticipation filled me as I was transported upstream on one of the smaller royal barges. The trip took two hours, rowing against the tide.

The wind whipped at my cloak and icy spray dampened the hem of my skirt, but I refused to take shelter in the tiny cabin. I did not want to miss a moment of the experience. I had traveled through London by water before, but in the past I had not been free to sightsee. Princess Mary preferred to remain inside the tiny cabin and her maids of honor perforce stayed with her.

On this occasion, although I was accompanied by Master Kent, two yeomen, and Edyth, I was free to remain in the open air. The tide was at the ebb, allowing the barge to "shoot" London Bridge. I stared up at the closely packed houses in fascination as we approached and at the underside and "starlings" as we passed beneath. At high tide, passengers disembarked on one side of the bridge and walked to meet their watercraft on the other . . . if the barge or boat made it through.

We passed ships anchored in the Thames and a shoreline filled with warehouses, tall buildings, and church spires to dock at Paul's Wharf. Although we had but a short distance to travel on land, there were horses waiting. I rode on a pillion behind Master Kent. Edyth was mounted behind one of the yeomen. The other, clad in the princess's blue and green livery, walked ahead of us to forge a path through the narrow, crowded streets.

The Great Wardrobe consisted of a large town house, several smaller houses, and a number of shops. Within these buildings were both storage rooms and offices. Master Kent escorted me, with Edyth in tow, to one of the latter and told me to wait there for Mistress Pinckney.

The office was sparsely furnished, containing only a table heaped with ledgers and several storage chests. It had but one window, opening onto a courtyard. I passed the time watching men unload bales of material that had just been delivered, but I could not see them very clearly through the thick, wavy window glass.

Behind me, the door opened. I turned with a smile on my face, prepared to greet the silkwoman, and found myself instead confronting her son.

Rafe Pinckney had filled out in the year since I had last seen him. His shoulders seemed broader, his arms and chest more muscular. I felt certain that he noticed the changes in me, as well.

Although I was still uncommon tall for a woman, the shape I had grown into was now abundantly womanly. I did not look at all like my father's aunts. I fought a blush as Rafe's deep brown eyes devoured the increased lushness of my body.

I cleared my throat. "I was expecting to meet with Mistress Pinckney."

"She sent me instead."

I hesitated. I was not certain how to address him. He was not a gentleman, so "Master Pinckney" was not appropriate. "Silkman Pinckney" did not sound quite right, either, nor was it correct, for I was sure he had not yet completed his apprenticeship. Rafe might not be the humble servant I'd first thought him, but neither was he a merchant trading in his own right.

If the silkwoman's son noticed that I did not greet him by name, he made no mention of it. Instead, he suggested a tour of the silk store at the Great Wardrobe and I agreed. With Edyth trailing after us, eyes wide and mouth agape at the wonders rising on high shelves all around us, he displayed bolt upon bolt of the expensive fabric. It came in every color imaginable, as did spools of silk thread. At last we reached a storage rack that held a dozen varieties of silk ribbon, the sort of thing his mother supplied to the court.

"Most of this is imported. That is cullen ribbon." The disdain in his voice as he indicated one particular bolt made it clear that he thought this product far inferior to ribbons made in England.

"Cullen?" It looked very fine to me.

"From Cologne. It is used to make girdles and key bands." He jabbed a finger at another sample of ribbon on the rack, sneering as he identified it. "That is called towers ribbon. From Tours. It is a fine silk used to make decorative roses."

We moved on. Rafe made derogatory remarks about every sample of imported silk goods we encountered. After a bit, his superior attitude began to amuse me.

"I suppose your mother is the only one in the whole wide world who is truly skilled at making trimmings of silk," I said, thinking to tease him.

"No one can produce a better hair-lacing ribbon." He turned, a challenge in his deep brown eyes.

His intent gaze fell upon my face. I stared back at him, transfixed. For a moment, I forgot to breathe. Then he reached out and lightly touched my cheek. His fingers—ungloved again!—feathered across my skin to tuck an errant lock of my hair back into place beneath my headdress.

I shied away from him, my face flaming. "You are bold, sirrah!"

He grinned at me. "A trait I come by honestly."

"Never tell me you are descended from pirates!"

He laughed. "Some might say a merchant adventurer and a pirate have much in common."

I bristled, thinking for a moment that he knew my grandfather and great-grandfather had been merchant adventurers of Bristol, but Rafe was speaking of London men . . . and women.

"Did you know that the profession of silkwoman is the only one that London wives are permitted to pursue without their husbands' permission? My mother trades as a *femme sole*. She purchases imported silk goods on her own and has negotiated contracts with all the most prominent Italian silk merchants in the city."

Hearing the pride in his voice, my irritation with him faded. And *what* he said intrigued me. "Is Mistress Pinckney permitted to keep her profits? Or does your father claim them?"

"Father lets well enough alone. He says running her own business keeps her busy and out of trouble."

We resumed our perambulation through the warehouse. "What does she do with the silk after she buys it? Does she dye it?"

Rafe shook his head. "Most raw silk is already dyed. A silkwoman is first a throwster, making the silk into thread, and secondly a corseweaver. She and the women she employs make the silk into small items like points and fringe. But you know all that already."

"Then tell me something I do not know," I challenged him.

We wandered deeper into the storage facility. The high shelves rising on all sides created an illusion of privacy. When we turned a corner, we lost sight of Edyth, who had stopped to gape at a basket of gold trim.

"Something you do not know," Rafe repeated. Then he chuckled. "Shall I tell you what men talk of in London these days? Perhaps I should not. You chided me for repeating rumors the last time we met."

I was astonished that he remembered what we'd talked of, even though I could still recall every word of that conversation. "I enjoy hearing a good story," I quipped, "even when the tale is untrue."

He looked offended. "I do not need to make up stories. What I observe around me every day far surpasses any fancies a poet could conceive of in his imagination."

I stood with my head cocked expectantly, silently waiting for him to give me an example.

"The princess is at Greenwich, is she not?"

I nodded.

"And her mother, the queen, is there also?"

"Yes. The king will join them soon. He, in case you did not know it, is currently residing at Bridewell Palace, just outside London's wall." Bridewell was, in fact, only a short distance from where we stood.

"I am well aware of where the king spends his days . . . and his nights." Rafe snapped out his words. His mouth turned down in disapproval and his tone was grim when he added, "So is all of London."

After a cautious glance to each side of us, he placed one hand on my upper arm and drew me close enough to smell the hint of sandalwood that clung to his clothing. Even through many layers of fabric, I felt the imprint of his fingers on my skin. I shivered, but I did not try to free myself.

He spoke in a low voice. "Before Queen Catherine left for Greenwich, she was at Bridewell with the king. There is no chapel there. Anyone who wishes to hear Mass must cross the River Fleet by way of a gallery that leads to the friary on the other side."

"Blackfriars," I murmured, still distracted by the pleasant warmth of the hand wrapped around my arm. "The Dominican friars who live there wear black mantles over their white habits, hence the name."

He rolled his eyes. "Pay attention, Mistress Lodge. This gallery is well over two hundred feet long. Anyone who stands in the street below has a fine view of those who cross it. When the queen was in residence, her loyal supporters among the citizens of London gathered daily to watch for her. Every time she appeared, they shouted words of encouragement."

"Encouragement?" I knew the queen was popular, but Rafe's choice of that particular word confused me.

Again he surveyed our surroundings, clearly wishing to make certain we would not be overheard. Edyth had reappeared, but was examining a bolt of sky blue cloth and she was not near enough to cause him any concern. No one else was in sight.

"They called out 'May you win your case!' and 'You must have victory, else England itself will go to ruin!' and other sentiments of the same sort."

My eyes widened. "Your Londoners are either very brave or very foolish."

"The people of London love Queen Catherine, and they do not approve of the concubine."

I did not have to ask whom he meant, but I frowned. "Mistress Anne Boleyn never rejoined the queen's household after she recovered from the sweat."

"Did you imagine that illness checked her ambition? Or her spite toward Queen Catherine and her daughter? When the king and queen returned to London in August, the concubine moved into Durham House. It is a goodly mansion with terraced lawns that run clear down to the riverbank, but Mistress Anne did not think it grand enough for her." He grinned suddenly, but it was not with amusement. "Or perhaps she did not feel safe there, for all that it possesses a strongly fortified gatehouse on the land side. The noisy mobs that gathered outside Bridewell cheered for the queen, but those that assembled on the Strand in front of Durham House made it clear they did not want the king's mistress living there. She moved to Suffolk House in Southwark and then, in early September, she retreated all the way back to Hever."

Sensing there was more to the tale, I asked, "What happened then?"

"A most peculiar thing. King Henry summoned the Lord Mayor

and the aldermen of London, along with an assortment of noble-men, judges, and other important people, to come to him in the great chamber at Bridewell. He . . . lectured them. As if they were schoolchildren who had failed to understand an earlier lesson. He explained that his conscience had troubled him for some time con-cerning his marriage to Queen Catherine. She was once married to his brother Arthur and His Grace said he feared that he and the queen had therefore been living together, most abominably and de-testably, in open sin. There is a passage in the Bible that forbids any man, even a king, to uncover the nakedness of his brother's wife."

"Oh, no," I murmured. Did the king truly believe that his mar-riage was invalid? If he did, then matters were far worse than I had imagined.

Rafe's grip on my arm tightened to the point of pain. "King Henry insisted that he only began nullity proceedings to set his conscience at rest. He even claimed that, were he free to choose again, and were there no impediments to the match, he would take Catherine of Aragon as his wife above all others."

"Did his listeners believe him?" Wincing, I tried to pry Rafe's fingers loose.

Abruptly, he released me. I rubbed the spot he'd been holding, wondering if he'd left a bruise.

"The citizens of London are not fools," he said angrily, oblivious to the fact that he'd hurt me. "What they believed was the warn-ing beneath the king's words. For anyone to voice support for the queen after hearing the king's explanation would be an act of mad-ness. And no one now has any doubt but that His Grace intends to proceed with the divorce. He will set his wife aside and take a new bride."

"But surely not Mistress Anne! A foreign princess—"

"Yes, Mistress Anne. King Henry sent the queen to Greenwich alone and within the week the concubine was back in London. His Grace has installed her in Bridewell Palace in the apartments adjacent to his own, where she now lives in royal state, just as if she were already queen of England!"

22

He's a toothsome lad, that Rafe Pinckney," Edyth remarked when we boarded the barge for our return trip to Greenwich.

"He's a silkwoman's son."

"If you don't want him, I'll take him!"

For some reason, Edyth's playful suggestion annoyed me. "Since neither of us will see him again, he's best forgotten."

But I could not forget the intelligence Rafe had shared with me. The king's statement boded ill for his daughter, and for all of us who served her. That Lady Anne had moved into Bridewell had been even less welcome news.

"You look troubled," Maria said a few hours later, after she had admired the ribbons, laces, and other trimmings I'd brought back with me.

Under cover of showing her a particularly pretty piece of fringe, I repeated all that Rafe Pinckney had told me. "Do you think we should warn the princess?"

Maria's hand clenched around the lace. "The king will leave

Bridewell shortly for Greenwich. His Grace always comes here for Yuletide. Do you suppose he will bring his mistress with him?"

"He is the king. He can do whatever he chooses."

In the end I did not tell Princess Mary what I had learned in London. I should have. It might have been less of a shock to Her Grace when Mistress Anne Boleyn not only took up residence in her own wing at Greenwich Palace, but dared hold her own Yuletide revels. Although Queen Catherine still presided over all the formal celebrations of the season, courtiers flocked to this rival court, anxious to ingratiate themselves with the woman who had the most influence with the king.

Princess Mary was almost thirteen years old. She was naïve in many ways, for she had been sheltered all her life, but it was not long before even she had heard about Mistress Anne. She hid her feelings well for one of her tender years. Only those of us who were close to her knew how much she resented the favor that king and courtiers alike showed to her mother's former maid of honor.

At night in the maidens' dormitory, we speculated about the queen's claim that the king had no grounds to annul their marriage.

"Do you think the queen is telling the truth?" Mary Fitzherbert wondered aloud as the four of us gathered on the bed Maria and I shared. "She was old enough to consummate the marriage when she wed the king's older brother, and it is said he boasted afterward that he had been in Spain the night before." The annulment hinged upon this point. If Catherine of Aragon had never truly been a wife to Prince Arthur, then there was no impediment to her marriage to his brother.

Mary Dannett giggled. "All men boast of their conquests." She helped herself to a dried and sugared orange slice from the box of comfits she'd brought with her, then passed it around.

"The wedding to Arthur was nearly thirty years ago," I reminded them, "and only the queen knows for certain what happened in the marriage bed." And she, I thought to myself, would most certainly lie about those long-ago events, if she thought it would preserve her daughter's right to inherit England's throne.

Queen Catherine's first husband, Arthur Tudor, Prince of Wales, had died shortly after they were wed. She had languished in England for years afterward, until King Henry succeeded his father and married her himself. It had been a love match, or so I'd always heard. It was sobering to realize that people could fall out of love as well as into it.

"I do not understand how it is possible for a man, even a king, to set aside his wife," Mary Fitzherbert said. "A marriage is supposed to last until one or the other of the couple dies. What difference does it make if she did lie with his brother first?"

"That is just an excuse. What truly troubles His Grace is that the queen is too old to have more children. If the king wants a legitimate son, he has to take a new wife." Mary Dannett, who had recently acquired a suitor, considered herself an expert on such matters, especially since George Medley, the man who was courting her, was the son, by her first marriage, of the Marchioness of Dorset. The marquess, George's stepfather, was the king's cousin and a close friend of His Grace, although he held no important post at court. Through such tangled relationships much information could be gleaned.

"His Grace would never have thought to put aside Queen Catherine if not for Mistress Anne," Maria said. She looked as if she wanted to strike someone. Her hands were already curled into fists.

"I wish there were something we could do to break the concubine's hold on the king." I bit into a sugared comfit and found that it tasted bitter on my tongue.

"His Grace wants to marry her," said Mary Dannett, "and even some members of Queen Catherine's household must think that will happen. Several ladies have already abandoned the queen to join the concubine's retinue."

The phrase "rats deserting a sinking ship" passed through my mind but I did not give voice to it. Maria had gone very still, a pensive look on her face.

"What if one of us were to do the same?" she asked.

"I would never be so disloyal!" Mary Fitzherbert exclaimed.

"Nor I," said Mary Dannett.

I peered more closely at Maria's shadowed countenance. Only the light of one candle illuminated the darkness. We'd pulled the curtains closed around the bed, sealing the four of us inside a snug little tent. "What is it you are suggesting?"

A slow smile crept over her features. "If one of us were to enter Anne Boleyn's service, that one would be in a perfect position to cause difficulties for the concubine. More than that, she could gather information and pass it on to those in the queen's camp."

For a moment, the idea was tempting. Then common sense reasserted itself. "Your plan has a fatal flaw, Maria," I said. "Our devotion to Princess Mary is too well known and Mistress Anne is no fool. She would never trust any one of us."

23

At the end of Yuletide, the princess left court. Our lives went on much as they always had, filled with lessons, hours of prayer, shirts that had to be hemmed for the poor, and altar cloths that needed embroidering. I spent hours practicing my penmanship, even though I had no one to write letters to, and I continued to amuse the princess and the other maids of honor by telling stories.

One or two of the princess's gentlemen showed a flattering interest in me from time to time, but I felt no answering spark and I was wary of being courted for my inheritance. It occurred to me to wonder why Sir Lionel had not arranged a match for me, but I could think of two good reasons for him to delay any marriage plans. Once I wed, I could no longer be a maid of honor. Like Anne Rede and Cecily Dabridgecourt, I'd have to leave the princess's service. Then I'd be of no more use to Sir Lionel . . . not that I'd done him much good so far. But more than that, he would also have to cede control of my lands, chattel, and household stuff to a husband. That was the more likely explanation for him to leave matters as they were.

Whatever my guardian's rationale, it accorded well with my own wishes. The princess's household was home to me. I looked on Her Grace as the little sister I'd never had. My stepmother, for all that I had missed her when I first left Glastonbury, had faded in my memory. I had known, even at the start of my journey to Thornbury, that I might never see her again.

In May 1529, legal proceedings for the annulment of the king's marriage began at Blackfriars. We did not hear of this until some time later, in a letter from Maria's father. He wrote that Queen Catherine refused to acknowledge the authority of an English court. She insisted that they had no right to decide the validity of her marriage and that only the pope could rule on the issue. The pope seemed disinclined to do so.

In September, the king, the queen, and the princess set out on their usual hunting progress, moving slowly and stopping at Waltham Abbey, Barnet, Tyttenhanger, Windsor, Reading, Woodstock, Langley, Buckingham, and the king's new palace at Grafton in Northamptonshire. The building at Grafton had been completed only three years earlier and it was a fine, large house, big enough to also accommodate Mistress Anne and her entourage. They accompanied the royal riding household, part of the court and yet separate from it.

Queen Catherine dealt with her rival's presence by ignoring her.

Princess Mary tried to imitate her mother. One day at Grafton, when she was taking her daily constitutional, accompanied by Maria and myself, she caught sight of the king and the concubine on the far side of the garden. "My father has had mistresses before," she announced, "and eventually he lost interest in each and every one of them."

As she resumed her perambulation, Maria and I exchanged a look, but we did not contradict Her Grace.

In December, Mistress Anne Boleyn's father, Lord Rochford, was created Earl of Wiltshire. Afterward, outside of usual custom, the king decreed that all three of the new earl's children be addressed by what was now the earl's lesser title, that of Rochford. Thus, overnight, plain Mistress Anne became not just Lady Anne, but Lady Anne Rochford.

Once again, Yuletide was spent at Greenwich, but this year I was not dispatched to London to select silk ribbons and fringe for the dances and disguisings. Mistress Pinckney was sent for. All the maids of honor and at least half the princess's ladies-in-waiting crowded into the privy chamber when the silkwoman arrived to display her wares.

Rafe was with her, but in the presence of so many gentlewomen, he took care to efface himself. I could contrive no opportunity for a moment's private speech with him, and found myself strangely disappointed that I was denied the chance to question him.

I wanted to know how the citizens of London felt about the concubine now. No more than that. Or so I told myself.

Several hours later, as I was hurrying along a passageway on my way to fetch the princess's muff, forgotten in her bedchamber when we set out to attend Mass, a dark figure stepped out from a shadowy alcove to confront me. I gasped, then laughed nervously as I inhaled cinnamon and sandalwood and recognized the silkwoman's apprentice.

"You gave me a terrible start. You should not jump out at people like that."

His lips twitched. "I do beg your pardon, Mistress Lodge, but I have been waiting here in the hope of seeing you."

"Have you some new rumor to impart?" I blurted out.

His brow knit in puzzlement and I felt heat rise into my face. We had no arrangement that called for him to provide me with intelligence every Yuletide. It had just worked out that way. Was it possible he had not even been aware of passing on information of importance?

Feeling more awkward by the moment, I waited for him to speak again. He must have had some reason to lie in wait for me and I hoped he would hurry up and reveal it. My absence from the chapel would be noted if I took much longer to return with the princess's muff.

Instead of saying anything, he withdrew a small parcel from inside his cloak and thrust it toward me.

I stepped back, putting my hands behind me. "What is this?"

"It is a New Year's gift. I know it is early yet, but I doubt I will see you again before then." When he stopped mumbling and lifted his gaze from the stone floor, he saw my confusion. "It is for *you*, Mistress Thomasine Lodge."

"Oh." I did not know what else to say. I had nothing to give him in return.

"Take it," Rafe insisted, shoving the small parcel toward me yet again.

Certain he would let it fall if I did not, I accepted the gift. "This is most kind of you," I murmured.

He looked as ill at ease as I felt, shuffling his feet and avoiding my eyes. Just as I was forming the words to thank him again, he bolted.

"I must return to London," he called over his shoulder, "but I will see you again next Yuletide."

Then he was gone. Bemused, I continued on my way to the princess's lodgings, detouring only long enough to place the mysterious parcel in my trunk in the maidens' dormitory.

I intended to wait until New Year's Day to open the gift. My resolve had faltered by supper time. Inside the box was a delicate, burgundy-colored hair ribbon. I wondered if he had fashioned the pretty thing himself, and imagined his strong, long-fingered hands working the expensive silk threads.

The image was oddly unsettling.

24

After Yuletide, the princess's household settled in at Beaulieu Palace. By that time, Beaulieu had become Her Grace's principal residence. As usual, news of the king's court reached us in fits and starts, but we soon heard of it when the queen retired to Richmond Palace and King Henry, accompanied by Lady Anne, traveled to York Place in the city of Westminster.

Although Edyth was good about repeating what she heard from the other lower servants, her information was unenlightening. Not only was there nothing new to report, but Edyth was distracted. She was being courted by one of the grooms of the stable, a lad from Suffolk. She confided to me that she was trying to rid her suitor of his East Anglia accent, since she had almost entirely eradicated the sounds of Gloucestershire and Somersetshire from her own speech. Only the occasional colorful expression still slipped through.

From Sir Lionel directly, I heard nothing. It was the Countess of Salisbury who told me that his wife had died, but she knew no details of Lady Daggett's demise.

In the spring, we moved to Richmond Palace so that Beaulieu

could be cleaned and aired. I liked Richmond best of all the king's great houses. It boasted a wonderful orchard intersected by galleries that ran between the palace and the friary to the south. These galleries offered a splendid view of the gardens from above and also looked down on the tennis play at the northeast corner. The windows in that section were covered with wire mesh to protect spectators from stray tennis balls.

Princess Mary was less pleased to be at Richmond, since her mother had departed before we arrived. In June, however, the king came to spend the day with his daughter. He was about to embark on a four-month-long progress. For the princess, it was a joyous occasion. She basked in her father's attention and seized upon the opportunity to sing her mother's praises.

I trailed after them through the gardens, in company with the other maids of honor. From ground level, the patterns of the knots and hedgerows were not as impressive as they were from the gallery, but the scent of the flowers in bloom was lovely. There were a dozen varieties of roses and honeysuckle, too.

Like the princess, I allowed myself to believe all was well. We heard little to contradict that happy misconception in the months that followed.

25

When Yuletide came around again, I thought at first that matters between the king and queen truly had improved. The concubine was not in residence at Greenwich Palace. Queen Catherine presided over the revels, just as she always had.

I had thought about Rafe from time to time during the year, even dreamed about him once or twice. And I often wore the ribbon he'd given me. I pinned it to my sleeve the day he and his mother were due at the palace to show off their wares. In the noise and confusion created by a dozen women all exclaiming over silk trimmings, we arranged to meet in one of the gardens before he returned to London.

Bundled into my warmest cloak, I hurried toward him along a snow-rimmed path. I had changed from slippers into boots and scarcely felt the cold, especially when he held out both hands to catch hold of mine.

"Have you brought me another gift?" I teased him. I had hemmed and embroidered a handkerchief as a present for him.

"In a way." His voice sounded odd. It was even deeper than I remembered it, and he was looking down at me with an intense, almost brooding gaze.

Of a sudden, I felt leery of showing off my embroidery. I had a delicate hand with my stitches, but I was no professional. What had I been thinking, to offer something I had sewn to the son of a silk-woman? He was her apprentice, too. He was doubtless more skilled than I at plying a needle. I was glad the small parcel was hidden in the inner pocket of my cloak. I'd be embarrassed if Rafe saw what I had wrought.

He led me carefully over the icy gravel until we came to an arbor. In summer it was covered with roses. Bare, scraggly branches gave us only a modicum of shelter, but in that quiet spot it was private enough to permit Rafe to speak his mind. He gestured for me to sit on the stone bench beneath the arch. He remained standing.

"I did not think to see you this year," he said.

"When we parted, you promised we would meet again."

"Aye, I did. But I was not certain you would wish to see me."

I opened my mouth, then closed it again. I knew what he must be thinking. I was a gentlewoman, an heiress, and a maid of honor to a royal princess. I was very far above him in station. Rafe, although he was a year or two older than I was, was still an apprentice. I did not know a great deal about the ways of craft guilds, but I suspected that he had even less freedom than I did when it came to courtship and marriage. My actions were governed by a guardian. He was under obligation to a master or, in this case, a mistress. That he was apprenticed to his own mother might mean he would one day inherit her business, but for the nonce he was bound to her in a way that made him more slave than servant.

My feelings were in a jumble. Confusing desires tugged at me. My face grew warm, in spite of the frosty air.

I gave myself a mental shake. Why was I thinking about

courtship and marriage? No matter how old or how skilled in working silk Rafe became, he could have no permanent place in my life. He would never be a gentleman and therefore Sir Lionel would never allow a match between us.

Abruptly, I stood, intending to leave the arbor before I embarrassed myself further. Rafe grabbed my arm and hauled me back. My breath caught. My heart rate quickened. We were standing very close together, nearly touching from shoulder to toes.

"You have forgotten your gift," he whispered.

"There is no need for you to give me anything."

"There is every need. I want you to have something to remember me by."

And with that, he pulled me tight against him, planted his mouth firmly over mine, and kissed me. Of a sudden, I could neither breathe nor think. My blood pounded in my head. I felt near to fainting by the time he released me.

I inhaled sharply. My entire body tingled, especially my lips. Strange and powerful urges had me reaching for him when he stepped away from me, but I dropped my hand when I caught a glimpse of his face. Rafe looked as shaken as I was. His skin had gone pale. His pupils were enormous.

He started to speak and had to clear his throat before any words came out. "Remember me," he said, and then he turned and walked away.

I was still shaking when I came in from the frigid garden. Maria, catching sight of me, drew me close to the nearest charcoal brazier and bade me warm my hands. "What did he say to you?" she whispered.

So rattled were my thoughts about Rafe Pinckney that at first I did not understand what she was asking me.

"You are in the habit of returning from your meetings with the silkwoman's son bearing news of the concubine's doings," Maria reminded me.

"There was nothing this year." I shook my head, hoping to clear it. "He had no rumors to repeat."

Maria looked pleased. "Perhaps that means that the king has tired of Lady Anne at last."

We should have known better than to let ourselves hope.

Lady Anne Rochford was back at court in time for New Year's Day. Right after Yuletide, she and the king rode away together, leaving the queen behind.

In March, Princess Mary paid an extended visit to her mother. The king was elsewhere. Their Graces spent long hours talking together in private. The princess was quiet and withdrawn after these sessions, but she did not share what had been said with me, or with Maria.

Maria's mother and the other Spaniards who served Queen Catherine could add little to our knowledge. Mistress Vittorio told her daughter that the pope continued to resist granting King Henry his annulment.

"In time, they are certain the concubine's influence over the king will wane," Maria informed me when she returned to the maidens' chamber after spending the afternoon with her parents.

"But that does not appear to be happening," I pointed out, "and the king has been infatuated with Lady Anne for a very long time already."

"She has bewitched His Grace," Maria said. "That is what I think."

That was not the first time she had made this suggestion. "Would that the answer were that simple," I retorted. "If the concubine could be caught using spells, she'd be arrested and imprisoned."

Maria brightened. "No. She would be executed. Burnt for heresy. What an excellent notion!"

I thought about the times I'd seen Lady Anne, recalling the way people responded to her. Was that sorcery? Or merely the result of a compelling personality? Coupled with the power of physical attraction, something I understood considerably better after Rafe's kisses, I rather thought that Lady Anne had no need of spells to ensure the king's continued devotion.

26

We had been back at Her Grace's principal residence of Beaulieu only a few days when the princess was stricken with terrible pain in her head and belly. Her physician did not know what to make of her condition. He tried various nostrums. Her Grace could not keep them down. He bled her. That just made her weaker.

The next day, she refused to eat, rejecting nourishing broths and sweet confections alike. By the third day of her sickness, her eyes looked sunken and her cheeks were hollow. She kept her lips pressed tightly together to keep herself from crying out as each new pain racked her thin body.

I hurt for Her Grace when she pressed both hands to her belly, trying in vain to ease another spasm. She was panting by the time it passed.

"What can be causing this?" I whispered to Maria, terrified by this mysterious affliction. Maria swore in Spanish. Then she signaled me to follow her from the sickroom. She did not explain herself, only led the way to the kitchens. I watched in growing consternation as she inspected every clump of cooking herbs that hung suspended from the rafters. Apparently satisfied, she left again, still without saying a word.

"What were you looking for?" I demanded.

She was already outside. I had to run to catch her before she reached the still house, maintained to provide the household with cordials, sweet waters, and cosmetics. I stepped inside right behind her. The scents of a half-dozen perfumes greeted me, everything from lavender and rose water to the more exotic jasmine essence that the Countess of Salisbury preferred. Equipment for distilling stood ready for use on a table, but no one was present to oversee the process.

I seized Maria's arm, forcing her to look at me. "Why are we here?"

"I am looking for poison."

I gasped and released her, freeing her to rummage through the herbs. Her hands trembled as she took down bundle after bundle to look at and sniff and even taste.

In a faint, disbelieving voice, I said, "You think Princess Mary has been poisoned?"

"It stands to reason after what happened to the Bishop of Rochester. My father told me about it in one of his letters." She shoved aside an alembic and displaced a mortar and pestle.

"Tell me."

She did so as she continued her search. "It was late February when it happened. The bishop, John Fisher, was at Rochester House in London. His cook prepared a broth for him, but he did not eat it. He is a very holy man and fasts a great deal. In this case, that habit probably saved his life."

"What was in the broth?"

"No one knows. A powder of some sort. That is what the bishop's cook admitted later." She lowered her voice to add, "Under torture."

An involuntary shudder passed through me.

"The cook claimed he thought it was only a jest, that the powder was a laxative and would make the others in the household most uncomfortable for a time but not truly harm anyone. Instead, many were violently ill and two people died, one of the bishop's servants and a poor old widow who was among the beggars at the gate. She received some of what was left over when the household had finished their meal."

"But why would anyone want to poison a bishop?" I asked.

"Can you not guess? He angered Lady Anne Rochford. Bishop Fisher supports Queen Catherine in the king's great matter. And if Lady Anne would try to kill him, why not the princess, too? If one of the concubine's party is a worker in the kitchen, it would take but a moment to add something foul to a dish. Not all poisons have an evil taste or a bad smell."

"Is Her Grace going to die?" I whispered. "Has that woman killed her?"

"I may be wrong. I pray I am. But I know something of herbs from my father. I have to look. If I can discover what Her Grace was given, I may be able to compound an antidote."

"But you found nothing in the kitchen."

"No, nor here," Maria admitted, replacing a glass beaker on a shelf.

"And no one else is ill."

But Maria was already outside again. "The herb garden," she called over her shoulder.

Once again, I followed her.

"How can there be poisonous herbs here?" I asked as we stood in the chilly April sunshine looking down at the neatly planted rows of basil and borage, fennel and rosemary, sorrel and the like. My training in both cookery and distilling had been cut short when I'd come to court, although I did know how to make a poultice with self-heal, wine, and water to draw the infection out of a cut.

"Some herbs can harm as well as heal." Maria bent to inspect the neat rows of plants, reciting their names as she came to each one: "Betony. Parsley. Orache. Coriander. Clary. Dittany. Hyssop. Mint. Pellitory. Rue. Sage. Tansy." She hesitated.

"Surely tansy is not a poison," I objected. "We always have tansy cakes to eat at the end of Lent."

"Tansy cakes are made with tansy juice mixed with eggs. They *are* harmless. And oil of tansy, well steeped, can be used to calm the nerves and help female complaints. But in too great a dose, it is poisonous. It can cause convulsions and spasms."

"The princess has spasms of pain."

"But no convulsions."

Maria continued her inspection. "Violets. Fennel," she murmured, then passed by a few more plants without naming them, her forehead creased in concentration and her eyes fixed on the ground.

"Surely the princess's cook would know if he had a poisonous plant in his kitchen garden or among his dried herbs," I said.

"Not necessarily. Some poisonous herbs are easily mistaken for their more benign cousins. My father says that monkshood tops resemble parsley, and so do the leaves of cowbane. Young thimble flower plants look much like comfrey, but if you eat the leaves, you will die within a day. Even hemlock, which everyone knows is a poison, can be confused with caraway."

"I did not know hemlock was poisonous," I murmured.

"Well, it is. But in the normal way of things, no one would ever eat of it. The entire plant has a disagreeable, mousy odor."

Maria stooped to look more closely at a tall, hairy-stalked plant, but after a moment she stepped away, shaking her head. "There is nothing here."

"What did you expect to find?"

"Banewort, perhaps. It is often cultivated in herb gardens because it can be used as a sleep aid and to prevent miscarriages. And it can make one's pupils grow large and luminous. Some women squeeze the juice of the berries right into their eyes."

"If the plant is poisonous, why doesn't that kill them?"

"It is *eating* the fruit that is dangerous, although all parts of the plant contain the same deadly poison." Maria's attention had already shifted to the wooded area two bow shots distant from the manor house. "Some poisons grow wild. Henbane lines many of the roads hereabout and cowbane can grow in stagnant ditches."

For another hour, we searched among the trees. I learned a great deal more than I wanted to know about poisonous plants but we found nothing suspicious. It was beginning to grow dark when we made our way back to the princess's privy chamber.

"Her Grace is still suffering severe cramps, but she is no worse," Mary Fitzherbert told us. "She has been given borage. Master Pereston, the princess's apothecary, suggested it."

Maria nodded approvingly. When she'd stepped aside, out of Mary's hearing, she whispered, "Borage cleanses poisons from the blood. And it is easier to come by than a stag's heart."

I was not certain I wanted to know, but I asked anyway. "What would you do with a stag's heart?"

"If the princess were to wear part of a stag's heart in a silk bag around her neck, it would draw poison out of her body."

"I suppose we could ask for one in the kitchens."

Maria gave a derisive snort. "Some cures are simply old wives' tales and of doubtful use. Learned men like my father disdain them.

Another such is that wearing a bag of arsenic next to the skin can prevent someone from falling ill of the plague. Far more likely, the arsenic would seep through the bag and cause harm, for arsenic is a deadly poison."

"Arsenic?" I repeated, unfamiliar with the name. "Is that another herb?"

"It is a mineral, useful as a base for salves but very dangerous." She frowned. "That is all I know of it."

"Then perhaps we had better learn more."

I went in search of Thomas Pereston and found him not far away. Denied access to the princess's bedchamber, he lurked at the foot of the great stair that led to the royal lodgings.

"Tell me all you know about arsenic," I demanded.

The apothecary looked at me askance. "Why would you want to know such a thing?"

I hesitated, then glanced pointedly up the stairs.

"Ah, I see," said Master Pereston, "but you are quite wrong if you think arsenic is to blame."

"Tell me anyway. I would decide for myself."

He took off the tiny pair of spectacles he wore. Breathing on each lens to fog it, he used his handkerchief to wipe away the moisture. Only when both small circles of glass were clean and the whole was once again perched upon the bridge of his nose did he oblige me. "I suppose it will do no harm for you to know," he said. "And it may do you some good one day, although I pray you never have need of the knowledge."

"I see we understand each other." Even if the princess had not been poisoned this time, the threat of such a thing was very real.

"I fear we do." He cleared his throat. "Arsenic can kill if taken internally. It is tasteless and odorless in solution, and therefore dangerous. That is why only those trained to handle medicines that contain the substance—apothecaries and physicians—should meddle with it."

"What does it look like in its natural state?" I asked.

"It is a powder. Gray, with a crystalline appearance. But arsenic sulfide is yellow in color. It is even called yellow arsenic. There is also red arsenic—realgar—an orange-red powder that is used as a pigment by painters and in pyrotechnics. If you heat realgar, you produce white arsenic. The crystals then look something like sugar."

"And all of these forms are poisons?"

He nodded. "Oh, yes. Decidedly so."

"And their effects?"

"Severe abdominal pain." At my reaction, he hastened to reassure me. "The other symptoms of arsenic poisoning are not present in . . . in any patient I have seen of late."

He went on to enumerate them—clammy skin, dizziness, burning in the throat, vomiting, the bloody flux. Convulsions and unconsciousness were the heralds of imminent death. I felt rather ill myself by the time he came to the end of the list.

"Is there a cure?"

"Death comes quickly, Mistress Lodge. There is rarely time to attempt treatment."

"What if there *were* time?" I persisted. "Or if the victim had ingested very little of the substance?"

I sensed his growing impatience. Or perhaps it was nervousness. His gaze darted here and there as if he feared someone might be listening to our exchange.

"I have heard that patients who vomit up the poison and then drink large quantities of milk may survive even a large dose of the poison," he blurted out, "but I have no firsthand knowledge of anyone successfully brought back to health by that cure."

With that, Master Pereston bade me farewell, clearly disinclined to answer any more questions about poisons.

The physicians attending the princess, including one specifically called in to consult, studied their books, their astrological charts, and a sample of the princess's urine. They concluded that Her Grace was suffering from a disturbance of the mother and that this had caused hysteria. They delivered this verdict to the Countess of Salisbury, along with the opinion that the condition could prove fatal should internal swelling cause Her Grace to have difficulty breathing.

"Heaving of the lights," Lady Salisbury informed the maids of honor and ladies-in-waiting a short time later, using the layman's term for this condition. "It occurs when the lungs give out. The patient suffocates."

Although the countess was now quite aged, and walked with great effort because her joints pained her, she was still in charge of the princess's household. She had called us all together not only to report on the princess's condition but also to give new orders.

"There are to be at least four female attendants with Princess Mary at all times," she decreed, "to watch Her Grace closely for signs of greater contagion from the mother."

"What *is* 'the mother'?" I whispered to Maria.

"The uterus," Maria said, and frowned. "There are various roots—foalfoot, licorice, enula campana, and marshmallow—that can help alleviate this condition. And parts of other herbs can be useful, too, like maidenhair and hyssop."

She might have ventured to suggest these remedies to the countess had not a sudden anguished cry from Princess Mary's bedchamber sent us all rushing to Her Grace's side. Tumbling through the doorway, I stopped, stunned into immobility by the tableau before me. The princess stood between her bed and the close stool that had been moved out of the stool chamber for her convenience during her illness. Her Grace was staring in horror and disbelief at the bed she had just left. The bedsheets were stained red with blood.

"I am bleeding," Princess Mary whispered. "Am I about to die?"

Lady Salisbury, wavering between embarrassment and relief, hobbled forward. "Indeed you are not, Your Grace, and we have, at last, an explanation for Your Grace's pain. You have begun your monthly courses."

The princess was older than most girls for her first flowers. She had passed her fifteenth birthday a few months earlier, in February. But she had always been small for her age, thin and frail. And, it appeared, none of her senior ladies had ever troubled to explain to her what would happen at the onset of womanhood. Blanche had provided me with a surfeit of information and advice well in advance of my need for either.

Although it was clear that the princess continued to feel considerable discomfort from cramps, she was smiling when her lady mistress had remedied this oversight in her education. Her Grace was well pleased to have reached a natural and much to be desired milestone. She accepted that her pain, like the pain of childbirth, was a woman's lot, punishment for the sin of Eve.

Maria, however, saw no reason for Princess Mary to suffer. She urged Her Grace to drink crushed angelica in rose water to relieve the cramping. Lady Salisbury looked disapproving but did not stop her from administering the remedy. The countess then instructed her royal charge to rest and dismissed all the maids of honor in order that Her Grace could do so.

"We had no cause for alarm, after all," I said as the four of us made our way toward the maidens' dormitory for the night. Maria and I lagged a bit behind the other two.

"Not this time," Maria agreed. "My fears were groundless. But that does not mean that there is no danger. Only think of it—if the king were to lose his one legitimate child, would that not make him even more determined to take a new wife in order to get himself an heir?"

I glanced nervously over my shoulder in unconscious imitation of Master Pereston, hoping that no one was near enough to overhear. Talking of poison was dangerous enough. What Maria had just said came perilous close to speculating about the king's future. To do that, in these tumultuous times, could easily be misconstrued as treason.

27

We were still at Beaulieu in June. I had been for a walk in the gardens, enjoying an hour of solitude, and had stopped on a little footbridge to watch the fish in the artificial stream that ran beneath it when I noticed a man in a riding cloak watching me from the gate that led to the orchard. At first I did not recognize him. When I did, my heart sank.

Sir Lionel Daggett, a parody of a smile twisting his lips, stalked toward me along the graveled path. When he joined me on the footbridge, he doffed his feathered bonnet. It was a meaningless gesture. He'd never had any respect for me, nor any liking, either.

"Mistress Thomasine, you appear to be in excellent health."

I quickly curtseyed, which allowed me to hide my face from him. I was afraid my expression would give away my dismay at seeing him again and this odious man was still my guardian.

It had been more than three years since I'd last seen him. His raspy voice was the same, but he had continued to put on weight. He now had triple chins, and the veins in his nose bulged, a sure indication that he overindulged in drink as well as food.

When he extended a hand to help me rise, I was obliged to take it. Even with the two layers of our leather gloves between us, his touch made my skin crawl.

He wasted no time on preliminaries. Gripping my hand more tightly, he said, "You have been little help to me, Thomasine."

"You cannot blame me for failing to advance your political career," I objected. "How was I to win you an appointment at the king's court when his daughter so rarely sees him?"

Long service in the hinterlands had not improved Sir Lionel's temperament. He snarled. "A clever puss would have found a way. But it no longer matters. I've another use for you. My wife died some time ago. I am in the market for a new bride."

A terrible sense of foreboding came over me. I took a step back, but there was nowhere to run. I bumped up against the railing of the bridge. Over the thundering of my heart, I managed to croak out a response: "What has that to do with me, Sir Lionel?"

"Why everything, my dear. I propose to marry *you*."

The horrifying words hung in the still air between us. Bile rose in my throat. My innards clenched in dread. For a long moment, I simply stared at him. Then I blurted out the first objection I could think of that might have a prayer of convincing him to change his mind: "The princess must give her permission."

He laughed. "Your young mistress has no say in this matter. Nor does Lady Salisbury, if you are thinking you can persuade the old countess to stand against me. It is none of her concern."

"But . . . but I have an obligation to the princess." I turned away from him, gripping the railing with both hands. I stared down into the shining water below. For one mad moment, I considered flinging myself in. *Anything* would be better than being forced to marry Sir Lionel.

Seizing my upper arm in a painful grip, he tugged me off the bridge and toward a nearby grassy knoll surmounted by a wooden bench. He shoved me down onto the seat and lifted one booted foot to rest beside me, pinning the side of my kirtle. He leaned closer, until I could smell the cloves he'd been chewing on his breath. The scent made my stomach turn.

"There is no longer any benefit to me in leaving you in Princess Mary's household," Sir Lionel said. "A fool could see which way the wind blows and I am no fool."

A scream of frustration was bubbling up inside me, but I dared not let it out. My thoughts raced in frantic circles, seeking an argument that would persuade him to change his mind, but every avenue of escape was neatly blocked. He was my guardian. As such, he had the right to arrange my marriage, even if it was to himself. The powerful Duke of Suffolk, who had once been married to the king's younger sister, had acquired a girl's wardship to wed her to his son, but when his wife died, he'd married her himself. She'd been but fourteen at the time.

A girl could, I'd heard, refuse a match that was offensive to her. But I had also heard of brides beaten into submission by their parents when they attempted to do so. In lieu of a father, a guardian could likewise take up a switch, or a rod, or even use his fists on his ward. He could strike her with impunity until she agreed to do his bidding . . . or was dead.

I could not help but remember that Sir Lionel had kidnapped his late wife in order to force her to marry him. He'd no doubt raped her, too. My sense of desperation increased tenfold. The idea of lying in Sir Lionel's arms, obliged to allow him liberties with my person, sickened me. I could not bear the thought that he would kiss me as Rafe had kissed me. I was on the verge of descending into mindless panic when I began, at last, to *think*.

There *was* a way out of this. All I had to do was persuade Sir Lionel that it was to his advantage to change his mind.

Forcing myself to lift my face to his, I met his eyes. "I can still be of use to you as a maid of honor."

He sneered at the very idea. "I do not see how."

"By joining Lady Anne Rochford's household."

There! A spark of interest lit his expression. Putting every bit of enthusiasm I could muster into my argument, I sketched out my plan.

"Lady Anne's entourage grows larger by the day. Some of them formerly served Queen Catherine. The lady would delight in obtaining the services of one of Princess Mary's attendants. She would see it as a victory for her party."

I had no idea if that was true, but a calculating look came into Sir Lionel's eyes. I scarcely dared breathe while he turned my proposal over in his mind, weighing the advantages and searching for flaws.

"If it is possible to install you in that household at all," he mused, "I will arrange it, but you must first become my wife."

I knew why he wanted to marry me. In that way he would gain permanent control of my inheritance. On the other hand, so long as I did not wed anyone else, he would remain in charge of my lands until I reached my majority. "The lady's damsels," I reminded him, "must remain unmarried. That is the very definition of a maid of honor."

"Gentlewomen of the privy chamber have husbands."

"But the maids of honor are the ones closest to their mistress and therefore best able to whisper in her ear." This statement stretched the truth, but I did not suppose that Sir Lionel knew much about the workings of a woman's household.

He was silent for an agonizing length of time. Had his extended absence from court, I wondered, left him without influential friends there? I remembered what Lady Anne had told me, back when she was still plain *Mistress* Anne—that the king did not like Sir Lionel.

But money and gifts had bought me a place in the princess's household. Surely they could achieve similar results now . . . *if* Sir Lionel thought it worth the expense.

Abruptly, he removed his boot from my skirt, leaving a dirty footprint behind, and stepped back. "I will see what I can do," he said, and left me sitting there.

Barely a week later, word came to Beaulieu that I was to pack my belongings and be ready to depart for Windsor Castle the next morning.

28

The chamberlain of Princess Mary's household also received notice of my impending departure—authorization for me to leave the princess's service. He told Lady Salisbury where I was going and she, regarding me with undisguised disgust, thinking me a traitor, announced to Her Grace and all her ladies that I was abandoning them to join the concubine's household.

I started to object, then hung my head. What could I say? If I told them the truth, it might get back to Lady Anne. I was certain she had spies among the princess's servants.

In spite of the risk of being exposed, I begged for one final private audience with Her Grace. That meant there were only two yeomen in the chamber, well in the background, together with Her Grace, Maria Vittorio, and Mary Dannett.

Princess Mary turned on me the moment Maria shut the door behind us. "How could you?" Her hands clenched into fists at her sides and her lips formed a hard, thin line, but I could see the hurt in her eyes.

I flung myself to my knees before her. "Your Grace, I am as loyal to you as ever I was. I swear it."

The whole story tumbled out then, how Sir Lionel had planned to take me away and marry me and how, in my desperation, I had suggested an alternate plan. And now I added the thought that had come to me after he'd agreed.

"Maria once made a suggestion, Your Grace, that one of us should enter the concubine's household to spy on her. Now, under these circumstances, I believe such a scheme can succeed."

The princess's expression mellowed. She reached out a hand to touch my shoulder. "You serve me well, Tamsin."

Maria said something in Spanish.

The princess nodded. "That woman must be stopped." Her Grace rarely allowed herself to acknowledge Anne Boleyn's existence but, when she did, she never referred to Lady Anne by name. She was either "the concubine" or "that woman."

"I did not expect Sir Lionel to act so quickly." I rose at Her Grace's signal. "We have little time to plan, or to devise a means by which I can send messages to Your Grace."

"Invisible ink?" Mary Dannett's eyes lit up when she made this suggestion. "I have heard such a thing can be made from the juice of a lemon."

"One of the stories you told us talked of a code," the princess reminded me.

"Yes, but it did not explain how to use such a cipher." I glanced toward the two yeomen to make sure they were not close enough to overhear what we were saying. "Plain writing will do, I think, so long as we have a secure way to deliver a letter." I thanked the good Lord that I had been taught to write since joining Her Grace's household.

"That may be difficult," the princess acknowledged.

"It is a pity the dovecote contains no carrier pigeons," I said.

My quip produced a fleeting smile. "I fear it would be noticed, Tamsin, if you carried away a cage full of birds when you left us for court."

"There must be some other—" I broke off as the answer came to me. "Maria's father is at court. Could he—?"

The princess clapped her hands together in delight. For a moment she looked like the fifteen-year-old girl she was. "How perfect!"

Maria nodded slowly. "Father writes to me several times a month." Messages arrived for her almost as often as letters from Queen Catherine came for the princess.

"You must approach Dr. Vittorio as soon as you reach Windsor Castle," Her Grace instructed me.

"I do not want to arouse suspicions. If I enter that woman's household and immediately ask to speak to one of the most loyal members of the queen's entourage, it will raise questions."

"Not if you do so because you have a letter to deliver to him from his daughter. What could be more natural? And in that letter, Maria will explain, in Spanish, where your true loyalty lies. All that will remain to do is to devise a way to continue to cross paths with Dr. Vittorio at court." She chuckled. "I suggest you develop some minor ailment soon after you arrive."

"An allergy to the concubine?" I suggested.

On that light note, I bade the princess farewell, but I was anything but lighthearted by the time I returned to the maidens' dormitory. I felt as I had when I'd been ripped from Hartlake Manor. I was leaving behind my home, my friends—all I held dear . . . except for Edyth.

My faithful tiring maid was no happier to be joining Anne Boleyn's household than I was. I had to listen to an entire litany of complaints. In the end, I snapped at her to be quiet.

"We have no choice, Edyth. It is Windsor Castle or some godfor-saken spot in Cornwall with Sir Lionel Daggett."

"Oh." Her face was easy to read. She had no more liking for Sir Lionel than I did. Without another word, she resumed packing.

I had one last, uncomfortable interview to endure before I could leave. The Countess of Salisbury sent for me. I thought she would deride me for abandoning the princess, but instead she sent me an approving look as soon as we were alone in her closet, the small room she used for private devotions and letter writing. Princess Mary had told her my plan.

The chamber was opulent, boasting a fireplace, a writing table, and not one but two comfortably padded Glastonbury chairs. The countess looked me up and down, as if she were inspecting every inch of me for flaws, before she waved me into one of the chairs. I perched on the edge of the seat cushion, uncertain what to expect from the old woman.

"You are going to the royal court," she said. "I doubt you will be called upon to die for the princess there, but lie . . . aye, it may come to that. Are you prepared to take that sin upon your immortal soul for Her Grace's sake?"

She made telling a few lies seem as great a sacrifice as dying, and a mortal sin besides. "I will do all I can for my true mistress," I vowed, "and if I must sin, then I will confess my transgressions and be given penance for them."

Lady Salisbury chuckled at that. "You are bold, I will give you that. Let us hope you are also clever. You never struck me as such, but perhaps you will learn. Be on your guard, Mistress Lodge. You will have no friends in Anne Boleyn's household. Trust no one, not even your confessor."

I promised to heed her warnings and the next day I departed on schedule. Only Maria came to see me off, giving me a hug in farewell and slipping the letter she had written to her father into my hand. I quickly secured it in the inside pocket of my cloak.

When I stepped back, tears pricked the backs of my eyes. "I will miss you," I whispered.

"Then you should not have asked to leave," she shot back, speaking loud enough for everyone in the courtyard, including my escort, to hear.

Her aggrieved tone of voice shocked me. Dismayed, my feelings hurt, I sent her a reproachful look. She was already turning away but, at the last second, when she was certain only I could see her face, she winked at me.

29

The journey from Beaulieu to Windsor Castle took three days. I might have traveled faster without the baggage cart, but I was obliged to take all my possessions with me. I rode a palfrey borrowed from the princess's stables. I had not had a horse of my own since I'd left Hartlake Manor.

Three days was long enough for me to realize the enormity of the task before me. I fretted over how I would be received. Somehow, I had to convince the concubine that I no longer felt any loyalty to the princess. Otherwise she would never trust me or allow me close to her. The first step, I decided, was to stop thinking of her as the concubine. To anyone who supported her, she was Lady Anne Rochford, the future queen of England.

I had stayed at Windsor Castle before. It had been to Windsor that the princess had come first when her household left the Marches of Wales for good. But now that I was to be part of the royal court, everything seemed different. Approached from the Thames, the towering edifice had a forbidding appearance, looming atop an escarpment. The approach by land was less daunting, but once inside the ancient stone walls, I was immediately struck by how gloomy the place was, despite its size and grandeur. Windsor Castle contained neither galleries nor gardens. There was no respite from the brooding atmosphere that pervaded the place, not even in the apartments in the upper and middle wards, made bright by a multitude of decorative windows. These overlooked a steep cliff so frighteningly high that it made me dizzy to peer out.

My arrival at court caused only a small ripple of interest and might not have been noticed at all had I not assumed that I would be lodged in the maidens' chamber. When I presented myself there, expecting to find a bed and sufficient space to store my traveling chests, I was informed that I was in the wrong place. Sir Lionel had arranged for me to be given the post of chamberer, not maid of honor. A chamberer was a much less exalted person, although the position was one that would place me even closer to Lady Anne. I would serve her in her bedchamber, attending to her most personal needs.

I was not overly concerned by my demotion, but there was a serious drawback inherent in my altered status. A maid of honor was not permitted to take a husband. A chamberer could be married. I spent my first day at Windsor Castle fearful that Sir Lionel intended to force me into wedding him, after all. I did not draw an easy breath until I was certain he had left to return to his duties in Cornwall.

The Lord Chamberlain, who was in charge of such things, assigned me to a tiny, windowless room at some distance from Lady Anne's apartments. There was barely space for my boxes and a field bed—a portable folding bedstead—with a truckle bed for Edyth beneath.

"It is very small." Edyth stood, hands on her hips, regarding the tiny space with disdain. As I had come down in the world, so had she.

"But it is ours alone," I said, trying to find something positive about our situation. "And the bed is already supplied with a tester and a ceiler and curtains."

Edyth did not bother to reply. She could see as well as I could that the hangings were made of dingy dark green wool, much faded and somewhat moth-eaten. No tapestry hung on the wall to mitigate the chill that came off the cold stone. Since there were no coals for a brazier, we could not light a fire to heat the chamber. In fact, there was no brazier. Even though it was June, that night we had to sleep together for warmth, wrapped in extra clothing and with our outdoor cloaks on top of us.

The next morning I reported to the head chamberer and was informed of my duties. They were simple but menial—brushing clothing, refilling pitchers, and carrying away the pewter chamber pot concealed in the close stool in Lady Anne's stool chamber.

My new mistress ignored me for the first few days I was at Windsor. She had spoken to me only twice before. Those occasions had been several years earlier. But she was as sharp-witted as she was sharp-tongued, and sharp-eyed, too. Nothing and no one escaped her notice. I was certain she knew I was there and exactly who I was.

"Thomasine Lodge," she murmured on my fourth day in her household. "You will comb my hair."

The hair in question was thick and beautiful and Lady Anne was inordinately proud of it, refusing to wear gable headdresses because they covered it completely. She preferred what was called a French hood, and sometimes went about with no more than a net and a cap to contain her tresses.

I took up the ornately bejeweled ivory comb she indicated, feeling considerable trepidation as I did so. I felt sure she had singled me out for a reason.

"As I recall," Lady Anne said as I began to work the sleep

tangles out of her long, dark hair, "you were Sir Lionel Daggett's ward."

"I am so still."

Lady Anne laughed—a high-pitched, unnerving sound. "That is extremely doubtful. How old are you?"

"Nineteen, my lady."

"And as yet unwed?"

"Yes, my lady."

"Well, then, Thomasine Lodge, let me educate you in the law as it applies to wardship. I am well versed in this subject, as I have several wards, including my nephew, Henry Carey, my poor dear sister's son."

She spared a fleeting smile for that lady, Lady Mary Rochford, widow of a courtier named William Carey who had died of the sweat. Lady Mary bore little resemblance to her younger sibling. Where Lady Anne was slim, dark, and in constant motion, Lady Mary was gently rounded, fair of complexion, and of a placid disposition.

"You had not, I take it, attained your fourteenth year at the time your father died?"

"No, my lady."

"A pity. If you had, you would have received his lands into your own hands at his death. You would never have been subject to the court of wards at all."

"So I have been told, my lady."

She turned on me so suddenly that I almost snagged the comb in her hair. I pulled my hand back just in time, then tried not to fidget under the force of her disconcerting stare. Her eyes were very large and very dark, even darker and more intense than Princess Mary's, and her gaze bored into me, as if she sought to touch my very soul.

"Since you were under fourteen at the time your father died, you entered wardship."

"Yes, my—"

She swung away from me, once more facing a standing glass of steel in which she could see both our reflections. "And at sixteen, you came *out* of wardship."

"I . . . I . . . I beg your pardon, my lady?" I had been about to resume combing her hair. My hand froze in midair. The comb fell from suddenly nerveless fingers.

She reached out, quick as a cat, and caught it before it could tumble to the floor. Then she laughed again, and all those within hearing distance—a half-dozen assorted females from among her gentlewomen of the bedchamber and her maids of honor—laughed with her.

While heat flooded into my face, I struggled to make sense of Lady Anne's words. It seemed impossible to me that she was telling the truth, and yet she had no reason to lie. Was I such a great fool that I had not realized I'd been free of Sir Lionel these three years and more?

"Still," Lady Anne continued when the laughter died down, "you remain dependent upon the advice of others, Sir Lionel most of all. You cannot contract or alienate your lands, by will or otherwise, until you reach the age of twenty-one. Although, naturally, if you marry, everything you own at once becomes the property of your spouse. I shall have to think about a husband for you. In the meantime, have you some trustworthy man to make decisions about your estates?"

"I believe so, my lady." I choked out the words, hoping they were true.

Not once since I had left Glastonbury had I thought to ask for an accounting of my inheritance. I had assumed that Sir Lionel and my steward, Hugo Wynn, would take good care of Hartlake Manor and the other properties, since their income, too, derived from them. How naïve I had been! Perhaps Sir Lionel had looked after the property and the people on it, anticipating that it would one day belong to him, but I had no proof of that. For all I knew, everything I owned had fallen into ruin by now, bled dry to provide Sir Lionel with funds to bribe court officials to grant me this post with Lady Anne.

My mind awhirl, I continued combing out my mistress's hair long after she lost interest in me. That task at last complete, I drifted after her into the privy chamber.

Lady Anne's apartments were packed with expensive furnishings. The privy chamber was hung with colorful tapestries depicting mythological scenes, and carpets graced the floor as well as the tables. There were no fewer than three elaborately decorated chairs, one of iron and two of wood. All three were covered with crimson velvet fringed with silk and gold. Lady Anne sat on one and took up her lute. She was immediately surrounded by young gallants. As she played, laughter and song filled the air.

Forgotten, I sank down onto a window seat, my hands clasped tightly in my lap, and desperately tried to order my scattered thoughts. It did not surprise me that my stepmother had known as little of the workings of the law as I had. Women were not expected to be well versed in such matters. Even the Countess of Salisbury, I realized, had not thought anything was amiss when she watched me sign a document for my guardian just *after* my sixteenth birthday. That document, I recalled, had been written in Latin so that I could not read it. Sir Lionel had known *exactly* what the law on wardship decreed.

And that document? Authorization, no doubt, for him to continue running my estates.

My sense of guilt was so intense that I trembled with it. I should have done more to look after what had been built by my father and my grandfather and his father before him. I should have been in correspondence with Hugo Wynn from the start, asking after the horses and the home farm. Were there any horses left? There might not be. Sir Lionel had been quick to dispose of Star of Hartlake.

Instead, I had selfishly immersed myself in my new life in the princess's household, reveling in the attention I received for telling stories and in the new friendships I formed. Bound together by that friendship and by our devotion to Princess Mary, we had all been content to be cut off from the outside world . . . until the outside world forced itself upon us.

I looked up, startled, as a figure all in black stopped in front of me. "You must not mind my sister," Lady Mary Rochford said. "She has a peculiar sense of humor."

I slid over to make room for her on the window seat. When she had settled there and rearranged her skirts, she reached out one plump hand to squeeze mine. "Do you wish to speak with a man of law, my dear? If your guardian has deceived you, I am certain there are measures that can be taken to protect what is yours by right."

I started to say yes and stopped. "There was a paper all in Latin," I confessed. "Sir Lionel had me sign it just after I entered my sixteenth year. I think I must have given him control over my estates." Tears filled my eyes. I had not been just foolish, but stupidly so!

"You may still have legal recourse," Lady Mary said. "It would not hurt to inquire."

I sniffled. "At least I cannot have given my inheritance away forever. Lady Anne said I had to be twenty-one to do that."

Lady Mary's sympathy soothed me. I let her persuade me to talk to a lawyer she knew, although I did not have much confidence that anything would change. Only one thought gave me ease: In two more years, I would reach my majority. Then there would be a reckoning.

30

During the next few days, I heard a few hastily stifled chuckles whenever Lady Anne's gentlewomen caught sight of me, but other than that, no one paid me any particular attention. I was not ridiculed, nor was I regarded with suspicion because I'd come to Lady Anne from Princess Mary's household. Everyone, from Lady Anne herself down to the lowliest kitchen boy, assumed that my motivation was the same as their own—the desire to be at the center of court life. Personal advancement, to their minds, took precedence over loyalty.

Lady Anne had never made any secret of her dislike for the king's daughter. She seemed to consider Princess Mary, rather than the queen, her foremost rival for His Grace's affections. She did not know how little attention King Henry paid the princess.

"Tell me about your former mistress," she commanded during my second week in her service. "I have heard she is not strong—that she is a weak, puling girl who often takes to her bed."

"She was ill for much of the month of May," I said cautiously.

It had taken a full three weeks for her earliest symptoms to resolve themselves into her first flowers.

There had been no attempt to poison Princess Mary by Lady Anne or anyone else. Her Grace was simply one of those unfortunate women who were cursed with terrible pain when their monthly courses came upon them. Even so, I remembered Maria's story about what had happened in the Bishop of Rochester's household. Since I could readily believe that Lady Anne Rochford would order the deaths of her enemies, I remained wary of my new mistress.

"Why does the girl continue to annoy her father with her constant petitions to visit his court?" Lady Anne demanded.

I knew of only one such request, and that one had been made in the desperate days when the princess thought she might be dying.

"Her mother is just as bad," Lady Anne continued without waiting for an answer. "She is always begging the king to invite the girl here to live."

I struggled against a nearly overpowering urge to berate Lady Anne for her coldhearted attitude. I wanted to defend my former mistress *and* her mother the queen. I came very close to blurting out my true feelings and caught myself only just in time. Instead I murmured something unintelligible, hoping the concubine would take it as assent.

I had come to court to gain Lady Anne's trust, I reminded myself. To do so, I must tell her what she wanted to hear. Silently asking God's forgiveness for my lies, I put my storytelling abilities to work and invented several incidents that made Princess Mary sound like the worst sort of spoiled brat. I emphasized her poor health, her lack of beauty, and her tendency, in imitation of her mother the queen, to spend far too many hours fasting and in prayer.

"Then the French ambassador had the right of it," Lady Anne remarked.

"My lady?"

She laughed, but it did not come from the heart. The sound was too loud and somehow unnatural. "Do you know what he said of her, all those years ago when she was betrothed to the French prince? He proclaimed that she would never make a breeder. Too thin. Too pale. Too small, he said."

Again, I held my tongue. It would do me no good and possibly cause much harm should I contradict her. I also resisted the impulse to point out that Princess Mary had been a mere child at the time.

"There will be no marriage to a French prince now," Lady Anne declared. "King Francis is looking to Italy for a bride for his son. Some Medici girl, or so I hear from the very highest sources."

Her dark eyes glittered. The concubine derived great pleasure from any opportunity to boast of her intimacy with the king. I hoped he did not share any secrets with her that he did not want repeated.

Lady Mary Rochford looked up from her sewing. She had been a silent witness to our conversation, so quiet and self-effacing that I had all but forgotten she was there. "I am certain there will be other offers," she said. "The marriage of a princess has great value when it comes to sealing alliances."

Her sister glared at her. "There *have* been offers, but none of any importance. A son of the Duke of Cleves. The king of Scots. A prince of Transylvania." Lady Anne laughed again, and again there was something not quite right about the sound. "Send her to Transylvania, I say. That godforsaken principality is far, far away from England."

Transylvania? The name struck me as familiar and an involuntary shiver ran through me when I remembered why. I hastily crossed myself. People who knew of my ability to tell stories often shared with me their favorite tales and legends. In that way, I had heard of Vlad the Impaler. His story was not one I would ever repeat, no matter how desperate I was for something to provide an evening's entertainment. Prince Vlad had been a terrible man . . . if he had *been* a man. My stomach twisted at the thought of sending my gentle, sweet-natured princess into exile in the land that could spawn such a monster.

Distracted by her sister, Lady Anne abandoned her interrogation of me. I fancy that I hid my relief, but it was some time before my breathing steadied and my heart ceased beating so loudly that I feared the sound could be heard at the far side of the chamber.

I watched the concubine closely from the moment I entered her service, and tried to discern what it was about her that the king found so compelling. I soon dismissed the notion that she had bewitched His Grace and bespelled half the court. Anne Boleyn had simply been born with the ability to charm and dazzle.

A few resisted her allure. Bishop Fisher was one and Cardinal Wolsey another. Once, Wolsey had been the most powerful man in England after the king. In February, he had been banished to his archbishopric in York, far to the north. He'd left behind the two magnificent palaces he'd built—York Place and Hampton Court— making a "gift" of them to King Henry.

The concubine made a dangerous enemy. At close quarters, waiting on her in her bedchamber, I saw her moods shift like quicksilver. In an instant she could go from giddy good humor to white-knuckled fury. Time and time again, I saw her rein in her temper before it could explode, but I also sensed the rage still simmering just beneath the surface calm. I did not want to be in the way when all that anger finally burst free.

Almost as frightening was the ease with which Lady Anne succeeded when she set out to charm someone. She had an energy about her that was capable of infecting all those around her with the same high spirits. So often was there nothing but music and gaiety in her rooms that even I occasionally forgot that the concubine had a darker side.

Living in Lady Anne Rochford's shadow was a heady experience. It was fortunate that my new duties were so time-consuming, else I might have been tempted to do more than hover at the edges of the bright, gaudy circle of the concubine's friends and family. They loved music, dancing, and disguisings. They had quick wits and wicked tongues. Lady Anne's rooms were lively from dawn till well after dusk, and never more so than when the king came to visit.

King Henry and his Anne together were a powerful force. They seemed to feed off each other's strong personalities, so that each of them grew even more compelling when in the other's presence. Being with his lady love put His Grace in a jovial mood. He smiled on everyone. It was impossible not to smile back.

In truth, King Henry was the sort of man I would have looked upon with favor even if he had not been my liege lord. In spite of the fact that he was more than twice my age, he still cut a fine figure, being very tall and well muscled from regular practice in the tiltyard and long days of hunting and hawking. He wore his beard neatly trimmed and his hair cropped close to his well-shaped head. When he was amused, his blue-gray eyes twinkled and his laugh boomed out, filling the entire room.

For the most part, His Grace took little notice of anyone but his mistress, but one evening, when I was dispatched to another chamber to fetch Lady Anne's lute, he regarded me with a look of puzzlement when I returned with it. "Who are you, mistress? Your face is familiar."

"I am Thomasine Lodge, Your Majesty. Of Hartlake Manor near Glastonbury."

I wondered if I should add that Sir Lionel had been my guardian. I had done nothing yet about reclaiming my estates save write a letter to Sir Jasper, asking my stepmother's favorite priest to discover, if he could, what conditions were at Hartlake Manor and whether Hugo Wynn was still steward there. I had not received a reply.

For a moment I thought Lady Anne might regale her lover with the tale of my ignorance in the matter of my wardship. I was not certain what the result of that would be. The king might be very angry indeed with Sir Lionel. Or he might laugh, as everyone else had.

"Go away, do, Tamsin." Lady Anne was clearly displeased that His Grace's attention had strayed to someone besides herself. "You are too tall. It makes my neck hurt to look up at you."

As an adult, I had acquired a decidedly feminine shape, but I had also inherited my father's height. I stood a head taller than most of the women at court. I towered over tiny females like Queen Catherine. Although Lady Anne was not as short as the queen, I still had the advantage over her in inches.

I hastily curtseyed and took a few backward steps. Lady Anne began to strum her lute.

"You are a most becoming height, Mistress Lodge," the king said kindly. His admiring gaze swept over me from head to toe.

When I blushed, he chuckled.

"Now I remember," he said, turning back to his mistress as I continued my retreat. "The girl's father raised that magnificent stallion, Star of Hartlake. He made an excellent addition to the Royal Mews."

"So that was the reason for your interest in her," Lady Anne replied just before I moved out of earshot. "His coltish daughter reminded you of his horse."

31

This is Master Thomas Cromwell," said Lady Mary Roch-ford, indicating the stocky older man at her elbow. "He will assist you in the matter of your inheritance."

The fellow was plainly dressed for court, in a riding coat of brown and blue welted with tawny velvet. Leaving Lady Mary behind, I went with him to the small office he used as a member of the king's Privy Council. Since I had heard nothing from Sir Jasper and did not know what else I might do to untangle the legal intricacies of my situation, I told him everything.

He was careful to make no promises.

"Will you tell the king what Sir Lionel has done?" I asked.

"The king does not concern himself with such minor matters."

I was not sure why Master Cromwell should, either, other than as a favor to Lady Mary Rochford, but I left his room feeling that I had at last taken the first step toward reclaiming what was mine.

When I returned to Lady Anne's lodgings, I found everything in a state of confusion. Lady Anne was gone and her attendants, with Lady Mary in charge, had been ordered to pack their mistress's belongings.

"But where are we going?" I asked Lady Mary as I slipped one of her sister's velvet gowns into a protective linen bag designed for just that purpose.

"To Chertsey Abbey for the night. Then on to Woodstock." Her face wore a troubled frown.

"What is wrong?" I asked.

Her smile looked forced. "Nothing is wrong. On the contrary, all is well. For Anne."

"I do not understand."

Lady Mary had no need to answer me. I was supposed to be packing her sister's possessions, not asking impertinent questions. But she was a kindly soul.

"You know that here at Windsor it has been the king's habit to ride out to hunt nearly every day?"

I nodded and continued to pack Lady Anne's garments for transport.

"My sister and a few servants were accustomed to ride with him, but never the queen and yet, because she *is* the queen, King Henry has dined with her at least once a week and several times spent the evening talking to her while she sewed."

I knew all this. The concubine had complained of it in an aggrieved voice every time His Grace did so.

"Even though King Henry no longer shares the queen's bed, he customarily bids her farewell each time he rides off into Windsor Forest to hunt deer or other game. But today, he did not visit the queen before he departed with Lady Anne. His Grace is not coming back, Tamsin, and at my sister's bidding he did not even tell the queen that he is leaving her for good. Only once he was well away was Queen Catherine informed that she must be gone from Windsor by the time His Grace returns. The queen is to remove herself to The Moor, a house near Rickmansworth in Hertfordshire, which is to be her new residence. Further, she is not to write to the king, nor is she to see her daughter again."

Appalled by such cruelty, I whispered, "Princess Mary will be devastated."

Bess Holland, one of Lady Anne's maids of honor, overheard me. "Surely you cannot be surprised," she drawled. "There is no love lost between Lady Anne and the king's daughter."

I opened my mouth, then shut it again. Anything I said would be repeated to the concubine and it was now more important than ever that I remain in her good graces.

"Well I feel sorry for the princess," Lady Mary said. "She has done nothing to deserve Anne's dislike."

"Except *be*," Bess said. "Mary Tudor is to be sent to Richmond Palace to live. To my mind, that is far better than she deserves."

"Princess Mary has never been that fond of Richmond," I murmured. I was the one who liked that palace best. "She prefers Beaulieu. Perhaps the— Perhaps Lady Anne knows that."

Bess and Lady Mary both stared at me. Did they guess how close I had come to slipping and calling Lady Anne Rochford the concubine? I reminded myself again that it would be better to remain silent than to say too much.

At least Princess Mary would have her household with her, I thought, all those loyal servants who had served her for years. My friends.

I had never missed them so much as I did at that moment.

While I continued to tuck clothing into bags and bags into boxes and trunks, conversation flowed around me. My thoughts were in such a tangle that it was some little time before the full impact of what these changes would mean came home to me—once the queen was exiled to The Moor, I would no longer have any means of communicating with Princess Mary.

The plan we had devised before I left Beaulieu relied upon the queen's Spanish physician sending word in private to his daughter. I had met with him twice since I'd arrived at Windsor, once to give him the letter Maria had written and the second time to ask for a headache powder I did not need. I'd had little to report on that occasion, but now, should I learn something of importance, I would be in a quandary. I could not write directly to one of the princess's maids of honor without arousing suspicion. Worse, any such letter would most assuredly be intercepted and read.

After only a bit more than a month in Lady Anne's household, my usefulness to my true mistress appeared to have come to an end.

32

By November, the princess had been moved from Richmond to the Bishop of Winchester's palace at Farnham Castle, even farther away from court. The king and Lady Anne took possession of the king's manor of York Place at Westminster, formerly the residence of Cardinal Wolsey. Built of rose-colored brick with landscaped terraces, this palace rose up on the bank of the Thames just before that great river curved eastward toward London.

Westminster was a separate municipality, connected to the larger city by water and by a wide street called the Strand, which ran parallel to the Thames. South of York Place lay Westminster Abbey and the ancient palace of Westminster, much of it destroyed by a fire early in King Henry's reign. Only the chapel, the hall, and several minor buildings remained. Since the fire, when Parliament was in session, the House of Commons met in the Chapter House of the Abbey.

Rebuilding at York Place had been going on for nearly two years and was still in progress, but new lodgings for the king had been completed. He resided in these apartments while Lady Anne occupied the rooms that had formerly belonged to the cardinal, those that should have been the queen's. She had her own watching chamber, presence chamber, privy chamber, and bedchamber. The latter connected to a gallery with splendid views of the Thames. From its many windows, all filled with expensive clear glass, we could see across to Lambeth and even glimpse the spires of London's churches in the distance.

With Yuletide fast approaching and Lady Anne set to preside over the festivities at court in place of the queen, she declared herself in need of her own silkwoman. Candidates for the position were instructed to bring samples of their work to the gallery to be inspected. My heart was beating a little faster than usual as I trailed along behind Lady Anne, her gentlewomen, and her maids of honor. As a chamberer, I had no business accompanying them, but I hoped no one would notice. Or rather, I hoped that only one person would take note of my presence . . . if he was there.

Four silkwomen had answered Lady Anne's summons. One of them was Mistress Pinckney, but if she recognized me in Lady Anne's livery, she gave no sign of it. She displayed her wares, as did her three competitors, spreading out a vast array of beautiful silk goods. The selection delighted Lady Anne and riveted her attention and the attention of her attendants, leaving me free to slip away. I was about to do so when a familiar voice spoke softly from behind me.

"There is a bow window at the end of the gallery, directly across from the entrance to the garderobe. Meet me there."

By the time I turned my head, Rafe Pinckney had already moved on. I watched him deposit another armload of silk trimmings where his mother could reach it, then back away, head bowed, cap in hand, so quiet and unobtrusive that none of Lady Anne's ladies even glanced his way.

I could not imagine how he managed to fade into the background that way. It had been nearly a year since I'd last seen him and in that time he had grown even more toothsome. I felt sure that the breadth of his shoulders was greater. And his face—it was fully the countenance of a man now, even to the shadow of a beard.

The last time we had met, he had kissed me. My hands trembled as I remembered how I had felt when he held me in his arms.

While the other women were still distracted by tassels and hair-nets, fringes and belts, I slipped past them and made my way to the window alcove. It was so deep that I imagined three or four people could shelter there and not be seen from the rest of the gallery. Then Rafe joined me and I saw I'd been wrong. He filled all the available space, seeming to leave only just enough room for me. The smell of sandalwood engulfed me.

I sat on the padded wooden window seat, my legs suddenly too unsteady to support me. I had not thought beyond this point. At a loss for words, I waited for Rafe to break the silence. In the background I could hear the laughter and chatter of the queen's women. From farther away came the sound of hammering. The king had ordered his privy gallery at Esher dismantled and installed at York Place to link Wolsey's old house to the privy chamber of the new building.

"The princess sends greetings," Rafe whispered.

Whatever I had expected to hear, it was not that. "How—?"

"Are you still her devoted handmaiden?" One hand came up to rest against the window frame on my left side, adding to my sense of being hemmed in by his greater size and strength.

I glared up at him. "How can you even ask?"

A grin split his face and his dark eyes went from flat and suspicious to bright and delighted. I found myself smiling back.

"We cannot remain here long," he warned, serious again, "and there is much I must say to you." He sat beside me, leaning close and keeping his voice low. "Note well which silkwoman Lady Anne chooses. You will be able to send word to me through her."

"Are they all equally trustworthy?" Mistress Pinckney had an only one-in-four chance of being selected and I knew nothing at all about the other three.

He shrugged. "They are all willing, from time to time, to make use of an extra pair of hands. An offer to deliver their goods to court will not be refused. If there are no deliveries pending, then I will use the excuse of bringing a token from my mother to the lady. Such gifts are commonplace. Lady Anne will assume that Mother is trying to bribe her and thus usurp the place of one of her competitors. My visit to court will not rouse suspicion."

"Does your mother still supply trimmings to the princess?" I was finding it difficult to keep my mind on what Rafe was saying when his leg was pressed so snugly against my skirt from knee to hip. My throat had gone dry. My mouth, too.

"She does." He was staring at my lips, where I'd just moistened them with the tip of my tongue. He blinked, recollected his purpose in talking to me, and shifted his gaze to the cap he held in his hands. "I deliver orders to Her Grace myself, despite the distance I must now travel to do so. On the last occasion, your friend Maria brought me to Princess Mary's attention. I have agreed to convey messages back and forth for as long as you need me to do so."

My relief was so great that I nearly wept with it. Waving aside his concern, I sniffed once and then launched into an account of everything I had observed since entering the concubine's service. It did not take long. I had learned very little we did not already know. Nothing I reported was likely to come as a surprise to Princess Mary.

"Does Lady Anne trust you?" Rafe asked.

"I . . . I cannot be certain. She does not treat me any differently than she does her other female attendants. She does not confide in any of us, except perhaps her sister. And, in truth, she is more likely to talk to her brother than to Lady Mary." I did not count the times Lady Anne had boasted of some little triumph or other.

"Somehow, you must worm your way deeper into her confidence. And make certain that if she accompanies the king when he travels to France to meet with King Francis, you are among the ladies she selects to go with her. Otherwise, we will have no way of knowing what she does while she is out of the country."

"What do you think she will do?" I asked in confusion.

"There are rumors that she and the king may marry in Calais, with the French king as their honored guest at the nuptials."

"But the pope—"

"The pope has been under the thumb of a mutual enemy of France and England, Queen Catherine's nephew, the Emperor Charles. Some of the English lawyers working to free the king from his marriage are said to have argued that His Holiness therefore cannot rule on the issue with impunity."

I understood the seriousness of what he was saying and knew that Rafe was right. I must ingratiate myself to Lady Anne and somehow convince her that I was devoted to her cause. Then she would be more inclined to keep me at her side.

"If I had a truly splendid New Year's gift to give her, that might help. She is a most . . . acquisitive woman."

Rafe considered a moment. Then his grin—an expression I found most endearing—flashed a second time. "I think I know just the thing," he said.

We dared not stay longer in the window alcove. Rafe took only time enough to tell me how to send word to him through the other silkwomen. Mrs. Wilkinson was a widow with a house in Soper Lane, Mrs. Brinklow was a wealthy mercer's wife, and Mrs. Vaughan and her mercer husband lived in St. Mary le Bow, Cheapside. "I live in Cheapside myself," Rafe added, standing to let me pass out of our hiding place. "At the Sign of the Golden Hart near the Great Conduit."

In the confined space, I was obliged to brush against him as I left. Had I turned so much as an inch, I would have been in his arms.

I returned to the others in time to hear Lady Anne choose Mistress Joan Wilkinson as her silkwoman. Having made this announcement, the concubine left the gallery. Once again, I brought up the rear. I looked back once, giving Mistress Wilkinson a long, hard stare in order to fix her face in my memory. She was a little brown wren of a woman, with the most ordinary and forgettable features imaginable.

Two weeks later, when Mistress Wilkinson appeared without warning at the door of the long, narrow sleeping chamber assigned to Lady Anne's chamberers during our sojourn at York Place, I had to stare at her for a full minute before I recognized her. Fortunately, I was alone in the room at the time.

"Are you Tamsin Lodge?" she asked in a voice as high-pitched as a bird's chirp. When I nodded, she thrust a small package wrapped in silk cloth and tied with braided silk ribbon into my hands. "Young Rafe Pinckney bade me deliver this to you. For you to give to Lady Anne, he said."

The look of birdlike curiosity in her eyes prompted me to unwrap the parcel then and there. "You must keep my secret," I warned her as a deck of playing cards was revealed. "This is to be a New Year's present for my mistress."

"You may rely upon my silence. She is the hope of the future."

Her fervent declaration startled me. I had not realized that Mistress Wilkinson was so partisan. Then I frowned at the cards, uncertain why Rafe thought this particular gift would win Lady Anne's approval. In common with almost everyone at court, she loved to gamble, but cards were nearly as plentiful as dice.

"It is a very pretty deck," I said. Hand-painted, the figures were brightly colored and on the reverse of each was a stylized Tudor rose. "Please convey my thanks."

She chuckled. "These cards are more than pretty. Regard the queen."

I peered more closely at that card. The painted figure had a long neck, a long, oval face, dark hair and eyes, high cheekbones, a wide mouth, and a strong, determined chin—all of Lady Anne's most distinctive features except the tiny mole on one side of her chin. Although the artist had omitted it in an obvious attempt to flatter his subject, I suspected that Lady Anne would not have minded if he'd included it. I had heard the king call it a beauty mark. His Grace seemed as enamored of the tiny flaw as he was of every other part of her.

On New Year's Day, by which time the court had moved to Greenwich, I duly presented Lady Anne with the cards. She seemed delighted with my gift.

That moment was the brightest spot in an otherwise dismal Yuletide. In spite of the concubine's best efforts, the atmosphere at court was too tense for true mirth and merriment. More and more, in spite of the risk, the king's subjects had begun to speak out against his plan to set aside Queen Catherine. Even Lady Anne's own aunt by marriage, the Duchess of Norfolk, had left the court rather than be obliged to see her niece in the queen's place.

King Henry presented his lady love with a matching set of hangings for her bed and chamber. They were made of cloth of gold, cloth of silver, and crimson satin, the latter richly embroidered in heraldic designs. The concubine gifted His Grace with a set of intricately decorated Pyrenean boar spears, an exotic gift that pleased him mightily.

The king was less pleased when an expensive gold cup was delivered to him as a gift from Queen Catherine. His Grace had given orders that no one at court was to send gifts to the queen this Yuletide, or to any of her ladies, and he had not sent any himself. His exasperation, and his angry words to the hapless yeoman who tried to present the queen's cup to him, soured the day for everyone.

33

The following February I found myself at Hampton Court, another of the great houses the king had acquired from Cardinal Wolsey. Work had recently been completed on a new private lodging there for the king called the Bayne Tower. On the ground floor were offices and a strong room. The top level contained a two-room library and the king's jewel house. But it took its name from the placement, on the middle of the three floors, of a bath room adjacent to King Henry's private bedchamber and study.

That room was the talk of the court. It was said to house a large, permanent tub with two taps, one that ran with cold water and the other with hot. I should have liked to see such a thing but as a woman, and a mere chamberer at that, I had no business going anywhere near the place, not even into the new gallery that connected the Bayne Tower to the king's privy chamber in the older part of the palace.

I had access to almost everyplace else. No one noticed just another liveried servant when there were some two thousand people in residence. At my first opportunity, I went in search of Master Thomas Cromwell, having heard that he had an office on the premises.

I had not seen the lawyer since our brief interview at Windsor. In all the time since, I'd had no news of Hartlake Manor, not from Sir Jasper and not from Master Cromwell, who had promised me, in Lady Mary Rochford's hearing, that he would investigate Sir Lionel Daggett's dealings and that suspicious paper I had signed just after I'd turned sixteen. In but a few days' time, I would reach my twentieth year. In a bit more than twelve months, I would be entitled to take full possession of my inheritance . . . if I had any inheritance left.

Master Cromwell did not recognize me until I jogged his memory. "Ah, yes," he said with a rueful grimace, "you are heir to Hartlake Manor and other estates in Somersetshire and Gloucestershire. I sent a man to investigate."

"And has he returned?" It was a struggle to keep my voice even. I found Master Cromwell's condescension most annoying.

"A moment."

I expected the lawyer to search through the tall stacks of paper that littered his writing table. Some of them were so high that they threatened to spill over at any second. Instead, he closed his eyes. I could see movement behind his eyelids. It made me think of a clerk flipping over one page after another in a ledger, searching for the proper account. After a minute or two of this intense cogitation, his eyes flew open.

"Have you had any word of late from your stepmother?" he asked.

A dart of alarm pierced me and I clutched the edge of the table for support. "Blanche? Has something happened to her?"

Moving more rapidly than I'd have thought possible for such a heavyset man, he rounded the table, shoved a heavy law book off a stool, and plunked me down in its place. "Sit. I will not have hysterics. Lady Lodge is not dead, if that is what you fear."

"Then what? Why did you ask if I'd heard from her?" My first panic past, I was swamped by guilt. I had scarce given Blanche a thought in a very long time. Even when I did think of her, I pictured her living in her dower house in Bristol, placid and content.

Master Cromwell returned to his chair and sat contemplating me, his elbows on the table and his palms together. The fingers on one hand tapped against those on the other for a moment or two before he announced, "Sir Lionel Daggett married your stepmother a month ago."

I gasped. That Blanche and Sir Lionel might truly care for one another never crossed my mind. He'd married her for her fortune and to keep control of my property . . . and to control me. It made perfect sense. Having changed his mind about claiming *me* as his bride, he'd moved on to an alternate plan. A wife was entirely in her husband's power. Sir Lionel had taken a hostage against my good behavior. He counted on my affection for my stepmother to keep me from challenging his authority.

"Naturally," Master Cromwell continued, confirming my conclusions, "as you are not yet twenty-one, you will allow your new stepfather to continue to manage your estates while you remain at court."

"Have I no legal recourse?" I asked.

He narrowed his eyes at me. "You should be glad to have that good gentleman to look after your interests."

Swallowing a protest, I thanked Master Cromwell for his advice and fled. My tangled emotions overcame me only a few steps from his door. Tears blinding me, I stumbled on, nearly plowing into a passing yeoman of the guard. He righted me with a laugh and went on his way toward the kitchen court. I stood where he left me, in the middle of a passageway, shaking with a combination of despair, frustration, and anger. I had never felt so much like a pawn in a game of chess as I did at that moment. On all sides, there were people who wished to use me, and none of them cared a fig about what I thought.

I had no doubt but that Sir Lionel had bribed Master Cromwell to let matters stand as they were. What other explanation could there be for his attitude?

I could do nothing to help Blanche, and although I might still be able to find another lawyer to help me reclaim my lands, that would require that I leave court and return to Hartlake Manor. Leaving Lady Anne's household was the one thing I could not do, not now that I'd finally begun to make some headway in persuading the concubine to trust me. Ever since I'd given Lady Anne those playing cards, she had softened toward me. If I did not stay, it would be a betrayal of my vow to serve and protect Princess Mary.

A few days later, I received a letter from Sir Lionel. Within moments, I understood why my stepmother's favorite chaplain had never replied to my plea for help. Sir Jasper had died in November.

When I read through to the end, I crumpled the paper in my fist, barely repressing the urge to curse aloud. Somehow, after Sir Jasper's death, my letter to him had come into Sir Lionel's hands. Sir Lionel did not say so straight out, but his meaning was clear enough. My questions to Sir Jasper and the inquiries made by Master Cromwell's man—the beginnings of an investigation into Sir Lionel's stewardship of my estate—had prompted Sir Lionel to coerce my stepmother into marrying him. It was all my fault that Blanche was now his to do with as he pleased. He could beat her, lock her in her chamber, starve her—no one would say a word to stop a husband from disciplining his wife. And he *would* do all that, his letter implied, if I caused him any trouble.

With exaggerated care, I smoothed out the page and reread one particular sentence. Sir Lionel had been careful in his choice of words, but his meaning was as clear as a stock pond on a calm summer's day: "Your stepmother and your lands will be safe in my keeping so long as you remain my advocate at court."

34

The only event of note during the next few months was the April wedding of the Earl of Surrey and Lady Frances de Vere, the Earl of Oxford's daughter. Surrey's mother, the Duchess of Norfolk, objected to the match on the grounds that Lady Frances had no fortune. Lady Anne, however, favored their union, and so it came to pass. The new Countess of Surrey then joined the concubine's household.

In July, the court went on progress, leaving Hampton Court for Woodstock and Abingdon, heading toward Nottingham. The new French ambassador, Gilles de la Pommeraye, went along as the king's honored guest. Hunting, as usual, was the most frequent pastime, both shooting at deer with crossbows and coursing, but travel between stopping places was not so pleasant as it had been in the past. The crowds that gathered along the way to see their king were so hostile to Lady Anne that they greeted every glimpse of her with hissing and hooting and, sometimes, shouted insults. As there were too many malcontents to arrest them all, the king was forced to ignore the catcalls.

His Grace was already out of sorts, suffering from a toothache. I do not know where the progress might have gone that summer had Lady Anne's appearance been met with the shouts of joy that should have welcomed a future queen, but in August we turned back the way we had come. When we reached the manor of Hanworth in Middlesex, not far from Hampton Court, we were informed that the king and Lady Anne would remain there for the rest of the summer.

King Henry had already made a present of this house and its land to Lady Anne. Pommeraye stayed on as her honored guest, no doubt so that the king could complete his "secret" plans to visit France.

Hanworth, a redbrick manor house surrounded by a moat, was a pleasant place. It had been rebuilt by the king's father and refurbished by His Grace before he gave it to the concubine. Among the king's additions were terracotta roundels on the gatehouse, brought from Hampton Court, and new furniture for the great chamber, including a table for use by Lady Anne's gentlewomen.

The grounds were delightful. Bridges connected the house to the gardens, which were famous for their strawberries. Farther afield were an aviary, an orchard with a park beyond, and a series of fish ponds. I spent as much time as I could out of doors, but for the most part I was confined to the interior, trapped in a world full of heavy perfumes, pretended gaiety, and an aura of intrigue and danger. Whether the latter was real or imagined I could not tell.

Although I fancied that I had made myself useful to Lady Anne, I had as yet found no way to make my services seem indispensable to her. Each day began in her bedchamber, where she was dressed for the day. On one particular morning in mid-August, I stood nearby during this process, waiting to take charge of the green damask nightgown the king had given her. It was not so fine as the one made of black satin, lined with black taffeta and edged with velvet, but was more practical for everyday use.

At first I paid little attention when Lady Anne began to complain to her sister of the shortcomings of the French ambassador. Many things displeased Lady Anne and she had never been shy about voicing her opinions in the privacy of her chambers.

"I have already given the fellow one of my own prize greyhounds," Lady Anne muttered, "as well as a huntsman's coat, a hat, and a horn. And yet he still maintains that Marguerite d'Angoulême is not well enough to accompany her brother, King Francis, to Calais. If no French noblewoman of suitable rank is present, then I will not be permitted to attend the meetings, either."

"She cannot help it if she is ill," Lady Mary said in a soothing tone of voice.

"She is not sick. She is showing her disapproval of Henry's intention to marry me."

"They will find someone else."

"Who? The queen of France is out of the question. She is Catherine's niece."

Lady Mary handed me the nightgown. As its soft folds filled my arms, I inhaled the musky scent Lady Anne now preferred.

"Perhaps the Duchesse de Vendôme?" the concubine's sister suggested.

I should have taken the garment and carried it away at once. Instead I lingered, curiosity taking precedence over common sense. Lady Anne had been known to box a servant's ears for being slow. I had no reason to think she would spare me if I displeased her. And yet, there I stayed, watching Lady Anne's face go red with fury and hearing her voice rise until it was as shrill as a fishwife's.

"That whore? Do you think I want people to compare me to her?

It is essential that everything about this visit to France be conducted with the utmost propriety!"

"Perhaps it would be best, then, if no ladies were officially present on either side." Lady Mary's tart remark earned her a glower. "Think, Anne," her sister hastened to add. "If that is the way of it, you can still accompany King Henry to Calais and King Francis can visit you when he arrives there, *after* their first meetings have taken place on French soil."

"It is not enough. I deserve to be acknowledged as the future queen of England. There must be more I can do to make that toad of an ambassador sweet."

She reached into the comfit box kept on a nearby table, scooping out a handful of almonds coated with sugar to pop into her mouth. All the ladies at court were fond of these candies and I was no exception, but I could rarely afford to buy such an expensive treat for myself.

I gathered up my courage and offered a suggestion. "You might make him a gift of a fine horse, my lady, to go with the greyhound." Even kings could be swayed by good horseflesh, as I had reason to know, and Lady Anne had a fine stable. She bought her horses from Ireland.

She turned dark, luminous eyes on me, her gaze so piercing that it chilled me to the bone. But she was an astute woman when she kept control of her temper. After a moment, her expression turned thoughtful. "Perhaps that *would* work," she murmured. Then, sneering slightly, she cocked an eyebrow at me and asked, "Have you any other suggestions, Mistress Lodge?"

I spoke without taking the time to consider what impact my words might have. "You could ask the king to grant you a title in your own right, my lady. That way you would truly be the equal of any great lady of France, and of England, too."

35

On the first day of September in the year of our Lord 1532, Lady Anne Rochford, formerly known as Mistress Anne Boleyn, was created Marquess of Pembroke in her own right in a ceremony at Windsor Castle. She did not forget that I was the one who'd suggested that elevation into the peerage might make her more fit to meet the king of France. When she increased the number of her maids of honor, she rewarded me with a promotion.

The concubine chose blue and purple as her new livery colors. She redecorated her rooms at court. But she was far from content. She'd wanted more. She had already waited years to become England's queen.

The king talked openly of marrying his new peeress. The lady marquess herself made no secret of that fact that she hoped to be queen by the middle of the month. But matters did not fall out quite as she expected. Public sentiment continued to oppose their marriage and the pope continued to balk at annulling King Henry's marriage to Queen Catherine.

As the lady marquess's moods became more erratic, she took out

her frustrations on her servants. Her voice, at other times so pleasant, went high and shrill at the least provocation. She screamed
orders and threw things when she was not obeyed swiftly enough.
I soon became adept at ducking flying objects, but I had my ears
boxed twice for impertinence.

In this time of upheaval and uncertainty, only the ties I maintained with Princess Mary kept me anchored. I did not dare make
friends in the lady marquess's household. Any one of them might betray me. I could not even confide fully in Edyth, for she was a simple
woman and might, in all innocence, say too much to the wrong
person. Instead, I let her believe I was carrying on an inappropriate
and illicit love affair with Rafe Pinckney as my excuse for meeting
with him so often.

As Rafe had predicted, Mistress Wilkinson was not averse to
accepting his assistance when she delivered silk ribbons and other
trimmings to the court. Wherever and whenever we could, he and
I exchanged news, although there was often little to share. To the
concubine's frustration, matters remained in flux. Long stretches
passed in which nothing changed at all.

The tiltyard at Greenwich provided an ideal place for several of
our clandestine meetings. When it was deserted, we were assured of
privacy. When there were knights practicing at the barriers or the
ring, enough people crowded into the stands to watch that our presence went unnoticed.

"The princess is at Baynard's Castle," Rafe said on a sunny afternoon in late September as we pretended to watch two competitors
ride at each other with blunted lances.

"In London?" I had heard nothing of this.

He nodded. "She arrived yesterday."

"Will she come to court, do you think?"

"Maria sent word that Her Grace has been invited by the king to see his new palace, the one His Grace is building near York Place."

"I know something of that. The lady marquess is much displeased by King Henry's plans." I could not hide my smile, remembering how she'd ranted and raved when she'd heard of them. "The king intends to use the new palace as a London residence for the royal children, both Mary and Henry Fitzroy."

Rafe did not return my smile. "As if King Henry regards them both as bastards?"

"I had not thought of it that way. Well, then, the princess must make a special effort to charm her father when she has the opportunity. Warn her that she must avoid angering him. It would be best that she make no mention at all of her mother, no matter how great her longing to ask the king for permission to visit the queen."

"I agree."

Our eyes met. Somehow, during these brief meetings, widely separated as they were, we had come to understand each other very well. There were times when we almost seemed to read each other's thoughts. Gazes locked, I felt myself swaying closer to him and wishing that the tale I'd spun for Edyth's sake were true.

The clash of swords from the tiltyard pulled me back from the brink. I hastily drew the hood of my cloak over my head and turned away. "I have been gone from the lady marquess's lodgings too long," I mumbled, and fled.

It was the next day, as I was adjusting my mistress's new French hood over her long, thick black hair, that she broached the same subject Rafe and I had been discussing—the princess's plans to spend an afternoon in her father's company.

"I do not like it that Henry wants to be alone with her," she grumbled.

"Now, Anne, you know you are the one he loves," Lady Mary Rochford said. "Let him have his walk in the fields with his daughter. It will do you no harm."

"It is not the walking I mind, but the talking they will do at the same time." She scowled at her reflection in the looking glass. "I want to know what they say to each other and I do not think Henry will tell me, especially if his cat of a daughter spills poison into his ear."

At the mention of poison, I started and dropped the hairpins I'd been collecting from the floor. The lady marquess turned to look at me, annoyance writ large on her countenance. But after a moment, she began to smile. That second expression unnerved me even more than the first.

"Tamsin," she purred, "you served the princess for many years."

"Before I had any choice in the matter, yes, my lady."

"But you parted on good terms?"

"Well enough, my lady. I let Princess Mary think that it was my guardian's desire to place me in your service."

She laughed at that, remembering that by then I had been out of wardship but had not known it. "Mary did not know she could keep you if she wished to?"

"She is clever when it comes to the things she can learn from books, my lady, but she has little idea of how the real world works." Sadly, that was true, although I felt like a traitor for sharing my observation with Anne Boleyn.

"Nevertheless," said the lady marquess, "you must take advantage of this opportunity to pay your respects to your old mistress. You will accompany the king to St. James and when you return you will tell me everything they said to each other."

Elated, I made a deep obeisance, hiding both my face and my thoughts. I saw this assignment as proof that I had won the concubine's trust, and it had the added benefit of allowing me to see Princess Mary again.

St. James in the Fields was the name King Henry had given to the magnificent new house he was building near York Place. We traveled upriver from Greenwich on one of the smaller royal barges, since King Henry took only a few attendants with him. His Grace made no objection to my presence, but neither did he pay me any attention.

We docked in London long enough for the princess and some of her ladies to join us and then were rowed around the curve of the Thames toward the privy landing. Princess Mary's shortsightedness prevented her from recognizing me at first. When she did, she started to speak, then looked carefully at the other faces surrounding her. This evidence of excessive caution broke my heart. The innocent child I had met at Thornbury no longer existed. Naïve she might still be, but she had learned to be wary and trust no one.

I bobbed a curtsey. "Your Grace. It is good to see you looking so well."

"Tamsin." She gave a regal nod of the head. "I trust you prosper in your new position."

"I am content, Your Grace."

Just the faintest flicker of a smile appeared, enough to reassure me that she knew I was still her devoted servant, in spite of appearances. We were unable to say more to each other. There were too many people around.

It had not occurred to me before, but now I realized that any one of them might also be there as a spy for the concubine. Every word I spoke would be reported back to her.

Horses were waiting for us when we disembarked. Accompanied by only a handful of servants, myself among them, the king and the princess rode into the open countryside beyond the king's

manor of York Place in Westminster. Although I was close enough
to overhear what father and daughter said to each other, I had no
intention of repeating all of their conversation to anyone. I listened
hard only so that I might later pick and choose how much to share.
It was necessary to remain in favor with the lady marquess, but I was
determined not to betray my true mistress in any way that mattered.

To be honest, there was little said of a personal nature. The king
did not ask his daughter's opinion of his forthcoming marriage.
Queen Catherine's name was not mentioned. Instead, His Grace
explained how he had acquired the old leper hospital of St. James,
pensioned off the few inmates who'd remained, and razed the buildings. The new palace, I gathered, would have a large gatehouse with
octagonal turrets.

"It will be decorated with the Tudor rose and the initials H and
A," the king said.

The princess, although she paled slightly at this evidence of her
father's intent to remarry, said only, "Tell me more, Father."

His Grace showed her where each of the four courtyards would
be, and pointed out the location of the royal lodgings, the chapel,
the tennis court, and the tiltyard. "I am having some sixty acres of
marshland drained," he continued, "to create a park. This will be
stocked with deer. And I will add a hunting chase that will stretch
as far as Hampstead Heath and Islington."

Princess Mary showed proper enthusiasm for her father's plans. I
found them far less interesting, but I was able to repeat them in full,
mind-numbing detail to the concubine when I returned to Greenwich. The lady marquess found them even more boring than I had.

When I fell silent, she snapped at me. "So much for your much-
vaunted reputation as a storyteller!"

Stung, I blurted out a defense. "Tales that stem from the

imagination are always more stimulating than those that must rely upon dry facts."

Her lips quirked in amusement. "Tell us a tale, then. Perhaps I will repeat it the next time I am with someone in need of *stimulation!*"

I did not understand what she meant, but I obliged her with the story of Gammer Calista and her piskies, a rollicking tale of mistaken identities, lost gold, and magic.

36

On the seventh of October, King Henry and his lady love left Greenwich with a large retinue that included the thirty women who would wait upon the lady marquess in France. I need not have worried about being included among them. The concubine took with her almost every female in her household and added a sprinkling of noble ladies-in-waiting to augment her consequence.

En route to Dover, we spent one night at Stone Manor in Kent, another at Shurland on the Isle of Sheppey, and the third in Canterbury. On the eleventh of the month, we set sail for Calais. The king and Lady Anne were aboard the *Swallow* and her maids of honor accompanied them. Had I still been a chamberer, I'd have been relegated to less glittering company on a smaller ship.

I had never been at sea before. I did not enjoy the experience, even though it was pleasant weather with a fine wind and we reached Calais in less than five hours. Dressed all in blue and purple, the lady marquess's colors, we made a grand procession along cobbled streets lined with tall, narrow houses, stopping first at St. Nicholas to hear Mass and then, having given thanks for our safe passage, going on to the Exchequer, the grandest mansion in the English Pale, where the lady marquess was installed in a suite of seven rooms. One of them had a connecting door to the king's bedchamber. I caught only a glimpse of this room, but that was enough to see that it was hung with green velvet and contained an enormous bed.

Speculation was rife among the women the lady marquess had brought with her that the king would marry his mistress during their stay in Calais. The concubine herself certainly expected to be queen before much longer, ostentatiously wearing jewelry that had once belonged to Catherine of Aragon. Even so, the first ten days in the English Pale were spent not in wedding preparations but in hunting and hawking, gambling, and feasting. The constable of France sent many delicacies for the royal table, everything from pears and grapes to porpoises.

It was the twenty-first day of October before the two kings met at Sandingfield, near the border between the English Pale and French territory. No women witnessed this event, but we were there to watch King Henry ride out of Calais. In the bright sunlight, His Grace was a splendid sight, all in russet velvet bordered with gold-smith's work and pearls. He was accompanied by an escort of one hundred and forty noblemen and gentlemen and forty guards.

The lady marquess watched them until they were out of sight and then turned with a sigh. Four long days loomed ahead before the king was due to return. "His Grace might have left a few of the more interesting gentlemen behind," she complained to her sister.

"Do you not find the young Henry Fitzroy interesting?" Lady Mary teased her, referring to the Duke of Richmond, the king's il-legitimate son by Bessie Blount. He was thirteen years old and the

king intended to present him to King Francis when the two mon-
archs returned to Calais, but for the nonce he remained with the
women.

"We must see about a marriage for that boy, perhaps to our
cousin, Lady Mary Howard."

My fellow maid of honor, Bess Holland, gave a snort of laughter.
"Oh, *that* will please the lady's mother."

A satisfied smile lit my mistress's countenance, the kind that
made me think of a cat that has gotten into the cream. The concubine liked arranging marriages, even if she had not yet managed to
schedule her own.

Lady Mary Howard was the sister of that Earl of Surrey whose
wedding to Lady Frances de Vere the lady marquess had already
accomplished. Did she truly like playing matchmaker, I wondered, or did she just enjoy thwarting the Duchess of Norfolk,
her aunt by marriage, who had refused, out of loyalty to Queen
Catherine, to remain at court once the rightful queen was sent
away? It *had* been to taunt the duchess that Bess Holland had
been named a maid of honor. Bess was the Duke of Norfolk's
longtime mistress.

I liked Bess, who was country-bred like myself. She had a
nature every bit as acquisitive as the concubine's, but it was
fueled by the practical necessity of providing for herself should
the duke one day tire of her. Bess accumulated jewelry like a
magpie collected glittering objects, but she was also fun-loving
and cheerful. So were the other two maids of honor with whom I
spent most of my time, Anne Gainsford and Anne Savage. I had
to be careful around all three of them, for they had all been with
the lady for a long time and were truly loyal to her. It suited me
well that neither of the Annes paid much attention to me, but I

could not help but be pleased that they did not put on airs or snub me, either.

On the twenty-fifth of October, the two kings rode into Calais. Everyone turned out to welcome them, from serving men in tawny livery and red caps to soldiers in red and blue. The king of England outdid himself in the grandeur of his dress—a cloth of gold gown over a slashed doublet ornamented with rubies and diamonds. Three thousand guns sounded a deafening salute as the cavalcade entered the town. The French king, who did not look nearly as impressive as King Henry, was taken to the Staple Inn, on the main square of Calais, where he was to lodge.

That evening, King Francis sent the Provost of Paris to the lady marquess with a gift, a costly diamond. She was well pleased with this token of his esteem, although nothing would make up for the fact that no French noblewoman had ever been found to accompany her king to Calais. Protocol thus required any women in the English king's party to remain in the background.

On Sunday the twenty-seventh, King Henry planned a great banquet at the Exchequer. His Grace visited his lady's rooms before the arrival of his brother monarch. She laughed when she saw him.

"Is that the famous Black Prince's ruby?" She indicated a huge red stone the size of a goose's egg. It hung suspended from a collar that was itself bulging with large rubies, perfectly matched pearls, and glittering diamonds. Its splendor almost overshadowed the king's gown of purple cloth of gold.

"It is," said King Henry in an amiable voice.

I watched His Grace while he spent a few minutes speaking quietly with his mistress. Had he not been king, I thought, he would still command the attention and admiration of all who met him. He was the perfect image of all the golden knights in the tales of chivalry I told, the incarnation of splendor and refinement, of power and majesty. I admit it. In common with every other woman at court, I was a little in love with His Grace.

As soon as the king left the chamber, everyone sprang into action. Elaborate costumes had been prepared and were near at hand, loose gowns of cloth of gold held together with gold laces. Over these went crimson satin sashes decorated with patterns in cloth of silver. One outfit was for the lady marquess. The others went to the six ladies-in-waiting specifically recruited for this trip to Calais.

The Countess of Derby was Lady Dorothy Howard, daughter of the concubine's grandfather, a duke, by his second wife. She was married to an earl. Lady Lisle was married to a viscount, Arthur Plantagenet, the bastard son of King Edward IV. Viscountess Rochford was George Boleyn's wife and the daughter of a baron. Lady Fitzwalter was Lady Derby's sister, married to a baron who was heir to an earldom. Lady Mary Rochford was the daughter of an earl. The sixth lady was Elizabeth Wallop. Her father, like mine, was no more than a humble knight, but her husband was the English ambassador to France.

Since such grand ladies could not go anywhere unescorted, four maids of honor had been chosen to portray the four damsels who accompanied them. My costume was made of crimson satin. Over it I wore a tabard made of cypress lawn.

We were ready in good time. We had to wait until the two kings had supped before we could make our entrance. One hundred and seventy different dishes had been prepared for the occasion, so it was some while before the signal came.

When the music began, we entered the banqueting hall holding jeweled visors in front of our faces to conceal our identities. The huge chamber was bright as day. I counted twenty silver candelabra holding at least a hundred wax tapers. They illuminated walls hung with cloth of silver. Gold wreaths were encrusted with precious stones and pearls.

An abrupt silence fell at the sight of us, but there were exclamations of pleasure as soon as the seven ladies began to dance. King Henry beamed. He had been privy to his mistress's plans. King Francis merely looked bemused.

Once the performance was over, the lady marquess stepped boldly up to the dais and asked King Francis, in flawless French, to come down and dance with her. The other ladies chose partners from among the royals and noblemen at the high table while the damsels singled out gentlemen of lesser estate. I chose a Frenchman at random. I never did learn his name, but he was an excellent dancer. I enjoyed myself so much that I nearly forgot the purpose behind the disguising.

We had performed two pavanes and a cinquepace before King Henry, as if on impulse, whisked off the concubine's visor and revealed her identity to King Francis. The French king pretended to be surprised, but I felt certain he had already guessed who she was. Perhaps he even recognized her, since both Boleyn sisters had spent time at the French court.

Unmasked, we resumed dancing, all but the lady marquess. Instead, she retreated with King Francis to a window seat where they sat talking together for nearly an hour. She seemed to enjoy his company a great deal. Her distinctive laugh rang out more than once. Each time, King Henry's expression grew darker. He finally interrupted them with the pointed suggestion that it was time for the French monarch to return to his own lodgings at the Staple Inn. King Henry escorted him there to ensure that he went.

That the king could be jealous surprised me, but I suppose it should not have. His reaction pleased the concubine beyond all measure.

Back in her own suite of rooms, I helped her out of her costume and into her black satin nightgown. She had dismissed the rest of her servants. Only her sister and I remained.

"We will play cards to pass the time," the lady marquess announced.

I took off my tabard, leaving me in crimson satin. Lady Mary retained her glittering costume of cloth of gold. During the next hour I lost more than I could afford to playing Pope July and ended up forfeiting my next quarter's wages.

"Is she one with us?" the lady marquess asked her sister as she shuffled the cards for yet another hand.

I felt my heart stutter in my chest. Did she suspect my loyalty? I had been careful, but the tiniest slip might have betrayed me. It was not until Lady Mary nodded that I breathed freely again.

"I do not doubt Tamsin's sincerity, Anne. You may trust her to keep your secrets."

"Good." Abruptly abandoning the cards, the lady marquess stood and stretched with the sinuous grace of a cat. "On your oath, Tamsin, you must never speak of what you see and hear in this room tonight, not unless I order you to break your silence. Do you swear?"

What else could I do? I nodded, lied through my teeth, and vowed to keep all that transpired a sacred secret.

A short time later, the king joined us, entering the room through the connecting door to his bedchamber. His Grace went straight to Lady Anne and embraced her.

"My love," he murmured.

The passion that flared between them was so intense that I felt my face heat. Had I not been ordered to remain, I would have retreated to the outer chamber. In Lady Mary's expression, I found a reflection of my own embarrassment, but in her case the look was tinged with something more. After a moment, I realized that it was envy. If the rumors were true, at one time all that passion, all that intensity, had been directed at her.

"Are you ready to speak your vows?" the king asked, causing me to start and blanch.

The concubine smiled up at her lover and nodded.

"Then here and now, I take you, Anne, to be my lawfully wedded wife," said the king of England.

"And I take you, Henry," she replied, "to be my lawfully wedded husband."

The king's booming laugh rang out. "There. It is done. We are espoused, *per verba de praesenti* and before witnesses. Once we consummate our marriage, you will be mine until death do us part. Neither God's law nor man's will ever pull us asunder."

Lady Mary and I were not called upon to witness the consummation. Numb with shock, I let her lead me away. Neither His Grace nor his new wife paid any attention to our departure.

The king had married her. I had borne witness and I still could scarcely believe it. Trying to come to grips with the reality of what had just transpired, I started toward the room assigned to the maids of honor.

Lady Mary caught my arm and pulled me aside, out of the hearing of those members of the entourage who were not yet abed. "I have vouched for your loyalty, Tamsin," she reminded me. "Do not make me regret doing so. If one word of this leaks out, Anne will know whom to blame."

"I will never speak of it," I promised. I did not even want to *think* about what I had just witnessed.

The king had married his concubine, as he had long promised to do. But until he took this final step, the hope had remained, however faint, that he might tire of Anne Boleyn, and perhaps even return to Queen Catherine.

That possibility was now gone. Although clandestine, the ceremony was just as binding as a wedding performed by a priest.

And I had helped to make it so.

My loyalty to the new queen might no longer be in question, but to achieve that state, I had betrayed Princess Mary in the most unforgivable way imaginable.

37

Two days later, King Henry accompanied King Francis back to the border of France. We should have sailed home to England then, but violent storms prevented a crossing. We were forced to remain in Calais until the weather improved.

Although nothing was said of their secret marriage, the king and his new wife did not try to hide their delight in each other. In spite of the rain and wind, they were full of smiles and laughter and disappeared for long hours together, even in the middle of the day.

"So, she's let him tup her at last," I heard one disgruntled courtier mutter after he'd watched the loving couple pass by.

I was so startled that I almost asked him what he meant by that. In truth, I understood far too well. And I realized, belatedly, as I scurried away from the gentleman, and struggling to control my flushed face, exactly how the concubine had held the king's attention for so long. She had flirted with him, dallied with him, no doubt allowed him all sorts of liberties with her person, but she had withheld the final consummation of their lust until he pledged himself to her before witnesses.

My guilt at having been a party to that marriage increased ten-fold. While the king and future queen spent the two weeks of our weather-enforced stay in Calais in blissful admiration of each other, I sank deeper and deeper into despair.

At last the storms ceased and, although the fog looked treacher-ous to me, the king's flotilla set sail at midnight on the twelfth of November. Once we had landed safely in England, we went to Leeds Castle, then visited Stone Manor again, and finally settled in at the king's palace of Eltham, near Greenwich.

All the while we'd been traveling, I'd tried to think what to do. I wanted to warn the princess that she now had a stepmother, but I did not dare send her a letter for fear it would be intercepted and read. For disloyalty to Lady Anne, I would instantly be dismissed from my post and most likely arrested and flung into a cell in the Tower of London, too. I did not know exactly what the punishment was for betraying a king's secret, but I had no desire to find out.

Eltham was a dozen miles from London and four miles inland from the Thames, making it more difficult to travel between those two points than it would have been if we were at Greenwich or Richmond or one of the other riverside palaces. It was also more dif-ficult to send a message to Rafe Pinckney, especially when the lady marquess showed no inclination to order new silk trimmings.

After considerable thought, I arranged an accident that damaged all my silk ribbons and points. I asked permission to send to Mistress Wilkinson for replacements. The sooner Princess Mary heard of her father's marriage, the better prepared she would be to protect herself from her stepmother's machinations.

Two days later, I was walking for recreation in the gallery when I caught a glimpse of a lone rider. The windows faced west, giving me a spectacular view of the Thames valley toward London. As man and horse drew closer, my heart began to race. I knew Rafe even at that distance. Before he reached the stone bridge that crossed the moat surrounding Eltham Palace, I was in the wardrobe of robes awaiting his arrival.

"Rafe," I whispered as he entered the chamber, and frowned when I heard the catch in my voice. In a slightly louder voice, I greeted him as Goodman Pinckney.

"Mistress Lodge," he replied, carefully formal. "I have brought the ribbons you ordered."

"I am most grateful. How does your mother?"

"Well, mistress. She sends her greetings, as does Mistress Wilkinson."

Bored with our stilted conversation, the yeoman of the lady marquess's wardrobe, soon to be the queen's wardrobe, wandered away.

"Follow me," I whispered, and set off at a brisk pace toward a small, unused storage room I had discovered in my explorations of the palace.

Eltham was full of nooks and crannies. I might have led Rafe to any of a dozen deep window alcoves, some of them hidden behind convenient wall hangings, but it was not my intent to sit on his lap and let him steal a kiss. We had serious matters to discuss. When I had closed a solid wooden door behind us and lit a candle to illuminate the windowless closet, I rushed into speech.

"You must send word to the princess. The king has married the concubine."

"Impossible! No clergyman would dare defy the pope."

"There was no priest. They said their vows in private, but they did so before witnesses. In a court of law, the marriage will stand. The king himself said so."

He gaped at me. "You were there?"

"To my sorrow, yes. It seems I have succeeded too well. The concubine trusts me." I let all the bitterness I felt pour into my voice.

Rafe's arms came around me. When he pulled me against his broad chest, I could hear the steady thud of his heart beneath the plain wool of his doublet. It felt soft against my cheek and smelled of the familiar scents of sandalwood and cinnamon. Of their own volition, my hands searched for his waist and, finding it, clung. I lifted my face as he lowered his and our lips met.

I had chosen our meeting place well. It was private. Too private. Somehow, my back was up against the door and his long, lean limbs were pressed against mine from top to toe. Although I wanted nothing more than to go on being kissed and kissing him in return, I forced myself to ignore the tingling sensation deep in my womb and lifted my hands to his chest to push him away.

"We cannot," I gasped.

He retreated a scant few inches. His head dropped forward in defeat, but his hands still rested against the door on either side of my head, pinning me in place. "Do you know how often I think of you?" he asked in a choked voice. "Do you know how often I dream of you?"

There was such longing in his voice that I nearly threw myself back into his arms. My blood sang and my body yearned to be held close to his. But I had not lived at court all this time without learning the terrible consequences of following the lure of desire. Nor was I ignorant of the fate of those who defied convention and married beneath them.

Not that Rafe had mentioned marriage.

Straightening my spine, I found the courage to speak the hard truth. "We must not indulge ourselves this way. We have no future together. You must know that."

Abruptly, he stepped back, although he could not retreat far in the confines of such a small room, even one that contained no more than a few storage boxes, a three-legged stool with only two legs, and a wobbly candle stand. "I beg your pardon, Mistress Lodge. That was not well done of me."

I wanted to tell him that he kissed very well indeed but decided such a remark would not be wise. Instead, I gathered my scattered wits and reminded myself of the reason we were together in the first place.

"Princess Mary," I said.

"Yes. She must be warned of this development. I will take word to her myself." He tilted his head, studying my expression. "Is there something more?"

"Only that I need a faster and more reliable way to reach you, Master Pinckney. Perhaps an order for ribbons made to your mother rather than to Mistress Wilkinson? Are you still her apprentice?" I knew that he was older than I, and felt certain that by now he had become a master of his craft.

He started to reply, then fell silent without answering my question. After a moment, he said, "A message will always find me if you send it to the Sign of the Golden Hart in Cheapside near the Great Conduit."

"Perhaps we should devise a code," I suggested. "An order for red silk ribbons means I have news the princess must hear at once."

"A code could also save time if the matter is urgent," he agreed. "Send for blue silk if the king is about to make his marriage public and I can convey that message to the princess at once."

I was pleased to find Rafe and I were of one mind. In short order, we had assigned a dozen items of silk goods to represent as many messages.

"Will you be able to remember them all?" he asked, looking doubtful.

"I have an excellent memory, but if *you* wish to write them down—"

"There is no need."

We stood facing each other as our single candle guttered. The flickering light made it difficult for me to read Rafe's expression. I thought he intended to kiss me again. I wanted that more than I wanted my next breath. My eyes had already begun to drift shut as my body arched his way in invitation when the unmistakable sound of footsteps reached us from the other side of the door.

I froze, alarmed by the thought of discovery and suddenly very glad that we had written nothing down. Rafe plucked up the candlestick and blew out the flame, plunging us into darkness. Then we waited, the air between us as thick with tension as with unfulfilled longing.

Two men, laughing, passed by.

"You had best return to your duties," Rafe whispered when all was silent again. "I can find my own way out."

I nodded, then realized he could not see me in the blackness of the closet. "Safe journey, Rafe."

"And you have a care for yourself, Thomasine," he said as he opened the door, peered out to make sure no one was in sight, and gestured for me to precede him.

Although it had been years since we first met, he had never before addressed me by my Christian name. I started to hurry off in one direction while he went in the other, but I had gone only a few steps before I gave in to temptation. Turning and walking backward, I called after him: "My friends call me Tamsin!"

38

Princess Mary was not invited to court for Yuletide that year.

Just before dawn on the twenty-fifth of January, Anne Savage and I were rousted from our beds and ordered to help our mistress dress. Escorted by two of the king's most trusted gentlemen, we followed the lady marquess to an upper chamber in the gatehouse. A priest waited there, together with the Earl and Countess of Wiltshire and their son, George Boleyn, Viscount Rochford.

By his robes, the priest was an Augustinian friar. His hands trembled visibly, making it difficult for him to hold on to the little book that contained the words of the sacrament of marriage. In a quavering voice, he asked the king if he had the pope's permission for the wedding.

The king mumbled an answer. Unsatisfied, the priest mustered all his courage and asked if the document granting authority might be read aloud.

King Henry's smile did not reach his eyes. They glittered with the threat of violence if he was not obeyed. "The license is among my private papers," he said in a voice so cold it made me shiver. "If I should, now that it waxes toward day, return there to fetch it, my appearance abroad so early would give rise to talk that would not be . . . convenient. Go forth, in God's name, and do that which you have been summoned here to do."

The priest did not dare call the king a liar. He proceeded with the ceremony.

As we were leaving the small room, I overheard my mistress's mother question her son. "*Is* there such a license?" Lady Wiltshire whispered.

Lord Rochford chuckled. "It exists. The pope gave his consent for the king to remarry."

"But?"

He shrugged. "The consent is conditional upon a declaration that the king's marriage to Catherine of Aragon is void. It does not specify who should make this declaration of nullity. If the pope remains unwilling to do so, the king will obtain it from his newly appointed Archbishop of Canterbury."

So the king had told a half-truth, I thought. It scarcely mattered. His Grace *was* the king. His word was law. Now that I considered the matter, I was only surprised that King Henry had delayed his wedding this long in the hope of winning the pope's blessing.

It did not occur to me until later that the king might be excommunicated for flouting Pope Clement's authority. When it did, my spirits sank even lower. His Grace must love Anne Boleyn very much indeed if he was willing to risk his immortal soul to have her.

I sent a coded message to Rafe. There was no need for us to meet. What had happened would be clear enough from the items I'd "ordered" from his silkwoman mother.

A few days later, I learned that there had been an additional reason for the king's haste. There was to be a child. King Henry had married to secure the legitimacy of the future heir to the throne.

Rafe and I had not worked out a code for this development, but I felt sure my message would be understood when I amended my order by the addition of one purple ribbon in a length too short to be of any practical use.

By the end of March, plans were well under way for the new queen's coronation on Whit Sunday, the first of June. Queen Anne's official household was also well on its way to being formed. As I was in high favor with Her Grace, I was to continue as one of her maids of honor.

In May, Anne Savage left our ranks to marry Lord Berkeley, and Anne Gainsford was soon to wed Sir George Zouche, the new queen's longtime equerry. They would both return as ladies-in-waiting. To replace them, fresh faces arrived at court, including Queen Anne's cousin, Madge Shelton, and a shy, quiet girl named Jane Seymour, who had previously served in Queen Catherine's household.

"I need more servants," Queen Anne mused one evening, tapping her long tapering fingers against her chin. I stilled, suddenly wary, for I could see that her dark eyes were alight with malice. "Ah, I have it. I will order the king's bastard daughter to join my household."

The queen's sister-in-law, Viscountess Rochford, laughed. "That sour, ill-formed creature? Maids of honor are supposed to be pleasing to the eye."

"I'll have her for a chamberer, then, and keep her out of sight. Or better yet, I'll assign her to the kitchens. Would she make a good scullery maid, do you think?"

"Better to keep her away from court altogether," I dared interject, knowing the princess would be safest for the nonce if everyone forgot her. "Did Your Grace not once think to marry her off to some foreign prince?"

"She does not deserve the honor! Besides, if I have my way, the king will strip her of her title. She will be plain Lady Mary and not a princess at all."

Queen Anne paused to study her reflection in the standing glass, turning this way and that to admire the look of yet another new gown. Then she slanted her assessing gaze my way.

"You may be right, Tamsin. Mary would be nothing but trouble at court. Perhaps I will find some lowborn varlet to marry her to, someone from Northumberland, perhaps. Or Westmorland. Yes, that would solve the problem very nicely indeed!"

I spent a restless night considering what was best to do. In the morning, I sent another coded message to Rafe. Her Grace needed to regain the king's goodwill, no matter what she had to do or say to accomplish that goal.

Whether in response to my suggestion or on her own initiative, Princess Mary wrote a letter to the king that pleased him mightily. I do not know what it said, but it effectively thwarted Queen Anne's plan to permanently remove her stepdaughter from King Henry's life. When the Archbishop of Canterbury formally declared the king's marriage to Catherine of Aragon invalid, Princess Mary retained both her title and her place in the succession.

39

In the days leading up to her coronation, Queen Anne made many changes in her household, some to ensure that her court would appear as respectable as possible. We ladies were ordered to increase the hours we spent sewing clothes for the poor. The queen intended to give these garments away during her summer progress. To enhance an air of piety, she presented each of us with a book of prayers and psalms and the silken girdle from which to hang it.

All the liveried servants in the new queen's household now wore blue and purple with livery badges inscribed with the motto *la plus heureuse*—the most happy. And Queen Anne's heraldic emblem—a white falcon with a crown and scepter, standing with wings elevated on a tree stump covered in Tudor roses—appeared everywhere I looked.

I spent the bulk of my time with the other maids of honor, but now there was one significant change. Queen Anne employed a "mother of maids," Mrs. Marshall. This worthy matron was charged with making sure the behavior of all the queen's damsels was seemly, especially at night.

Bess Holland openly flouted her authority, going to the Duke of Norfolk's bed whenever he sent for her, but the rest of us followed her rules. The post of maid of honor to the queen was highly coveted. No one wanted to be dismissed and sent home in disgrace.

Our primary duty remained the same—to provide an attractive, but not *too* attractive, backdrop for our mistress. Our fairer coloring made her dark skin, flashing black eyes, and ebony hair stand out in contrast.

I was still the tallest. Madge Shelton was the prettiest one among us. I envied the dimples that winked when she smiled. Like my old friend, Cecily Dabridgecourt, Madge was exceedingly soft-spoken. Jane Seymour had lovely blue eyes, although in general her features, save for a nose that was too thick at the point and a long upper lip, were too small for her face.

Queen Anne had decided that eight maids of honor suited her best. Of the four newcomers, two had previously served in Queen Catherine's household—Mary Zouche and Margery Horsman. Mary had bright yellow hair, a square jaw, and a good complexion, but she was no great beauty. Neither was Margery, who was most distinguished by her brusque manner and her preoccupation with detail. Margaret Gamage, plump as a partridge, brown as a wren, and barely past her eighteenth birthday, was a novice in royal service, as was Jane Astley, who had only just turned sixteen. Jane was small and slender, with wide-spaced brown eyes, fair brows, and regular features.

Three days before her coronation, Queen Anne left Greenwich aboard a sumptuously decorated barge. She was accompanied by the principal ladies of the court. We maids of honor, together with the lesser ladies of the household, followed on a second barge. Behind us came the king's barge, carrying His Grace's yeomen of the guard and the royal musicians. More than one hundred and twenty large watercraft and some two hundred smaller ones made up the flotilla. Among them were the fifty great barges belonging to the London livery companies. They had been rowed downriver to Greenwich only that morning. Their pennants and bunting and streamers of gold foil were impossible to miss when the little bells sewn at the ends made such a joyful sound.

I searched for Rafe among the citizens of London aboard the barges but there were too many people. They were all dressed in their finest, which was very fine indeed. Some prosperous merchants were wealthier than any peer could ever hope to be.

Other vessels carried cannon, fired off in celebration, that filled the air with a haze of choking smoke. One of the smaller barges transported a mechanical dragon that moved and belched out flames. A huge representation of the queen's badge had been constructed on a wherry. The white falcon stood on a golden tree stump growing on a green hill. This enormous device was accompanied by young girls strumming lutes and singing sweetly.

Until coronation day, Queen Anne was to lodge in the royal apartments in the Tower of London. I had never before been inside its formidable-looking walls and I was unsure I wished to be confined within them. The Tower might be a royal residence, but it was also a prison and a place of execution. Lady Salisbury's father and brother had died there.

My trepidation faded when we reached Queen Anne's lodgings, apartments newly built in the Inner Ward north of the Lantern Tower. With little cries of delight, Her Grace explored her presence chamber, dining chamber, bedchamber, and stool chamber. All the furnishings were new and very grand.

"Light all the quarriers," the queen commanded as she ran one hand over the smooth surface of a breakfast table made of walnut. "I wish to see into every corner."

The quarriers—square blocks of fine beeswax—illuminated bed hangings embroidered with entwined H's and A's and chairs with braided and tasseled cushions and footstools. Queen Anne laughed when she came to a round table covered with black velvet for playing card games. The half-dozen coffers filled with jewels brought tears of joy to her eyes.

The queen's procession through London two days later was accompanied by salutes of cannon fire and fireworks but the crowds lining our way remained strangely silent. Although members of the livery companies cheered and doffed their hats, some of the common spectators sent looks that were overtly hostile toward their new queen. Far too many kept their caps on their heads.

The coronation ceremony lasted nine hours. It was an exhausting experience for a woman six months gone with child. Afterward, Queen Anne needed time to recover. She retreated to her bedchamber . . . with the king. They spent long hours there together during the following days, excluding all others.

Left to their own devices, the queen's ladies, gentlewomen, and maids of honor sat and sewed and talked in quiet voices of the doings of their betters.

"I wonder," Bess Holland mused, "if His Grace will follow his usual practice during the last month or so of the queen's pregnancy."

"What is that?" Jane Seymour asked. She was old enough that she should have been able to guess, especially given Bess's well-deserved reputation for making bawdy comments, but in common with Princess Mary, Jane was more naïve than most other females of the same age.

Bess's laugh was bold and earthy. "Why that is the time when His Grace is most likely to take a mistress . . . so as not to 'disturb' his wife."

"That may have been the case with Queen Catherine," Madge

Shelton said, "but it is plain to see that King Henry is madly in love with this wife."

"And Queen Anne is still young and beautiful," Jane Astley put in, "not old and haggard-looking like—"

Mary Zouche reached out and pinched her, preventing her from completing her sentence.

A pained silence fell. We had all taken an oath to serve Queen Anne, but old loyalties died hard.

I dismissed Bess's prediction without another thought. His Grace's astrologers and the queen's physicians all agreed that the child she was carrying was a boy. The king made grandiose plans for a joust to celebrate the birth of his heir and his delight in his new queen seemed stronger than ever. It was only toward the end of July, after the king left a very pregnant Queen Anne and her ladies at Windsor while he went off to visit the homes of several courtiers, that the subject of the king's . . . appetite . . . came up again. He was gone nearly two weeks.

"King Henry is still in the prime of his manhood," Bess remarked as she and I sat side by side on a window seat to work together on hemming an altar cloth. "In the last weeks before a woman gives birth, it is common practice for her to avoid conjugal relations for fear of harming the unborn child."

Because of Bess's comments, I paid particular attention to His Grace when he returned to Windsor Castle. He seemed happy to see his wife, but he did not spend the night with her.

I was unsure what to pray for. The king had *married* Anne Boleyn. Even if he had now strayed from her bed, she was still queen. She still had influence over His Grace. She would have even more after their son was born.

But if his interest wandered, I wondered, could another woman's influence diminish the queen's power? Could such a one persuade the king to look out for his daughter and protect her from the machinations of her evil stepmother? It seemed possible, but as I had no idea who His Grace's current mistress might be, or even if he truly had one, there was nothing I could think of to do to advance Princess Mary's cause.

Then everything changed.

On an evening when the entertainment included the performance of an interlude about a chivalrous knight and his lady, His Grace danced with the maids of honor, bestowing compliments upon each of us in turn. When it was my turn, he held me close, running one hand along my arm beneath my loose sleeve as he bestowed upon me a smile that made me tingle all the way down to my toes.

Much later, back in the maidens' dormitory, the other maids of honor surrounded me the moment I entered the room. "What did he say to you?" Mary Zouche's lips might be pursed in prim disapproval, but her eyes were avid with curiosity.

"Pretty meaningless words," I said, "just like the ones His Grace showered on all of you."

In truth, I could not remember exactly what the king had said to me. I had been too nervous, and too shaken by the way he pressed me against his big, strong body while we danced. I'd never before felt such powerful sensations, not even when Rafe Pinckney kissed me. What I'd experienced was, or so I supposed, the difference between being wooed by a boy and being seduced by an experienced man.

"We all saw the look he gave you," Bess said. "There was more than a hint of amorous interest in his eyes."

"You are imagining things," I insisted, refusing to voice my own suspicions aloud.

"The queen most certainly was!"

Appalled, I stared at her. Bess shrugged, as if arousing Queen Anne's jealousy were of no consequence.

"His Grace meant nothing by it," I said again. The queen had once boxed my ears for failing to bring her the right pomander ball. I hated to think what she would do if she thought I was trying to steal the affections of her husband! "He is playing at the game of courtly love, nothing more."

But barely had the words left my lips than one of the royal pages appeared at the door to deliver one red rose and one white. "From your servant, mistress," he said, and winked at me.

"The king pursues you, Tamsin," Bess declared as soon as the boy had gone. "He wants to bed you."

"You are mistaken."

Bess shook her head, a knowing look in her eyes. "I am never mistaken about such matters."

"Then His Grace's pursuit of me is only a game. King Henry is enamored of the queen. Why, just look at the splendid gifts he's sent her."

Before we'd left Greenwich, he'd given his pregnant wife an enormous bed, one that had once been part of the ransom of a French duke. In this, she would give birth to his son.

"The king has healthy appetites, Tamsin." She drew me aside to add, in a whisper, "The king may be forty-two years old and past his first youth, but he still jousts regularly and is in good physical shape. And he can be charming when he wants to be. It would be in your own best interest to encourage his advances."

I shook my head, once again rejecting the possibility that the king wished to seduce me. "His Grace is not so much interested in coupling as he is in engaging in courtly love with a lady not his wife . . . and not great with child. King Henry loves to dance," I added, "and for the time being the queen cannot partner him."

"If you believe that, then you are a fool!"

I was a long time falling asleep that night. The idea that the king might desire me was both terrifying and tempting. If I pleased him, perhaps I *could* thwart the queen's efforts to turn him against Princess Mary. But that would mean becoming his mistress—giving my body to the king.

I had always supposed, when I thought about it at all, that I would one day marry. I knew full well that most marriages were not based on love, no matter how much the poets rhapsodize about that emotion. I expected to wed and bed a relative stranger. With luck, over time, we might grow fond of one another.

But that was marriage, sanctioned by God and man. Surrendering my maidenhood to the king in the hope he would grant me favors— that was something else entirely. I shuddered at the thought. Not only was fornication outside of marriage a sin, but all my knowledge of the physical act was based upon bawdy innuendo overheard at court and the fact that I had once seen a stallion mount a mare.

Even before Queen Anne decided that her maids of honor should have reputations pure as new-fallen snow, I had held myself aloof from both casual flirtations and romantic entanglements. I'd fixed my mind on my mission and, truth be told, barely noticed whether any of the gentlemen at court showed an interest in me. As for Rafe Pinckney . . . as usual, I forbade myself to wish for the impossible. Members of the queen's court did not wed the sons of shopkeepers.

I sighed, rolled over, and punched my pillow into a more comfortable shape. I prayed that in the coming days I would be proved right and Bess Holland wrong. For when I had considered the possibility that the king might choose a mistress who could diminish the queen's influence over him, I had never imagined that mistress might be me!

40

I woke still burdened by my dilemma. During the night, I had remembered Lady Salisbury's remarks about lying and sin, made on the eve of my departure for the royal court. In light of recent events, they took on new meaning. Were I to lie with the king, I would gain an opportunity to advance Princess Mary's interests. Had that been what the countess had meant me to do all along? Could she have intended that I catch the king's eye, become his mistress, and displace Anne Boleyn, just so that I could influence His Grace to favor his daughter over his concubine?

That evening, when the court gathered for music and dancing in the king's great watching chamber, Queen Anne watched me through eyes narrowed to slits. She disliked that the king had paid even platonic attentions to another female. I could feel her anger building, a palpable force, but King Henry, oblivious, continued to flirt with me and flatter me. It was obvious now, to everyone who saw us together, that he desired me in a very physical way.

The next time His Grace returned to the dais where his queen sat, she turned to him with fury in her eyes. Then she began to rail at him.

I could not hear precisely what she said, but it was abundantly clear that she was complaining about his behavior toward me.

His Grace did not take criticism well. At first he simply looked taken aback by his wife's anger. Then he lost his temper and no longer troubled to speak softly.

"You must shut your eyes and endure, as your betters have done!" he roared at the queen. "I can lower you in only a moment longer than it took to raise you up."

A stunned silence fell among the listening courtiers. Several of them glanced my way, making me wish that the floor would open up and swallow me.

"You would not dare!" the queen shouted back.

"Would I not? Do not question what I would or would not do, madam. I do what I will!" And with that, King Henry stormed out of the chamber.

I did not sleep at all that night. I half-expected one of the king's minions to arrive at the door of the maidens' dormitory with a demand that I follow him to His Grace's bedchamber.

Dawn came without any such interruption, but the king and queen did not speak to each other for two days. By the end of the third, however, they had been reconciled. My brief tenure as a woman in whom the king was interested was over.

41

On Thursday the twenty-first of August, the court moved from Windsor to York Place and on the Monday following traveled on to Greenwich, where carpenters had been busy during our absence. Queen Anne began her confinement on Tuesday, shutting herself into her apartments, her women with her, to await the birth of the future king of England.

It was a luxurious imprisonment. The queen's presence chamber was divided by a curtain. No men save the physicians could pass through to the inner half. Her Grace's newly enlarged bedchamber, which now contained an oratory for prayer, was hung with tapestries depicting the legend of St. Ursula and her eleven thousand virgins. Next to the magnificent bed the king had given her was a pallet with a crimson canopy, the place where she would actually give birth. And, in case the child should need immediate baptism to save its soul, a font sent for from Canterbury stood at the ready.

On the seventh of September, at three in the afternoon, the queen's child was born—a healthy, red-haired daughter. King Henry named her Elizabeth, after his mother.

I liked the king, even if I had little sympathy for the queen, and I felt sorry for him in his disappointment. At the same time, I secretly rejoiced. If the king were to die leaving only two females as his heirs, then Princess Mary, as the eldest, would have the better claim to the throne.

Or so I thought.

I was soon proved wrong in this assumption. Unbeknownst to me, the queen had persuaded King Henry that Mary should abandon the title of princess and call herself only the Lady Mary. Informed of this, Princess Mary wrote a hasty letter to her father, refusing to oblige him. Infuriated, His Grace became even more determined to force his daughter to accept his will.

The king was enthralled all over again with Anne Boleyn, despite the fact that she had failed to give him a son. He was even overheard to say that he loved the queen so much that he would beg alms from door to door rather than give her up.

Matters deteriorated rapidly after that. On the fourteenth of December, the king dissolved his seventeen-year-old daughter's household and ordered her to Hatfield to serve as her half sister's waiting woman.

At Yuletide, Rafe contrived to accompany Mistress Wilkinson when she delivered fringes and frontlets and other trimmings to Greenwich. He also arranged for the two of us to be left alone aboard the small barge the silkwoman had used to transport her goods downriver.

My lower lip trembled as I looked at him. "I failed the princess," I blurted out.

"That is nonsense. You did your best."

"Did I?" I wished I could be certain of that. There was very little I was sure of anymore, except that I could trust Rafe.

In a rush, I told him of the king's short-lived interest in making me his mistress and of my failure to hold on to His Grace's attention long enough to benefit the princess. Tears blinded me, so that I could not see his expression, but I'd barely stopped speaking before he closed the short distance between us and took me in his arms.

"There was nothing more you could have done, Tamsin. You cannot slay dragons for Her Grace, no matter how much you might want to."

In spite of myself, I smiled. I reached up to wipe the tears from my eyes but he was faster. He dabbed at my cheeks with the pad of his thumb. And then, his eyes locked with mine, he lowered his head with excruciating slowness and touched his lips to mine.

I wished that kiss could last forever. It was the sweetest sensation I had ever felt. At the same time, it thrilled me right down to the marrow of my bones. When Rafe started to step back, I clung to him, burying my face in the front of his warm wool cloak. As always, he smelled of sandalwood and cinnamon.

It was cold on the Thames. The wind whipped up whitecaps to make the barge strain at its moorings and rock from side to side. The motion kept us off balance and clinging to each other. Neither of us minded. For a time, we did not speak. Then Rafe lifted my chin with the side of his hand until our eyes met once more.

"Marry me, Tamsin."

I blinked at him. "What?"

He grinned at my surprise. "You heard me. Marry me. If you truly think there is no more you can do at court, come away with me and be my bride."

I waited for him to tell me he loved me. When he did not, a niggling little voice in the back of my mind suggested that he was only interested in acquiring the fortune that went with me to the church. Once I wed, full control of all my lands and chattel would fall into my husband's hands.

"I cannot just *leave*," I blurted out, using the excuse that came most readily. "I swore an oath to serve at the will and pleasure of Queen Anne."

"Never say you meant such a vow!"

"My intentions do not come into it. She believes I am hers to command and I am not permitted to leave court without the approval of her Lord Chamberlain. It would make her suspicious indeed, should I suddenly disappear."

"Then ask her to dismiss you. If you do not think she'll let you go to marry, then tell her you are ill."

"Rafe, I cannot." I was horrified by how much I wanted to. "Besides, Sir Lionel would make it his business to cause trouble if I vanished."

I had told him a little about my stepfather, but not much.

"We would not be helpless." His arms tightened around me. "I will hire the best legal minds in London to fight off any challenge to our happiness."

But you would have to pay them with my fortune, I thought.

"If I ran away with you, I would have to disappear, never to be heard of at court, or at Hartlake Manor again."

A picture of Sir Lionel as I'd last seen him, wicked and conniving, sprang into my mind. I remembered how he'd looked when he was wrathful. And then I thought of the king. An elopement might well anger His Grace, too. And if he wished it, King Henry had the power to find me and then ruin the entire Pinckney family. Rafe and his mother could not prevail against such odds. Rafe was barely out of his apprenticeship. He did not have the wherewithal to protect himself, let alone a wife.

I pushed myself free of Rafe's embrace and backed away from him, nearly losing my footing when another wave hit the side of the barge. "I must remain where I am."

In spite of my determination to sound firm, my voice shook. Rafe started to follow me, then stopped, waiting for me to say more. Once again, tears threatened. I had to blink rapidly to keep them at bay. I would not cry anymore. Crying solved nothing.

I cleared my throat. I had spoken truer than I realized when I voiced my first objection to leaving, but the pledge of loyalty I felt bound to honor was to Princess Mary, not Queen Anne. "Court is the only place where I have a hope of influencing the king to treat his elder daughter with more kindness. My first duty is to her, Rafe. To our future queen."

Rafe's face closed up. I felt certain that behind his stoic façade he was as torn by conflicting emotions as I was. He, too, was loyal to the lady we were now required to call the Lady Mary instead of princess. Helping her to survive her father's marriage to Queen Anne was a sacred trust neither of us could easily forsake, no matter how much we wished to, no matter how much we longed to be together.

"Your loyalty is commendable." His voice was bitter as aloes.

After a long, strained silence, I said, "We need to devise new codes. Enough of them for me to send a variety of specific warnings."

He nodded. "As you say."

The ease that had existed between us had vanished. With stiff formality, we spent the next hour matching silks with messages. Only one would indicate that Rafe should come at once to court. I told myself that would be safer for him. The rest of the messages could be conveyed directly to the princess.

"How do you go about passing on news?" I had no idea if he would send the actual laces, points, and ribbons to spell out my message, or go in person to speak to Princess Mary.

"It is safer that you do not know." He avoided meeting my eyes.

There was not much left to say to each other after that. I rose from the bench where I had been sitting and prepared to leave the barge.

"Have a care, Tamsin," Rafe called after me. He meant much more than to watch my footing as I scrambled across the plank that led to shore.

Plagued by the dismal possibility that I might never see Rafe Pinckney again, I returned to the palace in low spirits. To keep from dwelling on my sense of loss, I threw myself into the celebration of Yuletide.

42

On a sunny day in March, Queen Anne set out to pay a visit to her baby daughter at Hatfield. She took with her only a few of her ladies and the small dog she called Perky. Her Grace was inordinately fond of him and I had to admit to some liking for the little fellow myself.

Perky was different from any other dog at court. Small, sturdy, and playful, he had a curly white coat, round black eyes, a plumed tail that curved over his back, and long ears covered with flowing hair. He stood less than a foot high. Affectionate and inquisitive, he was into everything. That was why, after he had thoroughly disrupted order in Princess Elizabeth's nursery, I was told to walk him in the garden.

Tucking Perky under one arm, I set out to explore Hatfield, a redbrick palace that had once been the property of the bishops of Ely. Four wings had been built around the sides of a central quadrangle and a gallery led to the adjoining church. I had no difficulty picking out the great hall or the solarium that overlooked one of the gardens. Using these landmarks, I made my way to a prearranged meeting place.

When the princess—I would not, at least in my thoughts, call her the Lady Mary—had been assigned to wait upon her baby sister, she had been told she could bring only two of her women with her to provide services of the most humble sort. One of them came from the lowest ranks of Her Grace's household and was a maid-of-all-work. The other, voluntarily surrendering her status and privileges, was Maria Vittorio.

Thanks to the coded messages we had exchanged, Maria was on the lookout for me, ready to guide me to the small, cramped single lodging assigned to Princess Elizabeth's sister at Hatfield.

Upon entering, I made my deepest curtsey to Mary Tudor. She was still my princess, no matter what her father decreed.

It had been nearly three years since I'd last seen her. She had lost weight in the interim, making her look gaunt and unhealthy. But her smile was genuine. Her Grace embraced me, dog and all, and laughed when Perky nuzzled her hand.

"How tiny he is!" she exclaimed.

"He is of a breed much in favor at the French court. Lady Lisle sent him from Calais as a gift. I am told she wishes to place one of her daughters as a maid of honor."

"No doubt she will be successful. That woman loves all things French." Never one to blame an animal for its mistress's sins, she took Perky onto her lap, stroking his soft fur. "How do matters stand at court?"

"She is once again with child." Queen Anne had announced her condition to the king in January and then told her ladies.

Maria swore in Spanish.

"Your Grace still has many loyal supporters among the courtiers," I hastened to add. "You must not give up hope that you will one day be restored to your father's favor."

"That woman hates me."

"She *fears* you, Your Grace."

Maria, who had been guarding the door, interrupted before I could say more. "Someone is coming. You need to be away from here, Tamsin, before you are recognized."

Her Grace handed me the dog. Maria grasped me by the arm and led me out by a door covered by a wall hanging. I caught a glimpse of a messenger in Queen Anne's livery as he came in through the main entrance. I tried to free myself, so that I could linger and listen, but Maria refused to loosen her grip. When I glared at her, she pointed to Perky. She was right. If the dog barked, we would be caught.

A quarter of an hour later, after taking Perky into the garden to relieve himself, I returned to the nursery. The same liveried messenger I'd seen enter Princess Mary's lodging was waiting just outside. I recognized him now. He was a groom of the chamber. Tentatively, I touched his sleeve. "Are you ill, Dickon?"

The expression on his face was more closely akin to terror. Sweat beaded on his forehead, even though the antechamber was cool.

"Oh, Mistress Lodge! No. No. It is just . . . I dread the queen's anger."

"Why should Her Grace be wroth with you?"

Such was Dickon's consternation that he responded to my sympathetic manner. "Her Grace sent me to the Lady Mary with a message. Queen Anne offered to welcome her back to court if she would acknowledge her father's marriage and Her Grace's right to be queen of England."

"And?"

He swallowed convulsively. "Her Grace will not be pleased with the answer I bring her. The Lady Mary said that she knows no queen but her own mother."

I sighed. "A stubborn reply, but not unexpected."

"There is more. The Lady Mary added that if the king's *mistress* would intercede for her with her father, she would be most grateful."

"Oh, no."

"That is what she said, Mistress Lodge, and now I must repeat her words to the queen."

"Must you? Perhaps you could omit the last part."

But Dickon knew his duty. Helpless to change anything, I waited with him until Queen Anne left the nursery. I handed her the dog, hoping that holding Perky would keep Her Grace more calm.

"Well?" she demanded.

Dickon relayed the princess's answer. All of it.

Queen Anne's dark eyes glittered with a hatred so intense that I was surprised she did not order her stepdaughter beaten for her effrontery. I'd not have put it past Her Grace, in a fit of temper, to take a switch to Princess Mary herself.

To my amazement, she regained control of her anger. Still carrying Perky, she gave a haughty sniff and stalked out of the antechamber.

At the end of that month, Parliament having already declared that King Henry was supreme head of the church in England, the king signed into law the Act of Succession. It nullified "the Lady Mary's" claim to the throne and required that all of King Henry's subjects take an oath to support the legitimacy of Anne Boleyn's offspring. To refuse to do so was treason, punishable by death.

I took the oath.

43

A few months later, Princess Elizabeth's household moved to Eltham. The court was at Greenwich, only a few miles distant. On impulse, Queen Anne decided to make the short journey and spend a few hours playing with her child. While the queen visited her baby daughter, I slipped away from the nursery.

A few judicious inquiries led me to the chapel, where Princess Mary had gone to pray. The new chapel at Eltham had been built close to the hall, with two spiral staircases that led up to private closets, one each for the king and the queen. Her Grace knelt in the body of the chapel. She did not look up at my approach, not even when I sank down onto my knees beside her. I said a quick prayer, asking God to guide my speech.

The king's daughter had inherited a full measure of her father's stubbornness. I admired her principles, but of late she seemed determined to court martyrdom. I had found it surprisingly easy to lie when I swore to support the acts of Parliament that had made King Henry supreme head of the church in England and deprived the princess of her place in the succession. So, I suspected, had many others, especially when faced with the death penalty for refusing. Surely the person most affected by these statutes could force herself to follow my example, especially when her disobedience made her father so angry.

Infuriated by her refusal to do as he ordered, he had cut off all communication with her mother. "The Lady Mary" and Queen Catherine, who was now supposed to be called "the Princess Dowager," were already forbidden to meet. Now, until Mary took the oath, she was not permitted to correspond with her mother, either.

"Your Grace," I murmured in a low voice, "you must think of your future. You cannot help yourself or your mother if you do not moderate your behavior toward the concubine. It would not take much to restore you to the king's favor."

"I cannot acknowledge a bastard as heir, nor agree to my own illegitimacy. Nor can I put my father above the pope."

"An oath taken under duress is not binding," I argued, although the only precedent I knew of involved that long-ago kidnapping and forced marriage of the woman Sir Richard Egerton had later wed.

The princess continued to pray.

"Another baby is on the way. If this one is a boy, no matter how irregular his parents' marriage may be, he will at birth become heir to the throne of England ahead of either of King Henry's daughters."

Once again, the king was certain that the child would be male. He had already ordered an elaborate silver cradle from his goldsmith. I had seen the drawings that Master Holbein, the king's painter, had made for it. The pillars were decorated with Tudor roses and precious stones and more gems were set in a gold border around the rim. There were also golden figures of Adam and Eve in the design. To go with this cradle, Queen Anne had demanded gold-embroidered bedding and cloth-of-gold baby clothes.

"I know of the impending birth. The queen's apartments here at

Eltham are to be turned into a nursery for the new heir." Princess Mary grimaced. "The roof timbers have already been painted yellow. I am not certain why. The prince is to have a great chamber, a dining chamber, an arraying chamber, and a bedchamber."

"The king longs to see his elder daughter." I hoped that I spoke the truth. "He is willing to forgive you for any words you previously spoke in haste. Time and time again, I have seen someone mollify King Henry with gentle words and a subservient manner. Would it be so difficult to play the courtier?"

When she turned her nearsighted gaze on me, I saw that there were tears in her eyes. She opened her mouth to speak, but a flurry of activity from one of the staircases prevented her.

I wished I knew some of Maria's Spanish curses when I recognized the queen's groom, Dickon, and others in Her Grace's livery. Queen Anne and her ladies could not be far behind.

"Stay," I begged the princess. "Speak with your stepmother. If you make an overture toward her, she will accept it."

The look Princess Mary sent my way was as cold as the Thames during a hard freeze. Skirts rustling, she hastened out of the chapel, pausing only long enough to make her obeisance before the altar. She left by a side door just as Queen Anne reached the bottom of the spiral staircase.

I remained where I was, head bowed, hoping to blend into the shadows. Unfortunately, my height alone was sufficient to make me stand out, not to mention that the queen had already noticed my absence.

Queen Anne had come to hear Mass. It was not until the priest had completed the ritual that Her Grace's liveried servants came for me. I had no choice but to accompany them up the staircase and into the private closet at the top. As soon as I entered that small room, Queen Anne dismissed everyone else except her sister.

"You were speaking to the Lady Mary," the queen said in an accusatory tone of voice.

I sank into an especially deep curtsey, pressed down by the weight of her displeasure. She could do far more than box my ears if she chose to, and she already had cause to dislike me. Ever since the king had singled me out for his flirtation, she'd been suspicious of my loyalty. If I wanted to keep my post at court—and my freedom—I had to convince her that I had not gone behind her back to conspire with her enemy.

"I went to the chapel to pray and found the Lady Mary there before me!" The hateful form of address left a bitter taste on my tongue.

The queen fixed her steady, black-eyed stare on me. In that moment, I knew that nothing I could do or say would return me to her favor. Despite that conviction, or perhaps because of it, I made one last attempt to pave the way for a reconciliation between father and daughter.

"The Lady Mary has learned humility during her time in Princess Elizabeth's service. If Your Grace were to persuade the king to let her return to court, I am certain she—"

"That girl has been a thorn in my side for years," the queen snapped. "Why should I do anything to please her? Why should I listen to *anything* you suggest, Tamsin Lodge? You, who would have betrayed me with the king had I not intervened." She began to pace, both hands resting on the rounded belly where her child was growing. "I should turn you out, send you back to your stepmother and that charming husband of hers."

The threat sent a chill clear through me.

"Surely there is no need for that," Lady Mary Rochford interrupted. "Perhaps my eyes deceived me, but I thought I saw the Lady

Mary curtsey to you, Anne, before she so precipitously fled the chapel."

I had to bite my lip to keep from contradicting the queen's sister.

"Why did you not say so at once?" the queen demanded. "It will please the king greatly if she accepts me. I am even prepared to offer her my friendship in return, for His Grace has given me no peace since she refused to take the oath. We will set her up in her own household once she does. Somewhere far from court," she added in a mutter. Then she called for pen and ink and wrote a brief note to her stepdaughter.

There was no time for any reply from Princess Mary before the queen and her entourage left Eltham to return to Greenwich, but that evening Lady Shelton, the queen's aunt and Madge's mother and the person in charge of Princess Elizabeth's household, sent a message to her niece.

"Ungrateful chit!" Queen Anne crumpled Lady Shelton's note and tossed it into the rushes. She looked as if she wanted to hit something, and when the linnet that lived in a cage in her presence chamber began to sing its pleasant song, she ordered that it be removed from the room.

"At least she did not banish the poor thing from court," Bess Holland whispered.

The other maids of honor giggled. The peacocks that had been sent to the king from the New Found Land across the Western Sea had annoyed Queen Anne by being too noisy in the early morning when she wished to sleep. She'd insisted that they be kept elsewhere. To humor his pregnant wife, the king had ordered that bird coops be built at Sir Henry Norris's house in the village of Greenwich and moved the peacocks there, together with a pelican that had also been sent to him from the New World.

I did not laugh with the others. My place at court felt as precarious as that pelican's. People, too, could be banished. And they could be locked in cages.

I waited until Her Grace was distracted by the king's arrival to retrieve Lady Shelton's letter from the rushes. Late that night, after I was certain that all the other maids of honor were soundly asleep, I smoothed it out and began to read, careful to shield the single candle that gave me sufficient light to make out the words.

At dinner, Lady Shelton related, the Lady Mary had declared in a loud voice that the queen could not possibly have sent the message she'd received that day because Her Grace, Queen Catherine, was far away from Eltham. The messenger, she'd continued, should have said that the missive came from Lady Anne Boleyn. Then she'd stated, in no uncertain terms, that she would acknowledge no other queen but her mother, nor esteem any as her friends if they were not also Catherine's. The obeisance "Lady Anne" had witnessed, she'd declared, had been made to the altar, "to my maker and hers," and not to any earthly creature.

Thus rebuffed, it was no wonder Queen Anne was so angry.

44

The summer progress of 1534 was shorter than usual, to accommodate the queen's great belly. The riding household traveled to The Moor, Chenies, and Woking, but then returned to Eltham, where the queen took up residence in lodgings near her daughter and studiously avoided encountering the Lady Mary. The king went off on his own to visit Guildford, where the rest of the court was to join him in a few days' time.

Deprived of her husband's company, Queen Anne fretted. She was an emotional woman at the best of times, quick-tempered and subject to fits of nervous laughter. Now she clung to her favorite little dog, Perky, scorned the company of any of her women save her cousin Madge and the young Countess of Worcester, for whom she had developed a particular affection, and demanded, with increasing heat, to know why her sister had not yet rejoined the court.

Lady Mary Rochford had left in June to visit her two children. She had a daughter, Catherine, and a son named Henry. Some said his father was the king himself, but His Grace had never acknowledged him. That made me think it unlikely, since King Henry had been overjoyed to claim Henry Fitzroy, if for no other reason than to prove that he could sire a son.

It was after we moved on to Guildford, in the first week in August, that disaster struck. With no warning, the queen gave birth to a premature, stillborn boy. When she realized what had happened, she became hysterical, sobbing and laughing and beating on her pillows until she finally sank into an exhausted sleep.

King Henry felt the death of his heir as deeply as the queen did. Perhaps more deeply. I saw the stunned expression on his face when he came to her chamber and was told what had happened. All the light went out in his eyes. Then he turned away, shoulders hunched, so that Queen Anne's ladies would not see the tears flowing down his cheeks and into his beard.

When he had recovered himself a little, he went to his wife's side. Uncharacteristically, His Grace was at a loss for words.

The queen was not. She screamed at him. "This is all your fault, Harry! You forced me to go on progress. I did not want to. You know the common people hate me!"

At first the king did his best to calm her. He knew she was not herself. But His Grace had never been known for his patience. When he finally lost his temper, his voice boomed out loud enough to shake the tightly closed shutters.

"Silence! You will not speak that way to your liege lord!"

As if she suddenly realized how rash her accusations had been, Queen Anne shrank back on the pillows. She whimpered. So did Perky. Huddled together in the huge bed, they stared up at the massive figure of King Henry through startlingly similar large black eyes. His Grace loomed over them, fists clenched. For one terrible moment, I thought the king might strike his wife.

"Good day to you, madam," His Grace said through clenched

teeth. "I will speak with you again when you have recovered your health."

I do not know what impulse drove me but, when he stormed out of the bedchamber, I scurried after him. Catching them by surprise, I pushed past his gentlemen and dared to catch hold of the royal sleeve. When His Grace turned with a snarl, I threw myself to my knees, head bowed. I landed hard, jarring my entire body, and barely managed not to cry out.

"Tamsin," the king said in surprise. "Why have you followed me?"

"To beg a word with Your Grace, if it pleases you."

My head was still bowed, so I could not see his facial expression. I held my breath, waiting for his response. It came out in a whoosh when a large, heavily beringed hand appeared in my field of vision. I took it and let him pull me to my feet. I am not at all certain I could have stumbled upright without His Grace's assistance.

After a moment's hesitation, the king tucked my arm through his and led me into a nearby gallery where we could walk and talk without being disturbed.

"Well, Tamsin?" he asked when we had gained a little distance from his attendants.

"I . . . I acted rashly, Your Grace. It is just that I felt so badly. About the baby. I wished you to know that you have my sympathy for his loss."

Such darkness clouded his expression that I abruptly stopped speaking, fearing I had offended him beyond forgiveness. My words had been heartfelt, but it was not my place to commiserate with a king.

There was another long silence and then, to my surprise, he replied with equal honesty. "This is not the first time I have suffered such a loss." I could hear the anguish underscoring every word. "Has it begun again? Stillbirths and miscarriages and only a single living daughter?"

I had no answer to give him. He was thinking of all the children he and Queen Catherine had lost. There had been a son, I remembered, who'd lived only a few days. How many others had never drawn breath I did not know, but their loss had taken a toll on the king. This latest blow was all the more difficult to bear for what it had cost him to marry Queen Anne. He'd torn England apart, claiming that his first marriage was cursed by God to be childless— or close enough, since most people believe a female is incapable of ruling—and now his new wife had twice failed to give him the male heir he needed.

At that moment, I pitied the king. I even pitied the queen. But I also knew that I would never have a better opportunity to advance Princess Mary's cause. For the first time, there seemed to be a true lessening of the king's infatuation with his second wife.

"Your Grace?" I said, tentatively, when we had walked up and down the gallery a half-dozen times in silence.

"Yes, Tamsin?"

"You have two healthy daughters who—"

He cut me off before I could finish. "And there will be sons." He patted my hand. "I have said so often myself."

That had not been what I intended to tell him. I'd meant to suggest that his older daughter should come to court, restored as heir apparent. Uncertain how to broach the subject, I waited too long. His Grace brought my hand to his lips for a kiss and, bidding me farewell, left me there in the gallery.

A certain coolness persisted between the king and his queen for the next few days. On the seventh of August, King Henry resumed his progress into the Midlands while Queen Anne remained behind to recover her health. Her Grace's sister was still, unaccountably, absent, but their mother was with the queen and so was Queen Anne's brother, Lord Rochford.

Once Queen Anne realized that she might have lost the king's goodwill, she became determined to rejoin the royal progress as soon as possible. To this end, she followed the advice of her midwife and rested for a few weeks, but less than a month after she lost her child, she was reunited with her husband at Woodstock in Oxfordshire.

King Henry greeted his queen with apparent warmth, but his eyes lacked any sparkle when he looked at her. It did not take me long to come to a decision. If I was to influence the king in his daughter's favor, I must take advantage of this opportunity.

This royal manor was one of the largest, a modern and comfortable palace that boasted extensive stables and kennels, a park that had been fenced in for a menagerie by King Henry I, and a lover's bower set in the middle of an intricate maze. There was room to house the entire court, since Woodstock could accommodate up to fifteen hundred people for two months or more.

At my first opportunity, early on a sunny summer morning, I stationed myself on a prominent bench near the entrance to the maze, quills, inkhorn, and papers surrounding me. His Grace was in the habit of walking in the gardens every day. I heard his approach long before he caught sight of me, but I pretended to be too engrossed in my work to notice him.

"Whatever are you doing, Tamsin?" the king asked.

Feigning surprise, I nearly upset the inkpot. His Grace caught it deftly before any of the dark black ink could spill. Then he put a hand on my shoulder when I attempted to rise to make my obeisance to him.

"Stay, my dear. We will forgo the formalities if you will tell me what it is you are up to."

"Your Grace is most kind. It is but a small project of my own devising. Perhaps Your Grace will recall that I have some ability as a storyteller?"

He nodded, which was gratifying in itself. I was surprised that he remembered. I had not often been called upon to recount my tales since leaving Princess Mary's household.

"I thought to collect some of the best stories by writing them down for others to read. I have heard that there are some here at court who collect poems in this way, adding to a collection housed in a single manuscript."

"It is an excellent notion," the king said, beaming his approval. "You must let me read some of these tales." His smile broadened. "Better yet, you must tell them to me directly, especially any that bear a resemblance to the tales of Master Boccaccio."

I blinked at him in confusion. "I do not know the gentleman, sire."

"No, you would not." He laughed at a joke I did not understand, but I was too relieved to find him in such good humor to worry about such trivialities. "We will speak more of this anon," the king promised. Then he lifted my hand to his lips, kissed the back of my knuckles, rose, and went on his way, still chuckling.

I sent a rueful look toward the maze. I had been hoping His Grace might take advantage of its proximity to walk with me there, leaving his entourage behind. Perhaps it was better that he had not. I did not intend to yield too easily to his advances. Indeed, I held out some small hope that I might simply play at the "game of love" with His Grace, as I had once before, and still achieve my end.

Taking my time, since I had decided that it was, in fact, a worthwhile project to write down my stories, I did not return to the queen's lodgings for some time. I was still a considerable distance away when I heard Her Grace's screams of rage.

"What is it?" I demanded of Jane Seymour upon joining the cluster of maids of honor outside the queen's bedroom door.

"Lady Mary Rochford has returned to court," Bess Holland said, speaking up before Jane could utter a word.

Another shriek silenced us. Queen Anne's voice rose to a pitch so shrill it hurt my ears, but this close to the source, I could at last make out Her Grace's words.

"How dare you, Mary?" she demanded. "How dare you wed without my permission? And to a nobody!"

Lady Mary Rochford's voice was calm and firm. "He is not a nobody. He is a Stafford, a member of one of the greatest families in the realm."

"A cadet branch!"

"I love him, Anne."

"Love? Love!" If a screech could sound incredulous, the queen's did.

"Love," Lady Mary repeated. "And the proof of that love is already growing in my belly, so do not think that you can annul our marriage."

Jane Seymour stifled a gasp. The rest of us looked at each other with frightened eyes. Queen Anne gave an incoherent cry of rage. It was followed by a crash, as if she had thrown something breakable against a wall.

"Get you gone from my sight!" the queen screamed at her sister. "Get you gone from court! You are no longer welcome here!"

A moment later, the door opened and Lady Mary Rochford emerged. Her lips were curved into a secretive little smile that said she was well content with this outcome. By the queen's command, she was free to return to the "nobody" she had married—to the man she loved. She could bear his child far away from the turmoil and trouble of the royal court.

I envied her.

45

All the while we remained at Woodstock, King Henry lavished attention on me, offering me "knightly service" as his "mistress" and calling me his "lady to serve." Queen Anne, having made the uncomfortable three-day journey from Guildford to Woodstock when she had not yet fully recovered from her miscarriage, was in no fit state to welcome her husband back into her bed, but she did not like seeing him court another. She was quick to snap at everyone—not just her servants, but the king, too.

Rather than quarrel with his wife, His Grace took to stalking out of the chamber in search of more genial company. He seemed to find my presence soothing. One day we explored the maze together, but only after His Grace convinced me that he knew the way out.

"Tell me one of your tales, Tamsin," he commanded as we sat on the stone bench at the center. "I am in need of a cheerful story."

I was happy to oblige. I had begun to enjoy these private moments with the king, although it was rare that we were truly alone. There were almost always courtiers about, since the king was never supposed to be left unattended. But his minions knew to stay well in the background when His Grace wished to be private. I soon learned to ignore their presence.

King Henry was pleasant company, witty and charming. Once, he played the lute and sang to me. It was a composition of his own making and he had a fine voice. He did not press me to lie with him, although he did steal a kiss or two, and liked me to sit upon his lap while we talked. We were a man and a woman delighting in one another's company, aware of the physical attraction between us but not yet ready to act upon it.

I told myself I was biding my time, waiting for an opportune moment to mention Princess Mary's plight. I dared not risk falling out of the king's favor by being overbold. It would never do to come right out and ask him to change his mind about Mary's place in the succession, but I was certain *something* could be done to make the princess's life easier. I never forgot, no matter how much I enjoyed the king's company, that the reason I was encouraging His Grace's interest was to advocate for his daughter.

One afternoon, King Henry took me to visit his library, a high, brightly lit room filled with books. He had been talking about that fellow Boccaccio again, and someone called Ariosto. Laughing, His Grace thrust a book into my hands.

"But this is not written in English," I protested. "I cannot read Latin. Or Italian. Or whatever this language is."

His grin widened. "You do not need to read words. Just look at the pictures."

Suspicious of the twinkle in his eyes, I turned the pages carefully until I came to the first illustration. My mouth dropped open and I quickly slammed the volume shut. I could feel the heat rising into my face. "Those people have no clothes on," I whispered, truly shocked.

The king roared with laughter.

It was a precious moment, and what would have happened next I cannot say, for we were interrupted by Dr. Butts, who had just returned to Woodstock. He had spent most of the month of September looking after the health of the king's eldest daughter.

I started to leave, but King Henry gestured for me to stay where I was. I settled back onto a padded bench.

"Well?" the king demanded, when Dr. Butts straightened from his bow. "How does the Lady Mary fare? Is she malingering again?"

"Your Grace, your daughter has been most desperately ill."

My audible gasp drew both the physician's attention and the king's. His Grace frowned and sent me a narrow-eyed look, but still he did not banish me. Alarmed to see that my hands were shaking, I tried to make myself as small and insignificant as a little mouse. I needed to stay and hear what Dr. Butts had to say about the princess.

"What is wrong with her?" King Henry demanded.

"It is a complicated tale, Your Grace. At first I believed that the Lady Mary suffered no more than a recurrence of her old difficulties—severe headaches and stomach cramps preceding the start of her monthly courses. But Lady Shelton, her lady governess, in seeking to help assuage her suffering, sent for an apothecary, Master Michael. The apothecary, in good faith, dosed the Lady Mary with pills of his own making, but these pills did not agree with her and she became even more ill."

Poison, I thought, and fumbled for the rosary the princess had given me so many years ago.

"I'll have the villain's head!" the king bellowed. Hands on his hips, legs apart, he loomed over the much smaller physician with the look of a bull about to charge.

"No, no." Dr. Butts made little soothing motions with both hands as he hastily backed up a few steps. "There was no real harm done and the Lady Mary is recovering. But she *was* very ill. Her suffering, Your Majesty, is compounded by sorrow. Had she not been so deeply troubled, she would have mended faster and there would have been no need for the apothecary's pills in the first place."

The king turned his back on the physician, striding across the small room to stare out the window. As he passed me I could see that his brow was deeply furrowed. He *did* care about his daughter. He just did not know what to do about her.

After a long silence spent contemplating the gardens below, His Grace spoke. "What do you mean by *troubled*? What troubles her?"

"May I speak freely, Your Grace?"

"As you will."

"The Lady Mary would recover in a trice were she to be set free to come and go as she pleases."

King Henry heaved a deep sigh but did not turn around. "It is a great misfortune, then, that she remains so obstinate. She deprives me of any occasion to treat her as well as I would like."

Dr. Butts glanced at me. Our gazes met with perfect understanding, but I was not brave enough to make the obvious suggestion. I left it to the physician. After all, the king had given him leave to speak without fear of reprisal.

"Send her to her mother," said Dr. Butts.

I held my breath. Had he gone too far? It was not a simple request. If the king allowed his daughter the one thing she most desired, she might never renounce her claim to the throne.

I could hear the regret in the king's voice when he replied. "It is a great pity my daughter is so distressed, but it is entirely up to Mary herself how long she remains in her present circumstances."

Accepting his failure to sway His Grace, Dr. Butts bowed himself out of the library.

Boldly, I left my seat and insinuated myself beside King Henry in the window alcove. I dared to touch my hand to his.

"Perhaps," I suggested in a soft voice, "a small show of kindness might be enough to turn the tide. Your daughter loves you very much, Your Grace."

He did not look at me, but continued to stare out at the Oxfordshire countryside beyond the panes of glass. "Why will she not take the oath? It is a simple enough thing to do. Do you think I do not know that many of those who swear it are perjuring themselves? But I must have the words. I cannot back down about that."

"Let her come to court," I urged him. "Then make staying here conditional upon her agreement." I felt certain that if I could talk to the princess myself, uninterrupted, I could persuade her to cooperate.

The king's answer was a derisive snort and a muttered, "The queen would have my head!"

I sighed.

King Henry looked down at me. "Anne does not have a say in all that I do."

Clasping me tightly in his embrace, the king began to kiss me. From that point onward, everything happened very fast, but it never occurred to me to protest.

His Grace swept me up into his strong arms and carried me from the library into a private passage that led to his bedchamber and the "secret lodgings" beyond. The rooms we passed through were a blur, as were the voices of the king's gentlemen. I clung tightly, my arms around his neck and my face buried in the plush velvet of his doublet. One of the jewels that decorated it scratched my cheek, but I scarcely noticed. If it had not been necessary, I think I would have forgotten how to breathe.

What breath I had came out in an explosion of air when the king tossed me onto the top of a feather mattress so soft that I sank into it by at least an inch. With a rattle of golden rings, he closed the curtains around the bed, shutting me into a small, opulent tent. I heard him call for a servant to divest him of his clothing.

Heart racing, I sat up, but that was all I could manage. I did not know what to do next. I could not run screaming from the room. I had never given His Grace any reason to believe I would not welcome him as a lover.

Neither had I thought this far ahead. I suppose I assumed that our flirtation would follow the same pattern it had when Queen Anne was pregnant with her daughter, but this was no longer a game of courtly love and I was no longer safe upon a pedestal, worshipped from afar.

I looked down at my trembling hands, wondering a trifle wildly if I was supposed to remove my own garments or wait for His Grace's minions to help me. I jumped when I heard the chamber door close with a thud. The servants had departed. I did not know whether to feel relief or panic. Before I could decide, the curtains parted.

King Henry wore a night robe over his nakedness, a gorgeous thing of red velvet furred with ermine. He clambered up onto the bed, showing a flash of skin as one strongly muscled leg revealed itself. He smiled broadly at my reaction and then bade me turn my back to him so that he could undo my laces.

He seemed pleased to perform this service for me, and was not unfamiliar with the workings of female garments. He had me down to my shift before I could think of anything to say to him. Then that last item of clothing was also gone. A moment later, I was on my back with the weight of his body on top of me. I felt his nakedness against mine and was on the verge of panic when he began to whisper.

"Sweeting," he murmured. "Sweet, sweet Tamsin."

He calmed me the way he would a fractious horse, running one hand over my flanks and speaking softly. Only when he was satisfied that I would not bolt did he begin showering kisses on me.

I returned them, tentatively at first and then with more enthusiasm. I had known from the start that there was no way to retreat and the last thing I wanted was to turn the king against me by failing to respond to his lovemaking. I was prepared to pretend to like whatever he did to me. I had learned enough from listening to the other ladies talk to realize that I could not just lie there like a corpse. If His Grace was disappointed in me, I would be of no further use to anyone, not even myself.

King Henry knew that I was a maiden. He was careful with me and instructed me in what I should do to please him. I followed these instructions willingly and, to my surprise, my body already seemed to know how to react. I will not say that it was painless when he pushed himself into me. A few tears leaked out through my closed eyelids. But then I found myself distracted by the rest of the procedure. The strange, goodly feeling returned to my nether parts and began to build toward something more, although in my innocence I did not know what that might be. Before I could find out, the king was caught up in his own release. He gave one final gasp and collapsed on top of me.

I frowned. He was heavy, but I did not dare push him away. I wondered if he would fall asleep. One of the queen's ladies-in-waiting had complained just the previous week that her husband always did so after they coupled. She had been quite put out about it.

Abruptly, King Henry braced himself on his muscular arms and, still panting a little, grinned down at me. Seeing his pleasure, it was not difficult for me to smile back, but I could not help but wince when he rolled away from me and I tried to sit up.

"I believe," the king said, "that you should have a hot bath. I am told it eases the twinges that result from the loss of virginity."

My mind did not have enough time to fully absorb the king's meaning before His Grace bounded out of bed. Then the only thing I could think about was the sight before my eyes. My face flamed as I stared at him. Stark naked, he boldly eyed my equally unclothed body. My garments having been carelessly tossed outside the curtains, where they had fallen into untidy piles on the foot carpet, out of my reach, I fumbled for a coverlet.

"Delightful!" the king declared. "There is nothing as pretty as a blushing bride! Did you enjoy your initiation into the ways of lovers, my sweet?"

I told myself that what had just happened between us was indeed the same as what any bride endured on her wedding night. In truth, I'd had more of a courtship from the king than most wives enjoyed from their husbands. Marriages were arranged by families. Gentlewomen were as often wed to complete strangers as to men they knew well.

"My sweet?" the king prompted me.

"I . . . I can hardly describe my feelings, Your Grace."

"Harry," he said. "When we are in private like this, dearest Tamsin, you must call me Harry."

And with that, he leaned in between the bed curtains, took away the coverlet I was still attempting to wrap around myself, and once more lifted me into his arms. This time he carried me out of the bedchamber and into a privy passageway that led to a room that contained a bathtub attached to one wall. It was made of wood and lined with linen but, unlike any other tub I'd seen, it had two taps permanently affixed above it. The king turned both and water began to flow into the tub. The stream from one of them was hot enough to steam.

His Grace . . . Harry . . . chuckled at the expression of astonish-ment on my face. "There is a charcoal-fired stove in the room directly below this one. It is fed from a cistern, filled from the conduit that brings water to the house from a spring some eight hundred feet away. You have no doubt seen the pipes. They run across a series of pillars in the park."

He held me close enough to the tub to dip my hand in. "It is a wonder . . . Harry. Almost like magic."

Again, he laughed, as delighted by my obvious pleasure as by my use of his name. Then he eased me gently into the warm water. It was already high enough to cover my lower limbs and feeling it lap at my private parts was sheer bliss. As he'd promised, it soothed away the lingering soreness.

With a sigh of contentment, I reclined against the folded towel that padded the rim of the tub. As the level of the water rose, I let my head fall back, luxuriating in the experience, and found myself staring up at a ceiling decorated with gold battens on a white back-ground.

"Harry" slipped into a bathrobe stored in a cupboard beneath one of the deep window seats. Rather than call for servants, he retrieved two large holland cloth towels and placed them on the chair posi-tioned near the bathtub. He brought me soap scented with sweet bay and turned off the taps, stopping the influx of water just before the tub overflowed.

I glanced over the edge at the floor. It was made of deal boards with little holes for drainage. Then my gaze fell upon the largest article of furniture in the room—a bed.

"Does someone sleep here?" I blurted out.

"That is for reclining after a bath, something the most learned physicians recommend to prevent falling ill."

While I soaked in the tub, the king fetched my clothing, and when I was done, he toweled me dry. There was a fireplace in the room, generating sufficient heat to keep goose bumps from forming on my skin. Harry helped me dress, too, tying my laces with his own hands. I had begun to think this was all a long, strange, and sensual dream, when he broke the spell. He called for his groom of the stool to escort me back to the maidens' chamber.

46

I went to confession the next morning. The king's chaplain gave me absolution but, for the first time I could remember, I was not content to accept that a few prayers would suffice to mitigate my sin. I had committed adultery. My penance should be severe.

To my mind, and according to the pope, King Henry was still married to Catherine of Aragon. I had not betrayed my current mistress, but I had wronged the rightful queen. I was no better than any other concubine.

Rafe Pinckney crept into my thoughts despite my best efforts. As the day wore on, I could think of little else. It should have been Rafe to whom I surrendered my virtue. Now that it was too late, I knew that I should have *married* Rafe, even though doing so would have ended any hope of remaining at court.

I paid little attention to my duties. I did not think anyone noticed. We were preparing to leave Woodstock the following day for Grafton in Northamptonshire, another of the king's hunting manors, and everyone was busy. I should have known better than to make any such assumption. Queen Anne had spies everywhere.

"I have no more need of your services, Mistress Lodge," the queen said when she called me before her late in the afternoon. Her words were clipped and her dark eyes burned with ill-concealed hatred. She knew I had been in the king's bed. "You will leave court at once."

"Your Grace, I—"

She rose from her chair, fists clenched. Expecting her to strike me, I winced. "You dare talk back to me? You will go!" she screeched. "Now!"

I went. While Edyth packed my belongings, I sought the fresher air of the courtyard. I sat on a stone bench, staring blankly at the bustle around me. The first of the baggage carts was already being loaded for the journey to Grafton.

The scene reminded me of that first day at Thornbury, when I joined the household of the Princess of Wales. Carts and liveried servants. Noise and confusion. Everyone moving with a sense of purpose . . . except for me.

I had been ordered to leave court. After so many years of royal service, the finality of it left me feeling dazed and shaken. I had lost my anchor.

Where was I to go? Hartlake Manor was no refuge, not with Sir Lionel there. After their marriage, he and my stepmother had moved into the manor house. To dispossess him, I would have to go to law and I had no ready access to the money it would take to hire a lawyer.

How much time passed while muddled thoughts churned inside my head, I do not know, but when I looked up, it was to find Bess Holland standing in front of me. "Are you ready to go?" she asked, her voice sharp with impatience.

I laughed without mirth. "Where?"

"To attend the queen while she sups."

"I have been dismissed, Bess. Her Grace ordered me to leave the court. You were there." All the maids of honor had been present to witness my disgrace.

"Aye, she did," Bess said with the flash of a smile. "And King Henry, hearing of it, countermanded the queen's order."

"Oh."

Bess laughed. "It appears His Grace wishes you to continue in your new role as his mistress. Come along. It will seem awkward at first, but you'll get used to it." Having been the cause of more than one row between the Duke and Duchess of Norfolk, she had cause to know.

That evening, when the king visited Queen Anne's rooms, she took him to task for rescinding of my banishment. The first part of their argument was conducted in whispers, but they were passionate people. Everyone in the privy chamber heard him when King Henry raised his voice.

"Your betters, madam, learned to put up with my diversions, and you must, too!"

After that, the queen did her best to ignore me. She never spoke of the fact that the king sent for me later that same night, the last before the court departed for Grafton.

His Grace—Harry—took me to visit the sunken bath at Woodstock.

The chamber contained a green glazed stove, unlit, and something that more closely resembled a cistern than a bathtub. We stood on the lip of it, looking down into a large square hole in the floor that had been lined with lead and filled with water. It was at least three feet on a side and appeared to be several feet deep. The water had a stagnant smell that made me wrinkle my nose.

"It is very . . . large," I said in a small voice.

"The old Roman baths that still exist in some parts of England look something like this," the king said, "but I have it in mind to turn this one into a heated steam bath after the manner of the Turks. A suite of six rooms, I think, one just to house a large boiler to heat water."

As had the other bath chamber at Woodstock, this one contained a bed. I avoided a dip in the cistern but could not elude the king's amorous embraces.

It was more difficult to yield myself to him the second time than the first. I was burdened with a guilty conscience. His Grace did not notice, nor did he make much effort at seducing me. The encounter was over quickly, for which I could only be grateful.

The next day, when we left Woodstock, I was not surprised to find riding uncomfortable. Bess noticed me shifting in my saddle and took pity on me, suggesting an herbal remedy that could alleviate the soreness. After we settled in at Grafton, she offered me further advice, not only on how to please a lover, but also on how to make conception less likely.

What I had learned from Bess met with the king's approval. He took me with him when he went hunting and, to my great delight, mounted me on Star of Hartlake.

The horse that had once been my father's pride and joy had passed his prime, but he was still a magnificent beast. I made certain the king knew how wonderful it was for me to ride him and how fond I had been of him when I was but a girl.

Grafton was one of the smaller royal manors, but like so many of King Henry's royal residences, it had enjoyed recent refurbishing. The newest addition, of which the king was justly proud, was a bowling alley. It was a substantial building, a brick and stone structure with a flat lead roof built on the north side of the orchard.

As a spectator, I watched from benches placed along the sides for our comfort. I had only ever watched the king bowl once before, at Woking, where the alleys were outside. Here windows and candelabra rather than sunshine lit the scene.

The players assembled in the waiting area at one end of the alley. At the other end servants waited, ready to collect the wooden bowling balls. Then everyone's attention focused on the king as His Grace stepped up to make the first cast. It was at that moment that Viscountess Rochford, Queen Anne's sister-in-law, who had seated herself at my right hand, leaned in close to whisper in my ear.

"Whore," she said, quite calmly. "You do not belong here. Crawl back into the gutter whence you came."

I turned toward her in astonishment. "My lady, I—"

"You are the worst sort of creature, disloyal and untrue," her low whisper continued, reminding me of nothing so much as the hiss of a snake. "It would not surprise me if you had been planted here to spy for the Lady Mary."

I gasped.

Her eyes went wide, and then she laughed. "Have I stumbled upon the truth? How delightful. I cannot wait to tell the queen."

I grabbed her arm. "You leap to conclusions, my lady. I do not mean the queen any harm." I spoke, of course, of Queen Catherine, but there was no reason for Lady Rochford to know that.

"Unhand me!" she shrieked, loud enough to have heads turning our way. "You are hurting me!"

Too late, I understood that she had been ordered to pick a fight with me. She'd hoped I would do just what I had done—appear to assault her. She . . . and the queen who'd sent her . . . counted on the king's displeasure falling on me, so that he would dismiss me from court.

I swallowed hard as I watched Lady Rochford stalk off. There were strict laws about violence within the verge—the area within a twelve-mile radius of the king's person. What was intended to prevent courtiers from dueling could be applied with equal force to the queen's attendants. Had I gone so far as to strike Lady Rochford in the king's presence, I could have been sentenced to lose the hand I'd used to hit her.

King Henry continued playing at bowls, if for no other reason than that there was heavy wagering on the outcome of the match. He waited until I was escorted to his bedchamber that night to ask for my side of the story.

When he'd heard me out, he banished Lady Rochford from court.

47

King Henry was still behaving with considerable coolness toward the queen when the royal progress came to an end for that summer. I continued to warm his bed. I became comfortable enough with His Grace to call him Harry in our most intimate moments, but I was never tempted to do so at any other time.

By roundabout means, I broached the subject of his daughter. I told him stories of my time in the Princess of Wales's household. I strove to make him understand how much Queen Anne's hatred of her stepdaughter had colored his opinion of a young, innocent, and loving girl, his own flesh and blood.

Toward the middle of October, I asked permission to write a letter to "the Lady Mary," who was by then living at The Moor in Hertfordshire. She continued to serve as a lady-in-waiting to her younger half sister.

"I am surprised you have not asked to write to her sooner," King Henry remarked.

We were lying side by side in one of the king's massive beds—any one of them would easily have accommodated a half-dozen people—and he was in a mellow mood.

"I did not wish what I wrote to be read by the queen's spies."

One of his hearty laughs reassured me that I had not been too impertinent. "You need have no fear that *anyone* will read your letter. Not even *my* spies."

The next day, I composed a message full of encouragement, telling my princess to take heart. "Your Grace's tribulations will come to an end much sooner than you expect," I wrote. "Should opportunity occur, I will show myself to be Your Grace's true friend and devoted servant."

Although I had King Henry's promise that no one would intercept my letter, I did not dare be more specific. In truth, I could not have said what form my help might take. The king doted on me now—not unlike the way the queen doted on little Perky—but in time he would tire of me. He could be testy and irascible. The wrong word at the wrong time might well cost me all the ground I had gained in softening His Grace's attitude toward his daughter.

The proof of my success came in the gift King Henry sent her—a litter made of velvet that was the twin of the one Princess Elizabeth used. Courtiers read this as a sign that "the Lady Mary" would soon be restored to her proper place. A number of gentlemen and ladies, both singly and in groups, paid visits to her at The Moor and even more of them did so when the princess's household moved to Richmond.

On the twenty-second of October, a Thursday, the queen went to visit Princess Elizabeth. The maids of honor served in rotation, so it was by chance that I accompanied her. The Dukes of Norfolk and Suffolk also accompanied the queen. She was in the nursery when she realized that the two dukes had slipped away to pay their respects to the king's *other* daughter.

"Let the Lady Mary come here to me," Queen Anne ordered.

Her messenger returned almost at once. Dickon was literally shaking in his boots. "The Lady Mary refuses to leave her room until Your Grace has departed," he stammered.

"She will be punished for this affront," the queen promised, and sent for Lady Shelton, lady governess of the sisters' household.

I do not know precisely what instructions the queen gave, but as soon as I was able to send word to him of what had happened, His Grace countermanded the order.

This odd life, serving the queen by day and the king by night, continued through October and into November. On the twentieth day of that month, a special envoy from King Francis of France arrived. He was Philippe Chabot de Brion, the Admiral of France. I never did learn much about him or his mission, but whatever he was asking for put the king in a surly mood. Despite this, in early December, the queen hosted a banquet in the French envoy's honor. Queen Anne sat next to Brion on the dais.

I was not supposed to be present. Bess Holland and I were not on duty, but Bess had convinced me that we need not hide ourselves away. We might not have places at the banquet, but no one was likely to stop us from lingering in the doorway to admire clothing and jewels and exchange pleasantries with courtiers we knew.

I did not anticipate that the king would notice me, or that he would leave the dais and seek me out. He appeared at my side without warning.

"Tamsin," he murmured. That deep, throaty rumble was something I had come to associate with the start of an amorous and enjoyable interlude. Just the timbre of his voice sent a little thrill of anticipation through me. Despite my earlier misgivings over the state of my immortal soul, I'd come to enjoy the earthy pleasures His Grace indulged in.

I did not discount the tangible rewards, either. A ring the king had given me sparkled on my finger. Beneath my shift hung a golden locket that contained His Grace's likeness in small. And in the royal mews, Star of Hartlake remained in the care of the king's master of the horse, but he was mine once more, yet another gift from "Harry."

I dropped into a deep curtsey, as did Bess. The king bent over my hand and kissed it, pulling me to my feet as he did so.

A peal of hysterical laughter rolled toward us from the dais. The king turned to look at the queen, as did everyone else in the hall.

The French envoy, in French, demanded to know if Her Grace was mocking him. His voice carried clearly.

So did the queen's reply. "It is only that the king went in search of your secretary, Admiral, that he might present the fellow to me, and entirely forgot what it was he set out to do when he found a fair damsel instead."

The king's face darkened with annoyance. I prudently stepped out of his way as he stalked back to the dais. The look Queen Anne sent my way was filled with loathing, as if she blamed me for her own ill-advised outburst.

A few days later, without warning, I fell violently ill. Terrible pain gripped my innards. My throat burned. My skin felt cold and clammy to the touch. I was dizzy and weak.

Edyth held my hair out of the way while I rid myself of everything I had eaten that morning. On the other side of the maidens' chamber, Bess Holland also retched into a chamber pot, though she was not as sick as I was. Jane Seymour had also complained of belly gripes and been excused from her duties for the rest of day.

Through the pounding in my head, a memory stirred. My symptoms might have been due to sickness, but there was also a frightening alternative. I had never forgotten the time when Princess Mary had been stricken with sudden, inexplicable pains or the fears Maria and I had harbored before a natural explanation was found for Her Grace's suffering.

Poison? Was it possible. I found it difficult to think clearly, but with an effort I remembered that Bess, Jane, and I had all eaten from the same little box of comfits. The king knew that I was fond of sugar-coated almonds and I'd assumed he sent them as a gift. I'd shared my unexpected bounty with Bess and Jane. They'd each eaten a handful of the comfits. I'd devoured considerably more.

What if someone else had sent the almonds? What if they'd been poisoned? The queen was also fond of these comfits. There were always some in her chamber.

I remembered more of that long-ago day at Beaulieu when we'd thought Princess Mary might have been poisoned. I'd learned something of poisonous herbs from Maria. And from Master Pereston the apothecary, I'd heard about a poison called arsenic.

White arsenic, he'd said, bore a resemblance to sugar. If someone wanted to dispense with a rival, what better way than to add a poisonous crystalline powder to a sugar-coated treat?

"Edyth," I croaked, my throat raw. "Find a feather."

She produced a fine, long one from a costume I'd worn in a recent disguising. I thrust it into my mouth and down my throat, attempting to rid myself of more of the poison.

Aghast, Edyth tried to make me stop.

I pushed her away. "This is necessary. I have been poisoned."

"Poison?" Her eyes widened in horror and disbelief.

Once my stomach was as empty as I could make it, I gave a new order: "Fetch milk. As much milk as you can find."

"Milk? Oh, no, mistress. You do not want to drink that nasty stuff. It is fit only for children and the aged. Imbibing it will make you feel worse, not better."

"Do as I say, Edyth!" I shouted at her.

Momentarily cowed, she asked, "Shall I heat it and mix it with fruit or spices?" That was the way milk was most often served to elderly persons, or else with chunks of bread in it as sops.

"It does not matter," I said through teeth clenched against a new round of belly cramps. I panted as pain racked my body. "Just be quick about it."

"Cow's milk or ass's milk? Or mayhap a goat would—"

"I do not care! Only hurry, Edyth. I could die while you stand there dithering."

By this time, Bess and Jane, alerted by the increasing volume of my demands, hovered beside my bed. Jane, one hand clamped over her abdomen, looked even more whey-faced than usual. Bess's long yellow hair hung in disorderly clumps.

"You think we have been poisoned?" Bess asked. "How can that be?"

"The comfits."

Jane started to weep. "I do not want to die."

"Then cast up the contents of your belly and drink the milk Edyth is bringing." I glared at my tiring maid and, at last, still looking mutinous, she left to follow my orders. Like most people, Edyth was certain that drinking milk caused headaches, agues, and rheums and should only be used to make cheese.

"I thought the king sent you these comfits," Bess said when she and Jane had duplicated my course of treatment with the feather. She picked up the small, ornate wooden box that contained the sugared almonds and opened it. When she saw it was still half-full, she quickly closed it again.

"I thought so, too, but they could have come from someone else. Someone who has similar boxes in her lodgings at all times."

I did not name Queen Anne. I did not have to. I saw the anger flare in Bess's eyes. She had supported the queen from her earliest days at court, back when Anne was plain Mistress Anne Boleyn, and now she had come close to dying by the queen's hand, a random casualty of Her Grace's jealousy.

"Send to His Grace and ask if this box came from him," Jane suggested, delicately wiping her mouth with a linen handkerchief. She was a very fastidious person.

"I do not want the king to hear that I am ill." Fighting another wave of dizziness, I had to wait until my head cleared before I could finish my thought. "You know how His Grace feels about sickness."

Everyone at court knew. King Henry went out of his way to avoid any contact with contagion. Even in the days when he'd first fallen in love with Queen Anne, he had left her behind when one of her maidservants, Edyth's friend Rose, had contracted the sweat.

It was some time before Edyth returned with milk, but when she did she brought great quantities of the stuff. We drank as much as we could hold. I do not know *how* it worked against the arsenic, but work it did. Bess and Jane were restored, save for some lingering weakness, by the next day. I needed longer to mend, but I gave out that I had my monthly courses and thus prevented the king from inquiring too closely into my absence. The queen did not trouble herself to ask after my health at all.

When Bess offered to dispose of the box and its deadly contents, I gave it to her willingly. I could not accuse the queen, and I did not want to risk anyone else accidentally ingesting the arsenic-laced candy.

I was half-asleep two nights later when Bess returned to the maidens' chamber. The maids of honor slept two to a bed. Since both Bess and I sometimes passed part of the night elsewhere, the other damsels had decreed that we be bedfellows, to avoid disturbing their rest. I heard the swish of fabric, felt the mattress depress, and breathed in Bess's musky perfume. I expected that in a moment she would settle and I could continue my drift into slumber.

Instead she put her mouth close to my ear and spoke in a whisper. "I had to be sure. Now I know. The sugar on the almonds did contain poison."

My eyes flew open and every muscle in my body tensed. "*How* do you know?"

"How does anyone test for poison? I fed some of the comfits to a dog."

This statement sparked a terrible premonition. "What dog?"

"The one whose loss the queen will feel most deeply."

"Not—"

"Yes. That annoying little white dog Her Grace is so fond of—Perky."

"Oh, Bess." I felt genuine regret. I'd been fond of Perky and I never liked to see any animal suffer, not even the mastiffs and bears purpose-raised for fighting each other in the ring. That poor little creature must have died in terrible pain.

But hard on the heels of that thought came a truly horrifying realization—the queen would be sure to think that I had killed her pet. I sat straight up in the bed. "What have you done? She'll blame me."

"Do you think me a fool?" Bess laughed softly. "No one saw me and as soon as I was certain that the sugared almonds had made him violently ill, I picked him up and threw him out a window. The cobbled courtyard below was deserted. It is well after midnight. When the body is found in the morning, it will appear that he died in an accidental fall. You know how he was always racing about, heedless of stairs and balconies . . . and windows. No one will guess the truth."

Sickened by her callousness, I could not speak. Unconcerned, Bess rolled over and fell asleep.

The next day, it was Edyth who brought me official word of

Perky's death. I was still weak, but well enough to leave my bed. I was sitting on the window seat, bundled up against the draft that crept in through the glass and contemplating the dismal December landscape outside when she came into the maidens' dormitory. The bare branches of distant trees stood out in eerie silhouette against a leaden sky.

"They found the queen's favorite dog dead this morning, its neck broken in a fall," Edyth announced as she put away the freshly laundered linens she had just collected, "and because Her Grace doted so on her pet, none of her ladies dared tell her. The king had to give her the news. For once," she added, "when Her Grace started carrying on, King Henry didn't stomp out of the room. He stayed with her and offered comfort."

"The king has a soft spot for dogs," I murmured.

After a few more days of rest, I was well enough to return to the king's bed, but something had changed. I could not put my finger on a reason, but I no longer felt comfortable in His Grace's company. When we were together, I was tense and uneasy, but that was nothing compared to my emotional state when we were apart. Then I was afraid.

With each passing day, I became more certain that it was only a matter of time before the queen made another attempt to kill me.

48

The court went to Greenwich for Yuletide as it always did, but, for the first time in many years, I did not encounter Rafe Pinckney there. He did not accompany Mistress Wilkinson when she delivered silks to the queen.

I had been of two minds about seeing him again. I might easily have avoided such a meeting altogether, as it was Madge Shelton whom Queen Anne had sent to inspect the silkwoman's wares. At the last moment, I persuaded Madge to let me accompany her on her errand to the queen's wardrobe of robes.

In spite of sharing duties and a dormitory with Madge, I did not know her well. She was a quiet young woman, soft-spoken and self-contained, although I'd often seen her laughing with courtiers who frequented the queen's chambers. Madge could flirt with the best of us.

She did not seem to notice my distraction, or even find it odd that I did not return with her to the presence chamber after we'd finished our inspection. I made myself visible, in case Rafe was lying in wait for me along the way, but he did not appear. More disappointed than I wished to acknowledge, even to myself, I returned to the maidens' chamber to give myself a moment's privacy and regain my composure.

"It is better he did not come," I told my image in the looking glass as I fussed with the angle of my French hood.

I would not have known what to say to him. I prayed he would never know how far I had gone in my attempt to advance the princess's cause. Or how much I had enjoyed some of it. Heat rushed into my face as I remembered one particular guilty pleasure.

Our use of coded messages had ceased once I was allowed to communicate directly with the princess. The last one I'd sent to Rafe had informed him that I had permission to write to her. I'd had no reply and had not expected one.

Once again, I resolved to banish Rafe Pinckney from my thoughts. I still had the king's ear, and my mission was still incomplete. I had not yet persuaded His Grace to restore his daughter in the succession.

Throughout Yuletide, the king and queen sat side by side under their cloths of estate—gold tissue, embroidered with the king's arms—and the king's red and gold liveried servants mingled with the queen's in blue and purple, but all was not well. Rumors flew. The king, it was said, had consulted members of his Privy Council, asking what grounds he might use to annul his second marriage. Having been the cause of the king putting aside one wife, Queen Anne had good reason to fear that His Grace might do so again.

On the evenings devoted to dancing, the king sometimes partnered his wife but more often danced with me. He also danced a great deal with one other lady—my fellow maid of honor, Madge Shelton.

"Madge is prettier than I am," I confided in Bess Holland late one night in our shared bed. "I wonder why she never caught the king's eye before."

"She never before made any special effort to attract His Grace's attention," Bess murmured in a sleepy voice.

"Why should she do so now?"

Bess's only answer was a soft snore.

I wondered if Madge had seen the jewelry "Harry" had given me and wanted baubles for herself. She knew he'd given me Star of Hartlake. She might even know that His Grace had presented me with an extra, early New Year's gift, a solid gold toothpick garnished with diamonds.

It was not until New Year's Day that the truth dawned on me. The queen was generous with her gifts, presenting each of her ladies with a palfrey and a saddle, but she also gave Madge a new gown and a specially blended perfume and a chemise made of lawn so fine as to be nearly transparent.

I saw everything clearly then. Having failed three times to rid herself of my presence at court, Queen Anne had devised a new plan. She had instructed her biddable cousin Madge to replace me in King Henry's bed.

49

By February, it was Madge Shelton whom the king's groom of the stool fetched from the maidens' dormitory and escorted to his royal master. My tenure as His Grace's mistress had come to an end.

King Henry granted me an annuity and sent me a jeweled broach as a parting gift, but neither could protect me from the queen's vicious temper and her desire for revenge. If I needed any further reminder of how unprotected I was, it came with the news that Princess Mary was once again dangerously ill with pains in her head and her stomach. I feared that, this time, she *had* been poisoned, and went weak with relief when I heard of her recovery. I took great care what I put into my own mouth.

Without the king's ear, I was of little use to the princess. Remaining at court became a perilous proposition. Since Princess Mary had no household of her own, and might never have one again, I was left with only two alternatives.

I could enter a nunnery. Aside from my lack of any vocation, I had another compelling reason to avoid taking the veil. Thomas

Cromwell had become a powerful figure at court since the long-ago day when he'd agreed to look into my legal affairs. Of late, he had been working hard to convince King Henry that all the monasteries and nunneries of England should be closed. Since dissolving the richest of the religious houses would transfer their wealth into the king's own coffers, I suspected it would be only a matter of time before His Grace agreed to implement Cromwell's plan.

My remaining choice—returning to Hartlake Manor to face Sir Lionel—also presented difficulties, but I told myself that I could deal with my stepmother's husband. I was of full age to claim my inheritance. By law, I was entitled to control my own property, even if my ogre of a stepfather did have physical possession of the estate. If necessary, I would go to law to have him thrown off my land.

Accordingly, I penned a letter to Hugo Wynn, my steward, ordering him to send an escort of loyal Lodge retainers to fetch me home. I took the precaution of warning him to say nothing to Sir Lionel of my plans. Then I waited.

Weeks went by without any answer. I began to wonder if Hugo was still there. I knew I would have to leave court soon, even if I'd had no reply. The queen's treatment of me had become well nigh intolerable. I had a dozen bruises on my body where she'd pinched me, and I'd become so fearful of poison that I scarcely dared eat. My clothing hung loosely on my body and my face was gaunt.

In April, one of the queen's waiting gentlewomen came down with a case of the measles. Leaving her behind, the rest of the court removed to Hampton Court. It was time, I decided, to resign my post, hire henchmen to escort me—if I could find any willing to be employed by an unmarried woman—and make the journey to Hartlake Manor.

I had not yet found an opportunity to approach the queen with my request to leave her service when Her Grace called for all her attendants to follow her out onto the balcony attached to her luxurious new first-floor lodgings. The king and a few of his favorite courtiers were hunting in the adjacent park. From the balcony we had an unobstructed view of the action.

The queen's groom, Dickon, approached me just at the moment when everyone else was distracted because one of the king's party had been thrown from his horse. Wagers were being made as to who he was and how badly he had been hurt.

"Mistress Lodge, you have a visitor," Dickon whispered. "The queen grants you permission to withdraw."

As I followed him inside, Queen Anne turned to watch me go, a malicious sparkle in her dark eyes. A sudden chill penetrated clear down to the marrow of my bones. As I'd feared, Sir Lionel Daggett awaited me in Her Grace's presence chamber.

Once again, the years had not been kind to him. His belly bowed out above his belt, preceding him as he advanced to meet me. His nose, a map of broken capillaries, red and ugly, led the way.

"Your family has need of you, Mistress Lodge," he announced for the benefit of the few courtiers within earshot. "Queen Anne has graciously released you from your duties so that you may accompany me back to Hartlake Manor."

The words *your family has need of you* filled me with trepidation. "Is Blanche ill? Has something happened to her?"

"My wife is well." Sir Lionel gripped my arm and propelled me out of the queen's lodgings and down a flight of stairs. "Or so I presume," he added when he was sure no one could overhear. "We have not seen much of each other since she decided to take a vow of chastity."

Digging in my heels, I finally managed to halt his progress. We had reached the middle of the courtyard. "Do you mean to tell me that Blanche has become a vowess?" It was a course followed by many devout women, but usually they were widows, not wives.

"I am amazed to hear you are unaware of that fact. I was certain you had put her up to it."

"I would have, had I thought of it." With a jerk, I freed myself from his grasp. "Where is she?"

"At Minchin Barrow."

"Good." With Blanche safe in the nunnery, at least until Master Cromwell had his way, I would have no qualms about evicting Sir Lionel from Hartlake Manor. I opened my mouth to say so, but he spoke first.

"She lives with the nuns with my permission and at my expense. Should I choose to withdraw both, she would have to leave Minchin Barrow and return to me. Will you come along quietly, or must I take out my . . . disappointment on your stepmother?"

"You would harm your own wife? What kind of man are you?"

"A determined one, as you will learn to your sorrow if you try to make trouble."

I did not doubt him for a moment. I might have called out to one of the yeomen of the guard—there were always a few about—but that would only save *me* from Sir Lionel. He had every right to do as he wished with Blanche. Although it had been years since I'd last seen my stepmother and she'd not troubled to communicate with me in nearly as long, she was still my father's widow. I did not want to loose this fiend on her.

"It will take me some little time to pack my belongings," I said, hoping to delay long enough to plead with the king to intervene.

It had been a mistake not to tell King Henry how Sir Lionel had wronged me, but it had never occurred to me to do so. All the favors I'd asked of His Grace had been for Princess Mary's benefit, not my own.

"I have already ordered your maid to pack for you," Sir Lionel said. "We will leave at first light for Hartlake Manor."

"Very well," I agreed. I would talk to the king after supper. I would beg His Grace, for the sake of all we had once shared, to protect me and my stepmother.

But I had reckoned without Queen Anne. She sent two of her grooms to ensure that I did not leave the maidens' dormitory once I returned there. When I wrote a note to King Henry and dispatched Edyth to deliver it, she was allowed to pass, since she had no hope of being admitted to the king's presence, but the missive was confiscated.

"Queen's orders, Mistress Lodge," Dickon explained when he returned it to me unopened. He looked embarrassed but determined.

"I do not blame you. You are only doing your duty." And hoping to avoid the queen's wrath I took the note back from him and burned it.

"You intended to return to Hartlake Manor in any case," Bess Holland reminded me when she and the other maids of honor returned to the maidens' chamber late that night.

"But I planned to take a few precautions first." I'd intended to consult a lawyer, and hire burly guards to protect me from Sir Lionel.

"Have you a cache of valuables close at hand?" Bess asked.

"Only the gifts the king gave me." Access to the wealth I had inherited was not possible so long as Sir Lionel controlled my finances.

"They will do," Bess said. "Do not tell anyone where you have hidden them. Is there a false bottom in one of your trunks?"

There was not, but I took her warning to heart. Before we left Hampton Court, Edyth and I sewed as many of my treasures as we could into our clothing.

I rode Star of Hartlake away from the palace, prompting a raised eyebrow from Sir Lionel. Edyth was mounted on the palfrey the queen had given me as a New Year's gift. The burly guards I had envisioned hiring accompanied us, but they were not in my employ.

"If you think to marry and deprive me of Hartlake Manor," Sir Lionel said when we had traveled westward for more than an hour in silence, "you are sadly mistaken."

"I have no immediate plans for marriage," I said in a mild voice.

"You will not marry at all. You ruined your prospects by your wanton behavior at court."

My hand clenched on the reins. "I had no idea my fame had spread as far as Somersetshire."

"Say rather infamy."

"That is rich, sirrah, coming from you. You are the one who first suggested that I try to capture the king's attention, and I was little more than a child at the time!"

"Back then, I planned to marry you myself, even if you were the king's leavings."

"You already had a wife," I reminded him.

"Wives are easily disposed of."

I sent a sharp look in his direction. He looked entirely too pleased with himself.

"Do you mean to rid yourself of Blanche now? It will avail you nothing. I will never marry you."

"I have changed my mind. I do not wish to wed another man's whore. You are no longer fit to be my wife, although I still might find you amusing as a mistress."

Too appalled by his suggestion to respond, I said nothing. We rode without speaking the rest of the way to the inn that would provide our first night's lodging on the journey. From his smirk, Sir Lionel thought me too cowed to object to his plans.

Once my first shock passed, I encouraged him in this misconception, riding with shoulders hunched and face averted. Let him think I feared him. It would make it easier to carry out my plan.

I told myself a story. The one Lady Catherine Gordon had once shared with me. If a kidnapped bride could escape her captors, reach London, and appeal to the Star Chamber, so could I.

Although we had ridden all day, we had not traveled far, slowed as we were by a baggage cart. We were still in sight of the Thames. The moment Sir Lionel left me alone with Edyth, to go down to the common room to sup and swill ale, I hastily packed a little clothing and all the treasures I'd acquired while at court into two small bundles.

Two of the pearls that decorated the front of my French hood were sufficient to bribe the innkeeper. He sent for his son and instructed the lad to row us downriver far enough to take passage on a tilt boat. For another two pearls, he agreed to hide Star of Hartlake and the palfrey. A third covered the cost of their care until I could retrieve the two animals. It was my fervent hope that the absence of our horses would make Sir Lionel think we had fled by land.

"What if he should discover where we've really gone and come after us?" Edyth asked as we were rowed downriver in a boat so tiny there was scarce room for the two of us, our bundles, and the boy. Darkness had fallen by then and the moon on the water cast eerie shadows.

"He will not know where to look."

"He is an evil man, Mistress Tamsin. One of his men told me that he's forced Griselda Wynn to warm his bed ever since your stepmother ran away to the nunnery."

"I doubt Griselda had to be forced into anything. She was always one to seize the main chance." But that explained why her father, Hugo, had never answered my appeal. "As for Sir Lionel, he'll never find us once we reach London. It is a very large city, Edyth. We can vanish into its vastness."

"That we can vanish, I do not doubt," Edyth said, her voice gloomy, "but how are we to *live?*"

50

We passed the remainder of the night in the flea-infested upper room of an alehouse. The innkeeper's son delivered us there to await the first tilt boat of the morning. They did not ply the river after sunset. Rather than sacrifice another pearl, which might rouse suspicion, I used half of my small winnings at cards to pay for the doubtful privilege of sharing a straw-stuffed pallet with my tiring maid.

Tilt boats, so called because of the tilt, the canopy that protects passengers from inclement weather, travel the Thames from Windsor to Gravesend. Once aboard, surrounded by a dozen or more strangers, I deemed conversation unwise. Instead I watched the shore and the other vessels on the river—tide boats, private barges, and large barges carrying produce from the country to the city.

Edyth's question had kept me awake most of the night. I had planned to escape from Sir Lionel's clutches at the first opportunity, but I had not thought beyond that point. We could live for some time on the profits of selling my valuables, but I might be cheated by some unscrupulous buyer, or robbed outright. We would also have to find lodgings. They could not be too respectable or Sir Lionel might locate them. But we dared not live in the roughest part of London, either. My head swam with the sheer number of matters I would have to settle by nightfall.

I did not know many people in London and trusted only one. When we docked, I began to walk northward. I had never been afoot in the city before. People crowded in on every side, pushing and shoving. Everyone seemed to be trying to sell me something . . . or pick my pocket. Pungent smells assaulted me from every direction.

A lad of no more than eight years grabbed my bundle and attempted to make off with it. Having kept a good grip on it, I retained possession, but it was a near thing. When Edyth cuffed him on the ear, the boy cursed her and fled into a narrow alley.

A nearby horseman laughed. The bay gelding he rode nearly trampled me as it surged forward through the crowd of pedestrians. "Quickly, Edyth," I said, and followed in his wake. We made good progress until he applied his spurs and left us in his dust.

When we reached Cheapside, I turned east and continued walking along that broad thoroughfare. I had ceased to hear the street cries. The noisome odors of cesspits and middens, unwashed bodies and animal waste had blended into one and the constant exposure had deadened my sense of smell.

Edyth clung to me like a leech as I pushed onward. I passed the ornate Eleanor Cross without even pausing to admire its intricate carvings and statues. Ahead, I recognized the Standard, one of several conduits that provided water to the citizens of London. Statues adorned it, too. As I walked rapidly past, I remembered that it was sometimes used as a place of execution.

A man carrying a full bucket bumped into me, sloshing some of the liquid onto my shoulder. He had come from the Great Conduit.

I stopped, searching for one particular sign along the north side of the street. Fine, high buildings lined Cheapside. Some were shops. Others were the houses of prosperous merchants. THE SIGN OF THE GOLDEN HART hung above the door to one of the latter.

A workroom took up the ground floor. A half-dozen women busily turning silk into points and laces looked up when Edyth and I entered. None of their faces was familiar to me.

I cleared my throat. "I am looking for Rafe Pinckney."

"He's not here, dearie," one of the women called out, "but his mother is."

She left me no choice but to follow her up a flight of stairs and into a richly appointed solar. Rafe's mother sat at a writing table, a ledger open before her. A pair of regals sat in a corner. A lute lay abandoned on a chair upholstered in the finest silk.

"Mistress Lodge!" she exclaimed in surprise.

"Mistress Pinckney. I must beg your forgiveness for intruding upon you without warning but—"

"You are most welcome at any time," she said, cutting short my apology. When she offered food and drink, I accepted with gratitude. Neither Edyth nor I had eaten since the previous day.

Over small cakes and barley water, I reconsidered my hastily conceived plan to ask Rafe for help in selling my valuables, finding a place to live, and hiring a lawyer. Rafe had once asked me to marry him. I still did not know why. But no man could want a bride who had lost her virtue. Even Sir Lionel had not. I could not bear the thought that Rafe would turn from me in disgust.

Mistress Pinckney, on the other hand, was a silkwoman. An independent businesswoman in her own right. She did not have to ask anyone's permission to offer me assistance. And she had no reason to expect me to have led an exemplary life.

I told her my tale, or at least the parts of it that I could bear to share. I did not admit that Sir Lionel's reason for threatening to make me his mistress was that I had already given myself to the king. Mistress Pinckney did not frequent the court. I doubted she knew I had ever been the king's concubine.

"Why have you come to me?" she asked when I had finished describing how Edyth and I had escaped and traveled to London.

"I have jewels and other small valuables I wish to sell or pawn for ready money, but I do not know whom to approach, or how. I must also hire lodgings." Another thought occurred to me. "And I must make haste to send a sufficient sum to the nunnery at Minchin Barrow, to ensure my stepmother's continued safety."

"Can the nuns protect her? A vowess is not cloistered."

"If her lodging is paid for, she will be safe enough." At least until Master Cromwell carried out his plan to dissolve the nunneries. "The sisters at Minchin Barrow are more fierce than Sir Lionel realizes. Two of them are my aunts. They will have no sympathy for the man who usurped property belonging to their kinswoman."

Mistress Pinckney nodded approvingly. "And how do you mean to reclaim what is rightfully yours?"

"That is what I will do with the rest of the money from selling my jewelry. I must hire a lawyer and bring charges against Sir Lionel for appropriating my land. And it may be necessary to hire men to help me evict my former guardian from Hartlake Manor."

"An ambitious scheme," she murmured, "and perhaps more expensive to carry out than you realize. As every merchant has cause to know, court cases can drag on for years. Have you the wherewithal to support yourself for that long?"

When I had described all the king's gifts save Star of Hartlake, Mistress Pinckney was shaking her head. "Such items sound very fine indeed, but for all you propose to do, I suspect they will yield

insufficient wealth. Moreover, most lawyers will advise you to
resign yourself to living under Sir Lionel Daggett's care until you
marry."

"Never!"

"Never return to Sir Lionel?"

"And never marry, either."

Mistress Pinckney looked thoughtful. I wondered if she was considering offering me employment as a silkwoman. "Wait here," she
said, rising. "Let me make a few inquiries."

I heard footsteps approaching on the stairs less than a quarter
of an hour later, but it was not Mistress Pinckney who entered the
room. It was Rafe.

I stared at him. He was the same, and yet so different. No one
would mistake him for a humble apprentice now. He looked every
inch the successful merchant.

He reached for me.

I stepped back.

"You have left the queen's service."

"I can be of no more use to the princess."

"Then you are free to do as you will."

I narrowed my eyes at him. "How much did your mother tell you?
How much did you know of my inheritance when you asked me to
marry you?"

A scowl replaced his smile. "Did you think I was after your fortune? It appears to me that any man who marries you will entangle
himself in legal battles for years to come!"

"That was not why I refused you. Not entirely. I feared to bring
Sir Lionel's displeasure down upon you and your family. And perhaps the king's, too."

"I inherited my father's business—he was a mercer—when he

died last year," Rafe said. "I have sufficient wealth to protect and keep you and take the odious Sir Lionel to court, too."

"Why would you *want* to?" I blurted out. "I'll bring you nothing but trouble."

His expression serious, he waited until our gazes locked before he spoke. "I fell in love with you the first time I saw you, Tamsin. I've never wanted to marry anyone else. I want to spend the rest of my life with you. Together we'll win back everything that is yours by right. For our children."

The future he described was one I longed to embrace with all my heart. How could I have denied the truth for so long? I loved Rafe Pinckney. I wanted to marry him and have his children. In that moment of revelation, I could not imagine my life without him in it.

And yet . . .

"How can I?" I whispered.

"Do you care for me, Tamsin? Just a little?"

"More than a little, Rafe." The confession was wrenched out of me.

"Then there is no impediment to our marriage."

"There is one." As much as I now wanted to wed Rafe, I could not agree to do so under false pretenses. Steeling myself for rejection, I took a deep breath and told him what stood between us. "I am not the innocent maid you imagine me to be. Before I left the court, I was the king's mistress."

Rafe's expression turned rueful. He clasped both my hands in his. "I admit I was not happy when I heard the rumors." He made a self-deprecating sound, almost but not quite a laugh. "I cursed fate, and the omnipotence of kings, and my own helplessness to intervene, but I never blamed you. What choice did you have? Even if the king had been willing to take no for an answer, you vowed long ago to sacrifice yourself in the princess's cause. You are an honorable woman, and I love you all the more for it."

"You *knew?*" I stared at him in stunned disbelief, scarcely daring to hope that he meant what he said.

The endearing grin that first drew me to him spread across Rafe's features as he pulled me close. "In spite of what members of the royal household might like to think, there are no secrets at the Tudor court. It is the future I care about, Tamsin, not the past. Share it with me." Then he kissed me, assuaging the last of my doubts about how he felt.

WE WERE MARRIED as soon as the banns could be read. It took five years to evict Sir Lionel from Hartlake Manor, but in the end we succeeded in reclaiming my inheritance. We settled there with our growing family. I told the children stories, including some about life at court, and I taught them to ride on Star of Hartlake, the girls as well as the boys.

AUTHOR'S NOTE

A letter from the Spanish ambassador, Eustace Chapuys, written on September 27, 1534, reported that the king had "renewed and increased the love he formerly bore to another very handsome young lady of the Court" and that the queen had tried "to dismiss the damsel from her service." Other letters from Chapuys reveal that this young woman was a "true friend" of the Princess (later Queen) Mary, Henry's daughter by Catherine of Aragon, and that Queen Anne's sister-in-law, Lady Rochford, was banished from court for quarreling with this mysterious woman in an unsuccessful attempt, at Anne's instigation, to provoke the king into sending his mistress away.

No one knows who this "king's damsel" really was. For the purposes of this novel, I created a young gentlewoman named Thomasine (Tamsin) Lodge. Her family, her servants, Sir Jasper Atwell, Sir Lionel Daggett, and Rafe Pinckney and his mother are all fictional characters, but the rest of the people in this novel are real, as are most of the events Tamsin narrates. In general, I've used the chronology of events found in David Loades's biography of Mary Tudor, as it seems the most logical as well as the most consistent. I've followed Eric Ives's account of Anne Boleyn's life rather than that of Retha M. Warnicke. It is to Ives that I owe my understanding of how the "game of love" was played at the court of Henry VIII. Also particularly useful were Alison Weir's *Henry VIII and His Court* and Simon Thurley's *The Royal Palaces of Tudor England* (source of the material on royal bathtubs). A complete list of biographies and other references used in writing this novel can be found at http://www.KateEmersonHistoricals.com/bibliography.htm.

In some cases, I had to choose between conflicting accounts of historical events, or make slight alterations in the time frame to fit the plot. I chose to make Sir Ralph Egerton Princess Mary's valentine, although at least one scholar not only places a different person in this role, but argues that the event took place on a different date. I moved Anne Rede's courtship a bit earlier than the dates on which her marriage was being discussed in extant letters. It is uncertain where Anne Boleyn was in 1526, but since she could already have been one of Catherine of Aragon's maids of honor, I made it so. It was probably not until 1533 that the silkwomen of London competed for Anne Boleyn's patronage, but she certainly employed someone as early as late 1531, when I have four of them vying for her favor. I did depart from Professor Ives's research in one regard. He makes a good case for the entire affair of the "unnamed damsel" to have taken place in 1534, rather than there being two stages, one during each of two of Queen Anne's pregnancies (1533 and 1534). For dramatic purposes, I kept the dating, mistaken though it may be, that is given in the *Letters and Papers, Foreign and Domestic, of the Reign of Henry VIII*, edited by James Gairdner in 1893.

WHO WAS WHO AT THE COURT OF HENRY VIII

1525–1535

Boleyn, Anne (later Lady Anne Rochford; Anne, Lady Marquess of Pembroke; Queen Anne) (c.1501–1536)
Does Anne Boleyn really need any introduction? She was a maid of honor to Queen Catherine, married Henry VIII, and was executed on trumped-up charges of adultery. For further reading I recommend Eric Ives's *The Life and Death of Anne Boleyn* and G. W. Bernard's *Anne Boleyn: Fatal Attraction.*

Boleyn, Jane (née Parker), Viscountess Rochford (c.1505–1542)
A maid of honor to Queen Catherine, she married George Boleyn and as Lady Rochford served in the households of Queen Anne Boleyn, Queen Jane Seymour, Queen Anne of Cleves, and Queen

Catherine Howard. She was banished from court in 1534 for picking a fight with the unknown damsel in whom the king was interested. She was executed for helping Catherine Howard meet in secret with her lover.

Boleyn, Mary (c.1498-1543)

Anne Boleyn's older sister, she was one of the many mistresses of King Francis I of France before returning to England to be married to William Carey. As Mistress Carey, she became Henry VIII's mistress. Her two children, Henry and Catherine, are sometimes said to have been the king's but probably were not. After her husband's death, she was at court in her sister's household. Mary's secret marriage to a minor courtier, Sir William Stafford, led to her banishment.

Butts, Margaret (née Bacon) (d.1545+)

Lady Butts, wife of Dr. William Butts, was in the household of the Princess of Wales by 1525.

Butts, William (c.1485-1545)

As one of the royal physicians, Dr. Butts appears to have been part of the household of the Princess of Wales in 1525. Later he was physician to the king. He was sent to look after Anne Boleyn when she fell ill of the sweating sickness in 1528.

Catherine of Aragon (1485-1536)

Queen of England until Anne Boleyn displaced her, she never recognized the annulment of her marriage or the illegitimacy of her daughter. An excellent account of her life is *Catherine of Aragon: The Spanish Queen of Henry VIII*, by Giles Tremlett.

Cromwell, Thomas (c.1485–x.1540)

A lawyer, Cromwell became the king's chief advisor after the fall from power of Thomas Wolsey. He remained high in royal favor until he arranged the king's marriage to Anne of Cleves.

Dabridgecourt, Cecily (1506–1558)

A maid of honor to the Princess of Wales, she was probably part of that household from 1525. She married Sir Rhys Mansell on June 19, 1527.

Dannett, Mary (d. before 1562)

A maid of honor to the Princess of Wales, she was probably part of that household from 1525. She married George Medley after 1526.

Egerton, Sir Ralph (c.1468–1528)

Treasurer of the Princess of Wales's household in 1525, he was by that time a very old man by the standards of the day. He was about fifty-seven. The story of the kidnapping of his future wife is true. She survived him. Some accounts identify him as Princess Mary's "valentine" on February 14, 1526.

Fitzherbert, Mary (d.1532+)

A maid of honor to the Princess of Wales, she was probably part of that household from 1525. Little is known about her except her name. She probably came from a Derbyshire family. In 1532, Princess Mary gave her a marriage gift but her husband's name is not recorded.

Gordon, Lady Catherine (c.1474–1537)

The daughter of a Scottish earl and his third wife, Lady Catherine was married to a man claiming to be Richard, Duke of York, son of Edward IV. Following their capture during an unsuccessful attempt to invade England in 1497, he was revealed to be one Perkin Warbeck, a commoner. King Henry VII imprisoned Warbeck but sent Lady Catherine to his wife, Elizabeth of York, to be a member of the queen's household. She remained in that position until the queen's death and later was one of Catherine of Aragon's ladies. She married three more times. During her third marriage, she was chief lady-in-waiting to the Princess of Wales from August 1525 until around 1530.

Henry VIII (1491–1547)

King of England from 1509. His love for Anne Boleyn prompted him to annul his marriage to Catherine of Aragon, ruin his former friend and advisor, Cardinal Wolsey, and break with the Roman Catholic Church to declare himself supreme head of the Church of England. The only two women it is certain were his concubines were Elizabeth Blount and Mary Boleyn. About all other women linked to him romantically, other than those he married, there is doubt as to whether the relationships were ever consummated. In the convention of the time, a knight referred to a lady not his wife as his "mistress" in the "game of love" but these liaisons were, more often than not, purely platonic.

Holland, Elizabeth (d.1554+)

A maid of honor to Anne Boleyn both before and after she became queen, Bess Holland had been the mistress of Anne's uncle, the Duke of Norfolk, since about 1526 and was still his mistress twenty years later. In spite of claims made by the duchess, Bess was a gentlewoman by birth and related to Lord Hussey. She may also have served in Queen Jane's household, since she rode in that queen's funeral procession in 1537.

Mary, Princess of Wales (1516–1558)

The future queen of England was never formally created Princess of Wales, but she was called by that title in documents and referred to herself that way. She was sent to the Marches of Wales in 1525, living at various houses but not, as is so often stated, at Ludlow Castle, which was in a state of extreme disrepair. David Loades's *Mary Tudor: A Life* should be read along with more recent biographies by Linda Porter and Anna Whitelock.

Perky (also spelled Purkoy and Purquoy)

Probably a bichon frise, a breed much in favor at sixteenth-century European courts, Perky belonged to Lady Lisle, wife of the Lord Deputy of Calais. She sent him to England as a gift for Queen Anne in mid-January 1534. On December 18, 1534, Margery Horsman reported that Perky had died in a fall and that because Queen Anne had "delighted so much in little Purkoy," the king was the only one who dared tell her what had happened to him. This story is found in *The Lisle Letters*, edited by M. St. Clare Byrne. Additional details surrounding Perky's demise are my own invention but are not beyond the realm of possibility.

Pole, Margaret (née Plantagenet; Countess of Salisbury), (1473–x.1541)

The daughter of George, Duke of Clarence, reputedly drowned in a butt of Malmsey, she was married to Sir Richard Pole. In 1513, during her widowhood, she was granted the title Countess of Salisbury in her own right. She was lady mistress of Princess Mary's household from 1516 to 1533. She was executed on trumped-up charges of treason. She was beatified by the Roman Catholic Church in 1886.

Rede, Anne (c.1510–1585)

A maid of honor to the Princess of Wales in 1525, she was courted by Sir Giles Greville in 1526 and 1527 and married him shortly before his death in 1528. Letters from the Countess of Salisbury and Lady Rede on the subject of this courtship still exist. Anne went on to marry twice more and to serve in the households of both Queen Mary and Queen Elizabeth. She retired from court life in 1566.

Savage, Anne (1506–1564)

A maid of honor to Anne Boleyn, she is said to have been a witness to her marriage to Henry VIII on January 25, 1533. Anne Savage married Lord Berkeley in April 1533. Numerous letters by and about her are extant.

Seymour, Jane (c.1508–1537)

A maid of honor to both Catherine of Aragon and Anne Boleyn, Jane attracted King Henry's amorous attentions in 1536 and became his third wife after Anne Boleyn's execution. She died shortly after giving birth to the future Edward VI.

Shelton, Margaret (Madge) (1505+–1583)

A maid of honor to and cousin of Queen Anne Boleyn, she allegedly seduced the king at the queen's command to distract him from his interest in the unnamed mistress of 1534. Although some believe this was her younger sister, Mary Shelton, Margaret is the more likely candidate. In addition to the king, she was romantically linked to Sir Henry Norris, a widower, and Sir Francis Weston (although Weston was married), both of whom were later executed on the charge they were among Queen Anne's lovers. Margaret later married a country gentleman by whom she had a large family. In 1538, Christina of Milan, then being considered as a possible fourth wife for Henry VIII, was described as greatly resembling the king's former mistress, Mistress Shelton.

Vittorio or Victoria, Mary (d.1536+)

A Mary Victoria was a member of the household of the Princess of Wales from 1525 until at least 1533. Her identity is uncertain. Dr. Fernando Vittorio was Queen Catherine's Spanish physician. In 1518, he brought his wife to England. They had a son and may well have had other children, including a daughter named Mary. The doctor's wife seems to have remained in Queen Catherine's household, along with her husband. She was left £10 in Catherine's will.

Wilkinson, Joan (née North) (c.1498–1556)

As the widow of a London alderman, Joan pursued a career as a silkwoman from her house in Soper Lane. She held the post of silkwoman to Queen Anne Boleyn from 1533 to 1535 and during that time was also engaged in smuggling banned Lutheran books into

England. During the reign of Mary Tudor, she went into exile. She died in Frankfurt am Main.

Wolsey, Thomas (later Cardinal) (1471–1530)

Henry VIII's chief advisor until he failed to secure Henry's divorce from Catherine of Aragon. When Wolsey fell from power, the king seized his property, including Hampton Court and York Place. The latter became "the king's palace at Westminster" and later came to be called Whitehall Palace.

For more information on the women listed above and to see portraits of some of them, please visit http://www.KateEmersonHistoricals.com /TudorWomenIndex.htm

⇒ The ⇐

KING'S
Damsel

BY KATE EMERSON

Introduction

The real identity of "the king's damsel" is unknown, but Kate Emerson has chosen to make her a fictional gentlewoman from Glastonbury named Thomasine Lodge. Thanks to the machinations of the stranger who becomes her guardian after her father's death, Thomasine is placed in the service of Princess Mary, only surviving child of Henry VIII and his first wife, Catherine of Aragon. Thomasine soon becomes one of her young mistress's confidantes. Later, when Mary asks her to go to the king's court to spy on Anne Boleyn, soon to be King Henry's bride, loyalty obliges Thomasine to agree.

At court, Thomasine not only finds favor with the queen, but also with the king, and experiences both the benefits and dangers of having done so. She also begins to realize that there is a wider world beyond the court, in particular that inhabited by Rafe Pinckney, the son of one of the royal silkwomen.

Thomasine's time as a royal mistress is brief, but it takes place at a particularly tempestuous time during the reign of Henry VIII—his marriage to Anne Boleyn. Thomasine leaves court before Anne's arrest and execution, but it is while she is there that the seeds of future disaster are sown.

Questions for Discussion

1. What is your impression of Thomasine's stepmother? Should she have done more to protect her husband's daughter? If so, what could she have done?

2. The definition of loyalty instilled in Thomasine at a young age by old Lady Salisbury, summed up as "be loyal to Princess Mary and willing to die to protect her," guides her during all her time at court. What do you think of this philosophy and of Thomasine for believing in it?

3. Thomasine also believes what her guardian tells her, some of which later proves to be untrue. Do you think she was naïve to accept his word, or just a product of an upbringing that taught girls to be guided by a man, even one they neither liked nor trusted?

4. Discuss the role of those who provided special services to the royal court, such as the royal silkwoman. In *The King's Damsel*, a silkwoman's son delivers secret messages. The mini-biography of Joan Wilkinson in the Who's Who section reveals that she helped smuggle forbidden religious books into England. What other possibilities can you think of?

5. Rafe surprises Thomasine when he doesn't condemn her for having been the king's mistress. Keeping in mind that the mindset of the times was very different from our own, why do you think he wasn't more judgmental?

6. How does the way Henry VIII is portrayed in this novel mesh with interpretations of his character in movies and on television? Which seems most believable to you?

7. Did the details about baths and bathing included in *The King's Damsel* surprise you? Henry VIII really was sensitive to smells and was an early advocate of cleanliness as a means of preventing illness. The baths and bathrooms in his palaces have been studied by archaeologists. What we don't know is how often he bathed or how many of his subjects followed his example.

8. Why do you think Anne Boleyn was able to hold King Henry's attention for so many years? By all reports she was not a great beauty. She had a temper and was subject to hysterical outbursts, at least during the last year of her life. Was it sorcery? Charisma? Or something else?

9. In an age when even university-trained physicians didn't know much about the causes of disease, people often put their trust in herbal remedies. Several "cures" and "preventives" are mentioned in *The King's Damsel*, as well as an antidote for arsenic poisoning. Discuss why some of these may actually have worked and why others probably did more harm than good.

10. Early in the novel, Thomasine learns that she has a niece, her late brother's illegitimate daughter by Griselda Wynn. In keeping with the times, the child, Winifred, is left with her mother and we hear no more about her, although Griselda later takes up with Thomasine's guardian. What do you think Thomasine might do once she reclaims her inheritance? Is she more likely to want to play a role in the little girl's future, or banish the entire family from Hartlake Manor?

Enhance Your Book Club

1. If you haven't already, read Kate Emerson's previous novels set at the Tudor court: *The Pleasure Palace*, *Between Two Queens*, *By Royal Decree*, and *At the King's Pleasure*.

2. Locate ornamental gardens near you that are open to the public and pay a visit. Look for typical Tudor features, such as knots, arbors, bowers, topiary work, and bridges over streams. Also seek out flowers and plants that were used to make perfumes in the sixteenth century, such as roses and sweet marjoram. As you smell them, think also of how they were used in pomander balls to block out less pleasant odors.

3. Read a biography of one of the real people Thomasine encounters. There are recommendations in the Who's Who section. Three more Kate Emerson suggests are Beverly A. Murphy's *Bastard Prince: Henry VIII's Lost Son*, Julia Fox's *Jane Boleyn, The True Story of the Infamous Lady Rochford*, and *Mary Boleyn: The Mistress of Kings* by Alison Weir.

4. Try telling each other stories without a script or notes, the way Thomasine would have done for the ladies of the court.